THE CAROLINGIAN CHRONICLES
BOOK I

WARRIOR, LOVER, KING

At Last Communications

Published by At Last Communications

Printed in the United States of America

ISBN-10: 0-9842768-1-5
ISBN-13: 978-0-9842768-1-3

Library of Congress Control Number: 2013921141

Acknowledgments

Thanks to those historians who investigated the life of Charlemagne, saw his greatness, and applauded his achievements, especially Thomas Hodgkin in The Barbarian Invasion of the Roman Empire; Alessandro Barbero's Charlemagne, Father of a Continent; Gregory of Tours, The History of the Franks; Pierre Riche', Daily Life in the World of Charlemagne; Paul Edward Dutton (ed.), Carolingian Civilization; and Einhard's The Life of Charlemagne.

Dedication

In memory of Dr. Frank Hoskins who challenged me to question my own assumptions and, so, opened my mind to new possibilities.

"A leader will find it difficult to articulate a coherent vision unless it expresses his core values, his basic identity. One must first embark on the formidable journey of self-discovery in order to create a vision with authentic soul."

—Mihaly Csikszentmihalyi

Chapter One
UNREST IN THE REALM

Cantering into the small clearing, King Charlemagne and Roland, his most beloved Peer, reined in their mounts. The men coughed. Smells from burned rushes and old timber caught in their throats. As the sky lightened, the blackened huts—their walls stretching upward like scarecrows—stood stark against the autumn sky. Roland's soft groan drew the King's attention. Charlemagne looked quickly into his friend's face. Roland nodded at a cart, tilted askew under a huge oak tree. One wheel leaned toward the ground, hacked almost through. A horse lay dead in its traces.

Seeing Roland's eyes lock on the cart, Charlemagne looked more closely. With a side of the cart resting on her left shoulder, a young woman lay dead, her neck bent in an awkward position. Just beyond her outstretched hand, an infant sprawled, its head red with blood.

The men dismounted and walked slowly around the small settling. Their eyes stinging from the acrid smoke, they scanned the modest plot of land and the two huts, one with a lean-to barn. The King peered into the torched huts, releasing his breath when he saw no bodies inside. Roland followed Charlemagne toward the barn. Charlemagne gasped and stood dead still. Roland moved two steps around the king and looked before him.

His throat closed; he swallowed convulsively, his eyes widened as he scanned the path before them. Dead animals littered the ground around the barn, their bodies splashed with dull red, bloody swatches. All lay in pools of blood, their throats cut: the ducks, the horse, a mother goat, a young kid, and some twenty or so chickens. Husks of threshed grain, saved for animal fodder, smoldered yet. Apples, onions, and turnips - trampled and mashed - squished underfoot.

For several years previous, Charlemagne's father, King Pepin, visited this settling and deemed it a prosperous one. It produced food enough to feed its people. Even now, buckets of nuts sat under the pecan trees. Apples and grapes dried atop a broad lattice-like platform which hung above the barn's curing room. Beside an old bench, lambs' wool waited carding. Here was the kind of success the King encouraged throughout his realm.

Charlemagne and Roland startled as the lean-to's burned walls collapsed. Behind the walls, exposed cages stood above the ground. Mother rabbits lay in their hutch unmoving, their and their babies' throats severed. The two men looked toward the fields, searching for more victims. King Charlemagne bent to scoop up a forgotten comb and heard a slight scuffing of foot on soil. There to his right, coming from the dense trees, was a young girl-child.

Perhaps eight or nine years, he thought. Her clothes were torn, her face dirty. Her eyes darted to him, to her right, in all directions. Charlemagne paused and stopped, moving slowly, so as not to startle her. He moved closer to his horse, Samson, and rubbed his ears. *If I am gentle with Samson, mayhap she will not fear me.* He smiled and nodded his head as he noticed her legs tremble. The child's eyes moved up — to his knees, to his waist, to his shoulders and, finally, to his face.

"Are you a giant?" she whispered, her arms hugging her

body.

"Nay, I'm a friend. Is this your family's settling?" he asked softly. He waved his hand toward the huts and, then, the barn. "Is your father or mother here? Are you hurt?" As he stroked Samson's head, the horse shifted and snuffled. The girl leaped back in fear. The King took a step toward her and reached out his hand. She backed up and did not speak. But her eyes moved to Roland as he came around Samson to stand beside the King.

"Are you hungry?" Roland asked. He offered the girl a flagon of water, then a battered tart which he pulled from his traveling bag. The young girl slowly reached out, grabbed the tart and gobbled it hungrily. Roland smiled, making soft, comforting sounds. She burst into tears.

"They came upon us so quick." She threw the words into their faces. "They rode fast, yelling and screaming! My uncle, he shouted to me. 'Hide! Hide! Stay quiet!'" She caught her breath. "I ran - fast. They didn't see me." Her eyes darted back and forth.

"They killed everybody...everybody, even the baby." She slumped down into the dirt, blackening her short tunic on the burned residue dotting the ground. The child rubbed a patch of black on her arm. "I was sweeping up the ashes." Her eyes clouded over.

"So, you moved the ashes from the fire pit?" Charlemagne asked. The girl nodded her head, staring off into the distance.

"Aye," she paused. "My aunt and uncle, they wanted new rushes..." She looked at the King. Her eyes widened, her mouth trembled. "I was throwing the ashes, there, in the wood...and, then, the screams began." The girl stopped speaking, her face immobile. The King walked slowly to her and gently squeezed her shoulder.

"You're safe now," he assured her. "What is your name, child?"

"Where's your family?" Roland asked. He walked closer to her, offering traveling bars (ground meat, oats, raisins and honey) in his outstretched hand. He stood to the girl's right and blocked her view of the bodies on the ground some ten feet away. A man and two women lay in their own blood, their heads hacked almost in half. Two children sprawled dead under a rickety cart, their clothing charred. A well-worn boot near the children had dull, dried blood all over it. Its color matched the autumn leaves of a near-by bush. Charlemagne saw Roland wipe his eyes and shift his body. The child seemed not to notice the bodies at all.

"Your parents, do you know where they are?" Charlemagne asked, picking her up slowly and gently turning the young girl's face toward his own, trying to keep her attention centered on him. Still dealing with the horrors of the previous hours, she wept quietly. Her eyes moved away from Charlemagne's face. He pulled her close to his chest and felt her arm steal around his neck. She shook her head back and forth at his question.

"Nay, not 'xactly. But we live another place." She whispered, pointing vaguely. "My name's Elsbeth."

"Then, this is your uncle's settling, Elsbeth?" The King asked, as he wrapped the girl in a woolen mantle. "These are your relatives here?"

"Aye." Her eyes wandered toward the huts. She frowned as she saw a huddled form on the ground. Elsbeth seemed not to understand the people were dead. Charlemagne patted the girl's back and tried, again, to get more information.

"And why were you here—visiting, mayhap?"

"Aye," she answered, "my cousin. There." She pointed at one of the fallen bodies. "She's dead. Klara...all of them."

Tears ran down her cheeks. Her thin arms clung to the King.

"And how far is your settling, Elsbeth?" The young girl shook her head. As the King spoke softly to her, she lifted an arm and pointed south. Charlemagne rubbed her back, cradled her in his arms, and made soothing sounds. As he comforted her, his other three Peers—Oliver, Rinaldo, and Grent—rode into the clearing. The King beckoned to them.

"The band attacked this settling, too." He said. "Please find a sheltered spot to bury the people. We cannot leave them here in the weather." The Peers dismounted, removed their mantles, and walked away from the huts, looking for a burial site. Soon, they began digging a grave.

"Nay, nay," Elsbeth whimpered as the Peers lay the linen-wrapped bodies in the ground. "Please, I want to go home." Her eyes locked on the turned earth.

"Aye, we are taking you. We start now," the King assured her. "Elsbeth, I must mount my horse. Roland here will hand you up to me." He put the girl into Roland's outstretched arms, mounted Samson, and reached immediately for her. "Now, little one, we ride for your home."

Some furlongs down the rough path, the girl tapped the King's hand and pointed to a clearing of three huts. Charlemagne reined in Samson and set Elsbeth on the ground. She ran immediately to the largest hut, then frantically from that one to the next, calling names. There was no answer. Roland circled the perimeter of the settling but found no one. The Peers spread out, moving in a circle from the huts.

"Could something have warned them?" The King asked Oliver as he rode up. "I see no blood or marauding here, no animals either." He looked around again, noting the neatly swept area between the huts. "People were here earlier; the wash water still boils. Of a certainty, they left in a hurry; mayhap they're hiding. We can't leave this child alone here, not after what we've seen." Suddenly, there was a cry near the river. Roland's voice called out, directing someone to stop.

In a few moments, Roland hurried into the clearing, followed by two men, six children, and three women. Elsbeth ran into one of the women's arms and began talking, talking and weeping at the same time. The King and his Peers watched the reunion silently, each lost in his own thoughts of death and grief. Charlemagne's hands trembled. His eyes, bright with unshed tears, gazed stricken at the young girl's weeping.

"No one should see this kind of killing," he said to his friends. "This butchery, we must stop it!" He rode Samson up and down, strongly resisting the urge to ride away in pursuit of the outlaws. The older woman took Elsbeth aside, talking to her softly and holding her close. The two men came to the King. Charlemagne questioned them, seeking any additional information about the outlaw band.

"They attacked just after sunrise, Sire. They rode in screaming and shouting." The older man said. He paused, remembering. "They had no concern for life—killed the adults, killed the children, slaughtered the animals. My brother, one stabbed him with a spear. The others—they used knives." He passed his hand over his eyes.

"I, I was standing among the trees. I stopped when I heard the hooves." The peasant pointed behind him. "I heard the bastards ride in, heard my brother's cries. He fought but they outnumbered him." He stopped speaking, tears traced down his face.

"You could have done nothing," Charlemagne reassured Elsbeth's father. "Had they seen you, you all might be dead. It's a good thing you didn't show yourself. They'd have killed you and, possibly, followed your trail back to your family." The man nodded.

"It was only a moment before they lit the fires. The thatch, Sire, it was dry, dry and old." Charlemagne dismounted, came to the man and clasped his shoulder. "I knew I couldn't save them, even thought my girl there," he nodded at Elsbeth, "was dead, too." He quickly wiped his eyes.

"I rushed back here, led my family into the forest to safety. I left them here alone, hiding in the trees, Sire. I went back, returned to those bloodied huts. By the time I backtracked, there was no sign of the outlaws. I found their hoof prints, veering off on a side path." He nodded his thanks when Roland handed him a flagon of water.

"The blood lust was on them, Sire. God knows the reason they took the trail west of us. Their choice saved our lives."

"They will never touch another settling." Charlemagne vowed to the sorrowing family and to his Peers alike. "They will not pass this way again. Trust me." The Peers nodded their assent. The King and his Peers took sleeping linens from their bags, as well as their mid-day meal, and piled it at the father's feet.

"This is all we have with us," Charlemagne apologized, wishing he had more to offer the struggling peasants. *I must improve these peasants' lives. I must! Poppa would agree, I know.* Thinking of their hunger, he remembered the carcasses of the animals killed in the first settling. Before heading here, Roland wrapped the meat in linens and slung it over his saddle. Charlemagne motioned for the man to take the linens from Roland.

"This is your brother's meat," the King said to the older

7

man. "I did not want it to spoil or to rot in the sun. Eat well, my friend. Build your strength. I may summon you to fight…in the next battle season." The peasant frowned at the King's words but said nothing. "Strengthen your body." Charlemagne drew a sword from his pack.

"Here, take this sword and practice. Any skill you develop will aid the realm, as well as your family." He handed the man the weapon.

Charlemagne and his Peers returned to the attacked settling and picked up the marauder's trail. The renegades' tracks were clear in the damp soil. As the sun began to sink in the western sky, Charlemagne and his friends came upon the outlaws. They sheltered under a stand of oak trees, wrapped in blankets, sleeping. The King and his Peers gathered around them. Rinaldo nudged one of them with his toe.

"Kill and maraud, then take your rest, I suppose." Roland observed.

"Aye, killing is exhausting work." Charlemagne intoned, looking at the six, snoring men. The heaviest outlaw in the group startled, jumped from his linens, and unsheathed his sword. His eyes widened. Seeing armed men surrounding him and his companions, he slipped his sword back into its sheath. Belligerently, he sneered into the faces of the men on horseback.

"What do you think you're doing?" He glared at Rinaldo, as he stepped back. "Who are you to sneak around us…some noble's lackeys, I bet? We be free men and sleep where we like." The outlaw looked into the Peers' stern faces. Thrusting his chest out, he demanded: "What noble house do you guard?" He noticed their well-formed swords, daggers, and well-fed horses. The King nudged Samson forward and stared into the outlaw's face.

"What house? ...the noblest house of them all." Charlemagne replied. "I, Charlemagne, King of the Franks, do sentence you to death...for mayhem, destruction, and murder. May God forgive you. None here will do so." The man's eyes widened, his mouth a big 'O' in his face. He fell to his knees, his head touching the earth.

"Ahh... great king!" he exclaimed. "Forgive me! I do bow to you!"

"Bow to those you brutalized, those lying dead in their own blood." Charlemagne's words hung in the silent air. "Your life is over. This day, all of you forfeit your lives. Only God in heaven can forgive such as you. Death to you." The other five men, now standing, made as if to run. "Take them." With the curses of the leader ringing around their ears, the Peers hanged the outlaws from the nearby trees.

"Such a quick death is too good for them. Let them hang. Leave the bodies there. Mayhap their slow turning on these ropes will discourage others of their kind." Charlemagne turned to his Peers.

"Roland, come with me. We must check on Count Hautgard's safety. He supplies 'sweet delights' to nobles' tables and was a loyal friend to Poppa. The rest of you, ride east, talk to the people, find out if other outlaws plague the region. But don't go too far. We'll meet you in two days' time at the old oak. From there, we'll catch up with the mobile court and journey to Aachen for the holy days. Be off with you!" The other Peers nodded, bade the two 'God Speed' and rode east.

"Let's pray this band did not, also, attack Hautgard's manor before turning to bed down here." Charlemagne said to Roland. "I hate killing our people, Roland; but such brutality must be punished. I wonder: will young Elsbeth ever put this horror behind her? And what was the reason for it? Her uncle's family had nothing of value. Those damn outlaws didn't even kill the animals for meat, just slaughtered the livestock and left the bodies lying in the dirt." The King rubbed his eyes wearily.

"Killing for the love of killing, this carnage must stop!" He gazed into Roland's face. "Tell me, can anyone explain this kind of slaughter? Are these men human?"

"Of a certainty, Sire, they are. But these are evil men, just as there are good men, those who sacrifice and forgive — even give their lives for others. Those are heroes. But, these men are villains. We must wipe them out; there is no choice." Roland stated firmly.

"Pray Hautgard's manor is safe." The line between the king's eyes deepened; he scanned the sky toward Septimania. "If he has come to harm…" Charlemagne refused to finish his thought. "Let's ride."

"He has not a single guard at his manor, does he, Sire?" Roland remembered the count's industrious but unprotected home.

"Nay, not one. There's my worry, Roland. I fear for his life and for his family. We must hurry!" Charlemagne turned Samson toward Count Hautgard's manor.

An hour or so later, the two men crested a hill and looked down into the count's stable yard. Two young boys hurried horses into the stable, looking over their shoulders as they pointed and shouted toward Charlemagne and Roland. Coming out of the barn and looking north, Count Hautgard waved as he spotted Charlemagne's banner. The count, a handsome man despite his years, with an open smile and a warm and ready laugh, hurried toward them. His pace increased as the King and Roland drew near.

"Your Majesty, it's good to see you!" Hautgard welcomed them, waited for the king to dismount, and, then, enveloped him in a huge hug. "Please accept again my deepest sympathies at the passing of your good father, Charles. I loved him well and was proud to call him my friend, as well as my king." The count turned to clasp Roland close. "Roland, welcome to my house."

"Thank you, Count Hautgard." Charlemagne replied as Roland got a hug. The King noticed a tear at the corner of the count's eye. His tear invited a few of Charlemagne's own. "My memories of being here with Poppa do deem this a homecoming, Sir. I am happy to see you again." Charlemagne embraced the count once more, determined to remember the happy times spent at this manor.

"Tell me, your majesty, how is your mother? Gisela? Carloman? What brings you so far from court?" Hautgard put his arm around the King's shoulders, just as he had when the King was but a lad. "I hope your court journeys toward us for Christmastide. I have new 'delights' to win the children's hearts."

"Gisela is fine, Sir. And you know my mother." Charlemagne replied. "She is nothing, if not resilient." The men smiled at each other, acknowledging their shared knowledge of the queen mother. They both knew of Bertrada's 'resilience' first hand. "We're doing as well as can be expected, except for Carl, with whom you know I share the crown. He began a journey to visit us for Yuletide but fell ill and recovers in Lombardy. We hope he will join us in Aachen for the Holy Days." Hautgard raised an eyebrow.

"...recovering in Lombardy, is he? I don't think King Desiderius' company will help an ailing man. How strange Carl lingers there." The Count replied.

King Charlemagne sighed in simple thankfulness for the count. When a boy he visited this manor often with his father and always received a son's welcome. He felt a deep sense of relief. All was peaceful. Responding to Charlemagne's questions, Hautgard confirmed the people of his manor had no contact with the marauders. He was unaware of any outlaw bands in the area. Reiterating his joy in seeing the two men, the Count led the king and Roland into the manor.

Hautgard was a simple man who loved people, who admired his king, and who felt blessed by Charlemagne's visit. He immediately made the women of his house –his countess; his daughter, Maria; and her visiting friend, Hildegard –aware of the King's arrival. He bade them prepare a banquet and cautioned them not to forget the 'sweet delights.'

In his youth the count traveled all over the realm, even into the Middle East. During these travels, he discovered Arabian pastries and Indian spices. Foreseeing the delight such sweets would garner, he obtained recipes and spices to prepare them at home. The count could read and write, one of the reasons noble families knew of his 'sweet delights.' Finding a noble who appreciated his unusual pastries, Haugard wrote or visited the nobles' manor to inquire if the families wished pastries delivered to their doors. If so, Count Hautgard would bake, wrap, and transport his wares to aristocratic mouths. His ingenuity made him a wealthy man. Now, he led Charlemagne and Roland into his library, filled with exotic artifacts collected from his journeys.

"We may speak here privately, your majesty," he assured the King. "I apologize for the sparse nature of my library, though." His library contained, mostly, account books and correspondence. Even he could not afford handwritten codices, copied diligently by Frankish monks. He owned two hand-bound parchments. One was a wood-backed binding of pages which outlined his family history. The other was a codex of the four Gospels which Charlemagne's father, King Pepin, gave him years before. It was his most precious possession. Haut-gard lovingly showed it to Charlemagne, praising King Pepin once again.

"Examine this, Charles." He held out the codex. "Your father was a generous man and a thinking king, an unbeatable combination." He paused for a moment, willing himself not to weep. "He is sorely missed, my son, sorely missed."

Roland sat silently, making notations, assessing soldiers and manor guards garrisoned within three leagues of the count's manor. In an emergency, they might be called on for help. If Charlemagne needed more men to deal with these marauding bands, Roland would have a list of local garrisons and manors - their locations and strength. As Hautgard praised King Pepin, Roland frowned, struggling to swallow.

Charlemagne noticed Roland's distress and swallowed hard himself, remembering his father was, also, a father to Roland as well. Roland caught the King's eye and shook his head slightly. Both men recognized the deep loss on the other's face. Charle-magne squeezed his hand into a fist and raised it slightly to Ro-land, trying to share his strength. He wrenched his mind from the black hole of loss which talk of his father always opened.

Charlemagne still turned unconsciously: to ask his father a question, to seek direction, to interpret his father's reactions, to crystallize his own thoughts. In the dark moments of the early morning, when he could not sleep, Charlemagne asked God the reason for his father's early death. *Had Poppa lived, Carloman and I both would better understand the art of governing.*

"If only Poppa were with us a little longer, Hautgard," he said to the Count, "Carl and I could move forward with more confidence. With only another half year, Poppa would have taught us so much more. I was just beginning to understand Poppa's views of a king's duties, his commitment to justice, his determination to improve the lives of the Frankish people." Charlemagne brushed away his own tears.

"Poppa taught without knowing it, by example. His expectations were high, of a certainty; but his patience was as well. His methods were different - quite contrary to those of my mother. Singlehandedly, he took the realm from the last Merovingian king, even obtained the blessing of the Pope in the process. He was a planner and a visionary. How I yearn to be half the man my father was." The king bowed his head, his grief as fresh as the day his father succumbed some eighteen months before.

"If I can only emulate his kindness, his understanding, his purity of heart, the Lord will be pleased with me yet." Count Hautgard dipped his head in respect for Charlemagne's praise of his father. His heart went out to the young man he had known since birth. Attempting to move beyond his recurring sorrow and to alert Hautgard, the King spoke openly to the count.

"Count, I need your help. Some hours ago, we overtook an outlaw band which is preying on small settlings." The King corrected himself as Hautgard's mouth dropped open in shock. "...nay, not preying. Six men destroyed a settling, the one just over the west hills. They killed men and beasts alike, even a three-month-old infant."

"Killing?" The count frowned, rose from his seat, paced. "...to what purpose? You mean - killing their own countrymen?"

"Aye," Charlemagne confirmed, "killing men, women, children, animals—anything which breathed. Have you heard rumor of them in your travels, Hautgard?"

"Nay, nay, Sire!" The count's eyes moved to his sword, hanging nearby. He shook his head vehemently. "I would have sent a missive to you right away, right away." He paced around the small library. "What is the reason for such killing? The harvests this year were plentiful. There was much opportunity for men to work, to gather the crops. Outlaws, you say? Killing people? A mad man must lead them."

"The Peers and I tracked this particular band and hanged them," the King declared. "But there are others. Are they evil, bent on destruction? Or does someone direct them; is there a purpose to their marauding? I must know." The King waited for Hautgard to respond. He could see the count understood what he was about to ask of him.

"You must listen and watch, Hautgard. Anything you hear or see, send me word. Not a single person must know of our pact, Hautgard, not even your countess." The King locked his eyes on Hautgard's face. "Do you understand me?" His voice was low and solemn, emphasizing the need for secrecy. While the count pondered Charlemagne's request, Roland leaned toward the King and whispered softly.

"Might we not offer the count a small guard, Sire? It would bring him comfort and would also remind him hourly of his duty?" King Charlemagne returned Roland's warm, slightly mischievous smile and wink. They had been sharing the same conspiratorial wink since they grappled in the practice yard together as young boys.

"Of a certainty." Turning to Count Hautgard, Charlemagne sweetened his request. "Count, I hope you will not take this amiss. May I post a small guard here, just to keep your manor safe? It would put my mind at ease." The king smiled, nodding at Roland. "You are easy prey out here, for desperate and driven men. Can you house them - in your stable, mayhap?" The count beamed with relief and thankfulness.

"My dear Charley, I would be much in your debt. Aye! I welcome such a guard and will treat them with all respect. I do pledge it." He obliquely referred to the King's need of his eyes and ears. "With regard to this other matter, I am, as always, your obedient servant. Be at ease. I will be diligent."

"I expected nothing less, Hautgard," the king nodded, "though I am much relieved. Watch and listen, my friend. No word is too small for you to note. Attend the upcoming harvest festivals, present yourself in the churches; take your rest in an inn from time to time." The king named the places which always provided information to an astute listener. "Linger in the common rooms. There will be plans and counter-plans discussed during the upcoming winter—in taverns, in brothels, at yuletide gatherings." He paused for the count to absorb his suggestions.

"These accursed men must be stopped, Hautgard! You will be my eyes and ears in this part of the realm. I'm relying on you." He watched the count accept his words and take a deep breath. "And I will long remember your faithful service at this critical time. You have my oath."

Chapter Two
HOPES AND DREAMS

Giving a quick knock on the door, Hildegard—the young woman from Swabia—entered the library. Charlemagne saw her before she spoke. The demure cast of her face, her shyness in entering the library, the liveliness of her intelligent eyes, her glowing face, all overwhelmed the king.

"Excuse me, Count, and your majesty," Hildegard said softly. "...just another few minutes before the meal can be served, Sire, if you are ready." Hildegard felt the king staring at her and blushed. She lifted her eyes to his face and held her breath. *He's watching me!* Her hand went to her headdress, then to the neck of her tunic. *How must I look? I'm flushed from the heat of the baking ovens. My clothing is disarranged from the bustle at the king's visit!* She swallowed and, immediately, controlled herself. *The king has nothing to do with me.* Hilde reminded herself. *He's visiting the Count's family.*

Having reassured herself, she smiled at King Charlemagne, her dark hair shining in the glow of the candles. Her curious eyes glanced from the count to the king. She smiled at Roland.

Hildegard thought her hair, curling about her face, unruly. But Charlemagne wished to touch it as she pushed one piece behind her ear. Her white, alabaster skin glowed, as her face reflected her regard. Noticing Charlemagne's stare, she blushed, embarrassed for him to see her interest. *He will think me wanton, if I stare into his eyes.* Hildegard looked quickly from the king to Count Hautgard.

"We are ready to break our fast, my dear," the count responded. "The king and I are just completing our reminiscences. Aye, we join you immediately." Hildegard curtseyed and hurried back to the cook room.

With their discussion completed, Charlemagne and Roland excused themselves, going to their bedchamber to change their linens for the evening meal. As they departed the library, they saw Hildegard hurrying down the hall as well. The king, nodding at her, spoke to Roland.

"What a ravishing creature she is! This meal will provide pleasure to both our eyes and stomachs."

"Aye, she is comely," Roland agreed. "She seems not as energetic as your sister, Gisela. But Lady Hildegard most certainly pleases the eye." Roland was happy to see the King's face lose its long-standing sadness. Since his father's death and his damaged son's birth, Charlemagne's famous eye for women seemed to have disappeared. Roland smiled at his comment about Hildegard. "...ravishing, Sire? Can it be you're recovering your adventurous spirit, your appreciation for 'God's best creation'? I agree; her beauty would delight any heart." The king stared in the direction Hildegard turned.

"It's certain her smile and laughter will decorate our evening meal. What a figure, Roland!" Charlemagne threatened to be poetic in his compliments. "You do see? She is healthy and beautiful both." He held up one hand. "Aye, before you say it, she *is* young, not more than thirteen or fourteen years; but she is blessedly curvy. Her eyes are clear, her back straight, her hair shining — all indications of good health and fertility."

Charlemagne frowned as he thought of the number of children lost every year in the realm. Because so many children died before their first birthdays, Germanic tribes much valued fruitful women. Healthy children, borne by a strong mother, guaranteed more hands for the difficult work of toiling in the fields. The more children each woman birthed and kept alive, the stronger was the realm.

"Name any maid in the court who is so tantalizing." Charlemagne dared Roland.

"I think not, Sire. I never disagree with a ruler's opinion of a beautiful woman, especially when the woman's face and figure invite comment. Mayhap, the lady from Swabia will lift your spirits, Sire, revive your hopeful view of life, hum?" Roland teased.

Replacing her every-day tunic with an embroidered one, Hildegard returned to the banquet hall. Count Hautgard, Charlemagne and Roland stood together in front of the great fire-pit at the far end of the room. Lined with stones, it supported a fire during much of the year. The men stood talking, enjoying the mellow light of the fire as much as its heat.

Hildegard's eyes focused on the King. His stature intimidated her; but his ready laugh, open affection for the Count's family, and seemingly close relationship with Roland reassured her. *He does seem a fun-loving man, though he has, of a certainty, arrived here to discuss serious matters.* When she announced the evening meal, the king's demeanor reflected substantive purpose. She hoped the Count's affairs were in order. But Hildegard was not seriously concerned. She was unable to imagine a mistake the careful, organized Count might make. Besides, the Count knew the King when he was a young boy; they clearly respected and loved each other. For another, though, the king would be a formidable adversary, indeed.

Charlemagne returned Hildegard's gaze. In fact, he stared at the body outlined under her clothing. A dark, green tunic appeared as Hildegard slipped off her mantle. Her waist was cinched by a belt embedded with small emeralds. Like gems hung from her ears, almost covered by her black, shining curls. The green pattern of her belt was re-created in her headdress, her veil more a frame for her face than a cover.

Comparing Roland's compact figure with the king's more robust one, Hildegard's attention was, again, caught by Charlemagne's stature. His size and strength promised an easy response to any threat. Although he stood more than six feet tall and was well-muscled, he was light in his walk. His fair hair reflected the glow from the fire and emphasized the golden brown of his eyes. In changing his clothing, the king replaced his plain, linen tunic with a soft, beige shirt. Over it he wore an embroidered silk tunic, rich in deep, azure tones. His breeches, pulled over the bands around his legs, were the same rich blue. He did not wear the matching mantle. Hildegard imagined he found the hall warm for his taste. Charlemagne's intense gaze rested on Hildegard. His pleasure in her was reflected on his face.

"I hope she finds me as pleasing as I find her." He whispered under his breath.

"Ahh, here come the ladies now." Count Hautgard beamed. "Sire, may I present my family? You remember the Countess Hautgard, of a certainty."

"Your Majesty, we are honored by your presence." The

Countess curtseyed deeply and smiled into Charlemagne's face.

"I am delighted to greet you again, Countess." Charlemagne bowed and kissed her hand, noticing her surprise. "You are as lovely as ever. I still remember your cream custard tarts with gluttony! It does make my mouth water to recall them." The countess laughed with delight and kissed him on the cheek.

"Aye," she smiled. "You were the most appreciative of my sweets, Charles. No matter what I offered, you ate with great glee. Why, I have never—before or since—seen a six-year-old who could eat so many custard tarts...at one time!" She laughed at the blush rising on his face. "Had I known of this visit, I would surely have prepared some for you, with my own hands." She smiled at her husband and nodded at the young women.

"Sire, may I present our young friend from Swabia, Lady Hildegard?" The count nudged a glowing Hildegard toward Charlemagne. "She is my Maria's best friend and often graces our home with her beauty and charm, not to mention her intelligence. She has some strong opinions for such a beautiful girl, but they are invariably good ones." He turned to his daughter. "And you remember our Maria." Hildegard and Maria curtseyed together.

"Maria," the King acknowledged the Hautgards' younger daughter and kissed her hand. "I am pleased to see you again, though you have grown up since my last visit." Maria smiled happily at the King and inclined her head, basking in the gentle kiss.

"And Jocelyn? Is she not at home?" Charlemagne asked the count.

"Nay. She visits her aunt. She needed a change of scene, she said." Count Hautgard smiled.

"Tell her I regret missing her." The King replied. "Although years younger than I, she was an enthusiastic companion when I visited your manor, Sir." Charlemagne turned to Maria's friend.

"I am honored, Lady Hildegard." He bowed, kissed her tiny hand lightly and, then, stepped back quickly, lest he lose himself in her cerulean blue eyes. Not allowing his eyes to linger on her, he addressed the three women. "I hope the count did not keep you overlong in the cook room, ladies. I know he advocates for culinary excess as long as he does not figure in the preparations!"

The meal was as rich and sumptuous as Charlemagne remembered. Platters were stacked with succulent, roasted fowl and savory, spiced meats, all dressed with the rare fruits and spices grown in Hautgard's sprawling gardens. Carrols, parsnips, and dried beans accompanied the meats, both blending with the smell of fresh-baked bread and honey-dough. Instead of cheese, nuts, and persimmons, the meal ended with a panoply of the Count's famous 'delights.'

When all ate their fill and left the table, Hildegard stepped into the small garden behind the prayer chapel to take in the fresh night air. In the afternoon, Countess Hautgard invited an itinerant minstrel to entertain for the night. As the man strummed, Hildegard made her escape. She sought just a bit of solitude. Her head felt full and ached, although she could not explain the reason. *The king makes me feel so strange. I feel both queasy and buoyant.*

In the garden, the weather was still balmy, not yet winter, but a welcome respite from the warmth and closeness of the banquet hall. Hildegard breathed in the crisp air and, suddenly, felt a chill. She was about to turn toward her chamber to get a light wrap when a looming figure stepped out of the shadows with her mantle folded over his arm. It was the king!

"I saw you slip out," Charlemagne stammered, suddenly tongue-tied. "I didn't want you to catch cold." He held out her cloak. "My herbalist says cooling off too quickly is bad for the digestion, as well as for the body." He stepped closer and threw the mantle about her shoulders. He fell silent, feeling the crimson creep into his cheeks. Hildegard giggled and, then, quickly covered her smile with her hand. She did not remember seeing a warrior blush.

"Excuse me, your majesty," she apologized hurriedly. "I did not mean to laugh. You sound so serious." She glanced at him from under lowered lids. "Thank you for your concern; but, honestly, I am very strong. My father taught me too much can be made of chills. They do not cause illness, he says. In fact, where I come from, some believe the cold prevents the development of serious body problems."

"I take your word for your strength." Charlemagne smiled, seeing the count was right about Hildegard's strong opinions. "The cold may, indeed, deserve this defense. I know little of healing. But, indulge me—just this once—and keep warm." The king carefully re-arranged her mantle across her shoulders, even unfastening her brooch to place it in her hand. "It's best to bundle up." He nodded at her to close the mantle with the brooch. Hildegard pinned her mantle shut and raised her eyes, looking directly into the king's serious face.

He stared at her. Hildegard took a step back. *How intent and mesmerized he looks!* A flash of fear ran through her. *Does he hope to read my thoughts?* Her initial smile faltered as she glanced quickly at the ground. *I have never received such a rapt look. I thought his attention to me arose from his admiration; but, if so, why does he not speak?* Hildegard was at a lost. *What did I do to subdue his spirit?*

Charlemagne stepped toward Hildegard, thinking to kiss her hand. But he noticed her unease and, instead, turned toward the garden gate. Her hesitation and less animated face stopped him. Having no experience with a woman's quietness, he did not know what to do. In times past, his attention to a woman and his concern for her comfort garnered him many thanks and much warm attention. But those women were neither shy nor silent.

"I should take my leave." He turned toward the manor's door. Hildegard did not reply. Entering the manor, Charlemagne turned back to her. "Good sleep, Hildegard." He pulled the door behind him. "Hold your mantle close."

Hildegard did not understand. Charlemagne spoke and joked with her during the meal. Now, he hurried away.

"What have I done? Why am I such a ninny? I can't expect constant attention from the king and, then, falter in my admiration of him." She despaired over her behavior. "A man pays me some small attention, and I can but giggle or misread his intention." Her dark hair bounced with her head's negative shake.

"I must spend more time with men," Hildegard decided. "I must learn to understand them — their moods, their expectations. I pray the King doesn't think me a baby." She sighed and pushed the heavy, oak door to re-enter the manor. Turning, she saw the count and Charlemagne passing, seemingly returning to the count's library. When Charlemagne spied Hildegard in the doorway, he winked and gave her a huge smile.

"Sweet dreams, my garden sprite." he whispered.

Chapter Three
CONNECTIONS AND REALITIES

The sun was well up when Maria and Hildegard awoke the following morning. Hearing servants' voices in the hall, both young women, still excited about the King's visit, jumped from their sleeping benches. Invariably prompt and conscientious, the two flushed with embarrassment when they realized the Count and Countess, King Charlemagne, and Roland broke their morning fast some hours ago. The two young women dressed hurriedly, taking care with their clothing. Mayhap an improved appearance would decrease their lack of punctuality. Countess Hautgard expected everyone to gather for the morning meal. They knew she would be disappointed.

"Do you think we'll see the King this morning?" Hildegard asked Maria, mumbling as she hurriedly rummaged through her trunk, moving clothing from one side to the other. *I'll wear my new scarf, if I can find it.* Pulling a silk scarf from under a tunic, she held it against her arm, judging its color near her skin. Hilde could hear Maria bustling around, searching for her most becoming headdress, no doubt. Hilde said nothing personal about the King—nothing about his concern for her health yesterday night in the garden or his attentions to her.

Even though Hildegard could not explain his long stares, she decided not to mention those to Maria either. She did hazard a guess or two and felt excited and flustered by the direction those thoughts took her. Remembering the King's intensity, Hilde was less uncomfortable about his stares this morning. In fact, she smothered her wish to sing out loud.

Whenever she remembered the King's eyes on her face, she knew he appreciated and admired her. *Could I be getting a fever? First, I feel overly warm and, then, suddenly, cool. It must be the change in weather.* Hildegard shivered and turned, placing her shawl around her shoulders.

"Oh, Hilde, I think the King will have left, don't you?" Maria asked. "At the evening meal, he reminded Lord Roland they should depart early this morning. And here, we overslept! I'll bet we missed their leaving."

"Aye, I remember." Hildegard knew the King would still be in the manor. *He will, of a certainty.* "He and Roland are, of a certainty, far away by now." She hid her smile beneath her clothing as she pulled her tunic over her head. Concentrating, she arranged her only silk scarf around her neck.

Maria, noticing the scarf, said nothing as she cinched her belt. She watched Hildegard take extra care with her clothing and wondered if the King's attention piqued Hildegard's interest in men. Maria hid her smile. Just yesterday, she lectured Hildegard on her tendency to ignore the young men who visited the manor. So far, Hildegard was singularly unimpressed with each of them, even when Maria praised them. But now, her shining eyes and low-key humming suggested interest in the King. Maria frowned, pursing her lips. She was not certain this interest was a good thing. The King was married after all.

"Come, Poppa will know the King's plans." Maria assured Hildegard as she took her friend's hand. They agreed they would return after the meal to straighten the room. Their tunics and breeches were scattered over the sleeping bench; their sleeping clothes crumpled in a heap on the floor. Their room, above the banquet room and, therefore, basking in heat from the firepit, was toasty. But once they opened the door, they were thankful for their shawls. Each patted her headdress one last time. Together, they descended the stairs. Both young women noticed the chill still in the air.

"What think you of Lord Roland, Hildegard?" Maria asked, giggling. "Do you find his looks pleasing? I should like to walk with **him** in the garden." Smiling widely, she tapped Hildegard's arm. "And how was your walk with the King?" Hildegard blushed and turned her face away so Maria could not see. Maria thought, again, of Hildegard's giddy behavior when she returned from the garden to their chamber yesterday night. She was both amused and curious.

"What do you mean? The King brought my mantle to the garden. He feared I would take a chill." Hildegard explained earnestly as she and Maria reached the bottom of the stairs. "We didn't walk at all far." Even as she corrected Maria's words, Hildegard wished the King had hours to spend with her.

"He does seem very thoughtful." Maria replied. Then, she burst out laughing. "Oh, Hildegard! King Charlemagne is elegant and speaks well but don't be too charmed by him. He has played with many of the maids at court..." Hildegard's stare stopped her in mid-sentence. "Well, the stable boys say so!"

"Guard your affections, Hildegard. There is no future with this King; he has a wife and son." She fixed her eyes on Hildegard's face. "Don't forget that." She gently squeezed Hildegard's shoulder. Smiling to soften her admonition, Maria led the way as she and Hilde entered the entrance hall.

"As for me, I favor Lord Roland. He's so handsome!" She gasped as she looked up; there sat the King and her father, intent over a map.

"Good day to you, stars of the morning." King Charlemagne greeted them as he stood. He bowed to Maria but kept his eyes on Hildegard's face. She murmured 'Good morrow' shyly, keeping her eyes downcast. She did not wish any of them to understand her happiness in seeing the King. Maria watched Charlemagne and Hildegard carefully. Although she felt some positive response in the King's face toward Hildegard, she could not see her friend's face and decided she made a mistake in thinking Hildegard interested. She detected no special reaction in her behavior. Still, she did well in cautioning Hildegard to guard her feelings, to remain aloof from this charming king.

"I trust the night gave you rest." At the King's soft tone, Count Hautgard looked up. He saw the King's eyes locked on Hildegard.

"Come; break your fast, my dears." The Count invited, a bit uncomfortable. "King Charlemagne, Lord Roland and I broke our fast 'ere you woke. But sit, you two, sit. I shall call for bread and cheese." The Count nodded to the King and disappeared into the corridor, calling his wife's name. As Count Hautgard left the room, the King wrenched his eyes from Hildegard and spoke to both young women.

"Roland and I must turn our mounts toward the mobile court; but it is such a beautiful morning that we agreed to linger a bit. It is to you fairies we appeal for entertainment. Would you honor us by indulging in a little fresh air and lively exercise? Please, accompany us for a ride along the river." Excited, Maria and Hildegard shook their heads vigorously, excusing themselves to retrieve their mantles. A moment later, coming down the stairs, Maria flipped her mantle over her shoulder and turned to Hildegard.

"Please, Hilde, entertain the King a bit so I might have time to speak with Lord Roland." Maria begged. "I would ask him about training horses."

"Would you?" Hildegard frowned. "I didn't realize you were interested in horse training." Maria laughed gaily, put her fingers to her lips, and shook her head. She shrugged and smiled widely at Hildegard.

"Nay, I'm not. But it's a subject Lord Roland delights in discussing." She winked at Hildegard. "I can ask questions, seek his advice, respond to his enthusiasm…and learn much about interacting with a man." She hesitated and frowned. "Don't you think so?"

"Don't ask me, Maria." Hildegard replied. "I know less than you about men—talking to them or anything else. Come, we must hurry or they will leave without joining us for a ride." She did so want to see the King again.

"We cannot ride overlong." The King warned them, opening the manor door for Maria and Hildegard. "Roland and I must rendezvous with the rest of our party before mid-day. We can waste no time in making for Aachen. There's snow in those clouds in the east." At the young women's sparkling eyes, he offered an invitation.

"You must visit my sister, Gisela, when you can, in Aachen. The warm pools in the caves are God's gift when snow and ice cover the trees. The water never goes cold." Maria and Hildegard gasped. No one ever told them of such pools. They nodded eagerly at the King, their faces full of wonder at being invited to court.

"Help me understand more about these pools, Sire," Hildegard said to the King. "The ones you mention, they are warm year round, even in winter?"

"Aye," Charlemagne answered. "They are warm from…" Hildegard raised her hand, motioning for him not to speak.

"Do you mind if I try to explain their warmth?" she asked.

29

"Nay," the King answered, his interested piqued. "What do you think could produce such a thing — warm pools of water all year 'round?" He looked at Hildegard bemused, positive her incapable of providing a plausible explanation for such a phenomenon.

"I read of such pools in the cold lands," Hildegard responded. "I talked about them with our manor's healer who studied in Rome. Sire, he knows much about ancient peoples. We decided there must be hot rocks in the earth. The rocks somehow warm the water before it bubbles up into the pools. But we don't know how the rocks become hot. That is a mystery, for certain." Charlemagne's mouth fell open. *I never wondered why the water is hot. I just explained it as a miracle, a gift from a loving God.* His eyes twinkled. *This one is a thinker and not afraid to voice explanations. The Count is right. She is outspoken.*

"Maybe we should speculate about those hot rocks, Hildegard. What do you think can heat rock?" He replied, taking her bridle and leading her away from Roland and Maria.

"I believe those two are going to solve the mystery of warm pools, Maria," Roland commented. He laughed as he dipped his head toward the King and Hildegard.

"Aye, Sir," Maria answered. "Their minds do seem to delight in the same thoughts, do they not? I'm relieved. I'm afraid Hildegard's becoming bored here. She does so love to explain things. None of us can match her in thought...or in curiosity."

"And so does the King delight in figuring things out. They seem well-matched..." Noticing Maria's furrowed brow, Roland added, "...to discuss nature's ways. Aye?"

"So it appears," Maria confirmed. She hoped their shared interests would not compromise Hildegard's good reputation. The King was famous for his conquests of women — willing women, mayhap. But, in an affair of the heart, *his* reputation would suffer no damage, of a certainty. The same could not be said for Hildegard. Maria turned back to Roland.

"Tell me how to choose a horse, Lord Roland."

Charlemagne smiled as he crossed over beside Hildegard. "And where do you wish to..." Charlemagne's voice died away, as a rabbit darted in front of Hildegard's horse. The horse reared, whinnied loudly and cantered away. Hildegard, a very good rider, had the horse under control immediately. But seeing the King wave Roland back as he turned Samson toward her, she gave her horse its head, though she pretended to pull on the reins.

Quickly, the King rode up beside her, caught her horse's bridle, and slowed down both horses. Hildegard pulled on her reins, this time in earnest. Charlemagne stopped the horses, dismounted quickly and hurried to Hildegard's side.

"My dear, are you hurt?" Charlemagne's wide eyes and flushed face convinced Hildegard he truly believed she was in danger. She felt immediately guilty for feigning distress, for attempting to encourage the King's attention. *What am I doing*? Hildegard asked herself. She dropped her head. *As Maria reminded me, the King is a married man. Despite that, he worries for my well-being.* He just has a good heart, she thought. Immediately contrite, she turned to him, solemn and apologetic.

"Oh, I fare well, Sire, thank you." She tossed her curls. "Just for a moment, I lost control of my mount. Thank you for such an immediate and gallant rescue." She whispered, suddenly shy. "You are a good rider." She added the last comment to emphasize her thanks for his concern. The relief in his eyes, his broad smile - both frightened Hildegard. He does over-react to my danger, she thought. *But, mayhap, he has a special concern for the safety of women.*

"I want no harm to come to you," the King answered seriously. "How would it look if the King's riding companion were injured?" He flashed a quick smile, though his serious demeanor startled and puzzled Hildegard. He reached up, put his arms around her waist, lifted her from the saddle, and set her on the ground beside her horse. "Do let us walk a little so you might regain your balance."

Hildegard scarcely heard his words. Her body tingled where his hands lifted her. She had just lost something to be cherished when he removed his hands from her waist. She felt light-headed and began to breathe deeply, hoping to slow her racing heart. Hearing her deep breaths, the King looked into her face.

"Are you winded, Hildegard?"

"…not at all, Sir. I am used to riding." Hildegard ducked her head. "I'm honored and pleased…to walk with you." Hildegard answered before she thought. She startled, confused by both the laughter bubbling inside her and by her fear of displeasing the King. I have never felt so giddy, she thought to herself. Clamping her urge to giggle, she looked at the King. He was staring at her, almost as if he did not realize where he was. As she watched, he shook his head, as if to clear it, and looked back at her intently.

"I'm relieved you're not injured. Your horse lunged before I saw the rabbit. Thank God Samson runs quickly!" His eyes moved to the river. "I do so love the water. Have you done any fishing during your visit?"

"Aye, Maria and I fished a few days ago, Sire. There's a grassy spot, there."

She pointed to the left as Charlemagne saw the river through the trees. He held his hand out to Hildegard, leading her across the field. Hildegard looked toward the bushes and stumbled over a hole in the ground. She gave a small cry as her ankle turned. Charlemagne tightened his hand reflexively, preventing her from falling.

"Flex your foot," he directed. "Here, I'll hold you steady." Hildegard moaned as she moved her foot. Charlemagne lowered her to the ground.

"Hildegard," he said, "I must examine your foot." He kneeled on the ground and touched her ankle. "Move your foot back and forth, from side to side, for me." As Hildegard complied with his requests, she gasped. Her face turned pale.

"You have a sprain." Charlemagne touched the puffiness in her ankle. "Your ankle is swelling, even as we watch. Here, let me help you up. We should go back to the manor." He took her arm, steadying her as he whistled for the horses. As Hildegard held her arms out for balance, the King put his hand around her waist.

"Your Majesty, I appreciate your concern. My foot is throbbing quite..." She stopped speaking as Charlemagne's lips touched hers. Later, Hildegard was unsure the King kissed her, so gentle and soft was the kiss. But she knew she could never have imagined such a thing, so the kiss must be true!

Chapter Four

CONFUSIONS AND REGRETS

Charlemagne excused himself and asked Roland to escort Hildegard and Maria back to the Hautgard manor.

"I must speak with the count one more time before we depart." He told them. He bowed to the two young women. "For the favor of the ride, I truly thank you." He scarcely looked toward Hildegard. "This morning was a wonderful end to our stay here. But, alas, duty calls and we must ride toward home." He turned and, then, caught himself. "Do think on my invitation to visit my sister at court. All of us would delight in your visit." Nodding at Maria and, then, at Hildegard, he turned his mount toward the count's library.

Charlemagne left Samson with one of he stable hands and hurried to Count Hautgard's library. Receiving a 'come' to his knock, the King bade a 'good morrow' to the Count.

"We must speak more of these outlaws, Hautgard." Charlemagne said as he entered the chamber. "But, first, thank you for the hospitality of your court. Our morning ride was very fine; you house two charming young women, Hautgard."

"They are both fine girls," the count agreed, beaming at Charlemagne. "I'm happy you are re-acquainted with my daughter and with her friend. Isn't Hildegard charming, though?"

"She is and an entertaining companion." Charlemagne agreed. His thoughts returned to his reckless kiss. *"I am surely losing my mind. What possessed me to kiss the young woman? I, I am a married king!"* Realizing Count Hautgard waited for him to speak, the King drew his mind from the morning ride and spoke to the Count.

"I am sorry I missed seeing Jocelyn. Countess Hautgard says she's visiting her aunt. Give her my greetings." The Count nodded and looked curiously at the King.

"You look worried, Charley? What is it?"

"These violent men pose danger for everyone in their path, Hautgard. God himself knows I don't wish to add to your burdens or disturb your dreams. But I must describe these outlaw's methods to you, all the better to warn you of their danger." He passed his hands over his eyes, hoping to block out his memory of yesterday's crushed settling.

"After discovering the destroyed settling, my Peers and I talked with those who saw the attack first-hand. We found the brother of the dead man. He confirmed my opinion. These are brutal, desperate men, Hautgard." The Count nodded and resumed his seat, stirring cinnamon and honey into the tea his countess left on the table.

"Is the threat only in this part of the realm, Charlemagne?" he inquired.

"Nay, there are reports of such bands every week," the King answered. "I heard of this particular one from an itinerant musician." He paused, his eyes boring into Count Hautgard's face. Charlemagne shook his head and seemed to make a decision. "I will describe their marauding. It's horrific, I warn you. I take no pleasure in sharing this but I must prevent your being lulled into believing these are typical robbers. I don't know their destination or, even, if they have one. Mayhap, they respond to every opportunity. I suspect the vulnerable are their prey. And I say 'prey,' Hautgard. They appear to hunt, seek out people to kill. They clearly are not hungry because they leave the animal carcasses, dead from a bow or a cut throat, on the ground to rot.

"They glory in the killing; I saw it in the sureness of their strokes. Finding such carnage is horrible, Count. There were blood flies everywhere!"

The Count's eyes grew large. He set his tea flagon on the table. Charlemagne's description made his stomach roll.

"As brutal as that," he replied. Charlemagne nodded, his face pale.

"Even in the best of times, Count," King Charlemagne added, "most of our people suffer. Their huts are barely adequate. Food is scarce and quickly eaten. People starve, even freeze, by the hundreds. Added to the people's daily struggles, these outlaw bands undermine the realm's stability. I beg you, keep me informed. We must break these marauders, decrease the fear they leave in their wake."

"I will watch, Sire, watch and listen. All of us working together should be able to eliminate this scourge from our land."

As one season folded into another, King Charlemagne's mobile court journeyed throughout the realm. Years before, King Pepin advised Charlemagne to move around the realm, to keep in touch with the people.

During the summer battle season, court members were busy: treating the wounded, repairing clothing and damaged weapons, rescuing those displaced by the battles. Priests and healers provided by the court cared for the soldiers and blessed the efforts of commanders as they marched into battle. Noble families, uneasy over the fighting and alert both to the pace of the battle and its fruition, supported the soldiers – their own as well as the soldiers in general.

Autumn was a time for healing, for preserving foodstuffs, for butchering livestock which wasn't maintained through the coming winter. Traveling toward its winter location, Charlemagne, his Peers, and his family interacted with the Frankish people, exchanged information, and renegotiated alliances. The King and the court nobles took advantage of hunting opportunities.

When the battle season ended, soldiers, peasants, and free men left the court and headed home. Their families and lords needed them to help prepare for the bitter, Frankish winter: to gather the harvest, to drop trees and cut fire-wood, to hunt game, to bolster hut walls and to protect their families.

And winter was the time of rest - the time when, finally, the year's circuit came to an end. There were leathers to repair, new clothing to sew, worn clothing to mend, and weary bodies to re-charge. Winters in Frankland were severe: days of bitter cold, snow and ice unending, sparse food, inadequate shelter. All men hunted and trapped during the winter, for certain. But the constant cold; the scarcity of food - despite clever planning and ongoing efforts to dry food and preserve it; and the migration of large animals brought the Frankish people to the verge of starvation. Many peasants, even landholders, were in danger of starving and, sometimes, of freezing to death. The constant travel, the lack of a home base, the wear and tear on clothing, spirit, and tempers made the winter stop a celebration, even had Christmastide not offered a reason for thanksgiving and rejoicing.

The harshness of the winters imperiled the tiny villages and settlings perched along the forest edge even more. Isolated and poorly defended, they were vulnerable to the random assaults of wanderers, outlaws, cast-offs - the degenerates of medieval society. The king's forays and the outlaws' fear of royal revenge did much to protect the peasants.

The annual, spring assembly brought nobles from all over Frankland to evaluate the realm's security and to plan for the upcoming battle season. Moving toward the first battle site, the court, again, visited nobles and paused in small villages, giving young and old, blessed and struggling, a chance to see the king.

It was both the people's need for his protection and his responsibility to them which drove King Charlemagne to follow the outlaw band to Septimania. Tracking evil-doers in increasingly bad weather was difficult but necessary. If the King ignored the attacks or postponed his retribution, the people's faith in him weakened. Criticism, threats, dire predictions from rabble-rousers and trouble makers would haunt the manors, churches, inns, towns and brothels - where ever people gathered.

Charlemagne and Hautgard hurried from the library. Roland waited in the courtyard; the reins of Charlemagne's mount in his hand. The commotion of the men's taking their leave occupied everyone's thoughts. After squeezing Count Hautgard's shoulder and bowing to Countess Hautgard, the King turned to Hildegard and kissed her hand.

"Forgive my forwardness, my lady," he whispered. "I don't wish to earn your poor regard. I'm an old, married man and must guard my little kisses more completely." He dropped his eyes. "Please, do not think ill of me. I did forget myself."

"I need no apology, Sire." Hildegard replied, too confused to say more. She was unable to decipher what happened. The King kissed her and, now, he begged her to forgive him. *His feeling must surely be brotherly to me.* "Truly, there is no harm done. I thank you for your rescue and for your worry about my injury, Sire. I will be well-recovered, even before you get to Aachen." King Charlemagne nodded, bade her farewell and nudged his heels into Samson's flanks, surprising Roland with his rapid departure.

"Is something amiss, Sire?" Roland questioned.

"Nay, nothing," the King answered. "I fear we lingered over-long on our ride. I would not wish the Peers to plant roots near the old oak, waiting for the two of us!" He laughed and urged his mount to a canter, attempting to eliminate any lingering thoughts of Hildegard's desirability...there beside the river.

"We make a late start, Sire," Roland confirmed. "But our horses are fresh. The Peers will likely be glad for a mid-day nap before we arrive."

"Aye," King Charlemagne answered. "But I don't want them to sleep away the day and keep us awake through the night, singing, drinking and recounting war stories. We must make plans for destroying these outlaw bands. All of us need clear minds." He patted Samson's neck, riding hard. It was no longer possible to talk together so Roland nodded and relaxed, allowing his body to match his horse's strides.

I'm a fool. Charlemagne reprimanded himself. His behavior with Hildegard filled his mind. *What was I thinking?* He shook his head in frustration, pushing his long, flowing hair behind his ears. *This lengthy conflict with my wife is clouding my judgment. I must take care. Young maids talk among themselves; they create great drama and involve everyone in their speculations. Once I had a reputation with women; but, thank God, my behavior since marrying Himiltrude is exemplary. I must control myself.* King Charlemagne smiled, thinking of the stolen kisses he once collected at every celebratory banquet held in his father's court.

Those young women's shock registered on their faces, just as Hildegard's face had. I remember. But they took great delight in a kiss from their prince. In past memories, his conquests delighted Charlemagne. But, now, his behavior with Hildegard felt dishonest.

King Charlemagne berated himself and made a vow. *I will give no more kisses. A less serious maid than Hildegard will read much into a little kiss. I must not think my marriage is over; Himiltrude and I will come back together. We must.* The King paused in his thoughts, surprised his mind dwelt on this one kiss. What is one little kiss, anyway? Suddenly, he remembered the last kiss he gave his wife.

His little son, bungling about to catch his balance, spit up on his mother's neck, just as the King bent to kiss it. The sticky milk quickly cooled Charlemagne's interest in kissing, as he and Himiltrude burst into laughter. Little Pippin shrieked, spraying them both with milk. The King smiled at the memory of his sticky little son and spurred Samson faster. But riding Samson like the wind did not help him forget his marital problems.

His first marriage was a joining encouraged by King Pepin because Charlemagne's younger brother, Carloman, was already a father. Pipin wanted both his sons to have heirs. But Charlemagne's joining proved much less amenable than all hoped, possibly because of the Queen Mother's constant interference. And the birth of his little, hunch-backed son, Peppin, was the final disappointment to the frayed couple. Charlemagne sighed and came back to the present. Roland, catching his eye, raised his hand and mimicked drinking from a flagon.

"It's time for a mid-day meal, Sire," he mouthed. "I'm hungry." The King nodded and turned Samson toward a near-by stand of oak trees, welcoming in their shade.

"Let's stop here, Roland," Charlemagne said. "Didn't I notice the Countess quietly putting food in our traveling bags?"

"She did, Sire," Roland confirmed, patting his own bag. "I hope she included venison left over from yesterday night's evening meal. My slice, even on top of all the other food, was sweet, indeed." The two men sat under the trees, eating the delicious fare Countess Hautgard provided. Roland unpacked hardboiled eggs, several rounds of cheese, slices of roast venison and boar, hunks of rye bread, and onions. He discovered walnuts, pecans, dried plums, bits of oatmeal, honey, and pork fat pressed into 'traveling bars.' The King laughed at his delighted expression when he held up the bars.

"Traveling bars are meant for munching in the saddle, Roland," Charlemagne pointed out. "Their sweetness increases one's energy for riding."

"Not if I eat them for a sweet treat now!" Roland retorted. The king laughed with Roland. But, then, in an instant, his face changed dramatically.

"Roland, what am I to do?" he asked. "I have a failed marriage; I have a damaged son. What is to become of my realm?" His eyes clouded; his back bent with sorrow. He gazed into Roland's face. "My brother, Carloman, worries me. He's unable to command the empire, has no understanding of the difficulties of rule. And he barely understands the concept of defense. He holds his own lands carelessly and thinks of battle only after someone attacks. Why must I maintain the realm, establish a Christian rule, oversee everything, if I have no able heir?" Roland, hearing the despair in his friend's voice, looked at the King, willing him to meet his eyes.

"My liege, are you asking me for advice?" At Charle-magne's mute nod, Roland answered. "Then, I must speak frankly. You may not like my words." Charlemagne grimaced but motioned for Roland to continue.

"Like them or not, I have need of your thoughts," he replied.

"...very well. My advice is this: do as you think best." Seeing the King's dismissive smile, Roland continued. "You must follow your own choices—not those of the Queen Mother. She argues, derides, demands until she wins you to her decisions, good or bad. You make strong, well-reasoned choices; but you never hold to your own opinion." Charlemagne raised his hands in supplication, as if begging Roland to understand his position.

"Stay. Stay and listen." Roland urged. "Who decided you would marry Himiltrude? Who chose the time for the marriage to take place? Who chose the color of your banner, when King Pepin decided to give both you and Carl colors separate from his own? Who argues, each year, about our Yuletide location? Who demanded you accept Ganelon at court? I know he is my stepfather but he does not belong with us. He wants only to fight and conquer—not to build." Roland stopped counting on his fingers."

"...unimportant decisions? I think not. Queen Bertrada influences too many decisions, decisions which people credit to you. She is not wise as was King Pepin; she is not competent to rule or to decide policy. She often alienates the court's nobles. Many of those decisions – the nobles who could participate in the spring joust, the counts who sat beside you at the Yuletide banquet are ill-advised."

"She is the Queen Mother, Roland," the King replied, suddenly realizing his docility to his mother painted him weak and controlled.

"Aye, but she is *not* the king, Charlemagne." Roland's words burst out, even as Charlemagne's face begged for understanding. Roland took a deep breath, hesitant to be frank but determined to give his best advice. "A failed marriage, you say? If that's true and the marriage ends, what will you do then?" He hurried on before he lost his courage. "You know the Queen Mother will demand you re-marry. She will not wait a fortnight. And she, of a certainty, will arrange your next betrothal."

"Aye," Charlemagne answered, hoping - with his monosyllable answer - Roland would desist. But Roland did not.

"You will have, again, a bride not of your own choosing, but one your mother chooses. Is that what you want? The regard you feel for Hildegard of Swabia," Roland suggested, "what will you do?" He searched the King's face, waiting for any response. Charlemagne did not reply. Roland shrugged, seeing his words had little impact. "Though Himiltrude brought an alliance and rekindled family bonds, she seems uninterested in your dreams for the Frankish people. Mayhap, you should get to know a woman before you marry and bed her, Charlemagne."

"I know you say these things for my own good, Roland." King Charlemagne rubbed his temples for long moments. "But you do advise without sufficient knowledge. Himlitrude received training to manage a household and to be gracious. She was and is now fully capable of organizing the daily activities of the court; of smoothing over in-court rivalries; of dampening courtier ardor; of supervising a peaceful court. But my mother will give her no authority and over-rules her decisions repeatedly."

"Within the last few months," the King explained, "Himiltrude ceased making an effort. Now, she concentrates on caring for our son. Alas, little Pippin is deformed. You know, Roland, his hunch-back disturbs his balance, as well as his posture. Fighting men will never follow him." Roland shook his head slowly. There was nothing to be done about the child; fate often decreed such things. But he heard with relief Charlemagne's understanding of the difficult position in which Queen Himiltrude found herself. He listened closely to Charlemagne's explanation. The King seemed unable to stop talking.

"I urge Himiltrude to expect more from Pippin, as he grows older. Then, his skills and his spirit might be strengthened. But she thinks my demands are unreasonable, my methods too harsh." The King dipped his head. "We do little now but argue about the boy. Finally, I chose to stay away. You noticed, Roland, surely. I sleep in the soldiers' tents, more often than in my own."

"Aye," Roland responded. "Do not dally in your decisions and, later, be moved by the Queen Mother's wishes. Look among the nobility's daughters, get to know these young women, determine their value. Surely, there are healthy, interesting, educated daughters who would make a fitting partner. Mayhap, passion must come from someone else. You need a woman who will be a queen, Sire, a woman who looks to the good of the people. Leave your mother out of it." Roland prayed the King would heed his words and decided to be specific.

"I can't remember your being so taken by a woman in a long time—even it if is only dreaming from afar. Hildegard nibbles at your heart, doesn't she?" Roland held his face somber, though the idea of his lustful friend moon-eyed over a maid delighted him.

"I want only a little peace," Charlemagne mumbled to Roland. But the king knew he lied to them both. *Nay, nay, I want a partner.* Charlemagne admitted to himself. *I want a woman who will support my concern for my people; a woman who can reassure me, rekindle my enthusiasm in dark times; a woman who will share my life. If she cares for me, all the better. But I ask only that she help me, help me to help our people.*

"If I might have a partner, Roland, instead of an alliance, it would strengthen my life!" He thought again of Hildegard. "She is perfect, but I'll not sully her. If I demand my Franks and my conquered peoples live Christian lives, I must do the same. I cannot seduce innocent, young women—no matter my physical needs or my reputation. "Roland, I must live as the Christ exhorted us. I must...and my next wife must be my last one."

Roland nodded, carefully listing the King's wishes in his mind: a wife who shares his dreams for the Frankish people, a supportive wife who guards his enthusiasm and shares the realm's burdens. Roland munched slowly on a traveling bar, considering the King's requirements.

"Mayhap you should talk to the Abbot, Sire. Only he can advise you on your current marriage. Surely he sees your quandary— the reason you seek another wife, a mother for your heir."

"I'll approach him," Charlemagne agreed. "But, for present, we must get to the court. Come, let us ride quickly. If we meet the Peers, we ride toward the court and sleep within our own tents tonight. With less speed, we'll be wrapped in linens on the ground once again." Roland cantered his mount behind Charlemagne on the narrow path through the woods. The King hurried Samson, heedless of small animal burrows, ruts, and dangers hidden in the narrow path.

Roland thought back. Charlemagne appeared anxious to leave Count Hautgard's manor. But Roland saw the yearning in Charlemagne's eyes as he bid Lady Hildegard farewell.

Thinking of the King's intensity, Roland considered Charle-magne's dilemma as they rode. He unearthed no solution. He and the King rode less than an hour before they spied a group of three mounted men hailing them.

Chapter Five

DEPENDENCE AND NEED

Roland stood in his saddle, pointing toward the group at the forest edge. "That's your banner, Charlemagne." King Charlemagne nodded as he snapped his bridle.

"It's our brothers." Charlemagne sighed as he raised his hand in greeting. In a moment, Roland's hand, too, shot into the air as he waved to the rest of the King's Peers: Oliver, Rinaldo and Grent.

"Well met, friends." Rinaldo greeted Roland and King Charlemagne. "Thank God we've met you early. We bring bad news, Sire." He looked to the King. "It's as you feared. Our spies uncovered an Aquitainean plot. The traitor is none other than Hunald." Charlemagne nodded, his glance taking in all of them.

"He betrays me, does he?" Charlemagne looked to Oliver who reined-in beside Roland. Oliver glanced once into Roland's eyes and, prodding his horse, moved to the King's side.

"Aye, he marches to attack us, Sire," Oliver confirmed. "Before starting out, he explained his battle plan to other nobles, trying to recruit them. He moves toward us, deliberately moving the fight far from his own lands. The battle, then, will not adversely affect his crops and livestock."

"He cares nothing, though, for his neighbor's fields, does he?" King Charlemagne asked. His face darkened, his brow wrinkled; his lips tightened. "Let's see how many others he's willing to sacrifice." The King rattled off orders. "Call in our scouts; we need their reports. Order the army to march west. Summon our commanders. We'll drive Hunald back to his own lands and defeat him there. He chooses a bad time for battle; the weather changes moment by moment." He lifted his hand to dismiss them but paused. "Oliver, has Carloman arrived?"

"Nay, Sire; our scouts report no movement on the roads. We have watched for days—no sign of him yet. Is it possible Carl is marching from a different direction, approaching from a route we haven't anticipated?" Oliver twisted in his saddle to look at both Roland and Charlemagne. "I trust Count Haut-gard's manor is safe?"

"Aye," Charlemagne replied. "The Count is well. He agreed to be our eyes and ears in Septimania." He rubbed Samson's neck, scrutinizing the thick forest and thinking aloud. "I antici-pated Hunald's discontent. I sent for Carloman so we could stop this rebel together. But I must confess: I didn't expect his move this soon. If we are to surprise the Aquitaineans, we need Carl's troops." He considered Oliver's question.

"Carl's marching from a different direction, you ask? Nay. Is it possible he doesn't understand the threat?"

"He may not," Roland answered. "You know Carl. He un-derstands a threat only when he sees a raised battle axe and a furious assault." Roland's forehead wrinkled. "His outlook is strange. Even when he sees a wrong which must be corrected, he avoids battle, even more assiduously than most clergymen."

"You're right," the King allowed. Charlemagne understood his brother so little; he was unable to explain Carloman's thoughts, much less his behavior. "Come, let's join our sol-diers. We'll be in the thick of battle before too much longer."

Two leagues later, the muted sounds of a rider cutting through the thick underbrush halted the King. Spotting a flash of color in the distance, Oliver eased his horse from the King's side and rode slowly toward the approaching rider. Lord Janlur, one of the King's trusted commanders, emerged from the deep forest.

"We've yet to spot King Carloman," Janlur reported gruffly. The King's face flushed. His voice, raised and irritated, broke the morning stillness.

"Where the hell is my brother? Aquitaine must be taught a lesson. They'll rue the day they rebel against the Frankish realm." He paused. "This is our first challenge after Poppa's death, the first test of our combined strength. Today, the Frankish brothers defend their rule, prove their mettle.

"Fear not, Sire, he'll come. King Carloman will come." Oliver reassured the King.

"When? I need him now!" Charlemagne shouted, frightening a flock of birds into flight. "A show of force, an assault with us working in tandem, will put these rebellious dukes down. They do not even guard their camp perimeters." Roland rode up beside Charlemagne and reined in his mount.

"The Aquitainean army camps less than a league to the east."

"Where can Carl be, Roland? Damn it; where is he?" The King asked, his face a study in disappointment. Standing upright in his saddle, Oliver deflected the King's attention. He stretched his hand southward.

"Sire," Oliver raised his voice, "riders on the left." Charlemagne and Roland turned, just as the King spied his brother's colors through the trees.

"Thank God, he comes." The King muttered. Did Carl march slowly or meet resistance on the road? Let's find out. He motioned to Roland.

"Follow me," he ordered. With Roland and Rinaldo carrying his banner between them, the King cantered his horse toward the curve in the trail. He could see nothing ahead of him. Then, remembering the proximity of the Aquitainean enemy, Charlemagne slowed Samson's trot. As he did so, the almost-constant mask of exhaustion and grief framed his face.

Above, the towering trees stood leafless and stark against a bleak, gray, October sky, almost as if the forest itself were mourning. King Charlemagne thought of his father's passing, the father who died unexpectedly — well before he thoroughly prepared his two sons to stand in his stead and protect the Frankish realm. Charlemagne, the older of the two kings, looked as lifeless and grim as the barren trees above him. He loved his father dearly and very nearly fell himself from the grief of King Pepin's passing.

"Of a certainty, my father's death did not still the needs of the realm. No matter how heavy my heart, I have responsibilities to the people. Here in Aquitaine, I must begin to fulfill Poppa's expectations." Charlemagne knew this battle required strength and determination. He possessed those in abundance, but did he have his brother's support and his loyalty?

Must I fight alone? Charlemagne asked himself. *God knows, Carloman has little training for rule or battle. And Poppa's death will bring out the jackals. Hunald's rebellion is the first test of our strength. I pray Carl will support my plans.*

Just as Abbot Fulrad - the court priest - and Oliver predicted, others looked with envy at the Frankish realm. With King Pepin's last breath, Charlemagne at twenty-six and Carloman at twenty became joint kings of their father's empire. Each ruled specific lands; but, together, they shared responsibility for the realm. Only after Charlemagne's angry insistence did Carl agree to march to Aquitaine, to assist in putting down the rebellion. The rebels were lackluster soldiers; but led by Hunald, Aquitaine's ruler, they were devious. Signs pointed to their employ of 'out-of-realm' (mercenary) soldiers to aid them.

"I never dreamed we must fight to prove our strength…to our own lords." Charlemagne admitted to Oliver as they rode toward his brother. Across the ravine, Carl meandered toward them with none of the urgency Charlemagne felt. "We must be steadfast." Charlemagne declared. "Hunald and his ally, Duke Lupo of Gascony, risk much. Hunald fought Poppa and my grandfather before him. We shall end this; I weary of their constant rebellion. They cannot adequately defend their own lands without our aid. But, I daresay, several others promise them support." Oliver nodded, agreeing with the King's words.

At long last, rounding the curve in the rough trail, King Charlemagne met his brother's escort. He hailed Carloman's men at arms and joined his brother at the head of the large contingent.

"Carl, you're here at last. Greetings and welcome to you." Charlemagne rode beside his brother and clapped him on the shoulder. "Thank God you've arrived! Come, we must discuss battle plans quickly." He frowned and rubbed Samson's neck to disguise his impatience. "I did expect you three days previous."

"Aye," King Carloman grinned, "but I wished my soldiers fresh for the fight, so we did not hurry. My men are energized and eager, brother." He turned in his saddle and looked at the giant trees surrounding the road. "Thank the Father we found you. I dreaded searching these forests." His eyes moved upward. "Frankland will never be at a loss for wood. Look at the size of these trees, sentinels to the very sky."

Charlemagne side-stepped Samson, then nudged the horse to step back...anything to hold in his frustration. *Why think of trees now? We have a battle to fight, a realm to protect.* He watched his brother through resentful eyes. *Look at him, making pleasant talk while the battle waits. Carl still does not understand. He thinks being a king frees him to argue philosophy, to compose long religious treatises, to plan outings and jousts. Never does he think of tactics, of supply movements, or even of improving his own sword arm...or of his duties. Aye,* King Charlemagne allowed, *Carl is adverse to the duties of a king. He wants only the rewards.* Carloman raised his head, smiling at Charlemagne's Peers as they moved around him.

"Do you scout with Peers only, brother? If the rebels must be stopped, why not march our army straight into theirs? The combined size of our armies will undermine these proud Aquitaineans' plans. Or do you want, instead, to plan and to organize, to plot and to scrutinize?" Carloman sat patiently on his horse. He knew Charlemagne would not answer his questions. The Peers were in battle gear but appeared relaxed and greeted him eagerly. Carloman called each one by name.

"Does my brother need my army?" He asked them. "Or does he merely want to command more soldiers, make a show of his military prowess?" Charlemagne frowned. *Carl's teasing is out of place.*

"Neither, brother. Aye, I do scout with few companions...for stealth. I feared the enemy forces would be on the march, so late is your arrival. We saw their camps but have observed no troop movement. Military prowess? Nay, I want a large force to show Hunald I consider him an enemy, not just a misled, disloyal noble." He smiled at Carloman, refusing to rise to his taunts. "Did you see any movements, any maneuvers,

Carl?"

"… none." Carloman shook his head. "We did not even see a scout, thank God. My soldiers camp two leagues to the west."

"Send for your men," Charlemagne commanded. "We must make haste." King Charlemagne lifted his reins as his brother spoke, shaking his head negatively.

"I see no need for war, Charley," Carloman protested. "The rebel soldiers, have they threatened you? Are they a-horse, ready to attack? Where is the enemy?" He held his hands open, as if baffled. "Your eagerness to battle… you over-state the threat. There's no reason to fight." He spat out his words and glared into his brother's face. Charlemagne grimaced.

"Come, Carl," he growled, "let me show you the tactics we'll use." Charlemagne pulled Samson's reins, expecting Carloman to follow.

"One minute, if you will," King Carloman replied. He wished to talk with the Peers. He was genuinely happy to see them. At his father's death, he relocated his court, halfway across the realm. He missed these men. Carloman made eye contact with each one, smiling and nodding to each man in turn.

"My friends, greetings to you; it is good to be back among you." Each of the Peers greeted Carloman. All had served King Pepin together and were brothers in arms, if not always in spirit. "If only we could share sword practice and attack skills again…" Carl wished aloud, looking toward Charlemagne.

"But I am summoned," he emphasized, seeing the annoyed look on Charlemagne's face. "I go for my lesson in battle strategy." He turned his horse toward Charlemagne. The Peers dismounted and talked quietly among themselves. They saw King Charlemagne draw battle movements in the dirt as he talked intently to Carl.

"What is the threat then?" Carloman asked Charlemagne some minutes later. "I feared Hunald's legions would be lined up, ready to attack. They haven't deployed soldiers to the field. They don't fire upon us. This threat you fear...it appears non-existent to me. Where is our enemy?" His voice was sharp; his eyes alight with questions.

"The threat lies in the opportunity it opens to all dissatisfied popinjays, brother." Charlemagne answered, the words darting from his mouth. "They do undermine our reign by this demand for independence." He swiped at an insect buzzing near his ear. "But you are correct. I, too, can discover no battle readiness."

"Then, except for pompous posturing, no harm is done." King Carloman turned in a circle, peering into the thick trees. "Words are not very costly. Where's the harm in avoiding this battle?" He added thoughtfully.

"No harm? Aye, there is harm...and danger," King Charlemagne insisted.

"They rebel against our rule, Carl." The veins on his neck stood out like cords of wood. His rapid pulse was obvious, underneath his right ear. "If they splinter the realm, counts and nobles will follow them, all demanding freedom to control their own borders, to maintain a standing army, to choose their battles. We'll have a rash of little dukedoms, none with any strength." Charlemagne bristled with impatience.

"Hell, Charley, let them take care of themselves - stand, support and defend themselves - or fall. It's their choice. We have no duty to them." Charlemagne opened his mouth to speak but Carloman's voice over-rode his words. "How can a rebellion of such weak dukes as Hunald and Lupus spread? They are all talk. Send a peace offering and let's go home." Charlemagne spoke with exaggerated slowness to his brother.

"If they fall to an overnight invader, what then? Do we let the invader—Saxon or Moor or Avar—take this corner of our realm? Nay, never."

Seething with fury, Charlemagne bit back his next words. Noting his brother's pale face, his stiff back and his aggressive stance, Charlemagne dismounted to sit on a near-by stump, clamping down on his smothering frustration. *I'll give Carl a little more time. He must see the sense in my words.* Carloman walked closer and placed his hand on Charlemagne's arm.

"You are the realm's soldier, brother," he said gently. "It's your job to anticipate clashes which might arise. I don't deny that. But we need to seek counsel as well. All my advisers—military and ecclesiastical—urge caution, measured deliberation. They beg we not be hasty." He gazed into Charlemagne's face, surprised at its bleakness, the hopelessness of his expression.

"You must be patient." Carl advised as he pawed through a handful of walnuts, searching for the largest pieces.

"Nay," Charlemagne answered. "In war, patience is an over-stated virtue. I remain steadfast. Saddle up; we are to battle." Carloman looked around wildly.

"I believe your mind unsound, brother. You ignore Roman-based rules of engagement. Do you wish to prove we are barbarians? I absolutely will not follow you in this." Carloman's voice rang with anger.

"We are not Romans, brother. We fight when someone challenges us." Mounting Samson, he turned, again, to Carloman. "Remember, Carl. I am your liege of first resort - should you need counsel, additional troops, or armaments. Do not compromise the safety of your lands through studied indifference or foolish argument. God be with you." He cantered off.

Chapter Six
BATTLE JOINED

Seeing Charlemagne settle into his saddle, the Peers mounted and fell in behind him. Sighing, Carloman motioned his own escort forward and reluctantly pointed his horse toward his army's camp. Once, there he conferred with his commander.

"This is a good tactic, King Carloman." Commander Harrels – a commander with thirty years battle experience - assured Carloman. "King Pepin would approve. I can see his huge smile. During spring training, your brother repeatedly tested his 'pincer movement' in mock maneuvers. I advise you to follow him."

"But I see no immediate threat! Where is the enemy?" Carloman protested.

"Hunald's rebellion is a test of your battle worthiness and of your courage." Harrels emphasized his words. "Neither Hunald nor Lupus expect a battle today. Our soldiers are fresh; this terrain is of no consequence. It's time to strike!" He looked under his brows at his king. "The surprise, Sire, the surprise may win this battle for us." He remembered Harrels' words when he returned from talking with Charlemagne.

"King Charlemagne sees the threat more clearly than you, Sire. These rebels must be stopped. You are too good, thinking the best of men. Your brother does not make this mistake. He sees the ambition, the jealousy of the nobles. Pay no attention, give no value to the advice of your churchmen; they know little. This battle is necessary." And so Carloman followed his commander's unwavering support of King Charlemagne.

Charlemagne and his Peers rode swiftly to the waiting Frankish army which camped not far from Fransec. Mounted on Samson, King Charlemagne watched as his commanders rode toward their own troops.

"Sire, is all well with King Carloman?" Roland asked. He pointed to Carloman at the bottom of a nearby hill. His stiff head, his ramrod posture, radiated anger as he sat atop his horse, looking over Duke Lupus' camp.

"He seems prepared to attack with us, Roland," Charlemagne replied, despite his worry. "I had to convince him the fight is necessary. He's not happy but he marches, even as we speak." The King spread his arm to his left. "I'm relieved. It proved more difficult than equipping our infantry — my effort to ensure Carl's cooperation. Pray he remains with us. I'm unsure of his steadiness in battle." He turned to spot his brother.

"There, Roland. He moves; he's aligning his troops." Roland spied the very tip of King Carloman's banner as his soldiers topped a small rise and came into view.

"Then, I return to my men, Sire." Roland breathed a sigh of relief. *Carloman always tries to negotiate. Thank God he didn't suggest doing so here today.*

"Hold your men steady, Roland." Charlemagne commanded. "I don't want our mounted men ahead of the infantry. Consider walking the horses for a time. Even if your men must dismount, control the destriers. Listen for Oliver's horn. Two blasts leave you free to charge, as usual."

"God be with you, Sire." Roland called as he rode away.

"And with you," Charlemagne answered.

In addition to being close friends and counselors, each Peer was a specialist in a specific type of fighting. Ganelon led the archers; Roland commanded the cavalry; and Rinaldo ordered the infantry. Their skills - developed in service to King Pepin, honed through mock-battles and practice drills, and proved in heated battles - always served the troops well. The King's uncle, Bernard, was second only to Charlemagne in command. He, often, led auxiliary troops, tangential forays, and parallel attacks. Each man commanded in his own right. They all were soldiers with insightful minds.

Many of the soldiers came from the nobility, outfitted and supported by dukes and counts to help the King protect the realm. But, once they were secure in their skills, their loyalty and obedience was to Charlemagne alone. The people's most important expectation of the king was for him to keep them physically safe: to protect them from invaders and marauders. Charlemagne, more than most, took his responsibility seriously and constantly labored to increase the size of his army and to improve the abilities of his soldiers.

Once he saw the enemy, King Charlemagne signaled his commanders. Leading the army, the king raised his hands so the men could easily see his hand signals. When the fighting began, Oliver took directions from the King and passed them on through his horn. Commanders and soldiers stood patiently; their confidence in the King complete. At this moment, all were silent, waiting for the single note which began the fighting.

As the King directed, Ganelon, commander of the archers, held them back. Charlemagne hoped the unexpected attack and a slight delay in launching the arrows would confuse Hunald's soldiers. As usual, the archers moved to their places on both sides of the infantry and hid behind small hillocks above the camped enemy. Individually, they shot men they could pick out in the enemy camp. But they did not loose their arrows in the standard volley.

Rinaldo and Bernard rode up beside him. "Battle is joined, son," Charlemagne said to Rinaldo. Charlemagne nodded to both men but looked into his youngest commander's face. Rinaldo's brow wrinkled, his lips pressed together. He nodded his head.

"You have the most difficult task, Rinaldo. Restrain your fighters. Take your time before attacking."

"When do we charge, Sire?" Rinaldo asked. He rubbed his whip, jiggled his left foot in anxiety. "Will we implement the 'pincer' movement?"

"Aye, in good time." The King answered. "Begin the infantry's charge right after Oliver's third blast. Fight as you normally do. Today, we just move a little more slowly." King Charlemagne explained to the nervous man.

"I fear Hunald's archers will be upon us, Sire, upon us before we raise our swords." Rinaldo seemed to leak the words from his mouth.

"Nay, not today." the King answered. "Ganelon's archers stand ready to deflect them. And the cavalry attacks ahead of your men. We change our order of attack."

"Aye, Sire, we shall do as you command." Rinaldo assured the King as he rode away. Bernard, Charlemagne's uncle, moved closer.

"Am I to deploy my troops, Sire?" he asked.

"You are," the King replied, "in your own good time. You decide when to attack; it's your decision alone, Bernard. You're the best commander here; we all know it." Bernard, the King remembered, loved to fight. He was as much a soldier's soldier as was the King. When he and Bernard discussed strategy yesterday night, Bernard agreed to lead a second column parallel to Charlemagne's troops but some distance behind them. Now, seeing King Carloman on the left, Bernard believed his place given to the King's brother.

"Carloman apparently has my place," he stated a little mournfully.

"Nay, he does not. As I move from the right and drop my column toward Carl, close in the space between the two of us." King Charlemagne suggested Bernard's direction. "That way, we'll soon surround the enemy. We attack first with mounted cavalry, next with archers, and then with infantry. "Our three contingents will be a vise!" *If Carl is not steady, Bernard will be in place.* King Charlemagne thought.

"It may work." Bernard's voice strengthened as he visualized the troop movements. "Ahh..." he said smiling. "This is your famous 'pincer' movement."

"That's my name for it, Bernard. Come, our battle begins."

King Charlemagne raised his hand over his head and dropped his hand in an aggressive chop. He felt and heard his army snap to order. Thousands of footsteps echoed in the still air. The voices of the Frankish soldiers rose—almost like a cyclone—throbbing, undulating, rising into a peak of shrill sound. Their battle cry always stirred the King. He leaned into Samson's strength, as the horse leaped eagerly under him. Samson cantered quickly before the main column, prancing back and forth to the sound of the marching drums. Boom! Boom! Boom! The drums vibrated in the King's ears.

Charlemagne's army advanced on the undefended, main camp of the Aquitainean forces. The cavalry horses' eyes were wide, their feet kicked up dust. Men shouted shrilly. Commands and quick retorts battered back and forth. King Charlemagne showed no hesitation. At the front of the line, he led the army forward. Bernard, waiting for the long columns to move, watched the legions surge; stop as if for a second breath and;

then, move slowly ahead in stately procession. The banner men and those with signal flags rode beside and to the front of the army columns, ready at a moment's notice to transmit a change in the King's orders.

Ganelon held his arm upright for long minutes, restraining his archers. Hearing Oliver's single blast, he let his arm fall. In the front line, archers pulled their bows and released a volley of arrows. The arrows fell among the Aquitainean foot soldiers who rushed in and out of tents, grabbing their weapons. Blop, blop, blop, the arrows found their marks. Enemy soldiers fell to the ground, fatally wounded or dead.

For today, Roland's mounted infantry rode in front of the archers, waiting for their third volley. When it came, the infantry spurred their horses and overran the scattered, confused foot soldiers of the Aquitainean army. Blood, smashed weapons, tattered clothing, and cries — from the attackers and from the defenders — filled the air. Hunald's calvary, confused by the Frankish archers' precise strike, desperately clumped together. Many held their shields up but refused to move. Commanders brayed and shouted at their men, doing their best to draw the legions together. Their barking, frustrated commands slowly aligned the disparate units. While still trying to position themselves, Hunald's soldiers marched toward the Frankish army.

Rinaldo led his infantry in a steady march. Suddenly his swordsmen hurried forward, skirting around and beyond the cavalry. The double blast of Oliver's horn seared the air and seemed to wake the infantry. With a huge roar, the men ran toward the enemy, slashing with their swords, and flinging their knives quickly. It seemed only moments later when Oliver's horn sounded again, calling Carloman's army to turn south, to trap the enemy between the two Frankish legions. Charlemagne's commanders, knowing to ignore the long-short blasts, continued their steady march.

The King looked to the rise on his left, searching for Carloman's troops. He swallowed once, twice, a third time and reined in Samson. He cursed vehemently under his breath. Just a hundred yards from the merger of the two armies, Carloman put his hand in the air and motioned his army from the battle. He pulled his horse hard to the left and descended the hill on the other side. King Charlemagne lifted Samson's reins to ride toward his brother. But his hand dropped. He cursed into the murky air.

"By all that's holy, what in the hell is Carl doing?" Charlemagne shaded his eyes with his hand. "Curses! I cannot get to him! He deliberately ignores the battle plan." Charlemagne felt his heart drop. *Carl understands exactly what he's doing. He never even looked back. He abandoned us, left us to fight alone!* Oliver, atop the highest hill, repeated his two blasts but knew his summons was futile. Carloman made his decision. He withdrew from the battle; he refused to fight.

Charlemagne tried to swallow, again and again; struggled to force down the lump in his throat. He felt it would never completely dissolve. His eyes watered at the betrayal of his brother. He dropped his head, bowed his shoulders.

"'Twas better he told me outright, better he refused to fight," the King whispered. "Better not to take the field than to abandon us, leave our entire left flank open and undefended!" The King paused for a moment, looking toward the expanding space as Carl's troops moved away.

Bernard's troops slowed their march behind Carloman, clearly unsure of Carl's intent. In a moment, they appeared to have stopped marching altogether. The King shook his head, back and forth, back and forth.

"I did not foresee this," he said as Oliver rode up beside

him. "At the least, I believed Carloman would engage the enemy and, then, retreat. It never occurred to me he would avoid the entire battle! Damn him; damn him to hell!" Charlemagne tried to arm himself against the slaughter to come. At his side, Oliver blew the same horn blast for a third time. Charlemagne sat unmoving. *God forgive me. Hundreds of our soldiers will be slaughtered. Carl condemns them to an early death.*

As Charlemagne rubbed Samson's neck to calm him, on the far ridge Bernard rode back and forth before his legion. He tried to ascertain what just happened. Quickly, he returned to the head of his column, waved his men forward, and increased his pace. Bernard's soldiers followed. With a sudden burst of speed, they melded into the route Carloman deserted.

Charlemagne's hand went up to punch the air; he pressed his legs against his horse. Oliver's horn sounded two staccato blasts. Samson bounded forward, increasing the King's marching pace. The horse was wild with excitement.

Charlemagne and Roland saw Hunald outlined on a faraway rise, gesturing to several mounted commanders who rushed toward the battlefield, ostensibly carrying his orders. Charlemagne could hold back no longer.

He snapped Samson's reins and rode into the battle, yelling at the top of his lungs. Not for a moment could he imagine directing from the sidelines. He relished being in the thick of the battle. His blood ran hot; he reveled in the danger, in the power of the army, in the live or die battlefield. His blood surged amid the effort to stay alive. Only in the middle of the fighting could he evaluate the efficacy of his maneuvers and the readiness of his men.

King Charlemagne startled as an arrow zipped across his shoulder, heralding a storm of arrows from Hunald's archers. The Aquitainean soldiers didn't seem to realize their arrow attack concentrated on only one-half of the attacking enemy. Hundreds of Aquitainean arrows filled the air above the King and toward his forward line. Hunald's archers began reloading for a second volley. The Frankish archers held their bows taut once again, just as Charlemagne ordered. Rather than seeing, King Charlemagne felt his bowmen raise their arrows. He galloped into the advancing enemy line, slashing right and left with his sword. With Hunald infantry attacking, the Frankish archers pulled their arrows back and loosed them. They fired again, then stepped back to allow Roland's regrouped cavalry to move.

The unexpected volley of arrows and Roland's charge, together, overwhelmed Hunald's infantry. The two forces battled each other, neither giving an inch. Charlemagne plunged his sword into enemy soldiers, again and again. The leather jerkin over his tunic was wet with sweat, his right arm dripped blood. Frankish archers and infantrymen swarmed around him, attempting to protect him and to quell the advancing Aquitainean soldiers. A mounted, enemy cavalryman veered toward a Frankish archer. Samson quickly headed the mounted man aside. Another soldier kicked with his unbridled foot and rode over an archer, raising his sword toward the King. Samson pulled away, the sword grazing his left flank. Charlemagne dropped against Samson's neck and jabbed his sword at the man's torso. The sword caught in the man's gut, almost jerking the King from Samson's back.

The fighting was brutal. Men now fought to stay alive, rather than to defeat the enemy. The sound of screaming horses, moaning men, bones crunching as people fell from and under their horses melded into a cacophony. Men fought with arms hanging useless at their sides, with blood pouring from neck and stomach wounds, with eyes incapable of measuring the extent of the battle.

Samson, feeling the King slip from side to side, fought to move to the edge of the field. Charlemagne kept reining him back, thrusting viciously with his dagger. Finally, there were three short blasts from a horn, then another three short blasts. There was a momentary pause as men heard the signal to end the battle. But no one could stop the fighting. There was still too much danger, too much blood lust among the soldiers. Charlemagne felt a hand on his shoulder and heard Roland's shout.

"We have prevailed, Sire! We have prevailed. Sire? Sire, are you hurt?" Roland demanded.

"Nay! Nay!" Charlemagne answered. "I am well, just a little flesh wound." Roland grabbed Samson's reins and spoke directly into King Charlemagne's face, the better to make him understand.

"Sire, we do prevail. Sheathe your sword. The fighting ends. Most of the Aquitainean army is overrun. They're surrendering." He looked over his shoulder and continued. "Aquitaine's cavalry is dismounting, your Majesty. I must see to those horses." He hurried away, hoping Oliver would be there to lend him a hand.

"Broken horses....they are the worst result of a close battle. It's a rout, Sire, a rout!" Roland shouted as he rode through the decimated ranks of the enemy. The battle was over, well fought and won.

"Thank God!" Charlemagne laughed, finally having the wit to comprehend Roland's words. He glanced around, the blood lust draining from his mind. He saw Roland's cries were accurate. No one was fighting. Charlemagne swung his right leg over Samson's back, dismounted and kneeled. He must thank God for this victory...and for his own safety. The wound on his arm was nothing, a small price to pay for Hunald's defeat.

This is the worse time. Charlemagne thought. *Just as the battle ends, we don't know who is injured...or loss. It is a somber moment.* Charlemagne steeled himself as Rinaldo rode up. Rinaldo shook his head negatively.

"No reports yet, Sire, on those killed," he said. The King nodded.

"We shall rest tonight." Charlemagne declared as Fulrad and Bernard cantered up a moment later. "We have Gascony to defeat on the morrow."

"Will you speak to the prisoners before we rest, Sire," Abbot Fulrad asked, "or after moonrise?"

"... after moonrise, Abbot." Charlemagne replied. "Before speeches, we shall bind their wounds, as best we can. Next, we feed them and send the priests through the camp. They must bless the dead and breathe hope and thanksgiving into the living. We shall pray and praise God together. Our enemies, seeing God's victory for us, will have an opportunity to denounce the error of their ways. Let us pray, Fulrad, you and I. Pray our next battle is so quickly won."

Soon, Oliver's victory blasts rang over the now quiet battlefield. As men searched for comrades, mourned those lost, and bound up wounds, King Charlemagne sent scouts south, seeking information on the movement and strength of Gascony's troops. He met with his commanders, inquired about their wounds and any comrades who were lost. For hours, he toured the army camp: praised the wounded, noted the names of those who perished, and thanked the men for their courage. Near dawn he slept, rising to lead his army into Duke Lupo's Gascony at mid-day.

Chapter Seven
First Battle Success

Marching toward Bordeaux next morning, Charlemagne and his Peers waited for updates on Hunald. It was unlikely he died in battle and the Frankish reconnaissance teams reported his body unfound. So, it was critical to determine his present location. Considering the number of soldiers who protected him, he was likely in good health. If wounded, he was not in the field, of a certainty. Abbot Fulrad, Ganelon, and Janlur speculated on Hunald's location. All ceased speaking as Theo rode up beside the army column.

"Hunald flees, Sire," Theo reported. "Some of his commanders swear he left the battlefield mid-day yesterday, riding south with a large escort. A scout returned and confirmed the retreat of such a host—more than three hundred soldiers, he said."

"I guessed he fled to Lupo," Charlemagne nodded at Theo, "even though I doubted Lupo would shelter a coward." He smiled slightly. "I imagined Hunald...on his knees, begging for succor. I wonder what he offered Lupo to protect him. It will not be enough." The King fingered his signet ring.

"My mind is at rest, Fulrad. We held our own. Nay, we won this battle! Now, I know what I needed to understand. I don't need Carloman—his approval or his army—to support my efforts. This army, the one we lead now, can protect the whole of Poppa's legacy. Thank God grandfather Martel created our core of standing soldiers." He nodded as Bernard rode up. "Good job, Uncle Bernard. You saved our left flank! Poppa would be proud of us all."

Later that day, King Charlemagne understood there would be no battle against Lupo of Gascony. The Aquitainean soldiers had the right of it. Hunald fled the battle and asked Lupo for protection. The Duke of Gascony, receiving reports of Charlemagne's success at Fransac, surrendered and admitted Hunald sheltered in his camp. Knowing his meager numbers made him helpless before King Charlemagne's force, he capitulated and offered to surrender. Before the Frankish army crossed into Gascony, Lupo's surrender missive arrived. Unbidden, he volunteered to retreat to a monastery for the duration of his life.

King Charlemagne, thankful to contain the rebellion with so little loss of Frankish blood, took Lupo's oath of fidelity at sunset. Minutes later, Abbot Fulrad and Hunald set out for the nearest monastery. King Charlemagne ordered Hunald to live in the monastery for the duration of his life and suggested he spend the time contemplating his foolishness. The King confiscated Lupo's lands for the crown and sent him, too, to a monastery. He ordered Lupo to oversee his former lands from his new monastic home. Lupo was never to benefit from this stewardship.

"He now maintains lands for me." Charlemagne told Fulrad, his eyes glinting with satisfaction. "Lupo will serve as a reminder to other nobles. They must prepare to lose everything, if they challenge their king." He turned to Roland.

"How many soldiers have we lost? Has a count been made?"

"No more than fifty, Sire. Two fine commanders died from their wounds and a number of bowmen. Overall though, the fight was short; the victory sweet." Roland added, as he imagined the soldiers' thanksgiving. They would feast and drink into the night, rejoicing at their swift victory. As always, King Charlemagne was a hero. The soldiers toasted, praised, and acclaimed him into the small hours of the morning.

King Charlemagne, thinking of his father-as battle invariably led him to do- and accepting the betrayal of his brother, felt his thankfulness and his energy fade. Seeking solace, he turned, again, toward his soldiers' tents. Roland, knowing the regret of battle, sought the services of an itinerate minstrel to entertain at the commanders' evening meal. Then, he sought out the King. He found Charlemagne at a campfire, sharing nuts and freshly-picked persimmons with his soldiers.

"I pray you are not over-full, Sire. A minstrel happened by and, for a meal, is eager to entertain us. Please, return to the banquet tent." Nodding at the soldiers, Roland added: "We'll send the singer on to you after his songs and stories to us." King Charlemagne, taking a handful of walnuts, took his leave.

"We are fortunate to have a minstrel," the King commented to his commanders. "Of a certainty, we will all be better for lyrics and bold stories this night."

Leaving a trusted count to rule in Aquitaine and to oversee Gascony, King Charlemagne turned his army toward his court. Knowing the mobile court could not keep pace with him, he had bade them wait at the site of the recent spring assembly. The conspiracy of Hunald and Lupo had delayed the onset of the battle season; but, now, it was time to fight.

Each annual assembly brought together the strength of the realm: the king, the nobles, and the few independent men who made their homes in the Frankish realm. The independent men, farmers and tradesmen, were - more often than not - soldiers no longer young enough to fight who had earned land, position, and success serving in the Frankish army. Anyone with power or influence attended these assemblies where negotiations identified the season's battles. Invaders: marauding tribes, people fleeing persecution, bandits, and those with visions of conquering the 'backward barbarians,' all looked with keen interest to the Frankish empire.

Charlemagne's father, King Pepin, had first served as the master of the palace, governing a realm under the command of a Merovingian king. But the last Merovingian was so inept a ruler that Pepin appealed for clarification to the Pope.

"Who should rule a realm," he asked Pope Hadrian, "the man who does the work or the man who wears the crown?" The Pope, in search of military might to buttress his position, decided in Pepin's favor.

"The man who governs the kingdom, who protects its people is the true king of a realm," he responded. Hearing this, Pepin called an assembly of the Frankish nobility and asked them to name him king. Pepin held the power of the realm in his hands so the nobles acquiesced. They named him king, as did Pope Hadrian a short time later. The Pope named Pepin's two sons, Charlemagne and Carloman, his heirs. King Pepin fought to expand the Frankish realm through war and conquest. He left his sons a large realm, one governed largely by resident dukes and counts overseen by Pepin's court. But these men governed very much as they pleased. They interpreted the *capitalaries* (laws) as they wished, little concerned with consistency in interpretation or in the application of justice.

Pepin often spoke of the realm to his sons about the need for a new governing structure for Frankland, as well as his dreams of a 'Christian' kingdom. Carloman attentively followed his father's devotion to the Church while Charlemagne became a wonderful military tactician and a soldier's soldier. Now, with Pepin dead, his sons must accommodate each other in the joint ruling of the realm.

Charlemagne and his Peers rode into the mobile court's camp. People, wrapped in their linens, heard the King ride in but knew to greet him on the morrow.

"I must let Ma-mam know we return." The King said to Roland. "First thing after we wake, I will determine the readiness of the court to march. Sleep well, my friend."

"As should you, Sire." Roland replied as he nodded and watched Charlemagne ride toward his mother's tent. The King dismounted and stepped inside.

"Where have you lingered, Charlemagne?" Queen Bertrada's voice cut into his thoughts - of Hildegard, riding across the fields. He shook his head and looked up. There stood his mother in the door of her tent, her eyes blazing.

"I've waited and waited. You are adept at wasting time, did you know that? There is so much to do!" Queen Bertrada's voice barked, even as her mouth turned down with displeasure. Her eyes bored into her son's, daring him to reply.

"I returned from Lombardy three days ago. But you...you were nowhere to be found. What are you thinking, leaving me waiting like this?" She held her hand up to forestall his answer. He hated when she did that—silenced him, as if she were the king and he one of her bothersome subjects. "I bring reports for you, important plans you need to know." Queen Bertrada raised her eyebrow and pointed to a bench, comfortable once more in her ultimate control.

Charlemagne saw the upturn of her mouth, the look of triumph in her eyes. *Dear God, please don't let her have done something for 'the good of the realm' again.* He groaned with exhaustion, feeling to his bones the effort required to deal with his mother. *Perhaps a conciliatory approach is best.* Charlemagne was weary and knew from experience not to cross his mother when she was in this kind of mood.

"Ma-Mam, you seem well." Charlemagne replied through clamped teeth.

"Welcome home. You enjoyed a fruitful journey, did you?" Again he noticed the sparkling victory in her eyes. He bit back his urge to confront her. "You seem ready to burst with delight. What is your news?"

"Come, come into my tent!" The Queen Mother smiled smugly, beckoning to her son. "Prying ears should not be privy to this news. Nay, it must be discussed in private." Charlemagne took a step back. His mother's beaming satisfaction boded ill for him, he knew. He was immediately wary.

"I must see to my court, Ma-Mam. I have been absent even longer than you. The court traveled weeks without me, without us." He turned back toward the door of the tent. "I must talk with Seneschal Egginhard, determine if all is well in my absence."

The King thought of Egginhard with relief. As seneschal/supervisor of the court, the seneschal took care of the court's retinue, of their foodstuffs, of their tents—not to mention the expenses, guests, daily support, and special needs of the nobles with them. Its successful journeys through the realm, taken to secure support for the King and to maintain allegiances, were all due to Egginhard's considerable skills.

"How good it will be to spend Eastertide in peace. Egginhard has spy reports for me. I must go to him now." The King added. He stood up and moved toward the tent's flap.

"By the way, we did quell Aquitaine's rebellion. You seem to have no interest in the outcome." At his quiet reprimand, Queen Betrada's head snapped around. "Carl finally responded to my request for help." His mother's lips curved in a wide smile. "But he was unwilling to help defend the realm. He withdrew from the battle, only minutes before the attack." Charlemagne watched his mother absorb the news. "You should, it seems to me, turn your attention and your influence to your second son." The King mounted Samson, urging him away from his mother.

"I must check on the court. I shall join you for the evening meal, Ma-Mam." *Her news, whatever it is, can wait.* He ignored his mother's open mouth, even as he saw her lips moving—demanding he return, no doubt. The King waved and nodded to Roland who rode up beside him.

Roland smiled gently, having seen this game played many times before. The King's most often-used tactic with his mother was to feign an emergency and hurry away. Seeming to have pressing duties, he escaped her without lengthy explanations.

King Charlemagne checked with Egginhard on the fitness of the mobile court for traveling: the packing readiness; the adequacy of their food provisions; the likelihood of sufficient grazing for the horses and livestock; and an update on members of the court who remained. He told Egginhard to disperse scouts ahead to evaluate the roads. The gray, hovering clouds on his way back suggested imminent rain.

"I must greet Himiltrude and see my son." Charlemagne turned Samson toward his home tent. When he was in camp, the king spent most of his time in his 'battle tent.' But Himli and Peppin welcomed him home in their own tent. Well, in the past, Himli welcomed him. Now, she seemed not to care if he appeared or not.

Charlemagne was sick to heart. So far, his efforts to comfort his wife about Pippin, their little hump-backed son, came to naught. She was still overcome with sorrow at his handicap. Now, months after the boy's birth, he and Himiltrude said little to each other. Each of them suffered separately. They were unable to find a way back to one another. My love and need for Himiltrude are gone, the King admitted to himself. *Though my feelings have weakened, she loves me still. And I, in my own way, still love the mother of my son.* He rode Samson slowly into the middle of the camp.

"Pleasant evening to you, Sire," a young groom said as he walked by the King. "Welcome home."

"Wait." Charlemagne said to the lad, looking around, puzzled. "Where is Queen Himiltrude's tent? Surely, it's not already dismantled for our upcoming march." He turned in a circle. Himiltrude's tent was always adjacent to his battle tent. "Where do I sleep this night, I wonder?" He smiled at the groom.

"Queen Himiltrude is not here, Sire," the groom replied, sensing the King's disquiet. "Let's see. Aye. She's been gone three days now, your Majesty — the queen and the babe both. Her escort's not returned yet; but, mayhap, they're to remain with her, not expected back – I mean." He paused. "There was a mountain of chests, baskets, and the like piled in the carts, Sire. It was a hurried leave-taking." The groom stood, confused by the King's stare. The lad bowed and hurried back to the horse lines. Charlemagne felt bewildered.

"Chests and baskets? Where has Himli gone? Surely, she does not need so much for a visit to her family. Ma-mam will know," he decided.

The King left his horse with a groom. Then, he stopped at the cook tent to obtain trenchers of food to take for his mother's evening meal. Because of packing preparations, there was to be no court meal this night. He had promised his mother to dine with her, to hear this 'news' which seemed so important to her. *I will eat sparingly, so I can share a later meal with some of my nobles. My canvassing of the court and my talk with Egginhard shows all are ready to march. There are two outlaw bands and a small group of barbarians toward the east which we must confront.*

Chapter Eight
Mother's Betrayal

"Thank God!" the King murmured. "There's not much need for fighting this summer. We'll be able to move toward Aachen for Yuletide. There we can rest." *The warmth of the mineral pools and the ease of the castle both draw me. Ma-Mam will rule the court as usual; but there, with more entertainments, I can escape her secrets and intrigues.* Charlemagne, balancing the food vessels on his shield, called at his mother's tent.

"Greetings, Ma-Mam? Are you here? My hands are filled with a cauldron and loaves." His mother stuck her head out, gave him a quick glance and stepped aside, so he could enter her tent. Once he was inside, she took the meal from him, setting the cauldron and basket on the table.

"You must drink ale this night," Queen Bertrada told him. "We are celebrating." The Queen Mother could wait no longer. She handed Charlemagne a cup of wine, bustling to offer him cakes and tarts.

"Ma-Mam," Charlemagne grinned. "I would gladly have sweets for my meal, but I have bought food for us." And he nodded at the trenchers on the table. The Queen turned away with the tarts, motioning him to the small table to eat. King Charlemagne first blessed the food and, then, thanked the Lord for his safe and successful journey, as well as for his mother's speedy return.

"Count and Countess Hautgard send their greetings, Ma-

Mam," he began, speaking as he cut the roasted boar. "They, in addition, sent summer wine from last year and..."

"Aye, aye. I do not wish to speak of them." She smiled broadly, even as she saw Charlemagne draw back. "Excuse me, son." Bertrada inwardly cursed her short-sightedness. "I didn't mean to suggest I do not value the Hautgards." In truth she could not stand either one of them. "I'm reminded of the many summers you and your father spent away from me, visiting their isolated manor." She sighed, obviously exaggerating. "I could never understand its attraction." She offered more boar, chick peas, and rye bread to her son, adding food to her own trencher. She patted Charlemagne's hand briskly.

"My dear," Bertrada began, deliberately softening her voice. "I'm happy you visited with the Count. He was always a good friend to your father. And the Countess is hospitable, indeed." The King relaxed, regaining his good humor, erroneously believing his mother shared his appreciation of the Count and his wife.

"I must share my news, Charlemagne," his mother purred. She spoke lightly, smiling all the while. Had Charlemagne cut his roast with less interest and attended his mother more, he would have been on guard. As it was, he did not see her gloating look and did not forearm himself. "You will be so impressed by my efforts."

"Ma-Mam, what have you done?" The King almost ignored her. His mother always plotted and counter-planned, trying to manipulate the nobles of the court to her way of thinking. "You battle to restrain your satisfaction. I fear such unbridled delight." He sat back, lay down his knife, and gazed into his mother's face. He didn't realize he held his breath. "What are you so eager to tell me?"

"My boy, King Desiderius and I spoke often during my visit."

"You were in Lombardy, Ma-Mam?" Charlemagne sat bolt upright. "...on the way to where? I thought you went to Aachen, to prepare the manor for Yuletide." He frowned. "You know I do NOT approve of this. Desiderius—that pompous, overbearing bastard – wants the realm! He is our greatest enemy. He believes his claim to the crown was as strong, if not stronger, than Poppa's! His many wars against us testify to his resentment. What are you doing? He even wants to take church lands from the Pope!" His mother dismissed his accusations with a flip of her hand.

"Nay, he's quite amenable to us forging alliances, becoming neighbors in spirit, as well as in geography. You do misjudge him, son. He's ambitious, it's true. But, aligned with his interests, our realm will garner more influence."

"It's not possible, will never be." Charlemagne re-iterated. "Do you understand me? Desiderius is no friend of this realm. I assure you."

"I spent considerable time with his family, especially his younger daughter. Her sister is Tassilo of Bavaria's wife. Desiderius placed her well, don't you think? The younger daughter's name is Desiderata. Why not be friendly with these courts, Charles, and with their friends? It would guarantee more stability in the realm. Besides, I found King Desiderius sympathetic to your need for a different wife." She smiled contentedly.

"Another wife? What are you talking about?" Charlemagne asked, amazed.

"You must have an heir, Charles. Peppin can never lead soldiers. No matter what accommodation we make for his deformity, he cannot fight...nor command men. You know that." Her voice softened, despite the harsh thrust of her words. "You need another son. And you need one soon."

"Are you insane? I already have a wife! This idea is reprehensible!" Charlemagne paced the tent. The King's horror showed on his face. Panting to catch his breath, he could not speak. He felt a slow trickle of blood run from the corner of his mouth. *I have bitten my lip.* The realization fed his anger.

"Such duplicity, Ma-Mam! You journeyed to Lombardy to speak with Desiderius about this? Are you unable to understand the contempt in which he hold us, this entire family! You negotiated my life with my enemy, never told me of it, never once asked my opinion? I will not accept such plotting!" The King shouted. He slapped his thigh.

"What do you think – I'm eight years old and need keeping?" The King's face drained white; his jaw clenched. He strode around the tent, back and forth. "You do overreach your duties." His stomach clenched. His mother ignored his anger.

"I heard Desiderius was anxious to secure a betrothal for this younger daughter." His mother answered smoothly. "You will be well-pleased with her appearance, Charley. She is more than a head shorter than you but, still, is tall and stately. Her hair is blonde and thick, falling to her shoulders. Her bosom, not as large as you might wish, is certainly adequate. She is quite lovely."

"She is much like I was at her age. Her manners are exquisite; but she is firm and in appropriate control of the maids in her service. Her expectations of court members are clear." The Queen was so excited she did not notice her son's silence. "She is friends with all the noble families and sought out by the duchesses, countesses and men alike. You are fortunate, indeed." Finally realizing Charlemagne voiced no reaction, she stopped speaking.

Charlemagne stared at his mother. He could not make sense of her words. "What have you done?"

"I've negotiated an alliance with Desiderius, King of Lombardy. And the prize is yours—his daughter, Desiderata! You now have a secure, military ally to help protect the realm. I expect a grandson in my arms by Yuletide next." She flashed her son a huge smile, overlooking his displeasure, anticipating his approval of her work.

"Nay. I have a wife and a son. Handicapped Peppin may be but he is still my heir! What will the Holy Father think of this?" Charlemagne asked.

Shaking her head from side to side, Queen Bertrada made an effort to control her temper. Enunciating her words, striving to speak calmly, she answered.

"I do you a favor, Charlemagne. For the sake of the realm, forget Himiltrude. You must strengthen your position; another wife will guarantee you a successor." She took a deep breath. "Surely, you understand. The Lombard princess brings you more advantages than any other woman. Believe me, I evaluated them all. Consider this carefully; you will thank me." Finally seeing his shocked face, she screeched at him.

"You never see the good I do! You are the world's biggest fool! I have every right to make a marriage for you. I'm your mother. You do nothing for yourself." She threw him a disgusted glance.

"You mull around, moaning about little Pippin's affliction. Unfair it may be; but you must produce an heir men will obey, one men will fear. You always resent my help - I who've given up everything for you. Think of Frankland; the realm must be secure! If you will not secure it, I shall…by any means necessary."

King Charlemagne, seeing his and his mother's anger building to the usual breach, visibly shook himself and attempted to clarify his situation to his mother. He grasped her hands, stared into her eyes, and spoke unequivocally.

"Ma-Mam, I'm already married. Himiltrude is my wife, the mother of my child. Pippin is my son. You think neither of them worthy. It matters not." He flung her hands aside. "The marriage exists; my son lives. The Pope blessed and sanctified my union." Queen Bertrada shook her head at his words.

"I cannot have two wives. This is not the Christian way. I cannot live one way and ask the people to live another. What have you done? Pope Hadrian will excommunicate us both. Do you wish to lose your Church, your hope of salvation forever?" His mother's eyes were unmoving. Her stubborn need to prevail will someday overwhelm the little good sense she possesses, the King thought.

"Peppin is my son, Ma-Mam, and my heir. I cannot deny my child; I will not deny my wife."

Queen Bertrada realized Charlemagne cared nothing for her anger. And she cared nothing for the Pope's anger. *The Church? Hah!* She feared neither. Hadrian needed Charlemagne. He might huff and puff but he would never excommunicate either of them. It would not happen.

However, she must not alienate Charlemagne. He guaranteed her presence at court. He allowed her any luxury she wished and never interfered in her control of court entertainments and festivities. She must maintain his good will and reestablish her influence over him. Immediately discarding her attack mode and her demanding tone, Bertada spoke lightly, her voice soothing.

"You must have another son, one who can lead." She dropped her eyes, seeming to regret the harshness of her words. Humming softly, she moved to the table to pour ale from the flagon. She stroked the King's hand and wrapped it around the cup.

"Surely, the Pope can find some dispensation in Church law to dissolve the marriage. He needs your protection; you must impress that need on him." She almost purred her next words. "Your union was a Germanic joining. It did not take place in the Church, under the hands of a holy man. You cannot argue its sanctity." She moved quietly, hoping to win her son's acceptance with sweet words and quiet speech.

"Nay! Nay!" King Charlemagne pushed the flagon away. He seemed not to have heard her. "I **will not** drink! Have you no shame, trying to soften my mind with ale and win my approval?" Queen Bertrada startled, embarrassed Charlemagne so easily saw her motives. The King gazed sadly into his mother's eyes.

"But my marriage *was* blessed later, Ma-Mam," the King reminded her. "The Pope acknowledged Peppin as my lawful issue, both in church and in secular law. You do deny the legitimacy of your own marriage if you hold to this reasoning. Newly revised Church law makes *me* illegitimate. Do not go down this road." The King's brow furrowed.

"What sorrow you unleash? Desiderius does not wish to 'influence' my court. Nay, he will try every trick, promise every noble, employ anyone he can to undermine me. And failing in those efforts, he will overthrow me. Make no mistake, Ma-Mam, he may well murder me...to take the realm. And you think an alliance will save my rule?" King Charlemagne laughed bitterly and walked toward the tent door.

"My God," he muttered, "how I need Poppa!" He left his mother quickly, alternately enraged and saddened by her mindless meddling. The Queen Mother stood immobile.

"Praying for his father as usual. Never does he see his faults—his excessive concern for the Frankish people." She sneered. "Those two are just alike; they would sacrifice themselves for others, but never think to advance their own power." Bertrada paused, thinking. She was certain Charlemagne would eventually embrace the betrothal. *There is nothing left between him and Himiltrude. He surely is not eager to bind himself further in the marriage. Church law we can overlook. Pope Hadrian will never excommunicate Charlemagne. He needs his might too much. This betrothal will still turn out well.*

Charlemagne ran to the horse line, flung himself on Samson's back and rode away. Tears streamed down his face. *No wonder I can't find Himli. Ma-Mam sent her away. Oh, God! There's no guessing what she told her. I was surely painted a monster. My poor son…what will happen to you?* He rode Samson for miles, forcing the horse to fly down the forest paths. Finally, Samson slowed down. Smelling water, he stopped at a nearby stream, gulping the water to quench his great thirst. Charlemagne patted the horse's neck, realizing he punished his mount because he dare not pummel his mother. He returned to the court's camp slowly, going straight to Abbot Fulrad's tent.

"Come in, my son," the Abbot invited, recognizing the King's outline in the dark night. Pulling his tunic over his sleeping linens, the Abbot stepped back for the King to enter. Abbot Fulrad was the closest to a father Charlemagne had. He came to the Frankish court just before Charlemagne's birth. He was Charlemagne's oldest counselor and friend, as well as his spiritual adviser. Now, exhausted from his mother's announcement, the King knelt to pray on the Abbot's prayer stool.

"My dear boy, what is it? What weighs so heavily on your

spirit? Share this burden with me." The Abbot put his arm around Charlemagne. He felt the King shudder.

"Charlemagne, what is it?" Fulrad repeated, almost afraid of the answer. He helped the King stand. "Tell me. Are you ill?" Does he know his wife and child are gone, the Abbot wondered.

"Himiltrude? Where is she, Abbot?" The King whispered, his face as white as an altar linen. "Where are my wife and son; do you know?" The Abbot caught his breath. He shuddered, wondering how much the king knew. He took the easy way.

"Himiltrude and Pippin? Are they not in their tent?" He looked again into the King's face, saw exhaustion and sorrow. "What are you asking? Your words make no sense." Abbot Fulrad placed his hand on Charlemagne's forehead, as if feeling for a fever.

Charlemagne shrugged the Abbot's hand away and sat at the writing desk. If he knows nothing of Himiltrude's leaving, I surely will not be able to find her. Charlemagne thought. He still could not believe his mother would go to such lengths. But Queen Bertrada's plotting was the only explanation for the disappearance of his wife and son. Charlemagne stood up, unsteady on his feet. The Abbot put his arm around Charlemagne's shoulder, giving him strength.

"I am very tired, Abbot," Charlemagne admitted. "Shelter me for tonight. I wish to see no one. Do you understand?"

"Of a certainty," the Abbot replied. "You will not be disturbed here. Come, come to my sleeping bench." The Abbot put his arm around the King's waist and walked him to the bench, holding the linens aloft as Charlemagne slid between them. Fulrad covered the King.

"After you rest, we will talk." The Abbot said. "There is much on your mind. I go for food and drink. No one will know you are here." The Abbot squeezed the King's shoulders, shaken by his blood-shot eyes, the gray pallor of his skin, his body's weakness, his trembling legs. "Lie down and rest." He tied the tent flap, assuring no one would disturb the King. For precaution, Fulrad summoned a guard, placing him in front of the tent.

"Let no one enter." He commanded. "I shall hasten in my return." The Abbot hurried to the cook tent. He brought back wine, blackberries in cream, and wheat cakes. Charlemagne did not stir as he entered.

Chapter Nine

WARNING

King Charlemagne stirred in his linens. A memory of Hildegard riding her horse across the plains woke him. His heart swelled as he quickly looked around the tent. Closing his eyes, he took himself back to the morning ride near Hautgard's manor: Hildegard's smile, her eyes as they brightened at his words, the trot of her horse, the sweetness of her mouth beneath his. Sighing, he turned and realized he was in the Abbot's bed. He slowly opened his eyes and understood he was alone. Then, all of it rushed back. He thought of his wife and his son. His heart fell in his chest; his eyes filled with tears. Sadness, regret, hurt, shame filled his mind. *Where are my wife and son?*

What am I to do? He asked himself. "Is there any hope of finding them?"

He heard scuffling at the front of the tent and turned. Abbot Fulrad came in, carrying baskets. The smell wafting from one identified hot bread. Charlemagne knew another basket held cheese, nuts and hard-boiled eggs. Fulrad smiled.

"Awake, are you? I've brought a bit of a breakfast, just bread and cheese. I thought you needed something before going to pray this morning. The air is nippy; a storm is gathering. Do we move today toward Aachen?"

"Mayhap, Abbot. ...today or tomorrow." He got up, wrapped a linen around his body, and motioned to the Abbot to sit. "We need to talk, Fulrad."

"Sire?"

"Do you know anything about Himiltrude and Peppin. Where are they? I returned and find our tent gone. There's not a sign of them anywhere. Tell me, if you know anything." Abbot Fulrad's face blanched white. He rubbed his hands together and looked into the King's face.

"They are no longer in this court." He said, his eyes downcast.

"I know that, dammit, Fulrad! Where are they? Did you see them leave? What day was that? Where were they going? And why...why did my wife and son leave the court...without a word to me?" He gazed into Fulrad's sad face and added: "Tell me. All of it, whatever you know."

"Queen Bertrada sent them away, Charles. One day they were here; the next day, they were gone. Your mother made her decision long before she confided in me. I told her she violated church teachings. An able heir or not, Peppin is your son; Himiltrude is your wife. Aye, I urged her to leave this to you. But she refused. She was unmoveable in the sureness of her decision. I don't know their destination, though they did have an escort."

"How dare she? What a way to treat Himli, Fulrad! What must she think of me? Do you know what my mother told her?"

"Nay, Sire, I do not. I suspect your mother confronted her, told her to pack her things, giving her little time for it. She and Peppin, with a military escort, left the camp before any were awake. It's been five, six days now. We woke; the tent was gone. She and Peppin were nowhere to be found and Himiltrude's mount was missing. That's all I know. Queen Bertrada told the court Himli went to visit her family."

"I cannot countenance it, Fulrad. It's too cruel and heartless. Punishment for two who did no wrong...no wrong at all!" He held his face in his hands as his body shook with grief. Fulrad sat with his arms around the King's shoulders. All he could do was give a little comfort.

Charlemagne felt Fulrad's grip lessen and understood the abbot slept. The king moved gingerly; found his tunic, leggings, and foot coverings; and dressed quickly. He left Fulrad's tent to stand outside.

"My mother banished them." He told himself again. "She sent them away. God knows where." Raising his eyes, he spied a large boulder in the distance and hurried to sit behind it, away from the eyes of the camp. He propped his back against the boulder, smearing his tunic with lichen.

"Ma-Mam will never give me Himiltrude's destination," he muttered. *God knows where she might have sent them. And she banished Pippin, too — on an unknown journey as summer is ending. They could easily be attacked, robbed for the linens and furniture in the cart!* His thoughts ran wild, but soon he slowed them down. He had to think. *Abbot Fulrad said Himli left with an escort. Thank God; they're protected in some small measure.*

He grieved at the banishment of his son, at the ill treatment of Himiltrude. His mother's action left him bereft of hope. He remembered his happy days with Himiltrude, especially as they anticipated the birth of their child. *How sweet those days were! And, then, the sorrow came with Pippin's birth, with his deformity. It almost broke us both.* Charlemagne knew his mother. She instigated all this while he was away. His face a mask of grief, he made a vow.

"I will ask nothing from Ma-Man, not ever again. I will never trust her nor listen to her wishes. If only, I could remove her from the court..." The King pushed his weary body to a standing position and hurried to his tent to change his clothes. This was the third day in this tunic and breeches…ever since leaving Hautgard's manor. Now, they were stained further with dirt and brown lichen from the boulder.

"No one must know of this," he told himself. "I'll say Himiltrude and Pippin are visiting her family, just as Ma-Mam said. But I'll send my own scouts to search for them. The changing weather might wipe out the route they followed; but, mayhap, I'm not too late." He sent for the captain of his guards, giving directions for a search party.

As the day wore on, the court buzzed with excitement. Unknown to Charlemagne, the daughter of the court—his sister, Gisela—was on her way home. A scout reported her escort crossing a near-by meadow and, then, a courier announced her arrival. Courtiers, servants, nobles and all the children of the court came forward to greet her.

Vaguely hearing calls and shouts from the court, King Charlemagne awoke, ignored everyone and went to bathe in the near-by river. With sad certainty, he realized he and Himiltrude could never repair their frayed marriage.

Their disagreement over Peppin's disability, the limits it placed on his future, efforts needed to strengthen the boy - they opposed each other's ideas with a vengeance. He wanted to push Peppin; Himlitrude wanted to spare and protect him. Himli withdrew from the affairs of the court. Since his birth, Peppin got all her attention. Charlemagne needed her spirit, her enthusiastic view of life to infuse the court. She refused to interact and criticized Charlemagne for the limited time he spent with their son.

He must think of another marriage; it was necessary for his future. But his mother's premature betrothal sickened him and made her ambition even more hateful in his eyes. *God, give me a wife focused on many interests,* he prayed, *not just on her own desires.* He worried little about the Pope's reaction. With the right explanation, Charlemagne knew the Pope would call his first marriage a 'barbarian union' and give him leave to remarry.

"Of a certainty, I do not want a Lombard betrothal. Mayhap, I can refuse it. After a suitable period and a dispensation from Pope Hadrian, I can take another wife. In the meantime, I'll approach Hildegard to determine if she retains feelings for me.

"Heavenly Father," the King prayed, "don't let Hildegard forget me. Keep her opinion of me positive, not frightened by my intensity. She is a gentle maid. Protect me from her disapproving judgment." He rose from his knees, hearing footsteps behind him.

"Gisela is here! Gisela is here!" A young courtier shouted in delight, waving at Charlemagne as he sped by on some errand.

"Gisela!" The King's heart leapt. "Gisela is here?" Of every court member, Gisela was his favorite. His sister stole his heart the very day she was born. Ever since, he protected her and sheltered her from the strains of court life. She adored him. He felt his heart beat with joy and found comfort in this unexpected news.

"Where is she?" He demanded of his mother as she, too, hurried by.

"Come; get ready for our meal." Queen Bertrada called as she half-ran toward the banquet tent. She stopped short and looked at him. "Where have you been since yesterday night? I was readying a regiment to find you."

Charlemagne did not answer. He was perfectly capable of ignoring his mother, if Gisela were truly here. "Where is she?" He stopped another courtier, not knowing which direction to go.

"I'm here," a clear, loving voice seemed to sing. The King turned, saw his sister running to him and hurried forward, whisking her into the air.

"How fine to see you," he boomed as he kissed her cheek. "Why didn't you let us know you were coming? I'd have welcomed you if I only…"

"Put me down, you brute!" Gisela laughed. "That's the point of surprise visits…that no one will know! Come, come; I haven't been locked in stocks. I wanted to see my big brother…and the rest of the court, of a certainty." She added, as her mother walked up and waited to escort them to the banquet tent.

"You go ahead, Ma-Mam," Charlemagne suggested, seeing his mother's impatient, tapping foot. "I must change this tunic. Gisela will hurry me along." Queen Bertrada nodded and turned away as Charlemagne pulled Gisela into his tent.

"You look a little pale, brother," Gisela said. "I was uncertain when Ma-Mam wrote of her plans for your betrothal. Actually, the betrothal is the reason for my visit. I must talk to you."

"Ha!" Charlemagne croaked, his voice devoid of laughter. "So you knew about it before I? How very like our mother…to publicize the event even before the groom was informed. How I loathe her meddling, Gisela."

"She considers only her own wishes, Charley, hers alone," Gisela answered.

"Nothing changes her, though Poppa did limit her meddling." Giving him a hug, Gisela patted his back in sympathy. "How did this come about? Ma-Mam wrote me from the Lombard court, bragging about her 'coup.' …if all of us were only as confident as she."

"I would wish her much less triumph myself." Charlemagne responded gloomily. "I didn't realize the force of her will, Gisela. She considers no one but herself. Finally, it's clear to me."

"Aye, you're correct," Gisela agreed, nodding. She looked at her brother closely. "What was Himiltrude's reaction?" Gisela liked Himiltrude. They spent many rainy afternoons comparing needlework and designing tunics. She couldn't imagine Himli's position in this.

"Gisela, I don't know what Ma-Mam is doing!" King Charlemagne admitted, ignoring the question. "She turns my world upside down...with no warning. She didn't even give me a chance to think about a betrothal! I was happy with Himli." He stopped and looked into his sister's face, seeing her doubt. "But, then, after Pippin came damaged, the worry of an heir reared its head again. Who knows if Himli can have a whole child?" Gisela squeezed her brother's shoulder, trying to give him comfort.

"In truth, I'm drowning in others' expectations. *I will not cloud Gisela's visit with my problems.* "But how are you? Still determined to enter a nunnery, are you? We won't dwell on my sorry state." He shrugged into an embroidered tunic. He startled on hearing the near panic in his sister's voice as she replied.

"Charley, I may not get you alone again, so listen. I made this trip to warn you." Gisela grabbed his arm to assure his attention. "Ma-Mam wrote she brokered this alliance and this betrothal for you. I wonder, how well does she know the Lombard king?" Gisela did not wait for an answer. "He is very ambitious, brother. Be careful with his daughter; she is totally under his influence. She does anything he asks. And he has designs on your kingdom." Charlemagne looked at his sister with new appreciation.

"Would Desiderius threaten my rule, Gisela?" Charlemagne asked.

"Aye, I believe he would," Gisela confirmed. "I was only a child the few weeks I spent at their court. Do you remember the summer I visited Lombardy? Ma-Mam was trying to create dynasties, even then." Gisela didn't pause for her brother to reply but tapped his shoulder.

"Heed me! You must protect yourself, Charley. Know this: if Desiderata is not happy in this marriage, if it is not to her liking, her father will punish you. He will demand your blood. He wants the realm and is willing to sacrifice his children to further his climb. He is very like our mother in the choices he makes."

"May God protect us all, then," Charlemagne answered. His sister nodded her head in agreement.

"Desiderata will report everything to King Desiderius." Gisela's face reflected the urgency of her words. "Desiderata will bring people from the Lombard Court here with her. Beware of each of them." She paced around the tent, then turned back to her brother. "And what about Himiltrude, Charley; what is her future in all of this?"

"Ma-Mam spirited her away...and Peppin, too." Charlemagne admitted, seeing the horror cross his sister's face. "I've no way to find them. Even Abbot Fulrad has no knowledge of their destination." He hurried to explain. "Ma-Mam always disliked Himiltrude, even though she hurried our marriage. Mayhap she thought Himli could tame my wild ways." Seeing Gisela's strained face, Charlemagne tried to ease both their minds. "I will explain it to Himli someday, Gisela. There's nothing to be done now." He considered Gisela's warning.

"It seems I have no choice of bride, anyway. Ma-Mam denies me that." He shrugged. "I only need a son, Gisela. The woman who births him is of little moment. Don't worry over-much." Charlemagne decided to try to forget his problems for now. He brightened to deflect his dear sister's worry.

"Most royal marriages seem to produce children. A child, a son … is now my single concern. If Desiderata becomes my wife, Ma-Mam will expect much and praise little. Desiderata will have years of demands ahead of her…learning to please our mother. Ma-Mam will surrender little to her; you can be sure—no matter how much she seems to approve of her." Laughing at Gisela's disgusted expression, he gave her a hug and sighed.

"I value your presence, Gisela," the King said. "You keep me clear-eyed about Ma-Mam. I forget too often her manipula-tive nature, if you are not nearby."

"I have far less patience than you, brother. Why think you I wish to become a nun?" At the King's start of surprise, Gisela laughed aloud. "Aye, I will escape her, and on my own terms." Charlemagne gave her arm a squeeze and nodded at her in-sight.

"For much do I admire you, Gisela," he answered, kissing her cheek. Then his thoughts returned to his own problem. "Oh, Gisela, Ma-Mam does create misery…misery for us all." His eyes were moist as he thought about the mother of his son and all they were to each other only a short time ago.

"Come, come. We're wanted at the evening meal. Please, Gisela, help me ignore our mother this night. I do wish to tear her tongue from her mouth. If only I could, it surely would be of great benefit to the realm." He heard footsteps approaching.

"Hurry! I want no messenger summoning me to table." He held out his arm to her. "Take my arm and *pretend* you're a princess."

Happy to join in a light-hearted moment, even a brief one,

Gisela assumed a coquettish smile, laid her arm on top of Charlemagne's massive one, and kissed his cheek.

"You command my world, my dear," she answered.

At the meal, everyone feasted and laughed. There was always an added gaiety when Gisela was in the banquet hall. Some of the young lords suddenly remembered news they must bring the King. They smiled and chatted with Gisela as they waited their moment to speak. Gisela was unfailingly pleasant but uninterested in any of them.

For years, she dreamed of joining an abbey. In fact, she spent most of her time in one already, learning the ways of the sisters and cementing her commitment. When informed of her choice, King Pepin supported and encouraged her interest. He knew all too well the pressures put on a young princess…and the added expectations of this particular one's mother.

Her light brown hair and green eyes, so attractive to the young nobles, was a contrast to Carloman's brooding, dark looks. Gisela's outspokenness and quick mind always delighted King Pepin and continued to impress her brothers. She loved animals and people, spending an equal time with both. *Gisela*, Charlemagne thought, *is the best of Poppa and of Carl. She thinks; she consults; she finds practical solutions; and, then, she acts — always with a loving heart.* He nodded as she promised to ride with him on the morrow. Then, Gisela retired for the evening.

The King was lost without his sister at his side. The merry fools bouncing around the banquet tent, the skilled musicians playing softly behind him, even a court poet reciting his verse did not distract the King's conflicting thoughts. In the midst of the court's gaiety, he felt alone, almost abandoned.

How sorely I need a help-mate, Charlemagne thought, as the sheen of dark curls caught his eye. His heart soared, even as he laughed at himself. *How can a mass of curls so please me?* Understanding, he nodded to himself. *They are but a symbol of the wife I dream about — not a wife of my mother's choosing, but of my own.*

He imagined a wife who was bosomy; who laughed easily and with great innocence; who was a caring, loving woman thankful for her blessings and eager to share them with others; who would work to improve the lives of the people in his realm. *Hah!* He berated himself. *It's not likely I shall find such a desirable woman, not at all likely.* His thoughts stopped abruptly. At that very moment Hildegard's face popped into his mind. He caught his breath. Then, he smiled, his face suffused with delight and wonder. *Hildegard is just such a woman. Even the dark curls are hers.* His mind danced with joy.

King Charlemagne rubbed his temples, trying to dislodge the thought from his mind. But, too late - the thoughts lay there. *It's Hildegard you seek. Hildegard should be your wife.* In a moment, he sobered. *Hildegard doesn't remember you...at least, not with positive thoughts. You had no right to kiss her and, then, apologize. She is many leagues away, well-content in another world.*

"If only she were in my world," Charlemagne muttered. "I could bear all misfortunes, even the meddling of my mother." The thought crowded every corner of his mind. Trembling, he excused himself from the table and left in search of a courier.

"Ride quickly." The King commanded. "I wished this missive delivered yesterday." The messenger startled, then laughed aloud.

"I cannot bring such a miracle to pass, Sire," he answered.

"But I will get it there as quickly as the horses can take me."
And he galloped out of the camp. Charlemagne counted as the
days slowly inched by, wishing with all his being he could be a
sparrow sitting in Count Hautgard's cooking room when the
messenger arrived.

Chapter Ten
THE FATEFUL JOURNEY

Winter finally arrived in the garden of the Hautgard manor. Since the King's departure, Hildegard whiled away the days, watching the garden plants shrivel and re-living the moments she shared with King Charlemagne. In the herb garden, she spun her dreams of him and smiled with no worry of anyone's questioning the smile or asking her thoughts. Even though the herbs she loved were dormant, hiding in the earth, their dried stalks and dead blossoms comforted her because the King once stood among them. *Charlemagne won't give me a thought. He's married and is, I am certain, sought by many noble women. I heard some say they hope his marriage will fail. In any case, I'm away from him now, lost here in the wilds and wooed by local lads – buffoons each and every one.* She laughed aloud, admitting it tragic to compare these young men to the king.

"What a fool I am!" Hildegard exclaimed. "How many women garner such concern from their King? I should feel gratified, even smug. After all, he did more than speak to me; we rode together." Even now, days later, her memories of the King's words and her confusion over his attentions made her feel unsettled. When Maria spoke to her from the garden gate, she startled.

"What do you here, Hildegard?" Maria asked. Hilde shied, her thoughts interrupted by her friend's appearance. "Are you unwell? Should I fetch yarrow to ease your belly ache?" Maria assumed Hildegard's monthly pain was upon her. "I wouldn't interrupt, but I need your advice on gifts for the manor's children. Yuletide will soon be upon us." Maria waited, standing at the side gate. Her arms held balsam boughs and bags of chestnuts, gathered for decorating the banquet hall for Yuletide celebrations. Immediately chagrined for giving Maria worry, Hildegard hurried to the gate.

"Nay, I am well, Maria," Hildegard replied. "And the yarrow, I do not need." Hildegard answered, pulling herself away from her conflicting thoughts. "The children are always so excited at Yuletide, as was I. Let's plan some special surprise for them, something they will not expect."

"Aye, that's a good idea. But what can it be?" Maria's face lit up, her enthusiasm immediately kindled. "We usually include nuts and sweets in the baskets. I always liked any sweet when I was little." She wrinkled her nose, trying to think of a new gift. "It must be simple, though. There are twenty children under the age of twelve in the manor families. And we have less than eight days to concoct a surprise."

"I was thinking," Hildegard replied. "What if we create something special for each one…like embroider a flower on the new tunics for the girls? The boys might like a deer or a bear on their hats. You know, Maria, something to make the gift unique…for that child alone?" Hildegard looked out over the garden. "I only wish we could help their parents. Now, there would be a gift for certain!"

"Help their parents?" Maria asked, not understanding.

"Aye," Hildegard replied. "Help them improve their lives: have a bit more food for their children, a warmer hut for the coming winter, cloaks lined with fur. They live, throughout their lives, Maria, with so very little." Maria nodded her head, frowning.

"Life is hard, Hildegard," she agreed. "Mother and Father do all they can; but, sometimes, the crops don't grow. Then, hunger follows. But what can you and I do?"

"I don't know, Maria." Hildegard admitted. "But there must be some way to relieve this hunger. The winter brings cold and want. It haunts us year after year, sapping the strength and hope from everyone."

"Aye," Maria replied. "Let's see what we can do to make the children happier now. We'll start with them." Her natural buoyancy returned. "Come, we'll ask Mother's advice. She'll delight in the idea and will help us make plans." Maria and Hildegard sought direction from Countess Hautgard who heartily agreed a surprise for the children would be welcome.

"We have a few days yet," she pointed out, "to work on this. But don't strain for skills you don't have. You have more than twenty gifts to prepare. Simple creations will please the children and will prove easier for you to undertake."

The two young women gathered the items designated for each family's Yuletide basket: tunics, nuts, sugared fruit, fruit spreads, wool hats, and new linens. The day before Count Hautgard delivered the baskets, the manor's cooks would bake tarts. And the following morning, Maria and Hildegard would pack tarts along with the other items. Countess Hautgard told them she wanted to add a ham and a fat duck to each basket as well.

Laughingly teasing each other about their embroidery skills, Maria and Hildegard each brought a sewing basket to the cooking room. They sat together at one of the large tables to weave their magic.

"Now, Maria," Hildegard said, her face intent. "Tell me something about each one of the children: a favorite animal, a skill, treasures they value." Maria began describing the children in each family, trying hard to remember any special skills or interests which set them apart one from the other. The serving girl heard the girls talking and came to the table. The three of them soon identified special interests of each child in the manor. Maria and Hilde girls began sewing and embroidering — placing names, animals, and symbols on the caps and tunics. Near mid-day, as they ate chicken pie and lentils, Count Hautgard came into the cook room.

"Stretching those busy fingers, hum?" he asked, smiling at them. He held aloft a piece of parchment and looked steadily into their faces, smiling widely. Taking his time, he settled down on a bench at their table.

"I have heard of your Yuletide plan for the manor's children. You have a wonderful idea, very kind and caring. I do commend you for your good hearts." He praised them. Then, he rose and gave them both kisses on their cheeks. Maria and Hildegard felt their hearts lift. They knew the Count doted on them. He often brought them ribbons, jewelry, and exotic sweets found in his travels. But he very seldom commented on their virtues.

"Thank you, Sire," they replied in unison.

"Perhaps good deeds are rewarded," the Count said mysteriously. "I have here a missive from King Charlemagne." He unrolled the parchment in his hand. Hildegard and Maria looked at the Count in surprise. Hildegard unconsciously held her breath as she waited for Count Hautgard's next words.

"A big honor, he extends to us — a big honor. I have here," he tapped the parchment slowly, "an invitation for you to join his court — you as well as Jocelyn. I'm quite overcome. I never thought daughters of mine would have such an opportunity."

Maria, her twelve-year-old heart fluttering, jumped from her seat, shouting her excitement. She immediately kissed her father, Hildegard, the cook, and the baker. Count Hautgard beamed at his daughter, holding up his finger to quieten her squeals.

Hildegard's face was pale and still. She did not know how to feel. *How can the King invite Maria and Jocelyn and not me?* She asked herself. *Mayhap he forgot me, overlooked I am, here at the Count's manor.* She smiled at Maria's excited face. *I cannot bear it! The King excludes me! All my dreams of his interest now are proved untrue, hopeless dreams of a foolish girl.* She steeled herself, determined not to destroy Maria's happiness or show her own disappointment. The Countess nodded toward Hildegard, just before the Count looked over to see the shadow, the question, in the young woman's eyes.

"Oh, you're included, of a certainty, Hildegard." The Count hurried to reassure her. "You and Maria are invited to serve as maids to Jocelyn. Just last month, Jocelyn begged to join the court. But I had no relative to invite her, no power to grant her wish. And I would move heaven and hell to make it so. Since the death of her husband, Ehren, she has been so unhappy. And I could think of nothing..." He paused, then smiled. "Mayhap, King Charlemagne has heard her prayers."

"Are you certain, Count; I am included in the King's invitation?" Hildegard asked, her excitement beating in her ears. *If I am to go,* her heart sang, *he does not forget me.* "Mayhap, the King believes I am back in Swabia by now." She was afraid to think her dream was true. "I never expected to go to court, Sire." Count Hautgard glanced back at the parchment.

"Of a certainty," he confirmed, tapping the missive. "Your name is listed with Maria's and Jocelyn's; he expects the three of you." Hildegard nodded, smiling widely into the Count's kind face. *But you must not put undue hope in this invitation. The King includes you because you are a good friend of this family.* He has not singled you out, Hildegard reminded herself. Still, she felt alternately excited and worried: excited at the promise of seeing the King again; worried at the heartache she knew awaited her, if she did not end her infatuation. *The King will dally and compromise you, then go on about his life. You must be strong. Forget your feelings. There is no one to protect you but yourself.*

Count Hautgard knew the girls must have time to talk, to think, and even to weep about the offer. "I leave you to consider this."

He and his countess returned to the banquet hall. She looked at him knowingly as they sat to enjoy a cup of tea. "I suspect none of them will reject this invitation, my dear." He smiled at his wife as they listened to Maria's and Hildegard's delighted voices.

"This does guarantee all three of them a bevy of eligible young men. My dear, I feared much for our girls' futures. Isolated out here in the byways, we are far removed from society and the possibilities which social gatherings encourage." Countess Hautgard explained. "And Jocelyn so needs a change in her life. I fear her grief over Ehren's death will eventually overwhelm her."

"Aye, she suffers as much as on the day of his death. I know you worry." The Count admitted. "Now, Charlemagne answers our prayers with his offer. I am as relieved as you. I want the best for our daughters. But it will be difficult here without them. In a new environment, mayhap Jocelyn will recover her spirits."

"I do wonder, though. Do you think the young men might fancy one of the girls above the other two? Coming from the royalty of Swabia, Hildegard may be more desirable than our two girls." Count Hautgard asked, unsure if he should mention his suspicions to his wife.

"I do fear Hildegard is unlikely to secure a young man's interest." The Countess replied. "I noted the look on the King's face whenever she entered the room." She frowned at the Count. "If the King fancies her, no other man will dare to look." The count did not reply. King Charlemagne would have been surprised at the Countess' insight. Even though he might pressure Pope Hadrian to see things his way, the King still was not able to initiate an illicit liaison. He dare not flaunt the scruples of Church law. Looking into his wife's face, the Count voiced his question.

"Do you think Charlemagne interested in Hildegard? Oh, I think not, my dear. He is married. Surely he dare not compromise the young woman's reputation."

"Aye, I denied his apparent interest until...." Countess Hautgard broke off her sentence and held up a finger. "Do you remember my telling you Roslie, Countess Bretagne, visited last week when you were away?" The Count nodded. For four days, he visited inns and way-stations, spying for the King.

"Aye," he confirmed. "I was on an errand for King Charlemagne."

"Well," his wife continued. "Roslie's daughter, Miriam, is serving in the Lombard court. Miriam wrote her mother the court is rife with speculation about a marriage for Princess Desiderata." The Count frowned.

"I don't understand," he answered. "What has this to do with our King?" His Countess hurried to explain.

"My dear, Desiderata turns down every suitor. Who's left for her to wed? She alienated almost all the nobility months ago. Why, I even heard she told one young noble's mother that her son is not good enough for her! Who would she consider her equal? ... no one but the King of Frankland." The Countess smiled at her husband, certain she identified the key player in

Desiderata's upcoming marriage.

"But...but," the Count replied; "this is of no consequence. The King is a married man!" He looked at his wife in shock and confusion.

"Mayhap not for long, dear." The Countess answered as she rose.

Taking his wife's hand, Count Hautgard walked her to the cook room. His kind eyes crinkled, his mouth widened in a smile as he watched the young women's excited behavior, still accompanied by squeals of delight. Maria and Hildegard hugged each other, alternately shrieking and laughing — celebrating their good fortune.

"I shall send a messenger to your sister's manor to direct Jocelyn to shorten her visit. She has a different kind of journey to make now." Count Hautgard snapped his fingers to get the two young women's attention. "The King requests you begin your journey quickly. We hope for good weather, despite the lateness of the season for traveling. If the court journeys toward Aachen, you will likely overtake them." Maria and Hildegard stared at each other. They stood quickly.

"Oh! Excuse us, Father," Maria blurted out. "We must look to our clothes. New gowns must be cut and stitched. Oh! Oh, Hildegard! What an exciting life we are going to have."

Countess Hautgard checked on the stew, bubbling on the hearth. "Let's have rye loaves with this stew, Elsa." She suggested to the baker. Turning to Maria and Hildegard, she smiled at their enthusiasm. Hildegard pulled Maria beside her on the bench. In a moment, they were both standing again. The Countess, quite pleased with this turn of opportunity, smiled warmly at all in the kitchen.

"Calm yourselves," she urged. "Leave the Yuletide sewing here. Go to your chamber and evaluate your clothing. Consider the tunics and gowns you will need. Describe them to each other, so we may sketch them out for cutting and sewing. And do not forget your small clothes. When you finish, come back here and continue with this stitching."

The two young women nodded and took each other's hands. They rushed from the cook room, identifying tunics they would never take to court, but including a few pieces which would fit into their sterling future wardrobes. The Count and Countess listened to the muffled sounds of laughter from the room above.

"I fear they will succumb to a heat malady," the Countess said. "The heat from the baking ovens and their own excitement will sicken them for certain." She smiled as the Count laughed.

Hildegard wrote her father of the King's invitation. She described the excitement in the Hautgard manor, including her own. Hildegard admitted her conflicting thoughts about accepting the invitation and added a description of her first conversation with the King. Then, she mentioned her worries.

> *While I am honored by the summons, Father, I doubt I shall have the ability to hide my opinions and deny my thoughts. I fear I will offend every noble at court. As you are well aware, I am outspoken. The King does appear to value forthrightness; but that may have been a ruse or a tolerance for Maria's friend. I know not which.*
>
> *Please, Father, give me your best advice. I suppose I am asking you if it is possible to refuse this request, not that I would choose to do so.*

Poor Father, he will think I do not know my own mind. Hildegard smiled to herself. *I hope being at Charlemagne's court will afford me more contact with him. But is being around him wise, considering his marital state?* She sighed, already understanding the complications of her infatuation with the King. *Certainly, I cannot say these things to Father.*

Hildegard waited with great impatience for her father's reply. One day, she wished he suggested she return home. Another day she wished for his blessing of a calm journey to the King's court. She honestly did not know which advice she wanted. Although her messenger rode rapidly back and forth and delivered her father's missive, his reply came only one day before Jocelyn arrived back home from Reims.

My dear Hildegard,

Your mother and brother join me in sending you our heartfelt greetings. We are comforted in hearing your visit to Hautgard's manor has been so pleasant. You may imagine my surprise at the King's invitation. But, truthfully, my dear, it is not possible for you to refuse it. To do so would be suspect; it would be taken amiss. And foregoing such an opportunity is unwise.

I understand your trepidation at the thought of the royal court. Who would not be frightened by the protocol, formality, and seriousness of that entire place? But do not despair. Were you unable to impress them or unequal to the demands, I daresay King Charlemagne would not have invited you.

I am prejudiced, certainly; but I believe you capable of anything you set your mind to do. Go, my dear; accept the invitation. If you wish to leave, to return home, that will be possible...after you've spent some weeks there learning court protocol and meeting all the illustrious souls who fill that court. Such acquaintances can only serve your future. We are in

despair your journey home must be postponed, but that can-
not be changed. I have every hope this experience will be a
positive one. Never under-rate yourself, Hildegard, nor allow
anyone else to cause you to doubt your value! You are my pre-
cious daughter, head and shoulders above the rest of the young
women of my acquaintance.

We love you dearly. Never doubt that; we live for the day
you return to us.

Your loving father,
Poppa

I shall visit the King's court in the spring. You may re-
turn home then with me, if you so choose.

If I told Father King Charlemagne stole my heart, he would bring
me home now. The King is married; nothing will change that. So my
feelings for him must wither. I'll see him little and living with that
fact, as he moves around me, should curb my heart.

Not wishing to anger the King or bring any reaction against
her family, Hildegard decided to join in the excitement of planning for this new adventure. Besides, she must guard herself,
do nothing to raise Maria's suspicions. By methodically moni-
toring her words, she successfully convinced Maria her interest
in the King was over. She described it as a 'passing fancy.'

The Countess, Maria, Hildegard, and manor maids filled
the following days with sewing, packing, re-packing and
wringing of hands. With Jocelyn—eighteen months older than
the other two—finally returned, the three young women
packed expeditiously for their journey to Charlemagne's court.
Determined to shed no tears over their departure, the Count
and Countess bid them farewell with smiling faces, though
they beamed through eyes moist with unshed tears. The King

sent a small contingent of soldiers to escort Jocelyn, Maria, and Hildegard to the mobile court's location.

'I want no one inconvenienced or neglected, Count,' King Charlemagne wrote. 'My soldiers will give their lives, if need be, to keep your young women safe.' Of a certainty, Count Hautgard's delight with the soldiers is plain to see, Hilde thought to herself. *But, if possible, he's less excited than the Countess. She is ecstatic with the excitement of our departure and all aquiver, as she supervises the loading of our trunks and baskets into the carts.*

Three days after the King's escort arrived at the Hautgard manor, the three young women journeyed toward Charlemagne's court. After many miles and rough weather, the forward rider spotted the court banners. Immediately, Hildegard was nervous.

"It can be," she murmured to herself, "the King will not remember me. Or, he asked me to join the court to make Maria's transition easier. As maids in waiting, both of us learn to serve. We practice on Jocelyn but will be called on to attend to court ladies as well." Her mind skipped to another subject.

I hope Charlemagne did not see my delight in him. Hildegard worried. *He did regard me with approval. I know he did. But his coolness as he left told me. I have no reason to dream as I have.* Hildegard's feelings wavered. She was still confused by the King's abrupt 'good night' in the garden and his quick 'goodbye' as he left the Count's manor. But in their extended conversations, he evidenced little interest in hurrying back to his court.

"God help me," Hildegard whispered. "I must move beyond these feelings. I must bind my heart!" She tried to recall the vague gossip about the King before his marriage. All she could remember was the rumor of his popularity with the young women of his court—of their enthusiastic interest and of his eager response.

"There's the court!" Maria's shout interrupted Hildegard's thoughts. "I can see King Charlemagne's banners! Ohhh...I wonder how close to the King's tent we'll be. Do you see the King's banners, Hilde—right over there?" Maria pointed. "His is the purple one, the one shaped like a dragon." Maria climbed down from the cart and ran to the front of their procession. Hildegard held to where she was.

Chapter Eleven

REUNITED BUT APART

I don't know how to greet Charlemagne when I see him. He's my sovereign - nothing more, nothing less. I'll reflect cool friendliness and quiet regard. Everyone in the court will watch him greet us. Hildegard smiled at her own seriousness. *I must prepare myself. Others' judgments will spring unbidden here.* Waking from her introspection, she watched Maria skip forward in front of the soldiers, then back to their traveling cart.

"Maria!" Jocelyn cried out to her. "For the love of God, get back in your cart. You make a spectacle of yourself…and embarrass Hildegard as well as me. Show a little decorum." Jocelyn glared at her sister. "Control your enthusiasm or you go home." At that, Maria stopped in the middle of her latest dance.

"You dare not do such a thing!" She cried at her sister.

"I can and I will. If you don't act like a lady, I shall send you home as soon as the sun rises. Be certain of it." Jocelyn threatened as she motioned Maria back to their cart. "Father gave me leave to correct and to reprimand you. He said if you don't respond with mannerly composure, I am to send you home." Jocelyn glared at her younger sister. Her mouth was a thin line, pursed tightly. Her hands balled into fists.

"Return to the cart, Maria. Now. I tell you this one, last time." Extending her hand, Hildegard gave Maria a pull into the cart and whispered.

"Please, do as she says, Maria. She feels discomforted by your frivolous manner and won't hesitate to send you back to your father's manor. She will not suffer embarrassment, especially not from you." Jocelyn will be a difficult teacher, Hildegard thought; but she does protect our reputations from court gossip. *Maria thinks court life will be all sweetness. She believes men will seek her hand and imagines days of idleness and parties. She fools herself. We will work hard: run errands, placate noble women, and maintain clothes for us three and, possibly, others. With everyone here, we must be circumspect.*

Grudgingly, Maria nodded her head at Hildegard.

"Sooo, you agree with Jocelyn." She commented, her voice shrill with suspicion. "I thought you would surely share my excitement, Hildegard, and dance with me!" She watched Hildegard from lowered brows. "We're joining King Charlemagne's court. Can no one see the glory in that?" Maria waited for an answer. Receiving none, she rekindled her own enthusiasm.

"I'm eager to see Lord Roland again; aren't you, Hilde? He was so kind to us back home. Won't you be happy to see him — Lord Roland and, surely, King Charlemagne?" Maria cocked her head at Hildegard, barely repressing a smile.

"I wish to see the entire court, Maria," Hildegard quietly answered, "no one person more than another, though I hope to see both those gentlemen."

"...as do I!" Maria laughed, unable to control her excitement.

At that very moment, Hildegard heard hoof beats. Her heart skipped as she recognized Roland. *Charlemagne can't be far behind!* Stopping at the head of the soldiers' column, Roland said something to the sergeant, nodded and turned toward their carts. Recognizing Maria and Hildegard, he moved in their direction. Pulling in his horse, Roland bowed from his saddle to Maria. Hildegard sighed. *I so hoped the King would come to greet us,* she thought; *but he would not.* She shook her head.

I must adjust to court protocol. King Charlemagne probably doesn't meet a single person who arrives at his court...unless it's a fellow ruler. Mayhap even another king would first be welcomed by the seneschal or by the Queen Mother. Hildegard's attention turned to Roland as he spoke.

"Maria, welcome to the Frankish court...and you, also, Hildegard. Please consider yourselves a significant part of Charlemagne's entourage." Roland first turned his attention to Maria. She beamed from ear to ear. Maria thought Roland the most beautiful... nay the most handsome man in the world. Since they began their trip, she repeated this observation to her sister or to Hildegard at least three times a day. His dark, good looks; his white teeth flashing a wide smile; his carefully stitched tunics; his exquisite manners—not to mention his respect for women—endeared him to every woman he met. Hildegard smiled, watching Maria's face.

An idiot she may be, but blessed is she as well. Any man she fancies, she can dream might one day be hers. How hopeful it must be — to be fond of a man who has no wife. Hildegard consciously kept her face pleasant, though she realized anew the hopelessness of her attraction to the king.

"Please do acquaint me with your sister." Roland requested. "Is that beautiful creature, there in the other cart, she?" He bowed in Jocelyn's direction. "It's my honor to greet you, Lady Jocelyn. The King delights in your journey to his court. He told me you were the first infant he ever really liked...at the old age of twelve. He looks forward to greeting you in the banquet tent at our evening meal."

"Aye, Lord Roland." Maria replied. "This is my sister, Jocelyn?" She held out her hand, grinning first at Hildegard, then at Jocelyn.

"Lord Roland," Jocelyn inclined her head. "Please accept our thanks for your greeting. All of us look forward to becoming friends to all in King Charlemagne's court." Jocelyn was spell-bound by Roland's courtesy. No man ever granted her so much importance or spoke in such a courtly manner. After his greeting, she managed no more than a slight tilt of her head and a wide smile. Roland bowed from atop his horse and turned to Hildegard, smiling.

"Hildegard, my own and the King's welcome. It's good to see you again." He rode to Hildegard's cart and bowed low over his horse's neck.

"Thank you, Lord Roland." Hilde replied. "I'm happy to see you again and look forward to greeting our King."

"I beg your indulgence." Roland turned. "Please excuse me while I direct the escort to your quarters. Look everything over and settle into your tent before we gather for the evening meal. I shall delight in seeing you as we gather after sunset." He bowed to each of them and returned to the head of the escort.

"Oh, Maria! I must admit." Jocelyn finally found her voice. "Lord Roland is just as attractive as you said...mayhap, even more so! This *is* going to be a grand adventure."

Following Roland's directions, the young women's escort stopped in front of a new tent, a Frankish banner waving in the breeze beside it. Hildegard held the tent flap as Jocelyn and Maria went inside. She heard a cry of delight.

"What a cozy place!" Maria exclaimed. "Look, our sleeping benches are already arranged." Fluffy linens and wool blankets lay on the benches. Jocelyn ran her hand down the linens and sniffed. She smiled with satisfaction. She could almost feel the warm rays of the sun which dried the linens. A hanging tapestry between each bench provided some degree of privacy, as did the placement of the sleeping benches. Guards entered the tent, carrying the young women's traveling chests. Jocelyn asked the guards to slide the carry-all bags beneath the benches. Nearby were several wooden chairs covered with additional wool linens.

"We shall, of a certainty, be warm enough," Jocelyn declared. "Look at all the linens in this tent. It must get cool here in the night...for one to need so many covers."

"The court moves all over Frankland, Jocelyn. The weather is changeable, I think, from south to north, for example." Hildegard walked over to a small, wooden chest in one corner. "I wonder what this chest contains?" She looked at Jocelyn and Maria, questions in her eyes. "Why, it's filled with little drawers...as if to store things." Maria hurried over to stand beside Hildegard.

"It must move with the tent," she observed. "But what manner of things would one carry in it?" The girls opened and closed the drawers of the chest, intrigued by the many divisions in the space.

"Mayhap we are to store and transport our jewelry and hair ornaments," Jocelyn suggested. "The divisions would keep them in order and protect them, wouldn't they?"

"Aye," Hildegard agreed, looking at the chest. "If we wrap our jewels in cattail fluff, they will be doubly secure. Mayhap, it was not made for the purpose we suggest, but it is a useful transport...and so beautifully made!" Each of the little drawers had a nub of wood for pulling the drawer open and carved front panels held the image of a Frankish flower. "These carvings do much to beautify the front."

"You take the first row, Hilde; Maria shall use the second, and I'll put my things in the third." Jocelyn decided. "We'll store valuables in this beautiful and useful chest." Intrigued by the small chest, the girls transferred their jewelry to its little drawers. They, however, decided not to unpack further, not knowing how quickly the court might be moving. In moments, refreshments arrived from the court cook tent. They sat to relax and enjoy hot cups of cider when there was a slight noise outside.

Before anyone could stand, a hand pulled back the canvas of the tent. Roland requested permission to enter and, hearing Jocelyn's affirming reply, announced a visitor.

"May I present King Charlemagne, ladies," he said, bowing to them all and extending his hand behind him. Roland stepped aside as Charlemagne entered the tent. The King hurried immediately to the young women. His eyes passed quickly over Jocelyn and Maria and settled on Hildegard's face. He gave her a slow, searching smile and, then, wrestled his attention away. Hildegard, who watched him closely, saw him take a deep breath. He shifted his feet and seemed to steady his shoulders. His torso angled toward Hildegard but, imperceptively, he leaned his chin toward Jocelyn and Maria.

Clearly, he must greet them first. They are family friends. Hildegard approved of Charlemagne's courtesy. His loyalty to Count Hautgard required his attention focus first on the Count's daughters. She saw his right hand, held behind his back, wave slowly. *Ohhh! There's my 'hello'.* Hildegard consciously tried not to smile. No one must see any private communication between her and the king. But her heart beat faster. The King connected with her quickly and unobtrusively and in a special way.

Hildegard understood Maria's obvious excitement but sympathized with Jocelyn. Not having been around King Charlemagne, she—the oldest of the three young women—felt the most inadequate. *Jocelyn will soon understand Charlemagne is a gracious man. With her serious mind and insightful thoughts, she'll easily measure his true worth.* Hildegard was certain the King would impress Jocelyn. She watched as Charlemagne turned to Count Hautgard's daughters. Understanding that Hildegard saw and noted his surreptitious greeting, he was charming and gracious to the two sisters.

"My beautiful subjects! It is an honor to welcome you to the court. I hope your journey here was pleasant...considering the changeable weather. I am thankful you accepted my invitation to join us." He turned to Jocelyn and, then, to Maria.

"How are your dear parents? Having you here, I miss them even more."

Although he yearned to turn to Hildegard, he knew he must restrain himself. Roland, suspecting the King's impatience, watched him in admiration. Hildegard, the most striking woman of the three, stood back as the King welcomed Count Hautgard's daughters.

"Jocelyn, how fine to see you again. Why, you are a woman grown. Not to offend you, but my memory is of a mischievous, energetic little girl who did often best me in our games. You were strong and quick...and delighted in besting a lad ten years your senior." Jocelyn laughed as did Maria.

"Thank you, Sire, for the honor of joining your court." Jocelyn hurried to say. "This is truly the happiest day of my life!" Jocelyn, naturally reticent and often obscured by Maria's energy, could think of nothing else to say. She saw the lad she used to climb trees with in the King's dancing eyes and strong body. But, now, he appeared serious and grown, not the happy, careless young lad she remembered. Maria took a step forward and curtseyed.

"The pleasure is ours, my lady," Charlemagne responded. "The Queen Mother will welcome you this evening and introduce you to the court." He turned to Maria, putting out his hand to help her rise.

"Maria, I'm honored to see you again. Welcome to the court. I trust your father and mother flourish, though losing you both is a blow, I know. I am in their debt for allowing you to join us. Their loneliness, with you here, will test their strength." Charlemagne looked at the two sisters and, then, turned back to Jocelyn. While Maria gazed starry-eyed at Roland, Charlemagne and Jocelyn reminisced about childhood games and, their occasional altercations. Maria laughed with delight. Finally, she understood.

Jocelyn—the always well-behaved, docile, obedient child—once provoked her parents' patience, too! Charlemagne easily re-established his old comradeship with Jocelyn, teasing and complimenting her in the same breath. He, then, concentrated on Maria. She shimmered in his attention. Charlemagne almost turned once, twice...to look at Hildegard but controlled his body and continued to talk with the two sisters. Finally, Maria held up her hand and spoke to both Charlemagne and Jocelyn.

"Come, come, you two. Hildegard is being left out of our reunion. Hilde, please don't linger there in the corner. You are one of us. Come."

Hildegard did not respond immediately. She watched the King with her two friends. He is even more handsome than before, she thought. Her eyes scanned him from head to foot. At every remembered feature, she felt her heart beat a little faster. *His broad shoulders, his plain but immaculate tunic, his questioning smile—all brought back memories of their ride together at Count Hautgard's manor.*

At Maria's words, Charlemagne turned to look directly into Hildegard's face. She saw him blush, take a short step forward, and, then, smile broadly at her. He is happy to see me; it's not possible for me to mis-interpret that. Hildegard said to herself. The King's hands rose unbidden, reaching out as if to enfold hold her. But he caught himself and spread them widely apart.

"Hildegard! I welcome you with joy and excitement, just as I do Jocelyn and Maria," Charlemagne said. "It seems ages since I saw you last. I hope your journey here was pleasant and not too rushed." He looked at each young woman in turn. "You do honor us with your presence." Charlemagne turned to Roland for confirmation. "Roland invited you to the banquet tent this evening. We shall all talk and become better acquainted then." He turned toward Hildegard.

"Please, may I ask you to excuse Hildegard? I have a missive from her father which contains information for her." Hildegard gasped. *He asks specifically for me!* She almost shouted in relief. *He did come to welcome me! He did!* Her heart sang. The King held his hand out to Hildegard.

"My Father? He is ...well?" She could hardly speak the words. The King nodded and squeezed her hand, smiling into her eyes. She felt cared for, feeling her hand in his. Turning back to Jocelyn, Charlemagne added.

"We shall become good friends, all of us. Of that, I am certain." Jocelyn nodded, as did Maria.

Chapter Twelve

FORGING AHEAD

Charlemagne led Hildegard, her hand still in his, out of the tent and toward a small, near-by hillock. Hildegard walked slowly beside the King. His very presence seemed to call to her. She felt his large hand cover her own and wished they could walk like this forever. *He would not still hold my hand – not this long – if he were not happy to see me.* Hildegard longed to say she missed him but her feelings kept her silent. She felt hollow in the middle of her body and only noticed the feel of his hand in hers.

He led her up the hillock silently. They reached the top of the hill and disappeared as they walked down the other side. At the same time, Roland spoke again to the other two young women.

"If you're not too weary, I would talk with you a bit." Roland said. "Mayhap, you have questions about the court I might answer?" Maria and Jocelyn responded warmly to his invitation. Roland beckoned to a man at arms and motioned to his squire. "I will escort these ladies to the banquet tent. We can relax more comfortably there; and, if they pepper me with questions I cannot answer, there are others who can help me out. Jensen, we'll ride in the cart to the horse line where these animals can be wiped down and fed." Roland's squire took the head of the horse and led him forward. Maria chatted easily, thrilled Lord Roland was to spend more time with them.

Charlemagne held Hildegard's hand tightly, a little more tightly than was necessary in Hildegard's opinion. He stared at her, losing himself in her deep, blue eyes. How long he stood there, gazing at her, he didn't know. As Hildegard glanced at his hand around hers, he realized he was rubbing her forefinger with his thumb.

"I'm delighted to see you again, Hildegard." He looked into her eyes, barely able to keep himself from pulling her close. "You look wonderful, just as beautiful...nay, nay....much more beautiful than I remembered." He placed his hands on her shoulders, unable to believe she finally stood in front of him. "These past few weeks have been a misery." he whispered. He drew her arm through his, giddy from her body's closeness. "Hildegard, my love, how *are* you?"

"I'm wonderful, now you're here." Hildegard answered, feeling the deep thump, thump, thump of her heart. "You are a joy to my eyes. But, then, mayhap I should not speak in this manner." She looked quickly away, unsure of the King's reaction.

"Your words delight my heart, Hilde," the King whispered as his hand raised her chin toward his face. "I have thought of no one but you since I left Hautgard's manor. Can you forgive me such a leave-taking? I know I was abrupt with you, seeming only to want to begin my journey to the court." Hildegard held her breath. *Mayhap, I shall get some explanation of his mercurial behavior.*

"But I cannot escape, my dear," he continued. "There is no escape for me. I have wanted nothing, Hilde, for all these long weeks but to see you again." He smiled at Hildegard's intake of breath. She opened her mouth but he closed it with his finger. "Nay, do not speak. I must beg your forgiveness. I must make you understand." Abruptly, Charlemagne turned away, walked two paces from her and, then, returned. He quickly took a parchment from his tunic, unrolling it as he held one side and nodded for Hildegard to take the other side.

"We must pretend to examine this missive," he directed her. "You take it and read it through. I will walk you in the right direction...where we might be alone for a few moments." Realizing the King did, truly, care for her after all, Hildegard stumbled over a root crossing the path. The King immediately steadied her and put his hand against the small of her back.

"Be careful, my dear. We cannot have a new court member hurt on her first day here." He caressed her hand. "Was the rest of your visit to the Hautgard's manor pleasant? I know you wished to visit your family before coming here...to the court. But, this was not possible - not with the winter storms upon us. I pray your family doesn't think ill of me for spiriting you here to my court. Before this, I did not think of inviting young women to join us, though my mother often requests the presence of first one countess and, then, another." He gazed into her eyes, sighed and looked away.

"How do I explain? Do I need to explain?" He shook his head and walked a few steps toward the river. Hildegard did not understand. Why did he seem so unsure of himself? Something seemed to tug at him, a happy emotion; but, yet, something he saw as a problem overshadowed the joy. Hildegard stood still and looked out over the river. She smiled as he came back and took her hand.

"I will speak clearly, Hildegard. I know my words confuse you." Again, he rubbed her finger with his thumb and seemed to drift away into his own world. Hildegard did not know what to say. She withdrew her hand and stepped away from the king.

"This is a peaceful place." She said. "I hear only the melody of the river, the birds calling to each other and...there! A mother cow calls her baby. Mayhap, it wanders away from her." Charlemagne came to her and gently kissed her cheek.

"My dear, you are flawless." He whispered. Hildegard startled and, then, laughed.

"Because I hear the yearning in a mother cow's voice?"

"Nay...because you are wonderfully unique, because you are yourself!" Charlemagne laughed, grabbed her hands and twirled her around.

"You have my heart, Hilde! You stole it those days ago...there in Septimania beside the river." Hildegard gasped as he pulled her close to him. "I have no right to say this to you; I am not free." He dropped her hands. "Never-the-less, the words come from my heart. I simply must tell you my feelings." He looked into her eyes, seeing surprise but, also, a happy wonder at his words.

Taking hope from her silence, Charlemagne remembered their parting. "I fled Hautgard's manor so quickly because my feelings for you were deepening. I feared to continue our friendship. With it, you would be in a precarious position if my interest in you were publicly understood." He seemed to gather strength to continue. "You know I'm married. It is a fact; nothing has changed. But I do hope something, anything, will alter my condition." Seeing Hildegard's eyes open even wider, the King hastened to continue.

"Nay, nay. I do not yet know how this can be done or if it is possible." He admitted. "I only know it must happen. Life without you is intolerable. I could not bear it without you another minute...so I sent for you. Maria and Jocelyn are here to protect you, to deflect the court's attention from you and from our friendship." He paused, looked at his feet, and, finally, met Hildegard's eyes. "Do you understand me, Hilde?"

"I...I...I did not dare hope," she whispered. "Your behavior at the Count's manor was so contradictory." She paused, finally realizing the seriousness of Charlemagne's words. "I could not be certain of you..." She looked at him, still confused at the depth of his declaration. She never let herself think of this degree of feeling.

"I did not mistake your feelings for me; did I, Hilde?" King Charlemagne asked, holding his breath. "Tell me you care for me. If your feelings don't mirror my own..." Hildegard's head jerked around in surprise.

"...my feelings?" She asked, afraid to believe his words. "I tried my best to hide these feelings, to deny any attraction between us. You are, as you say, married, Sire! What could I do with my feelings but try to undo them, to forget about you. You did urge me to forgive your forwardness. Did you not?"

"I did." Charlemagne answered. "I thought our feelings, our love, impossible. But the simple fact is I cannot live without you. If you are in my world, I can persevere. Without you, I am nothing."

Hildegard withdrew her hands from his and sat on a nearby stump. She did not know what he asked of her. *He loves me but he's married. He wants me in his life so he invites me to court? How can this be?* She shook her head. He nodded toward the missive, indicating she should read it.

"Read this, just in case anyone is watching. It is a parchment from your father, thanking me for inviting you to court. I know it's not a choice he would have sought for you, but he seems content for you to come. He reports he had a long-lasting flux but is recovered." Hildegard took the letter from his hand. Trying to move her mind beyond the king's love declaration, she held the parchment out of the sun's beam, the better to read it. Charlemagne continued.

"I have no thought of anyone, other than you. You do care for me, do you not? Could you grow to love me?" His voice was quiet but agitated.

All the while, his eyes stared into hers. Hildegard found herself unable to think. She did not know what to reply.

"This sounds like affection without a future." She answered. "I cannot say how I feel. Your love, as you describe your limitations, has little to offer."

"In the time since I left Count Hautgard's manor, have you given your heart to another?" Charlemagne asked, ignoring her words. Hildegard, startled by the question, held her arms in front of her, seemingly to ward off his words.

"What?" she asked, bewildered. "What are you suggesting?" Tears filled her eyes. *How can he think me so vapid and inconstant? He cannot believe I could cease to love him!* "Nay, Sire, nay. I am incapable of denying my heart's choice." Charlemagne grabbed her hand, immediately tucking it under his arm.

"Forgive me, beloved." He answered. "I am not at my best. Forgive me! I will never wound you; I assure you, Hilde. May God strike me down if I hurt you." And he squeezed her hand. "My delight in seeing you again is confusing my speech, and my judgment, no doubt." Hildegard looked at him afresh and saw the love in his eyes. She held onto his arm, feeling her unreliable knees ready to buckle under her, as they did before.

Suddenly, Hildegard realized they were on display, just barely sheltered by this small hill. She dropped a curtsy to the King, rubbed her forehead as if in worry, and unrolled the parchment again. She shook her head as if she read ill news and, then, gave a small cry as she looked away. She mesmerized Charlemagne with her performance.

"Well done, my Hilde. We must fool the rumor-mongers in

the court." He breathed a sigh of relief. "This is the news you are to report, if anyone asks about our conversation. Is this acceptable to you?"

Charlemagne hated this last question. He was asking Hildegard to lie, after all. Their relationship was new, as far as anyone but Roland knew. But the King knew they must keep their passion a secret. Hildegard's safety depended upon it. If his mother found out, he would be unable to protect Hildegard.

"I understand, Sire. I do thank you for reassuring me about my father's health. But, now, you suggest we allow our attraction to grow? I cannot think you are serious." She raised her eyes, challenging the King. She saw him stiffen; he dropped her hand.

"I know nothing of your court, Sire; but my life would be forfeit if anyone suspected we were anything more than sovereign and subject." Hildegard did not drop her gaze nor smile to soften her words. "Swabia is a small place, your Majesty, not used to the ways of the King's court. Nonetheless, my father would count your words misleading and inappropriate. You speak of court rumor. But you do encourage it, do you not, leading me over this hill?" Hildegard stopped speaking; her heart thudded so loudly she was surprised the King didn't hear it. She treasured his sweet words; but she would not become his concubine.

"I am not naïve," she warned him, "nor a fool to treat in some frivolous manner. For my parents' sake, if not my own, I must guard my behavior. Neither would I garner wrong on your good name." Charlemagne's eyes widened at her words. He looked at the ground, his feet alternately scuffing the soil.

"Mayhap, I should describe my upbringing to you, Sire," Hildegard suggested. At the King's nod, she began. "My parents never countenanced large parties of young nobles or searches for excitement. They kept Gerald and me close to home: teaching us to consider the poor folk under Father's protection; nurturing our responsible instincts; and living modestly. They encouraged my naturally out-going heart to expand, to wrap itself around those souls who would benefit from my protection, and to work for the people." Charlemagne nodded his head slowly, impressed with her serious demeanor.

"Mother always said my concern would be repaid threefold by the people's loyal service."

"I must do good, Sire," Hildegard added, "so as not to disappoint my parents. They live and work for others, believing we are blessed and, consequently, required to return our blessings to the world." Charlemagne inclined his head solemnly, touched both by Hildegard's wish to please her parents and to help others.

"There is much need for good works in Frankland, Hilde. Challenges are everywhere: the hunger, the inability to trade freely, the severity of winter, outlaw bands, threats from invaders. The most pressing need is to decrease hunger throughout the land." Seeing her eyes widen, the King continued.

"With your dedication to the people, you can have a huge impact on the realm. The challenges and the problems never end, but neither do the possibilities." Hildegard, much taken by Charlemagne's words, beamed at him, content just to be looking in his face once more.

"At this moment, the world seems full of 'possibilities,' Charlemagne." She suggested. Hildegard let his name roll off her tongue. *It gives me such pleasure to address him by name.*

"Yes, *your* possibilities are endless, my dear," the King agreed. "Mine are much more constrained. I wrong you - I do - to speak of possibilities. My life, at this time, has far too few." Her dismissal of his words, her wish to 'do good,' endeared her even more to him. He closed his eyes, thought, and, then, looked once more into her face.

"Of a certainty, you speak the truth of it. I can only be your sovereign. I shall guard my words from this time forward." He smiled to show his acceptance of her reprimand. "I accept your correction and, at the same time, do beg your forgiveness." He bowed. "I, of a certainty, do not wish to jeopardize your reputation or your feelings for me. Neither would I attract the attention of the court to you ... or to us. My affection for you is already too deep, too deep to risk harming you. It's true. I summoned you here, but we must be only friends. I respect your forthrightness and your implicit warning. And I love you even more for your practical assessment of this situation." He smiled as he squeezed her arm. He felt Hildegard's slight tremor.

"You know I find you desirable—in every possible way. In my weakness, I allowed you to see it. I will not speak of it again. Know this, my dear Hilde. I shall carry you always in my heart…until I am free, until my heart can shout of my love to the whole world. If God is with me, my love will bind you to me so another suitor has no success in winning you."

Although Hildegard yearned to rush into the King's arms, she realized she must become an actress. She must not allow her feelings to show on her face. She must curb her impulsive reactions and bury her emotions deep inside herself. Although Charlemagne's declaration and looks warmed her heart, she could put no value in his words. He was not free. So, even though her heart cried with longing for him, with a need to see him smile, she gave her hand to him and curtseyed, as a subject before her sovereign—nothing more.

"Thank you for the reassurances on my father's health, Sire," she said. "He has suffered from this malady before. This episode, though, does seem to have been less dire for him than the one last summer. I appreciate your thoughts and gentleness in delivering the news." Hildegard curtseyed, once again, to the King and turned, barely brushing his hand with her own.

"Mayhap I might create a 'possibility' for myself." Charlemagne mumbled. "It's worth a try! Fulrad is straight as an arrow – one of his faults. I'll see how he reacts to my need for a new heir, a lad who can do those physical things Pippin is incapable of." He turned off the path to move toward Abbot Fulrad's tent. He scratched on the tent flap and called.

"Fulrad? It's me, Charlemagne."

"Come in, Sire. I hope the night gave you a good rest." The abbot pushed his prayer stool out of the way and gave the king a bear hug. "Do we journey today, Sire?"

"Aye, we're to Aachen, Fulrad! No more stopping along the way, no more banquets at the homes of our nobles. We journey ahead toward our manor and our well-earned rest."

"And none too soon, Sire, by the weather. Those heavy clouds in the northwest; there's snow in them, I'm afraid. We must hasten to Aachen. Let's pull out before breaking our midday fast. Don't you think? Berries, nuts, bread and cheese can serve today."

"Aye, we should, Fulrad. I gave the order to march early. Have you everything packed already?" Fulrad nodded his head.

"Like everyone else in the court, I can't wait to see the rooftops of Aachen. This circuit of the realm seems uncommonly lengthly, don't you think?"

"It's the battles, Fulrad. The more we have or the more intense they are, the longer the season seems. And, yes, this was worse than normal because we faced the threat from Hunald and Lopo. We marched earlier, remember? The Aquitainean threat blossomed even before the spring assembly. So, aye, it's time to end this year's circuit."

"Good," Fulrad replied. "Do you need me for something? What can I help do?"

"Nay, nothing. I wanted to ask you about Church teachings on marriages, Father. Can one ever be dissolved?" Charlemagne saw the Abbot's surprise and added a sentence, one he dreamed up to cover his reason for this question.

"I thought of Carloman, Fulrad, caught in a marriage of my mother's making, long before he would have chosen marriage for himself. Does church doctrine mitigate such pressure?"

"The church does not come between parent and child." The Abbot soberly pronounced. "At the time, Carl didn't object to the marriage. Had he, we might have avoided it. I admit. I thought Queen Bertrada too eager to betrothe him and in much haste to plan the ceremony. But Carl did not protest. And all is well. He has two sturdy sons, a devoted wife, and a kingdom to rule."

"Well, life is easier for him than me." Charlemagne declared. "He already had his sons and a wife when Poppa died. He had only to accept his part of the realm and rule. I, on the other hand, have no able son and a vanished wife." Abbot Fulrad frowned at the King.

"Charlemagne," he answered softly. "Neither you nor Himiltrude is responsible for Peppin's affliction. This is God's will, one of those things we will never understand. As for a 'vanished' wife, you know where she is, do you not? I thought Roland's best spy, Gottbert, finally located her."

"He did. But..." Charlemagne dropped his head, rubbed his

neck, and looked back into Fulrad's face. "She refused to return, Fulrad. Gottbert gave her my missive. I begged her to return to court. I told her I would come to get her, bring her back with me. But she said 'nay.'" He shook his head, although he understood his wife's reluctance.

"You'd think this place, her position, would be worth something to her, but apparently not. She reports Peppin is happy where he is; she does not have to listen to or obey my mother; and there are no court women to look down on her. She plans to run the manor herself to provide for our son. She believes both of them will have a better, even a happier life, away from this court."

"She's not far from correct." Fulrad answered. "The Queen Mother treated her abominably and you know it. If Carloman were still in this court, I predict his wife would no longer be with him. Your mother is a hard taskmaster, Sire. There's no denying it."

"Aye, in his last thoughts to Carl and me, Poppa urged us to establish a manor for Ma-Mam so she wouldn't travel with us on the annual circuit. She declares, though, her place is with me."

"It's a shame she so rules your life. The church teaches respect, even obedience to one's parents; but I think the commandment must be tempered with reason and a commitment to self-preservation."

"Fulrad! What a thing for a priest to say. Where is your humanity? Where is your Christian goodness?" Charlemagne laughed.

"I'm just suggesting," Fulrad replied, steel in his voice. "I'm suggesting a king should look to his own needs as well. He must rule, govern, protect, and maintain a realm. He needs an equal measure of peace. I wonder if Carl realizes his gift - his own realm, far distant from your mother." His eyes twinkled as he gazed at Charlemagne. "Think you King Desiderius, King of Lombardy, has his mother in court?"

"I believe she died not long after his father." The preist answered. "And so, he does not. But I wager this. Desiderius would control her completely, seeking no advice from her lips. His is a large kingdom; he has great authority – much like you and Carl. Seems to me the two of you together should be just as strong as the King of Lombardy."

Chapter Thirteen

TREACHERY AGAIN

Even as he appeared to discourage Hildegard's feelings, King Charlemagne plotted to see more of her. He appeared at the stables as she began her daily ride. He spoke with her at evening meals and visited the kennels when she was there. Her daily activities, as a maid-in-waiting, were filled with duties. The King had no difficulty in intercepting her, as if by accident, or in observing her as she moved around the court. Despite Hildegard's clear-eyed evaluation of the hopelessness of their love, she delighted in seeing Charlemagne at any time. As the days passed, she was unable to suppress her feelings, no matter how much she attempted it.

"Ma-Mam," the King said to Queen Bertrada, "please invite the young women from Count Hautgard's manor to your social gatherings. The Count's good will, his warm feeling toward us, must be maintained. He commands much respect in the region and leads the minor nobles in support of my army. Besides, here at Aachen, they will become acquainted with other members of the court."

"There's no doubt; you are my son. You know how to bind people to you." Queen Bertrada drew close to pat the King's cheek. "You reflect some of my qualities...in rewarding faithful service and cultivating allegiance." She clarified. She pulled her son's face toward hers and kissed him, full on the lips. Charlemagne recoiled. He hated this intimacy his mother began after his father died. His face hardened; he moved away quickly.

"Do not kiss me in this fashion, Ma-Mam," he told her. "It is unseemly and will start tongues wagging. You are unwise." Tell her you do not like it, he thought to himself.

"I do not want such a kiss. Do not repeat this." His voice was quiet and firm. Queen Bertrada looked quickly into her son's face. His jaw clenched; the furrow between his eyes was deep, his shoulders rigid as he stared at her. Realizing her mistake, she took a step toward him.

"Forgive me, Charlemagne," she purred. "You are such a fine-looking man. Your robust shoulders, shining hair, and firm stance do make my heart sing. I'm so proud of you!" She praised his manly virtues and, then, spoke of motherly pride. "Mayhap, I'm overly affectionate with you; but at this moment, I could not help myself." She glanced at the floor, rearranging her face in a sweet smile before looking up at her son.

"Control your feelings." King Charlemagne ordered curtly. "Do this again; I will embarrass you. I HATE it!" He turned the subject back to Count Hautgard, walking still further from his mother.

"The Count thinks his daughters blessed to be in the court. I hope he never realizes others may call them...prisoners." The King winced as he said the word. *I am more Hildegard's prisoner than she is mine. But I must dull my mother's interest in her, in any of the three of them.* "Hautgard and his Countess sent a missive, declaring their girls most fortunate to be among us." He added. He saw his mother's attention perk up.

"And well he should." The Queen Mother remembered again the visits her husband and sons had made to Hautgard's manor. "I could never do with the meager entertainments of that manor," she admitted, "so I never accompanied you, Carl, and your father on those visits. The hunting, fishing, mock battle games—they did so bore me." She thought of Hautgard's wife.

"The Countess should be grateful for our rescue of her daughters. We do, after all, take these boring country girls and transform them into swans." She nodded her head, pleased with the court's sophistication. "It's well they both thank us with service and devotion." Bertrada smiled broadly, delighted to consider yet another noble in the court's debt.

Suddenly, a blast of trumpets echoed through the air, cutting short Bertrada's words. The Queen Mother jumped in surprise.

"Who comes with such fanfare? Do you expect a visitor?" She asked, rushing toward the windows.

"Blessed Father!" she exclaimed. "It's Carloman...here at last." With a delighted cry, she rushed from the chamber toward the Aachen castle's courtyard. Charlemagne heard her calling to her grandsons as the noise of the trumpets faded away. The King followed his mother quickly, arriving at the front steps just before his brother's party reined in their mounts.

Waving to Carloman who was near the rear of the entourage, Charlemagne hurried forward to welcome Queen Gebnega and his nephews for this long-delayed visit. That duty done, he walked quickly to greet Carloman. Consciously holding his temper, he looked into his brother's face. Carl's eyes were sunk back in his head. His face, lined at the edges of his eyes and around his mouth, trembled. Although pale, his face was flushed—seeming, at first glance, to be burned by the sun.

"My God, Carl!" Charlemagne's shock colored his words. "You look peak-ed. Come, come into the hall." The King could not conceal his shock. This latest illness re-defined his brother's face, making it worn and gray. *Thank God we are here in Aachen.*

Carl couldn't travel further in his present condition. Charlemagne's angry thoughts, stored in his mind since the battle in Aquitaine, defused rapidly. He looked carefully at his brother again.

The planes of Carl's cheekbones stood out in bold relief, adding angles to a face which was once round and smooth. He moved slowly, like an old man, his limbs trembling with weakness. *Merciful Father! He is very ill. How can his present condition be an improvement? How did he manage to travel? He is more than exhausted!* The King swallowed quickly, surprised at the lump of fear in his throat. As he drew near, Carloman's hand grasped his shoulder. Carl shifted his body to lean heavily on Charlemagne.

"Come, come inside." Charlemagne urged. He turned to the cook's helpers. "…wine, ale, food. Hasten! Bring it to the library." Queen Bertrada shepherded her daughter-in-law and her grandsons to the banquet hall, increasing the boys' interest by pointing out the bowls of crystallized fruit, fruit bars, and fruit tarts heaped on the side table.

"My dear, this illness has ravaged Carl." The Queen Mother turned to her son's wife, Gebnega. "Are you certain he's recovering?" She asked anxiously as they drank tea. Her throat closed when she thought of Carloman's poor body. His gray complexion, his trembling, his stumbles — all denied his besting of the illness. Queen Gebnega nodded her head, acknowledging Queen Bertrada's words.

"Aye, Queen Mother," she replied. "He was very ill, indeed. But, as God wills, he begins to recover." The two queens shared a smile as the lads stuffed their mouths with pastries. "While the brothers make their peace, I will rest. This journey has all but destroyed my strength." Gebnega turned and looked at Bertrada with furrowed brow and halting words. "You did hear about the battle in Aquitaine, did you not?" Her voice lowered as two dukes came into the chamber.

"I did." Queen Bertrada responded, feeling her anger rise. "Charley told me Carl refused to fight, refused to help quell Hunald's rebellion. He would not engage the Aquitaineans." She pressed her lips together in order not to rant at her daughter-in-law. "He has much to answer for, Gebnega." She noticed Gebnega was hesitant to speak.

When she did, her voice trembled; she spoke in monosyllables and made no eye contact. She appeared ready to kneel on the floor in apology. Bertrada remembered Charlemagne's assessment of Carl's strengths.

"I'm angry and disappointed in him. Such cowardice should never strike dear Pepin's sons!" Her eyes blazed. Gebnega shrank into herself. "But his brother found a responsibility for him. He told me Carl is an excellent negotiator. I, myself, put little value in it; but Charlemagne tells me negotiation is sometimes useful. He assures me Carl's skills can be utilized in an effort to resolve problems peaceably — in obtaining allegiances, in trading goods, in dividing war's booty, in land-holding disputes." She shook her head at Carloman's wife, showing her disagreement with Charlemagne's defense of her husband.

"To my mind, Charlemagne is over-kind. But," she shrugged, "as a commander, he utilizes people's best strengths. If Carloman can polish his negotiating skills, the realm will have both an effective commander and an effective diplomat." Queen Bertrada noticed the dukes of Alamannia and Gascony eaves-dropping near-by. They were the primary reason she offered reassurance to Gebnega and in such a positive fashion. The dukes nodded discreetly to each other at the Queen Mother's words and walked away. Bertrada touched her daughter-in-law's arm, leading her forward.

"Your bedchamber is waiting. I'll hurry tea and berry tarts to you. Rest; reclaim your energy in the days ahead. I shall entertain the boys." After leaving Gebnega to rest, the Queen Mother retrieved her grandsons from the banquet room and, from there, led them to the stables, describing a spring colt she knew they would delight in seeing. Bertrada passed Charlemagne and Carloman as they walked together toward the library, Carloman leaning heavily on his brother.

"I was not certain I should come, Charley," Carl said as his mother waved happily, herding the two lads. "After Aquitaine, I know your disappointment and your anger will, hereafter, color our dealings together." Carloman was eager to put this subject behind him. If he found his brother unmovable, he planned to turn for home on the morrow. "But I had grave doubts about the wisdom of the fight. You, it turns out, had the better insight."

"I did my best to explain, Carl; but you would not listen." King Charlemagne replied, his voice growing harsh, even now many weeks later. "Even when we were boys, I never could understand your point of view, so contrary is it from mine." He stared out of the library window and nodded thoughtfully. "Your skills are diplomatic in nature and your religious convictions are sincere so...." Here King Charlemagne looked steadily into his brother's face. "So, I have a job for you. I will elevate you to 'court negotiator.' You will talk, negotiate, call upon God's name — if you see fit — to avoid as much fighting as possible." Carloman grinned broadly, opening his mouth to respond.

"I believe most combat cannot be deflected, Carl." King Charlemagne continued bluntly, ignoring his brother's wish to speak. "I need you to understand that. But if you help us avoid bloodshed and can obtain peaceful agreements without fighting, you shall get the credit when you're successful. However, when your negotiations fail, you'll support my battles and fight—not retreat from the field. Do you understand me?" He waited for Carloman to consider his proposal. "Given this condition, do you accept the role of negotiator?"

"I do accept it, brother, and willingly," King Carloman responded, relieved Charlemagne offered a way to smooth over the debacle he had almost caused in Aquitaine. If Charlemagne had lost to Hunald, Carloman thought, I would likely be banished by now.

"Then, let's talk of more pleasant memories." Charlemagne suggested. He slowly let out his breath, thankful Carloman agreed to the negotiating role. He could think of nothing else to do with him. And I must control him, Charlemagne thought. He is dangerous, going his own way, making cowardly decisions. When talk fails, his choice will be clear. And Fulrad and the other priests can say I gave peace a chance.

"Let's speak of the future, Charley." Carl answered, relieved to abandon talk of war. "Tell me of your betrothal." Charlemagne closed the library door and looked quickly into Carloman's eyes.

"My God! You've already heard about it?" He paused, incensed again at his mother's temerity. "But, of a certainty, you were in Lombardy where the treachery began."

"I know nothing about 'treachery.'" Carloman dismissed Charlemagne's response. "But, aye, news of it is all over the realm. When we stopped for the night, the taverns and inns were awash in speculation." He winked at his brother. "Incidentally, most men declare you have a good eye for beautiful women. Your bride's comeliness is praised all over the countryside." Looking into Charlemagne's face, Carl saw only resignation and fatigue. He sighed.

"No response, brother? I regret you anticipate so little happiness in this union. Ahh, your face tells the story. I hoped this was a choice you freely made." He waited for Charlemagne's answer. "Or is this Ma-Mam's doing? Tell me this betrothal was not a surprise to you." He said, hoping it was not true.

"Aye, you know the truth of it, Carl." Charlemagne confirmed softly. "I knew nothing of it until Ma-Mam announced it." His jaw tightened; he stared from the window.

"Aye, it was a surprise, Carl, and not a pleasant one. Ma-Mam's impatience to bring this about and her pride in her success have far outweighed her discretion." Carl moved to speak but thought it better to let his brother talk. "I had no notice of Ma-Mam's intentions…" Charlemagne's voice trailed away.

"And, even if I had, Carl, what would deflect her from her goal? She carries no doubt in her decisions and is not deterred by objections. Oft times, I think God himself would not broach her." Charlemagne sat down heavily on the bench beside his brother. He glanced at Carloman, noting again his pasty face, the fatigue around his mouth.

"But tell me," he turned his attention to his brother's health, "when did you fall ill and what manner of sickness is this? Frankly, you look like hell." Carloman raised his arm weakly.

"First, I wish to offer hope about this marriage. It may be your wife will become pleasing enough. Do not despair. Accommodations must be made, 'tis true. But there will undoubtedly be recompense." He smiled encouragingly at Charlemagne.

"Despite my initial lack of enthusiasm for her, Gebnega is an effective wife. She oversees court life, supervises entertainments and court nobles, and spares me the gossip and posturing of old and new nobility. She is much too ambitious for my taste but, frankly, her enthusiasm may serve my sons well." He shrugged.

"Nay, I was never eager for the match. For certain, I did not seek the marriage. Surely, you did not think Gebnega was my choice?" A mocking smile played around Carl's mouth.

"Aye, I did." King Charlemagne gathered his thoughts. "I believed you pressed for this union, that you declared undying passion for Gebnega, just after the spring festival that year." Charlemagne snapped his open mouth closed. He remembered thinking Carl enamored of Gebnega. *I fooled myself, hoped his marriage was more than a marriage of state. God knows, we had enough of such a marriage with Poppa and Ma-Mam. Are Carl and I doomed to repeat their mistake?* Charlemagne sighed deeply, not for the first time. *May a king never choose a woman he loves...and to hell with the needs of the realm?*

"Nay! I never swore undying passion for anyone. I loved Gebnega's cousin...insofar as a fifteen year-old can love any-one. But Gebnega, truthfully, I had no interest in her — no inter-est at all."

"But, then, why?" Charlemagne asked, still appalled at Carl's admission.

"Why?" Carloman repeated. "Why? ...because Ma-Mam declared it so. She sought my betrothal to bring Gebnega's un-cle, the ruler of Alsace, firmly into Poppa's kingdom. It was statecraft, plain and simple — and her way to control me, cer-tainly."

"I never knew," Charlemagne replied sadly.

"Nay...because you never cared. You spared little thought for me, brother. Your eyes were ever on the battle, the joust, the weakness of your enemy, the good will of your soldiers." Carl shook his head but, then, brightened. "No matter, I hoped for your happiness in this marriage. I know Peppin is not an adequate heir. But you know; Ma-Mam considers your prefer-ence unimportant. She's incapable of thinking of another's wants and needs. Her wishes are the only reality."

"Amen to that." Charlemagne replied bitterly, remembering his mother's haste to cement his first marriage and, now, this one as well.

"But you have a chance to defy her, Charles. You are not the callow youth I was. You are a man grown, twenty-seven years old. You must make your own choices." Carl paused. "Because I was given no choice, I press you to choose, actively make a choice of bride. Don't allow Ma-Mam to force you, as she did me." Carloman seemed almost to beg, his eyes downcast, his voice soft. He saw Charlemagne's frown and tried to soften his words.

"But, tell me," Carloman continued, "when does the wedding take place? We've heard no date, so I assume we are early enough for the celebration. I don't want to miss the parties and gaieties."

"You've missed nothing so far." Charlemagne laughed. "The ceremony won't take place for more than a fortnight. I have yet to send my final agreement to Desiderius." He looked at Carloman, smiling. "Nevertheless, hearing even a vague date, the nobles' drinking began in earnest some two days ago. Much celebrating, it appears, will take place well before the vows are taken." He offered his brother wine brought from Hautgard's cellar. Unsmiling and intent, Charlemagne spoke.

"I do thank you heartily for coming, Carl. It is a welcome gesture from the other ruler in Frankland. You will stay for the ceremony? I know it makes for a long visit, but many here wish to welcome you back."

"Aye, of a certainty, we will stay," Carloman confirmed. He looked closely at his brother. "Can you not find some joy in this marriage, Charley? It does not speak well of the nuptials—your mournful countenance." Charlemagne nodded reluctantly.

"I know; I yearn for joy but cannot find it. I do what must be done. Ma-Mam's signing of the betrothal, even in my name, locks me into this union. If I break the engagement, Desiderius will surely attack us. The integrity of my court rests on the vows Ma-Mam made. And I have not the troops to defeat Desiderius now. In another two or three years…with good booty and land conquests… we might withstand him, but not now." He dropped his head, trying to block out his memories of Hildegard.

"Aye, I see the quandary." Carl observed his brother closely. "But you are clearly not ready to marry. It does seem over-hasty. Why not set the marriage for Eastertide? Learn more of this woman and come to the marriage bed with a less-troubled heart. Why wed now? Is their merit to such a quick pace?" He gazed into Charlemagne's eyes, intent on the answer. Charlemagne glanced away, considering his brother's suggestion. His heart jumped. *Can I do that, postpone the ceremony?* Carloman would not be deterred; he spoke again.

"Is there some urgency I don't recognize…the need for an alliance, for land to pay soldiers' commissions—here at the end of the year? Mayhap, you hope to delay or prevent a war with the Lombard king?" Carl smiled; his eyes were still and fathomless. Charlemagne rose from the bench, uncomfortable with his brother's questions.

"You've a good idea, Carl." Charlemagne admitted, clamping down on the hope springing in his heart. "Ma-Mam is trying to hurry the marriage along, of a certainty. I wonder: did she agree on a wedding date with Desiderius and not tell me?" *I did threaten to not honor the betrothal. Mayhap she is uneasy because of my hesitation. Why should I follow my mother's dictates? I can move the wedding to the spring. It makes sense for those who must travel a distance for the ceremony.* But, then, the King's thoughts halted. He stared into Carloman's face. Holding his arms out in a helpless gesture, he re-iterated his despair.

"I don't want this marriage, Carl. I know, deep in my heart, it's a mistake." Then, thoughts of his little, deformed son popped into his mind. "But I need an heir. Ma-Mam is relentless. You've no idea..." Carloman smiled sadly.

"If not I, who? I'm your brother, for God's sake! I share your heritage, your realm, your future and this mother. Whatever duties you have, I share the same. But your reluctance toward the marriage, it must be obvious to all. If Desiderius were less ambitious, he would not tolerate your dithering. He would break the betrothal." He sipped his wine.

"I assume Himiltrude's gone." He reached out to squeeze Charlemagne's shoulder, guessing his mother drove his brother's first wife away. Charlemagne's face confirmed his suspicion; it filled with anguish and regret. Carloman's voice was urgent as he advised his brother.

"I love my boys...but, my wife, not much. She is my opposite: ambitious where I am not; bound by rules and social expectations which I don't value. She is blond and slender; I prefer women dark and busomy. You know my taste - it's the single thing you and I ever agreed on. And Gebnega was no princess...like Desiderata. I got no added benefits with my marriage." He noted Charlemagne's resigned face. He felt like slapping him. Carl's face flushed red; his voice hardened. He raised his voice.

"You're a fool, Charley. You're being manipulated and used. And you don't even see it! Your reluctance is obvious in every gesture. What does the Lombard princess offer? What have I missed—loyal Lombard nobles, the military prowess of her father, an elegant queen to grace your court, a caring mother to rear your babes?" Carloman spread his hands, begging for a response. "I have all night to listen." He offered as he rubbed his temples, sighing.

"Manipulated?" Charlemagne raised his eyebrow, seeming to return to the room. "Manipulated...by whom? Explain yourself! Who would DARE manipulate me?" He consciously controlled his voice, struggling not to let Carl upset him further.

"Who?" Carloman laughed deeply, clearly enjoying a joke Charlemagne did not get. "Who? Why, our dear mother, of a certainty. She plays you like a stringed instrument. Rub you against something, almost anything, and she produces a sound. Once the sound emerges, she convinces you it is the very one she's been looking for." Carloman shuffled about the room.

"Damnations, Charley. Admit you're a fool. You don't even think when Ma-Mam speaks. You jump as she points." He shook his head, pulled off his embroidered over-tunic, and turned back to Charlemagne.

"Well?" Carloman asked. "Will you answer?"

"Don't speak about Ma-Mam this way." Charlemagne warned, avoiding the question. "It's disrespectful!" Carloman interrupted, his face red, his hands waving.

"Disrespectful, you think so?" Carloman's voice rose in frustration. "Damn respect, brother! Think about our father. Did you ever see Poppa listen to Ma-Mam's demands? Did he ever ask her opinion about a treaty, an alliance, a single count's misconduct? Did Poppa even care about Ma-Mam's opinions or advice? Nay, nay! He did not."

"But she always explained the advice she gave Poppa." Charlemagne objected. "She told me the arguments she made to him—influencing his opinion, opening his eyes to undercurrents he didn't see!" Charlemagne's chin jutted forward; his face was red; his mouth quivering. "How dare you say such things? Ma-Mam was critical to Poppa's decisions. He listened to her."

Carloman fingered a parchment on the reading table. His frown deepened. He moved his eyes to his brother's face.

"If you believe that, brother, you're already lost," he answered quietly. Again, he rubbed his temples, then the back of his neck. "But I challenge you enough. I try only to make you think." He stood. "You're imprisoned by a clever jailer, brother. You could break free. You're stronger than I."

"Each of you—Poppa, Ma-Mam, and you—each of you always reminded me of your superiority, always pointed to my weaknesses." He challenged Charlemagne. "So be it. But, use your strength. Your mother neuters you. Do as she commands and you deny yourself. I cannot tell you my regret." His voice was weak and indistinct.

"I wanted to join the clergy, to become a monk." Charlemagne raised a surprised face to his brother. "Aye, of a certainty." Carloman confirmed. "I was more positive even than is Gisela today. But Ma-Mam wouldn't countenance it. She would not listen. Poppa, though disappointed, could have been convinced...but our mother? Do you know what she threatened?" He sat down wearily on a bench.

"She said she would tell every bishop in the realm I was lecherous, that she watched me day and night so I wouldn't despoil the court maidens!" Carloman's face reddened; his hands curled into fists; his breathing was labored. "She did, Charley, she did...my own mother. How I despise her!" Shaking his head, Carloman picked up his over-tunic and began examining the jewels held in place by embroidered threads. He let his pent-up breath out.

"Why do you marry this princess?" He repeated. "I want your answer." Charlemagne, irritated by his brother's repeated question and, now, more aware of his mother's duplicity, stared at Carloman. He rubbed his eyes and shrugged.

"I need an heir." Charlemagne answered. "In all your bitterness, you do forget I'm not as fortunate as you. Come, Carl, you've two sons to succeed you. I have none. I grow old; I need an heir."

"You have an heir." Carloman replied, holding up his hand to prevent Charlemagne's retort. "Maybe, he's not to your liking, but Pippin is your son. No one can deny that, not even you. He may or may not have the strength to lead. But another son may be weak as well. Who can say? Consider the weaknesses in the Merovingian kings. Or consider me. You agree; I am no soldier." He placed his wine flagon on the table.

"Let me be clear." Carloman made a final try, looking steadily into Charlemagne's face. "Although Poppa and Ma-Mam praised your abilities and your insight, you do not see as clearly as you should. You will wed Desiderata because Ma-Mam made the betrothal...even without your consent. This is her marriage: her idea, her alliance, her view of the future. It is her choice, not yours." Carloman walked to Charlemagne, swatting at his shoulder.

"You fool. You accept it; you do as she wishes. You, the most powerful man for five hundred leagues, let your mother choose your bride." He gazed into his brother's face. "What a waste. Ma-Mam beats you down, just as she did Poppa, just as she does me. In a few years, if you do not stand firm, the realm will be lost. She will make the decisions; she will rule. And you will garner the blame."

"Ma-Mam advances only herself, Charles. She does not understand ruling or fighting; she can do neither. She hasn't the necessary courage. She practices only intrigue and cunning. Intrigue cannot win on the battlefield. Remember, when she ar-

gues with you, you must not be her pawn. You must not sacrifice yourself and Frankland for Ma-Mam's ambition." He
kissed Charlemagne on both cheeks and left the room. Charlemagne followed Carloman from the library and ducked into
the near-by chapel to think, remembering his brother's impas-
sioned words.

Chapter Fourteen
CONFRONTATION

Charlemagne awoke to a harsh knocking on his door. Opening it, he scarcely recognized his brother. Carloman's hair was standing around his head; his face was flushed along the cheekbones; his arms flayed around his head.

"What is it, Carl?" Charlemagne asked, afraid of the answer.

"Come with me. Come!" Carl demanded. "Gisela is in her chamber, begging to talk with both of us. She won't say what's wrong. But, Charles, she's distraught. Her hair is uncombed; her face is blotched with crying. She is cold and clammy." Charlemagne was totally lost.

"What's happened? How has she come to this?" Charlemagne asked.

"In the early morn, I awoke hungry and left my bedchamber, looking for a sweet." Carloman began. "Passing the garden, I saw Gisela standing alone in the snow. Her lips were turning blue, so cold was she. God knows how long she was there." Carloman held his panic in with difficulty. "She wishes to talk to both of us. She asked me to come for you. Let's hasten."

"Aye, aye!" Charlemagne pulled on his tunic, hurrying out of his bedchamber with his brother. They walked rapidly down the corridor. Carloman flung open Gisela's door, grabbed a mantle of wool off the bench and wrapped it around his sister.

She stood in front of the hearth fire, uncovered expect for her sleeping tunic. She held her arms out to Carl, laying her head on his shoulder. Charlemagne rushed to her side.

"Gisela, we both are here. What's happened?" The words rushed from Charlemagne's mouth. "Why were you in the garden...in the cold of night? Are you ill?" He hugged his sister close, appalled at the chill on her body, at the dazed, hopeless look in her eyes. *If I didn't feel her breathing, I'd believe her dead.*

"Charley, Carl." She shuddered, tears standing in her eyes. "Ma-Mam has betrothed me. She declares I <u>must</u> marry — to secure the realm, for both your sakes." Gisela sighed deeply. "My marriage ceremony is to take place a fortnight after Charlemagne weds Desiderata." She felt her knees weaken and motioned her brothers to help her to the near-by bench. They moved in tandem, helping her sit and, then, arranging the wool linen about her shoulders. Carl added another two logs to the fire.

"What do you mean...marry who?" Charlemagne demanded. He hesitated to question Gisela. Her pale face and vacant stare frightened him. "There's no betrothal. This makes no sense."

"Ma-Mam...she said it. She came here last night. She said I was to marry Adelchis, Prince of Lombardy, as soon after your wedding as can be arranged. She betrothed us when she negotiated with Desiderata's father." Tears leaked from her eyes, bloodshot from previous weeping.

"What shall I do?" Gisela asked, almost whispering. "I belong to God; I have taken my first vow toward such a choice." She wrapped her arms around herself, huddling. "The Abbess, she will not understand. She won't reproach me, just gaze at me sadly with disappointed eyes."

"Fear not." Charlemagne answered. "You marry no one...not Adelchis, not the Duke of Aquitaine, not the ruler of Tuscany. No one, do you hear me?" He was rigid with anger. He never doubted for a moment his mother promised Gisela's hand to Adelchis. *This agreement we will not honor! Ma-Mam will not choose Gisela's future.*

"You will marry no one, Gisela." Carloman reassured her. "I am a King, a king of my own realm. And I will suffer our mother's machinations no longer. Nay, this is the end of her meddling."

Carl stood suddenly, motioning to Charlemagne, too, to comfort their sister. Charlemagne kissed Gisela's cheek, promising all would be rectified. The two brothers left Gisela's bedchamber, united in opposition to their mother's latest move. Charlemagne hurried down the corridor but slowed down for Carloman to catch up. As their feet slid on the stones, they slowed to a walk.

"I'm not sure I can speak," Charlemagne said to Carloman. "Poppa was ever calm with Ma-Mam; but I know my temper will best me." *And why shouldn't it? Ma-Mam betrays us all: me, Poppa, Carl and Gisela — most especially.* Charlemagne slammed into his mother's bedchamber door, flinging it against the wall.

"Ma-Mam?" He called. "Where are you, damn it? Show yourself."

Queen Bertrada turned from her clothes chest where she was removing small clothes. She replied quietly.

"Calm yourself, Charlemagne. How dare you shout? I'm right here." She closed the chest. "Why must you always make so much noise? What ARE you shouting about?"

Charlemagne rushed to his mother, grabbed her arm, and turned her face toward his. An angry flush covered his neck and chin; his face was turning cherry red, a vein pulsed beside his left eye. His hoarse voice demanded.

"What have you done?" His hand gripped her left elbow. He glared into his mother's face. "You do overstep yourself, madam," he growled through gritted teeth. "You have manipulated, promised, compromised, sacrificed, and sold your children. Each of us, you use to further your own damn ambitions!" He backed away from her. "What kind of a mother, are you—the remnant of some Greek goddess who sacrifices her children for her own designs?"

"I see you've heard." Queen Bertrada replied to her older son, taking a step back. A nervous tremble wandered across her mouth. Charlemagne pushed her down on a nearby bench.

"Don't dare say a word," he warned. "Your words, your actions are poison to me. You are an adder to your children: sighting, striking and devouring us as we stand innocent before you. This is the last time you will make any decision about my sister! Do you understand me?" His voice was low with anger and menace. Charlemagne trembled so strongly he could not control his legs. He glanced around at Carloman, whom he outpaced in the corridor, as he entered the chamber.

"You are a heathen- as evil and self-serving as any monster!" Carloman shouted at their mother as he hobbled into the room. He turned his ankle at the last corner and urged Charlemagne to rush on. "What in the hell have you done? How could you...encase both of your sons in a prison and, then, do the same for your daughter? Aren't the two of us enough for you? You sacrifice Gisela as well? Will your ambition never fail?" Charlemagne clasped Carl's shoulder.

"Help me, Carl, help me." Charlemagne begged, his great hands balled into fists. "I wish nothing more than to strike her!" He breathed deeply. "You and I, we will prevent this treachery. What will the Church say? God! What will the Pope say? One of his finest servants can no longer serve because of the matrimonial plans her mother instigated! Bah! …unnatural woman, you deserve to be whipped!" Charlemagne shook his fist in his mother's face.

"We heard your plan from our sister." Carloman interrupted his brother. "I found Gisela weeping in the garden, standing with snow falling around her—her tears freezing on her cheeks." His own eyes welled with tears. "Charles and I calmed her, assured her we will not honor this betrothal." He sat heavily, rubbing his forehead. "He and I are one on this, Ma-Mam. This agreement is a mockery. Gisela is promised to God, nothing changes that."

Charlemagne nodded, his eyes centered on Carloman. He could not bear to look at his mother.

"Come," Carloman said to him. "As kings of the realm, we will sever this misbegotten agreement. We can, also, banish Ma-Mam to a nunnery, though I would not wish her on them." Queen Bertrada made as if to object; but seeing her sons' faces, she stepped slowly backward. "This meddling is not to be borne."

Queen Bertrada gasped, unwilling to believe her sons' words. Her satisfaction with the dual marriage agreement negotiated with Desiderius of Lombard did not, all of a sudden, appear as advantageous as she assumed.

"Surely," she answered, "two marriages within families are far to be preferred to one. It is a perfect method for creating alliances, one to the other." She glanced at her younger son. "Carl, you are ill. You don't know what you're saying. You never spoke this way to me before. How dare you?"

"Charles, do not waste another word on her!" Carloman cried, holding his brother's arm. "She sees everything as she wishes to see it. She's earned our contempt, yet again." He turned, leading Charlemagne from the chamber. As they entered the corridor together, Charlemagne clasped Carloman's shoulder.

"You're absolutely right, Carl," he asserted. "We're the kings of the Franks. We will sever this betrothal between Gisela and Adelchis ourselves. Come! Let's find Fulrad. He shall journey directly to Lombardy. He must leave before anyone breaks his fast this day." He turned in the corridor. "First to Fulrad, then we must return to reassure Gisela. Her fear of this betrothal will make her ill." He and Carloman increased their speed. "There is much we cannot do, God help us; but we can and will do this for our sister."

The brothers hurried toward Fulrad's bedchamber. He was not there. Looking toward the chapel, they entered through the door which opened into the Abbot's office. Abbot Fulrad rose from his morning prayers. Hearing the door to his bedchamber open, he hurried to his office, looking alarmed.

"What is it?" He looked from one king's face to the other. They were both pale around the eyes, though the flush of anger rode their cheeks. "Has someone been hurt?" He would not think of anything more serious than an injury. "Are both of you well? You are flushed and are breathing heavily. I will summon an herbalist."

"You must go to Desiderius immediately," Carloman began. "A misunderstanding must be corrected. It must be corrected as quickly as you can present yourself to him."

"Aye, we must have rapid action on this, Fulrad." Charlemagne re-iterated Carloman's insistence. "Tell Desiderius his son's betrothal to Gisela is now null and void. It will not be honored." The Abbot fumbled for the bench behind him, almost falling onto the seat.

"What? What's the message?" The Abbot asked. He

blinked, aghast at the King's words. "I know of no betrothal for Gisela." He shook his head. "There is some mistake; she is promised to God."

"Exactly," Charlemagne replied, "our feelings exactly. Go to the Lombard king now, Abbot," he commanded. "This betrothal is Queen Bertrada's doing. It is to be undone immediately. Do not hesitate. Do not linger. Go now."

"No talk, no negotiation, Abbot," Carloman echoed Charlemagne. "The only words you need speak are these: Princess Gisela and Kings Charlemagne and Carloman of Frankland refuse the betrothal offer from Adelchis, Prince of Lombardy. It has long been Princess Gisela's intention, with her brothers' blessing, to give herself to the service of God. She is not free, nor does she wish, to marry." Carloman rubbed his eyes. "This is the only message you need deliver, Abbot Fulrad. We do not require a reply. And thank you. God speed."

"Be as diplomatic as you can, Abbot." Charlemagne directed. "Don't increase his anger toward us. In response, Desiderius may nullify my betrothal to Desiderata. That is completely acceptable. If such luck is with me, let us pray it comes to pass." The Abbot looked closely at the King.

"It's not likely, my son. Desiderius will never sunder his permission for your marriage." He explained. "His power will decrease without Gisela's betrothal to Adelchis; that is certain. But that union is as nothing compared to you and his daughter. You are the king; he will hold you to Desiderata. I have no doubt." Fulrad hurried from the chapel to retrieve his clothing and to begin his journey.

"I am caught, Carl." Charlemagne said to his brother. "Should I die without a whole son, my part of the Frankish realm may well be lost. My soldiers fight well; they will fight with your army, if need be. But they look for me. They want me fighting in the midst of them. There can be no release from my betrothal." Carloman nodded at his brother's evaluation. Charlemagne knew his brother was more interested in philosophy, religion, and agricultural methods than in tactics or command. *Carl might yet learn to fight fiercely, but men would never follow him unquestioningly as they do me. He, also, is easily duped, misled by those he trusts. The debacle in Aquitaine proved that.*

The advantages of the agreement for Desiderius are clear, Charlemagne told himself. *Gisela understood immediately. How can Ma-Mam be so blind? Desiderius need only do away with me, and he'll rule Frankland. If I die with no issue, Carloman will defer to Desiderius' interest in a hair's breath.*

"I must win Desiderius' daughter's support," Charlemagne said to Carloman. "She and I will produce a son whom she values more than her father. When the time comes, and it will, she will choose our interest before those of Desiderius. You and I must be of like mind, Carl. Only if we are united will our realm escape the bloodbath Desiderius' ambitions will bring upon her."

"Aye," Carloman agreed. "I learned my lesson in Aquitaine. I pledge you my support." He moved toward the door. "But, now, I return to Gisela. News of the Abbot's journey will bring her peace." He stopped. "Will you come with me, Charley?"

"Not this moment, Carl," Charlemagne answered. "I will wait to hear Fulrad has left the court. Tell Gisela we sundered the betrothal. She has no worry." He noticed Carl's drained face, his trembling hands. "Try to get her to sleep, Carl, and, then, sleep yourself. I will see both of you before the mid-day meal." Carloman nodded.

"Wait!" Charlemagne said. "Go to Ma-Mam. Tell her she's confined to her bedchamber until I say otherwise. We do not want her sending secret messages to anyone. And post a guard at her door. She's to have no visitors and send no messages. Spread the word in the court that she's ill."

"There will be many questions." Carl responded.

"No matter." Charlemagne answered. "She cannot be allowed free reign until Fulrad returns." Charlemagne watched Carloman leave. Unexpectedly, an image of Hildegard ran through his mind.

"I would see her," he muttered. "I must see her." His relief in saving Gisela's future must be shared with someone. *Hildegard will understand the implications immediately and be relieved for Gisela. Hilde will judge this a triumph for Gisela, that she may choose her own life.*

"And why should I care about Hilde's opinion of this?" Charlemagne stopped in mid-stride, considering the question. He smiled sadly. "...because I value her good opinion," he answered, "and because I defended Gisela's choice and trust my own judgment in this." His reply dismayed him. His own choices were so seldom realized. The King headed for the bedchamber Hildegard shared with Maria and Jocelyn. *I may not marry the woman I would choose; but I can look upon her face.*

No one was in the bedchamber. The King roamed the halls of the castle, looking for Hildegard. Finally, just as he was losing hope, he saw Jocelyn bringing flowers and linens for a visiting countess.

"Jocelyn, good morrow," the King greeted her, smiling. "I have a sick dog and wish Hildegard's evaluation of his health. Do you know where she is?" Jocelyn curtseyed.

"Aye, your Majesty," she replied. "She's in the stables with the puppies. She left but a short while ago."

"Thanks, Jocelyn. A good day to you," the King replied, waving and hurrying toward the stables. As he pushed open the stable door, he heard Oliver's voice and, then, Hildegard's soft response. Without thinking, King Charlemagne moved to the other side of the stable, hiding himself in a near-by horse stall, one close enough to hear their conversation. *They do talk often together. I wonder at their interest in each other.* Even as the thought occurred, he felt disgusted with himself—he who denied his heart's yearning for this woman. *I know she cares for me, no one else. Her allegiance is not so weak as to entertain thoughts of Oliver.* Charlemagne settled into the straw to listen to their conversation.

"This one," Hilde said, her voice fading as she turned her head, "is a certain copy of his mother." The King could hear the smile in her voice. "I think, Lord Oliver, he will be the best tracker. At six weeks, he is sniffing around the stables, trying to smell under the horses' hooves!" Hilde's happy laugh echoed in Charlemagne's heart. He sat mesmerized by her, peeking through a knothole in the stable's stall and watched the light play on her hair—her smile illuminating her face. Her dear hands stroked the pups' ears as she laughed in delight at their rough and tumble antics. Even as he smiled at her words, King Charlemagne felt a throb of deep pain. *God, how I love her! I love her more than myself. And I can do nothing about it. I cannot even show her my feelings...through my behavior or through my words. Must I always be punished or in pain, lose the people I need—Poppa and now Hilde? Why do I yearn for this woman whom I can never have?* The King wrapped his arms around himself, bowing his head. Through his pain, he heard heavy footsteps enter the stable.

"There you are." the Abbot's voice boomed. "Lord Oliver, how fare you this brisk, winter day?" Charlemagne heard Oliver's quiet reply.

"I am well. And you?" Oliver asked.

"Good. I am off on a journey and, so, brought my young

assistants to benefit from Hildegard's good teaching."

"Oh, Abbot." Hildegard laughed. "You give me far too much credit. What might I possibly teach your assistants? I am poorly schooled in the testaments, though I had instruction."

"My dear," the Abbot responded, "I know you teach these pups discipline and self-control. Please do the same for my assistants here." Two young boys stood meekly behind him. They were no more than eleven years old, all gangly arms and legs. He glanced back at them. "They fight for the silliest of reasons, Lady Hildegard. Neither of them is able to control his temper. They buzz around each other as bees to honey, but they never create any sweetness. They spout sarcastic comments or fling demeaning names at each other. Why, they even fight, hit each other in the most hateful way." He sighed dramatically, even as he winked at Oliver.

"They do want learning, Mistress. I hope, as you succeed with these pups, you might, also, pass like knowledge to these two wild boys here." He peered at Hildegard closely, holding his breath. Hildegard smiled at the Abbot and, then, beamed at the two boys.

"Do you really wish to learn about training puppies?" They looked eager and afraid at the same time. "I can discipline you; it's true." She said to them. "But to learn, you must have open minds and willing hearts. Will you best my pups in those two things?"

"We wish to please the Abbot, my Lady," the taller boy replied.

"I will be diligent, Mistress," the younger one whispered.

"Agreed then," Hildegard said, turning to the Abbot. "But I must warn you, Abbot; you may not like the results of my teaching. You pay a tall price for this learning, as you deem it."

"...a price for learning?" The Abbot replied, puzzled. "Any

price, my dear, any price is worth some peace between these two ruffians. I assure you." Oliver and Hildegard both chuckled. The Abbot smiled at their laughter. "You have several days, Lady Hildegard. These two lads must learn from you while I am away from court. I count on your dedication."

"He sounds desperate, my Lady," Oliver responded, rolling his eyes.

"You best explain the complications of your teaching to him." Hildegard nodded, all of a sudden solemn.

"Learning has two faces, Abbot." Hildegard included the two lads in her glance. "One kind of learning is the attaining of a skill. Then, if a man practices over and over—polishing the skill—he may, in time, become a master of his craft. The other kind of learning teaches boys or pups...to think. This is the learning which threatens people. Thinking always leads to change, and most people are very uncomfortable with it." She turned to the Abbot.

"So, you see, Abbot Fulrad, learning is not without its price, especially if the value of the learning—the deep thought which changes the learner and those around him—is not appreciated." She paused for the Abbot to respond. But he was mumbling to himself, not eager to answer her.

"Abbot," Hildegard asked, "are you prepared for these lads to change things...to change you, perhaps?"

"Nay, nay, I want no change! Teach them all you can of temper control. Make them skillful in holding their anger and their fists. I shall take care of any ideas about change...nip them without delay." He smiled grimly. "Trust me. I can keep these boys on a narrow path. But I have no time to teach them discipline." He glared at the two lads and turned, raising his hand in farewell.

"You do have a quandary, Hildegard." Oliver said. "Maybe,

you should have refused this task." Hildegard looked at him steadily and nodded her head.

"It does seem impossible. But I did warn the Abbot, Oliver. I shall teach the boys to analyze their anger, to puzzle out the reasons they irritate each other, and to learn to control their behavior. If they apply such knowledge to other things, what can I do?" She asked Oliver, smiling widely. "A mind freed to think is a better mind. Surely, you believe that."

"I do, indeed, my dear, I do," Oliver concurred. "But it does not make for an easy life."

"Nay, it does not," Hildegard acknowledged. "But it is our duty to think...and to be led by those thoughts. Otherwise, why did God give us minds?" She glanced at the two lads. "Only in thinking may we work for ourselves and for our realm." She pushed her hands against the hay and stood.

"You must excuse me, Lord Oliver. I now have boys, as well as pups, to see to." She walked toward her new, two-legged students. Oliver smiled, delighted to see someone render the Abbot speechless, though he knew Fulrad would never acknowledge his surprise at Hildegard's words.

Behind the stall, King Charlemagne sat on the stable floor, thinking and re-thinking the words which Hildegard spoke. "A mind freed to think..." I must strive to so free my mind," he vowed. "I must trust my own decisions and ignore unsolicited advice, especially from those with plans of their own. Doing so, I may yet find a way to protect Frankland and ensure a measure of happiness for myself." *Such happiness will never be complete without Hilde, but it is the most I'm likely to find.*

Chapter Fifteen

RAPID CULMINATION

Even before the lone rider was spotted from the castle turret, the captain of Charlemagne's guard heard the blast of trumpets.

"Whose banner is that?" Captain Gregory murmured to his squire. The burly captain shaded his eyes, peering over the wall. His body tensed; he held his breath, trying to determine the identity of the rider approaching the gate. He called to the guardian of the gate.

"Jonas, is anyone expected? Who do these trumpets announce?"

"I know not, Captain Gregory!" Jonas Styer shouted back. "We've had no messenger for the past fortnight." Jonas mounted his horse, his lithe, slender body becoming one with the animal. Signaling for the soldiers to open the gate, he galloped directly toward the rider who approached. Jonas, a brave man and always suspicious, ever eager to battle, was an excellent guardian of the gate—the man positioned to protect the castle. He and the oncoming rider met some three furlongs from the gate, far enough for the guards to arm themselves if Jonas were struck down. They spoke briefly and then turned together back toward the castle. As they cantered into the courtyard, Seneschal Eggihard hurried from the castle, eager for news from the incoming party. He must see to their housing requirements and to refreshments for the visitors. Jonas bowed to Eggihard and dismounted before him.

"The Princess of Lombardy arrives, Sire," Jonas announced. "This is Captain Daveed. He reports they've been riding since daybreak. He requests accommodations for the princess, her ladies, and his soldiers. Their party is comprised of Captain Daveed, twenty women, three other captains, and sixty soldiers, Sir. Eighty-four people embarked on this journey."

"Why so many people?" Seneschal Eggihard asked, his eyebrows rising in surprise. "Eighty-four people, Jonas?" He was dumfounded. "She is not expected." Eggihard could think of nothing else to say to Captain Gregory. "This is highly unusual…" But he clamped down on his surprise and hurried indoors, knowing he could voice no objection. He must inform the Queen Mother and, then, hurry to house and prepare - no stretch - the mid-day meal.

As he walked into Queen Bertrada's day room, Eggihard mentally listed vacant bedchambers, sleeping benches in the stables, soldier's quarters, sleeping places among the court workers. He would assure the Queen Mother everything was in hand. He prayed the Queen expected the princess' arrival and forgot to inform him. Queen Bertrada would be greatly vexed and even more demanding, if the visit were a surprise.

"What?" Queen Bertrada frowned at him, her forehead wrinkled with dismay. Her eyes held questions. Her mouth pulled down at the corners; she frowned. She looked as if she were unable to understand his message.

"The Princess of Lombardy comes to our gates? Are you certain, Eggihard; it is she?" The Queen Mother's voice was querulous as she rose. "Princess Desiderata? She cannot be *here!*" She turned toward the door, her face flushed with anger. *My God! For what reason does she come – without her father or her brother? How irregular…*

"I did not think to see her so soon." Bertrada remembered Eggihard, waiting her direction.

"If it is truly Desiderata, Seneschal; we must welcome her, of a certainty." The Queen swept aside her bewilderment. "See to the bedchambers. Inform the cook to move another table into the banquet hall immediately. It is fortunate we have delayed our mid-day meal, if we have more mouths to feed!" She exclaimed.

The Queen Mother was not overly concerned. Eggihard ran the court with an iron hand. Queen Bertrada gave him copious directions; but, in her absence, he managed fine without a word. These visitors, as all others, would be welcomed and pampered. This unannounced visit was irritating because planned activities — a picnic at mid-day and small, intimate parties this night — must be postponed. Queen Bertrada raised her voice to Egginard as he turned toward the corridor.

"Wait, Eggihard. Do we know the direction the King's hunt followed?" She asked.

"The hunting party headed west, my lady," Eggihard replied. "But who knows the direction they follow now, pursuing their quarry? I cannot predict it."

"Who knows, indeed?" Queen Bertrada repeated as she removed a more heavily embroidered gown from a near-by trunk. "There is no help for it. We must be hospitable. This is the Princess of Lombardy, for heavens' sake. Go, go and make preparations, Egginhard. Inform the noble ladies and the maids, of a certainty. Tell them an important personage is arriving. They are to ready their wit and their conversation."

"Alert the court with no delay. And send a messenger to the King. Hurry, bestir yourself!" Desiderata must be anxious for this marriage, the Queen told herself. Then, she smiled. *Ahhh, we have her. She and her father are truly committed to this betroth-*

al...if she arrives early to wed! Queen Bertrada gloated to herself, proud of the prize she secured for her son and for the realm in this upcoming union. *Although Charlemagne doesn't appreciate it now, later he will praise me for this marriage.*

Egginhard turned, calling orders to everyone he chanced to meet. People scurried like ants, well-trained to respond to just such demands. A maid-in-waiting rushed to the large chamber where court ladies gathered every morn. She burst into the room. Her eyes bulged, a broad smile covered her face. She pranced among the ladies. Clapping her hands lightly, she waited. She stretched up and down on her toes, smiling as the eyes in the room turned toward her.

"The court has important visitors." She announced. The women looked up eagerly, demanding to know who the guests were. "It's the Princess of Lombardy, Princess Desiderata herself! The Queen Mother directs us to welcome her in the courtyard." The noble women jumped to their feet.

"Come, come; there is not time to linger," the maid urged. However, nothing would do but the women fluff their hair, settle their headdresses, re-arrange their scarves and smooth down their long tunics. Only then did they rush toward the castle's courtyard, talking excitedly.

Just as Queen Bertrada opened the castle door, trumpets blared again. A host of hooves struck the stones as the unexpected party rode in. Princess Desiderata's guards — four of them before her, four of them behind her — entered the gate. Her twenty ladies, lounging in silk-bedecked carts followed. Eight guards rode each side of the entourage with the remaining soldiers bringing up the rear. The Princess sat upon her horse as her ladies moved from the carts; and still, Lombardy soldiers rode through the gate.

"My dear, welcome! Bring your ladies inside!" Queen Bertrada cried aloud as she hurried toward the princess. "This is an unexpected pleasure." From the height of her horse, Desiderata looked down on the Queen Mother. She looked around, a frown formed between her brows. Queen Bertrada's eyes widened as she gazed upon her future daughter-in-law.

Desiderata's bright, purple mantle and her yellow riding breeches strained the Queen Mother's eyes. But her orange tunic, adorned with strips of yellow, brought all conversation to a halt. She looked like some rather strange fungus. The Princess shook her head negatively as she acknowledged Queen Bertrada. Silence held throughout the waiting court members.

"Queen Bertrada, it is a great pleasure to see you again." Desiderata forced enthusiasm into her greeting. "Do forgive me for coming unexpectedly. I was so eager to see your beautiful court." Her mouth turned up, but her eyes did not smile. They were accessing the court personages, the flower beds, the clothing of the assembled women. Several maids and court workers hung back near the manor's façade. Desiderata was unimpressed with their appearance or their lack of awe as they gazed at her.

"My escort is large, I'm afraid." Desiderata acknowledged. "But I value each and every one of these ladies and, of course, my soldiers." She sat stiff and upright in her saddle, even though dressed like a serving wench or a minstrel's girl. Glancing over her shoulder, she gestured to the women accompanying her. "My ladies must have bedchambers close around me. My escort should be accommodated in your most comfortable barracks—with the King's guard, I believe." She waved her hands vaguely as the escort broke their formation.

"Aye, of a certainty." Queen Bertrada answered. "Eggihard and Captain Gregory will see to their comfort." She nodded as Captain Gregory assisted Desiderata in dismounting. Then,

Queen Bertrada took Desiderata's hand and beckoned her women forward.

Bertrada noticed the curious looks the castle guards gave Desiderata—one of surprise and, then, of forbearance. One or two shook their heads. Although the Queen's expression was serene, she gloated inside. Desiderata's taste in clothing is deplorable, she thought. *I shall have to take her in hand, improve her choice of dress. Clothed in this manner she will embarrass Charlemagne and the court.*

"Come, come." Desiderata urged the Lombard ladies as she looked curiously around the entry hall. "I daresay the castle's bedchambers will present a more pleasing appearance than this entrance room. Hurry. We must refresh ourselves—bathe and change our dress for the mid-day meal." The Queen Mother nodded in agreement. *A change in clothing would be highly desirable. Her plumage does seem a little wilted.* Bertrada kept her smile steady, doing her best to hold her laughter inside. Dear me, she thought as Desiderata stroked a huge feather that protruded from her rather severe headdress. *When Desiderata dips her head, she looks very much like a duck, the feather serving as an over-sized beak.* The Queen Mother glared at the soldiers arranged along the entry-room walls. They nudged each other, trying to deflect their own amusement.

"I hope your dishes are appropriately seasoned," the peacock princess said to Queen Bertrada, as she wrinkled her nose. "I find food outside our Lombard castle generally poor and ill-prepared." The Queen's head snapped toward the Princess, just as if slapped. Well, Bertrada thought, you look poor and ill-prepared for a state visit. *I name you a 'rare bird'… so the quality of food at my table is hardly as issue. I should think any grain or seed would suffice for such a brightly-decked spectacle.* Bertrada clamped down on her mean-spirited thoughts. *I shall refine your loathsome style. Until then, I must remember the military strength and noble alliances you bring to the realm.* Banishing her irritation, Queen Bertrada smiled.

"My dear Desiderata," she replied, "we shall do everything in our power to make you comfortable. Succulent dishes will be prepared to whet your appetite. You'll not be disappointed." Desiderata inclined her head slightly, shot another glance of despair at the huge entrance hall, and turned to follow the Queen toward the east wing. Suddenly, she stopped and spoke, feigning shock.

"Why, this hall is cavernous! I fear you must freeze in winter. There surely is a draft about my feet." Her loud voice rolled through the entry chamber. "Your entrance is not nearly as well-appointed as our Lombard castle, Queen Bertrada. We have tapestries upon the walls, somewhat larger ones than these. Do you not feel winter's chill here in Frankland? I thought all kings furnished their courts the same." Her disapproving eyes widened with surprise and judgment.

"The castle is more than comfortable, Princess. You must remember we have other castles throughout the realm. This one, though, is the King's favorite…for its warm springs. I daresay you have no such luxury there in Pavia." The Queen Mother bit her lips to control her fury. *How dare this emaciated girl criticize my home!* Bertrada's anger surged but she answered calmly. "We shall do all we can to make you happy here, Desiderata."

"Oh, I shall be," the Princess answered, a smile replacing her frown, "for a long, long time, I daresay." She turned to her women. "Let's hurry to our chambers. We eagerly anticipate bathing in those famous pools of yours, Queen Bertrada." Desiderata almost purred. "But I do hope there is a private, secluded spot for us — not one frequented by the common people of your court," she added. Queen Bertrada said nothing. *What a crass comment. It deserves no answer.* Desiderata hurried up the steps, oblivious or uncaring, about the bad impression she made.

"We shall need several linens each." Desiderata dictated when asked about her request for linens. "We must be thoroughly dry before we don our tunics. I should think three wiping linens will suffice for now, three for each of us." The Queen Mother nodded as she led Desiderata toward the most luxurious bedchamber in the east wing of the castle. The benches covered with silk linens and pristine white, woolen-stuffed bolsters were larger than normal. Thanks to Egginhard, heat blazed from the fire-pits - just the place for this demanding, little bitch, the Queen thought, feeling much less welcoming than before.

Some miles from the castle, Charlemagne and his hunting companions noticed clouds of dust rising around the Aachen manor.

"Seems someone is visiting the castle." Roland commented to King Charlemagne.

"Aye, with all that dust, the party must be large. I guess that ends the hunt for today." He looked over at Oliver, his most thoughtful, gentle Peer. "Take the extra mounts to the stable, Oliver, if you will. We'll follow right behind, as soon as we call in the dogs."

"I'll move on then, Sire. I have the horses right here." Oliver said as he pulled away from the hunters. "See you at the stables."

"Call the dogs in." Charlemagne told Rinaldo. "We end the hunt now. This one, of a certainty, yielded no roasts for the splits tonight." The hunters turned their mounts toward home.

Cantering with the extra horses, Oliver was much closer to the castle than the King and his companions. He counted more than fifty horses milling around in the coral. This was a large party to be unexpected. No one mentioned visitors to him. With a contingent this big, there would be feasting and partying to the wee hours of tomorrow's light. He sighed at the thought but, at the same time, thanked God the hunt was over. They found no elk, no moose, and few rabbits. Ground squirrels there were aplenty but no source for the roasts the King preferred.

The hunters were dispirited and weary. He overhead the younger Peers openly yearning for the entertainments and gaiety of an afternoon spent with the court ladies. Ranging ahead of the hunters, Oliver identified the banners of Lombardy flying over the Aachen courtyard. He rode back to the King.

"Were you expecting King Desiderius, Sire?" Oliver asked King Charlemagne as he returned to his side. "The Lombard banner waves at the door of your castle." Charlemagne frowned and shook his head.

"Desiderius? Nay, Oliver, I received no missive from him. This weather does not lend itself to long-distance travel. It's time for the snows. Why can he be here?" He turned to Oliver, a questioning look in his eyes. "Ma-Mam spent several days at his court; you remember, early in the autumn? But she didn't mention a visit." The King cantered closer. Now he recognized the Lombard colors.

With a dire sense of foreboding, Charlemagne settled back into his saddle, tightened Samson's reins, and urged him forward. Samson moved from cantering to a full gallop as the hunters followed him across the field. Soon, they reined in at the courtyard. Charlemagne dismounted, hailing Seneschal Eggihard as he hurried toward them. Even before the stableboys walked their tired horses away, Eggihard came to the King.

"Sire, the Queen Mother just escorted visitors inside." Eggihard announced. "The Lombard Princess arrived with quite a retinue, presumably for an extended visit." He waited. Charlemagne seemed about to ask a question but said nothing. "There are twenty ladies with her and thrice that number of trunks." Although Eggihard did not raise his voice, his opinion of the amount of baggage was clear.

"The Princess almost seems to command the Queen Mother, Sire." He stepped closer to Charlemagne. "I understand noble women do change their dress often, but the River Wurm itself has not enough water to clean the garments in all those trunks." King Charlemagne's jaw clenched but he did not respond, just stared into Eggihard's face.

"The Princess brought her twenty ladies and sixty soldiers, Sire." Eggihard watched the King's face as he gave the number of soldiers.

"Eighty people, Eggihard!" The King finally spoke, his face irritated, his lips pressed together. Dear God, Charlemagne thought. He pressed his left fist into his right hand, relaxed his jaw muscles, and consciously changed the expression on his face. *Since I did not send acceptance of the betrothal, Desiderius took events into his own hands. He sends his daughter who I am, king to king, compelled to receive.*

"Aye, Sire, actually eighty-four..." Eggihard smiled. He seldom saw Charlemagne discomfited and wondered at his reaction. "Did you expect this visit, Sire?" He asked softly, implying he would have liked notice of the Princess' arrival.

"Nay, I did not. But I will soon understand the reason for

her journey." Remembering his Peers' hunger, Charlemagne spoke. "It's past time for the mid-day meal. Come, let's eat." He turned toward the banquet room. He motioned to them, still considering the reason for Desiderata's visit. I will delay in presenting myself to the princess, he thought. His breath caught. *Oh, God! If Desiderata is here for the wedding, I have no hope. I cannot postpone the wedding. Desiderius will take offense and attack within a fortnight.* His brow furrowed; his heart dropped to his stomach. *I'm tricked! Damn, damn, Desiderius to hell!"*

"Nay, Sire, the meal cannot be served," Eggihard interrupted his thoughts, wondering at the look of panic on the King's face. "Because we wait for the Lombard ladies, the meal is delayed. The Lombard women...bathe, your Majesty." Eggihard looked at the stones underfoot. Bathing in the middle of the day was an unusual occurrence.

"Bathe? ...in the middle of the day?" Charlemagne asked, astounded. "Why?" He looked at Eggihard in total confusion. "I never heard of such! This princess, she seems an odd one, Eggihard. Mayhap she..." The King stopped speaking, trying to put a positive face on the unexpected visit.

"Bathing, is it? Well, if that's the case," he tried to laugh, "we have some time to wait, I imagine. You had best tell the hunting party, we eat late." He nodded to Eggihard and went into the castle to find the Queen Mother. As he paused in the corridor, he heard a soft, though determined, voice speaking.

"Never, never! Such a meal will not serve." The woman's voice was almost shouting. "Not one of my ladies here will eat suet. It is fit only for heavy-footed beasts, those that lumber or move slowly. We will have barley soup, white loaves, and pear preserves. You have that, do you not? Our mid-day meal must be light, to encourage nimbleness in our fingers as we weave, knit, and purl. The meal you suggest may serve as the evening meal, I suppose." The speaker paused. "I, myself, prefer fish or quail. Please add a sweet, dough with honey?" The King heard a low mumble in reply.

"Oh, I apologize for any inconvenience. You did ask our preferences; did you not? But... to be frank, these are not preferences. They are requirements. We partake of just this sort of food at each mid-day meal. I shall expect the same on the morrow, Queen Bertrada, and in the days after." The voice paused a moment as Charlemagne thought he heard another mumble. "Aye, that will do nicely," the first voice answered. "We shall all be in the baths." The voice faded away.

Yes, that's Princess Desiderata's voice. Charlemagne thought. She sounds just as demanding, proud and disdainful as I remember...and not at all apologetic for this unannounced visit. Charlemagne turned in the direction of the conversation and saw his mother, standing immobile at the juncture of the east and west wings. He walked toward her.

"Good morrow, Ma-Mam. Is King Desiderius here? I spotted his banners a half-furlong away." Charlemagne saw his mother startle, then she turned to watch his progress toward her. "I hurried home." He added, seeing his mother's distressed face.

"Oh, Charlemagne!" She exclaimed, relief washing over her. "Thank God you're here. Nay, it's not Desiderius who visits. It's Desiderata." She held her hand up to stop his questions. "She arrived alone, only her women and soldiers accompany her."

"What? Her brother is not with her? This is very strange...does Desiderius not concern himself with her reputation? Why is she here?" King Charlemagne asked.

"Well might you wonder. Has Desiderius communicated with you...a missive I don't know about? I daresay he's irritated by your tardiness in confirming the betrothal. And, so, he sent her to us." His mother frowned at him.

"It *is* inconvenient…with no notice. How do we provide for this great a party…and the special foods she demands? I pray this won't be a lengthy visit." Queen Bertrada was beside herself, anxious and angry. As she spoke, Charlemagne saw her realize the inconvenience and the expense this visit placed on the court: the special meals, armloads of linen each day, the entertainments to be provided. He was certain Desiderata required much fetching and coddling.

"I cannot believe her father sanctioned this — her making this journey alone." The Queen's eyes stared down the corridor. "She arrived with no male escort! Where is her brother? Doesn't she have an uncle?" The Queen's face was pale, her eyes darting about. The King saw the rapid tapping of her foot on the stone, a definite sign of frustration. She lifted her eyes to Charlemagne's face.

"Has she explained her visit? Did you expect her, Ma-Mam?" Charlemagne looked for any clue.

"She explains nothing." Bertrada declared. "She said only she expects to be here for a long time." She studied her son's face. "We must make plans. Desiderius must not expect more than…"

"Did you plan none of this with Desiderata, Ma-Mam? Did you invite her to visit, if just to be polite, during those betrothal talks?" The disgusted tone of his voice caught the Queen's attention.

"Nay, nay! I did not offer a visit; she didn't suggest one. It was unnecessary to woo her; she agreed to the betrothal forthwith. I never expected her to arrive here unbidden." Queen Bertrada repeated. "It's unseemly — without her father or mother. Not even her brother accompanied her."

"I fear I know the reason," King Charlemagne answered. He stared into his mother's face. "Desiderius hurries the wedding. He sent his daughter to hasten the ceremony. He wishes to imprison me all the sooner."

"Oh, don't be ridiculous, son." The Queen laughed. "Desiderius may be eager to gain you as a son-in-law, but I assure you he doesn't think of putting you in prison. What an imagination you have! Mayhap, he and Desiderata are eager for this wedding - eager for different reasons, of a certainty - but ready for it to be done." Queen Bertrada almost preened, gratified by the thought. "This will be the wedding of the century and the marriage of the entire continent! I'm so pleased!"

"God help me," King Charlemagne replied soberly. "May my approval of this bride match your pleasure in binding me to her, Ma-Mam." Charlemagne turned at the sound of running feet. He looked down the corridor as Gisela sprinted to their mother.

"The countesses are calling for you, Ma-Mam. They seek your counsel on entertainments for the evening meal. They are unsure what to select for a princess." Gisela knew her mother would send her to take care of it. She added: "I cannot help them. It would be unseemly for an aspiring nun to voice an opinion about entertainments. You must go to them, Ma-Mam, as soon as possible." The Queen nodded, turned quickly and hurried toward the ladies' chamber. Gisela turned to her brother.

"What's going on here, Charley? This visit of Desiderata's is presumptuous. Ma-Mam is the only one here who ever met the woman. Why would she travel here, all this way, unannounced?" She fumed.

"I suspect it was her father's idea, Gisela," the King replied. "He deliberately risks his daughter's good name. He counts on my marrying her immediately. A marriage would explain away her reckless arrival. No man would want such a smirch on his wife's behavior. He hopes I will agree to an early wedding to protect her reputation. Then, the realm will buzz, speculating I was over-eager for the joining." He ran his fingers through his hair, leaving it standing wildly about his head. "You and I spoke before about Desiderius' ambitions. He duped me."

"Carl suggested I delay the ceremony 'til Eastertide. It seemed an enlightened move. Damn it to all! Now, I don't even have that choice!" But," he squeezed his sister's hand as she took his arm, "such a choice only delays the inevitable. I am firmly caught, Gislea, just like a mouse in an owl's talons." Tears sprang into Gisela's eyes as she saw the genuine regret in her brother's face.

"Can nothing be done to sever this betrothal?" She asked.

"Nothing, Gisela," King Charlemagne replied. "There is nothing." Gisela's face paled. She caught her breath.

"My God, Charley, what will you tell Hildegard?" She caught his startled surprise and smiled sadly. "She's already in love with you; and you, I think, care for her." She saw Charlemagne's mouth tremble. "Oh, Charley!" He shook his head.

"Ma-Mam has put my word, my vow at risk. She does not consider a queen's duties or the personal characteristics a queen should have. Undoubtedly, she considers herself a fine model." He hugged his sister.

"Seeing this, I admire Poppa anew! The man was a saint. How did he ever deal with her? I ask you." Gisela shook her head. King Charlemagne sat down heavily beside her, his face in his hands.

"Come," Gisela urged him quietly. "Come. Let us talk in the library. We must consider this carefully, but not here in the corridor where anyone may hear." She took her brother's arm and turned toward the west wing and the library. On the way, Charlemagne calmed himself, gathered his thoughts, and outlined his options. They were few.

Chapter Sixteen
What Must Be

"How do you rule, if there is no good for you in the effort? Sacrificing yourself— it makes no sense!" Gisela shouted at her brother. She didn't expect an answer so she hurried on. "Let me but point out Hildegard's good points, Charley, before you make this choice. Your heart must be in your pursuits to garner success, especially in the choice of a wife." Charlemagne seemed to hang on her every word. She spoke quickly, cherishing his willingness to listen.

"Consider Hildegard's spirit, her commitments, as you think of the good of the realm." Gisela suggested. "You both dream of a different world: one unleashed from tradition, one which promises a better life for all the Franks, not only the advancement of the nobility. You speak eloquently about educating everyone, even young girls. Surely, there is advantage in selecting a wife who is equally forward-thinking, one committed to the changes you value." Gisela struggled to find the best words.

"I know Hildegard. She has her own passions; some align much with your own. She is well-educated, skilled, insightful and eager to correct wrongs. Although you two won't have a placid union, I describe her as an energetic, conscientious helpmate. You both seek the same changes!" The King raised his hands in surrender.

"Aye, I told myself this, Gisela." Charlemagne replied. "I

agree with all you say. But it is out of my hands now. Abbot Fulrad berates me for banishing Himiltrude, even though he knows Ma-Mam instigated it. Imagine his reaction if I choose yet a third woman! Think of Count Rastie, Count Bluntit, and Lord Sarren. They and other counts, here in our court, will denounce me. They'll demand a public defense of the decision. They might reject Hildegard, a woman whose family is virtually removed from the court. Each would be adamant for me to consider his own daughter. Even the Pope would find me hard to support." He let his hands fall to his sides.

"My choice no longer matters." He shrugged his shoulders, admitting defeat. "If I do not marry Desiderata, I risk the realm. Poppa counted on me to be strong, Gisela." His eyes begged his sister to understand.

He looked into Gisela's sympathetic face, saw the tears standing in her eyes. The King took his sister's dear hand, clutching it to his chest as he fought to control his despair.

"I cannot deny the feelings I have for Hildegard, Gisela. I cannot." King Charlemagne whispered. "She suits me perfectly. Her outspoken opinions, her open affection for the people, her planning skills, her competence, her cheery, hope-filled heart—all captivate me. But I am *not* free to choose her!" Gisela rubbed her brother's shoulders, trying to comfort him.

They sat quietly together until Charlemagne accepted his own words. He must marry Desiderata to win her father's support; he must marry for an heir; he must marry to protect the realm. It was his duty. He and Gisela watched the wood in the fire pit burn to embers.

"There is much unrest, Gisela, since Poppa's death. Carl and I have yet to be tested. Aquitaine was never a serious threat; it decreased none of the jealously among the nobility. Many of them, all over the realm, wish us to fail. They lick their lips in anticipation, hoping to share in power in a re-organized kingdom. Many scurry about, promising support and undermining each other in the hope of rising to the top." He nodded at Gisela as her eyes reflected her understanding.

"Lombard is the strongest threat we face. I have no land or booty to buy the loyalty of Lombard's nobles. And Desiderius' military strength is not to be ignored. With this marriage, Desiderius will be accountable for bringing his nobles to heel. If all goes well, his lands, Carl's, and mine will coalesce to form a larger and stronger realm." Charlemagne methodically ticked off the points on his fingers. "All in all, Gisela, I will be strengthened, rather than challenged by Desiderius and the willing nobles who join him." Gisela turned her eyes to her brother's face.

"If I could, you guessed it. I would, of a certainty, ask Hildegard to be my wife." As he thought of Hilde, his face softened; the tense, anxious frown disappeared from his forehead. "We do care for each other, Gisela. I find myself relishing the little time we spend together. These last few weeks—talking and sharing tales, joking and teasing, we appreciate one another." The King ducked his head. "She makes my heart sing. I feel anything is possible, if she is in my life." His face crumpled, stricken with the impossibility of his dreams.

"It cannot be, Gisela; it cannot be. The choice might undermine the realm."

"And it may not!" Gisela objected strenuously. Charlemagne shook his head and raised his hands in defense.

"No more." He whispered. He put his finger over her mouth.

"Are we merging our mid-day meal and our evening one?" The King finally asked. "I am beyond starving." Gisela roused herself, reluctant to return to the court's bustle.

"Let's go to the banquet hall," she suggested. "Surely, the cooks' additional dishes for the mid-day meal are now ready. Otherwise, you are right, Charley. We might just as well eat two meals in one. But you must agree, eighty-four more people for a meal is quite startling. Don't you think?" She rose from the bench and held out our hand, clasping Charlemagne's arm.

"You must speak to Hildegard, Charley. She hears the rumors which engage the court. You must explain this marriage to her. Please, Charley, be kind. Try not to break her heart," Gisela begged. The King's face paled; he looked haggard; his eyes were dull. He sighed, nodding at Gisela's pleas.

"Aye," he agreed. "I will go to her, tonight or in the morning. I promise you, Gisela; I will tell her. I know this message must come from my own lips." With that he and Gisela left the library. The following morning, Charlemagne dressed with care.

"This will be the most difficult message I ever deliver." he mumbled. His night was long—filled with unremitting sadness, filled with regret in raising Hildegard's hopes and, now, having to smash them. No matter how much his mind told him this was his only choice, his heart was unable to accept it. *Giving up the woman I love, the woman who shares my hopes for the people, the woman who would make a wonderful mother for...*King Charlemagne felt overcome with loss. He was physically ill: his belly ached; his throat constricted; his shoulders tensed with pain, so rigid were his muscles. He slipped to his knees.

"Heavenly Father, give me strength; steel my mind; numb my heart so I remain stalwart." He rose, forcing his steps toward Hildegard's chamber. "I do owe this much to her," he mumbled to himself. "I can't let Hildegard know the true depth of my feelings for her. She will understand even less, if I confess too much." Although his feet lagged, his thoughts were frantic, becoming such a jumble he forgot most of the speech he composed during the night.

"I imagine the worst," King Charlemagne reassured himself. "Her reaction will never be as dire as I fear." He felt a very old man, plodding along the corridor, forcing his feet to take his next steps. His eyes were dull, red-rimmed from lack of sleep. His face was gray, missing its usual enthusiastic eagerness. He felt nauseous and slowly rubbed his cramping stomach. How do I appear strong and determined? He wondered to himself. He paused to set a smile on his face.

"I will close off my feelings, state the realities and show no regrets. I will not speak at length with Hildegard. This pain mustn't be prolonged for either of us." Despite his unwilling feet, he finally came to the bedchamber which Hildegard shared with Jocelyn and Maria.

He knocked on the door, seeing recurring images of Hilde riding at Count Hautgard's manor. Her dark hair streaming in the wind, her eyes flashing with delight, her skilled hands controlling her mount—he visualized every detail of their ride. *Had he not thought of her constantly since her arrival at court?* Covering a groan with a cough, the King knocked on the chamber door, then stepped inside, calling Hilde's name.

"Hilde? Hildegard? Are you here?" He looked about for her. "I can't believe she's not here, not when I finally have the courage to speak to her." He consciously stopped speaking. He stomped his feet on the floor, hoping to attract the attention of anyone in the sleeping alcoves.

"Aye, just a moment," came Hildegard's voice. Charlemagne looked toward the back of the chamber, eager to see the owner of the voice, but just as reluctant to cause her pain.

"Hildegard? It's I, Charlemagne. May I speak with you?" He asked.

Hildegard, placing newly washed and dried linen into a trunk, knew the King's voice, but she startled when he called, nonetheless. She saw him pass her window but thought it unlikely he sought her. Her heart was heavy. Maria, anxiously at first, told her of the upcoming wedding yesterday night.

'Just so you know what's happening.' Maria said. Hildegard felt nothing. She did not believe, could not accept, that Charlemagne mislead her. *What would be the purpose of that?* She asked herself. "He showed me too much attention not to care for me. And, then, Maria says this princess is to be his wife? I cannot think her words are true." She shook her head, knowing she must go to the door. *But Maria has no reason to lie.* She quickly pulled a soft silk tunic over her plain one, pushed her unruly hair in place and left the sleeping alcove. Hildegard consciously gave a small smile as she curtseyed to the king.

The man she loved stood there, looking into her face. She thought him as handsome and kind, as thoughtful and dear, as she knew her mother felt her father. Despite his words, his warnings to her, she believed he cared for her. And she, long ago, admitted her love for him. Her feelings for him grew stronger every day.

"Your Majesty, did you call?" She asked quietly as she raised her eyes to him. Charlemagne took her hand, helping her rise from her curtsey. It took all his strength not to take her in his arms, though he did hold her hand over-long.

"My dear Hilde, I trust your morning pleasant. Forgive me for interrupting you so early; but we must speak." At Hildegard's surprised look, he added. "The truth is, Hilde, I must talk with you and quickly."

"It's too late to talk." She said to him, turning away. "...though I suppose I should offer you congratulations." She took three steps back, gathered her courage, and looked into his face. His eyes were large with surprise; the color drained from his face. Ever ruddy, his cheeks appeared white as snow.

"What do you mean, too late? Congratulations?" He looked into her eyes and saw the hurt. "Oh, hell. What have you heard?"

"...only that your wedding is upon us, Sire. The court buzzes with speculation about the reason for Princess Desiderata's arrival." Her voice trembled. "I was just told; there is to be a wedding...yours and hers."

"Hilde! Forgive me! I did not want you to hear this way!" He took a step toward her and stopped as she backed up again. "I can explain... Let me tell..."

"Explain? You've nothing to explain, your Majesty. Had I known sooner, I would be better prepared, better able to celebrate your news. But, no matter. I wish you much happiness, Sire." She paused, as if considering her words. "Mayhap, I am blessed...that no one thought this news of special importance to me." She stared into his face, almost like a statue. "I guarded my behavior. There is nothing I can be accused of." Because Hilde knew the court an uncertain place, she was discreet in her behavior with the King. And she spoke her feelings to no one.

"Nay, my Hilde," he replied, seeing her consternation. "No one suspects... You bring me only delight; be certain of that." He swallowed quickly, then turned his back to her and walked to the small fire burning on the hearth. "Please listen to me carefully." He turned toward her.

"The rumors are true. Desiderata and I are to marry. But...this is a choice for the security of the realm. It is not a marriage of my liking. Believe me."

"But you did agree to the betrothal, surely." Hildegard replied.

"I... well, not exactly." He stopped, knowing there was no way to explain this wedding — not to the woman he loved. Charlemagne saw her confusion and berated himself. *Deliver your message, you fool. You try, deliberately, to mislead her.* He dropped his head. *I cannot bear to hurt her. She has done no wrong, only loved me and hoped for a return of that love.* His heart squeezed so tightly he couldn't breathe.

Charlemagne gazed into Hilde's face, basking in her gentle presence. *My God!* The King's thoughts raced as he dropped his eyes. *How have I come to this?* He ran a weary hand over his eyes and answered his own question. *It does not matter. I must explain somehow.*

Charlemagne swallowed roughly. *I cannot bear this talk. I must get out of here.* But, try as he would, his legs would not obey. He glanced at Hildegard again, amazed by her patience. She picked up a tunic from her sleeping bench and placed it in a traveling bag. The motion seemed so sad. He looked at her closely and saw a tear trickle down her cheek. She turned away.

How can I deny her? How can I...when all my dreams revolve around her?

"Did you wish to speak with me for some reason, Charlemagne?" She asked.

"You must excuse me; I am packing...to return to my father's house."

"What? What did you say?" Charlemagne processed her words slowly.

"Your father's house? But why?"

"I cannot stay here, not in your court." Hildegard stared at him. "Are you without any feeling at all? You barge in here, confirm you are being married and think what? ...that I am unaffected by this? Can you understand this news is hateful to me? ...that I'm hurt, confused, embarrassed?" She sat on her sleeping bench. "Get out. Get out! And leave me in peace!"

"Hilde, please... I don't want to hurt you. I cannot bear to see..."

"You deliberately misled me. I thought we... you said... You spoke so lovingly to me I..." Suddenly, Hilde noticed the King's frowning face, the nervous rubbing of his hands. She held out a hand to stop his pacing. Her sob broke the stillness of the chamber as she confirmed the truth of his words in the blank, unfeeling face he turned to her.

"What kind of monster are you? Do you deliberately destroy me? Is this some joke, to see if I laugh at your marrying another?" Hildegard focused on the writing desk. Though she was composed, tears rolled down her cheeks.

"Ignore my tears," she directed him. "They will end, just not quite yet. Give me an explanation." Her mouth trembled, color crept up her cheeks. She suddenly felt very cold. "Hasten. I will not wait all day."

"Hilde, I cannot explain it," the King whispered. She saw the sadness and regret but saw, also, the decision was irrevocable. She thought her heart would fly from her chest. She sobbed in despair.

"There is nothing I can say," the King said. "Explanations change nothing. The fact is: I am betrothed to Desiderata. The wedding is to take place immediately. Please forgive me." Acting to control his own desperation, Charlemagne hardened his voice. His words came out cold and abrupt.

"But I did tell you I was married, many months ago. I did not mislead you." He remembered his vow to be kingly and tried to speak in a formal voice, even as his voice became louder. "I have not been false with you, Hildegard."

"But the marriage you spoke of was to another." Hildegard

objected. "You spoke of your marriage to Himiltrude. You never mentioned a new wife." She shuddered, then coughed. Her throat felt as if it were closing. "You said nothing of a coming marriage...not during our conversations, not during the rides we shared with Jocelyn and Maria, not at the court parties...not even when you called me 'your Hilde.'"

Charlemagne, shocked at the depth of his own pain, felt her every glance, every tear, every frown. They cut into his heart. I must end this, he said to himself. *I must get out of this chamber.* He deliberately pinched his ear. The pain helped him stifle his sorrow and regain his stiff, unbending control. *I cannot watch her grieve and know I am the source of such hurt.* He closed his heart, imagined himself on his throne and withdrew from his feelings. *If I do not deny them, they will overwhelm my sanity.*

Hildegard closed her eyes, as if to remove Charlemagne from her consciousness. She raised her hands to her ears, physically trying to block out his voice. Her shoulders shuddered as she sobbed softly. King Charlemagne stood with his head bowed, his eyes damp with unshed tears.

"I'm waiting," Hilde finally spoke. "How could you so ill-use me? Why did you summon me to court?" Her face was bewildered as she remembered her ridiculous hopes. Despite her burning eyes and the lump in her throat, she wanted an explanation. He stood there, his eyes locked on the floor.

Hildegard retreated to her own thoughts. She could not believe he was to marry another. When he came into the chamber, he gently stroked her ears with his words. And in a moment, he announced he marries another. *What kind of man was he? Even though he never spoke of a future with her, his eyes, his words, his whole manner conveyed deep feeling.* Hildegard caught her breath, now questioning her expectations.

"You are, I know, the most powerful king on the continent. I was foolish to think you would return my love." Her face flushed crimson; her eyes looked around the room, anywhere but at the King. "I was a child! God help me, I thought your heart joined with mine." Hearing the King stir, Hildegard looked up, thinking he would speak. He did not.

"But," she continued, "I am not such a fool...to have misunderstood so badly. Those chance meetings, the careful pleasantries in front of others, the soulful glances and whispered endearments — were they all a sham? Are you so treacherous you whispered endearments and, now, deny their intent? You are a monster." Anger finally overcame the hurt.

"Why tell me your plans now?" Hildegard wondered at his motives. "Do you fear I'll embarrass you before the court? You took overlong to tell me." She confronted him. "Did you not?"

"Aye, I did," the King admitted, finally speaking. "There were many things to consider; I had to rid myself of doubt or hesitation. And so have I done." He had to remind himself to talk in a normal voice. "With my vows to Desiderata, I cement two disparate kingdoms and assure the survival of the Frankish realm." Still unnerved by Hildegard's pain and anger, he spoke in an even firmer voice.

"My decision is made." He struggled to appear calm and in control. "It was not an easy one, I assure you." Hildegard did not react, if she even heard his admission. "The ceremony is three days hence." And, then, as if to wound her completely, he extended his invitation. "You, of a certainty, are invited to the celebration."

"Celebration?" Hildegard stared at him. "Ha! This is no celebration, Sire. This marriage is a mockery of the Church's words. You don't leave your family to cleave to your wife; you bring her to merge into you and your mother's strange union." Her eyes flashed; she was strong and in control.

"You do not begin a family of your own; you open your chamber door just enough to allow this unknowing wife to slink into Queen Bertrada's domain. Nay, nay." Her face seemed frozen in place. "This marriage is a cruel joke I will, with a certainty, not witness." Hildegard's eyes snapped, glaring at the King. "I would not view such sad events."

"You do over-react." Charlemagne was thankful for her anger. He would have welcomed a beating from her. *Hilde should strike me, not just throw words in my face. I deserve worse than she can imagine.* But he steeled his voice and betrayed none of his feelings. "I follow age-old traditions which define my Germanic heritage." Charlemagne began to feel righteous from the difficulty of his choice. "Do not tread on values which my family honors in each new generation." He thought his sentence well put and reasonable. "I warn you!"

"Warn me all you like," Hildegard shot back. "But do not dare mis-state your father's values. King Pepin abhorred marrying for alliances! He would never wish it. He asked your feeling for Himiltrude before he consented to your union. You told me so." She pointed an accusatory finger at him. "You do love her and little Pippin. Don't dare to deny it. God will surely punish you, if you say otherwise. Circumstances change, other choices are made, but love itself must never be denied."

Hildegard's mind overcame her mouth. "You *warn* me, do you? Dear Lord, what is the message in your 'warning?' What will you do if I displease you now or if your precious mother hears of my past affection for you?" She frowned, relaxing her pent-up breath in order to consider his words. "Is this the warning you give me? As I look into your face, I know I have no protector in this court. If anyone suspects I am unhappy with you, care anything about you at all, criticize your choices, my own life is worth nothing. With your impending marriage, I must rein in all feelings for you, scourge any suggestion of fondness for you from my face and from my actions."

King Charlemagne stared at Hildegard, furious she mentioned his father. *How dare she recall Poppa's values to me?* He cried inside. He rubbed his temple. Of a certainty, he remembered. *I told her of Poppa, of his hope my wife would be a loving help-mate, not a competitive one.* In that instant, the King remembered his father's comment about his own wife. 'As for your mother's helping me, I would not wish that on a son,' King Pepin told him. *My God.* Charlemagne was immobilized. *I did not understand Poppa at all. He was warning me, warning me to beware of Ma-Mam.*

His eyes returned to Hildegard. *Even angry as a wet cat, with blanched face and reddened eyes, she is beautiful. I am a fool to give up this incredible woman.* Holding his regret in check, he spoke of his first marriage.

"Nevertheless, my first union is finished. I move forward for the sake of the realm." He turned to leave but Hildegard's voice stopped him. She walked to stand in front of him and looked directly into his face. Despite her fear, despite her precarious position, she must remind him of his dreams.

"I am well aware your father wanted no alliances which imprisoned his children," she stated. "He forbade your mother to make such a betrothal for Gisela. Gisela told me of it, of her fear years ago!" Hildegard's voice changed. "But you, great King, you expunge his teachings from your memory. You battle and fight to make alliances as did the Merovingian kings of old." Here, her voice darkened with sarcasm. "...those fair, loyal, justice-inspired kings who exploited their own people, who treated the men like slaves and the women like sows — as breeders valuable only for their bodies. Your dogs live better than they." She paused, her face flushed, her eyes blazing, her thoughts crystal-clear.

Hildegard recognized Charlemagne's problem; he betrayed himself. Grabbing the door handle, she took a deep breath.

"I believed you a man of vision—a man so entranced by learning, by opportunities for the realm, by belief in a Christian kingdom. I believe you capable of moving heaven and earth to realize those hopes." Hildegard cast him a despairing look.

"But I made a huge mistake, King Charlemagne. You cling to the old ways, those which harm and limit and kill people's strivings. You honor the past, replaying the worse choices of those very Merovingian kings you did condemn." She stood erect, swallowed her fear and her pain, and blurted out her best choice to protect herself.

"I bid you 'adieu,' your Majesty. I return to my father's house." Charlemagne looked at her in astonishment.

"What?" He asked. *What does she say? Nay, she dare not leave. I will not countenance it.* "Nay, I will not allow it. I do not wish you to leave. I forbid it." Charlemagne searched for a reason to keep her at the court.

"The weather is too changeable, fraught with cold, ice, marauders—human and beasts. It is not safe...not now, Hildegard."

"If you will but send three men with me, they will be well-rewarded when we reach Swabia." She replied, ignoring his words. "Normally, I wait for my father's escort; but I would away as soon as possible."

"You may not leave," the King commanded. "I forbid it. When the winter ends, I shall supply an escort for your homeward journey—when the weather breaks, Hilde." So saying, he opened the door and walked into the corridor.

"Thank God, Charlemagne is gone," Hildegard murmured. She relaxed her tense face, releasing the noncommittal look she held there when Charlemagne was close by. Trembling with weariness and sorrow, she pulled a bench closer to the fire and sat down. She felt all strength drain from her body.

Chapter Seventeen

CHANGES

"What happens to me now?" Hildegard shuddered, imagining all types of punishments: removal from the court, scullery maid in the cook room, servant in the tanneries. More likely, though, Queen Bertrada and select countesses would scrutinize her behavior and her work. Sent on endless errands by the noble ladies, or ostracized by the maids-in-waiting, the daily demands on her would make her little more than a slave. *The King might confine me to this chamber — mayhap even refuse me free access to the stables.* Hildegard's breath caught. She stopped her panicked thoughts and mentally shook herself.

"Don't be ridiculous!" She chastised herself. "The King himself will ignore you. You have been discreet, regardless of your fears. If you play your part now, others in the court will know nothing. They may speculate about your renewed dedication to the noble women, notice you speak less to the King; but no one will confront you. Some few may note your less enthusiastic spirit. They may even gossip about the change in you. But, fulfill your duties and you will be left alone."

"Dear Father in heaven, help me get through the coming days — ever pleasant, uninterested in everything."

Hildegard shifted into a more comfortable position and began planning her transformation from energetic, conscientious maid-in-waiting to inconspicuous mouse: gracious and responsive to others, drawing no attention to herself. She bowed her head, overwhelmed at the effort such behavior would require.

"But I shall do it," she vowed. "I will learn all I can about the weaknesses of the people here and how to avoid those with power. I must, in order to protect my future." She bathed her face again, hoping the frigid water would remove the redness from her eyes, the fatigue around her mouth. Looking through her wardrobe, she chose another tunic, her most demure one — a plain, gray tunic with no embroidery. "To be unnoticed, I must blend into the background. And unnoticed I shall be!"

True to her vow, Hilde went about her daily affairs, though now with much less laughter and ready engagement than before. If any of the women noticed her subdued manner, they attributed it to a woman's monthly distress and gave her no more thought. In a surprisingly few days, she was a shadow about the court. She fetched, carried, brought, removed, and completed all the duties expected of a lady's maid. Her own time, she spent in the stable, among the puppies.

"Today the King takes his vows." Hearing her mumble, Maria approached Hildegard. She was so distant, so unapproachable, these days; Maria feared she was ill with some mysterious malady.

"You've not said a word about your gown for the wedding, Hildegard," Maria complained. "Jocelyn and I would have gladly helped with your embroideries, if you had but asked." Her forehead wrinkled. "You were so pre-occupied; I hesitated to worry you." Hildegard smiled at her scatter-brained friend. In the past three days, she felt thirty years older, well beyond the years of the other maids-in-waiting. Her carefree days at

Count Hautgard's manor—the days of embroidering and laughing, of dreaming fantasies about her future, of imagining so many intriguing possibilities—were done.

"I appreciate your concern, Maria." She patted Maria's arm. "But I have a gown from my cousin's wedding which will serve," she explained. "It requires no new handiwork and will be entirely suitable."

"May I help you dress?" Maria asked. She was giddy with excitement. The wedding was to begin in less than an hour. She could hardly wait to leave for the Church. "Come, come, Jocelyn," she called to her sister. "We must hurry. Let's help Hildegard into her gown and get to our seats." She sighed, raising her voice. "Are you ready yet, Jocelyn?" Her voice was shrill, impatient in having to wait for other people. "She probably is in there, dreaming of her own prince." She confided to Hilde.

"I'm almost ready!" Jocelyn called from the corner of the chamber. "...just arranging these glorious rubies father sent. It's a miracle. They came just as the wedding day arrives." She smiled sweetly at her young sister. "And, for your information, I don't need to dream of a prince. I already picked one!"

"Who? Who is it?" Maria demanded to know, rushing over to her sister.

"Why don't you guess?" Jocelyn teased.

"I know who it is." Maria replied seriously. "It's Lord Roland. How can anyone compete with him? He's so handsome, kind, attentive, gentle. All the girls gape at him. I have no chance!" Jocelyn and Hilde laughed.

"You are hopeless, Maria." Jocelyn replied. "There are many attractive men in the court: Rinaldo, Gotbrut, Oliver – for certain!" Maria shook her head. Laughing still, Hilde spoke up.

"Thank you both for your offer with my dress." Hildegard answered politely. "But I need no help. Maria, you have transformed my hair. How can I ever thank you for this new style? It's lovely." She twirled around her sleeping bench, deflecting Maria's attention from her behavior. "I have only to slip my gown over my head and I'm ready for the ceremony." Seeing Maria intended to wait for her, Hildegard began pawing through one of her trunks. "I'll meet you in the Church; please save me a seat." She took several headdresses and scarves from her trunk. "I promised to lend Countess Helga's daughter a head-covering." She opened the bedchamber door and stepped into the corridor. "See you there."

Hildegard did not even know Countess Helga's daughter. She had to avoid sitting with Maria and Jocelyn. Glancing up and down the corridor, she tucked the headdresses in a crevice behind the stairs and hurried away. She left the castle, walking toward the garden entrance to the Church. Yesterday night, she happened on a perfect location in the clerestory. Hidden high above the floor of the nave, she could observe the entire church without being seen. Even if she wept, no one would see her tears or worry her with questions about her emotions.

Hildegard quickly entered from the Church's garden and reached to open the small, secluded, staircase door. At that very moment, Countess Bologna entered the corridor and spied her. She called Hildegard insistently, her hands windmills as she beckoned.

"Come, come!" The Countess demanded. "I have need of you in the vestry. Desiderata is dressing there. We are still embroidering the Queen Mother's gown. Can you believe such last minute preparations?" She glared at Hilde as if she were to blame. "Come, hurry! We need your nimble fingers." Any other time Hildegard would have been pleased with the compliment, but not now. Still, she nodded pleasantly at the Countess and followed her.

The two women entered the vestry. Maids and noble women filled the space, stationed between bright swatches of silk and trunks piled high with clothing. Hearing raised voices, Hildegard realized they walked into the middle of a battle or, at least, a boisterous confrontation. Behind the closed door, the Queen Mother and Princess Desiderata were in a heated, verbal exchange. Their angry words punctuated the otherwise silent room.

Hildegard was shocked. This was not an auspicious sign: the bride and her to-be mother-in-law already argued! She listened. *Oh, it was about the wedding dress.* She looked from Queen Bertrada to Desiderata.

The younger woman wept, tears seeping from under her lids. The Queen Mother's face was red, her hair falling from her headdress. She held her hands, balled into fists, stiffly alongside her body. Charlemagne stood quietly between the two, munching an apple. He was, seemingly unconcerned.

"Charlemagne! Do something!" Desiderata demanded as she turned to her bridegroom. "Your Mother ruins my wedding. She says my dress is not appropriate!" Desiderata's voice broke as she sobbed. She buried her face in her hands, muffling her next words. "This is MY wedding. I will choose my own dress." Hildegard shrank away from Countess Bologna. I must not be seen here, she thought, as she slipped behind a stack of trunks.

"You will *not* wear this dress," the Queen Mother declared. "I forbid it." Her voice reverberated in the room. "It is both dowdy and ill-made. I will not have you embarrass this court with such a garment. I'll destroy it…before your eyes." Hildegard heard footsteps echo across the floor. She peeked around the tower of trunks.

Desiderata held herself like a warrior maiden. She walked

straight to Queen Bertrada and stood directly in front of her. The Queen Mother took a step back. Desiderata pulled herself up to her full height and glared into the Queen's face. She intimidated all in the room as she looked down at Queen Bertrada.

"Destroy my dress? Ha! I dare you. You'll not touch it, you harridan. Give it to me! Neither of you," she included King Charlemagne in her look, "makes any effort to understand. My mother, my mother made this dress. With her own two hands, she designed it, sewed it and embroidered it for months. How can I tell her I did not wear it?" Hildegard sat down where she was, stricken by the tumult in the room. "Have you nothing to say, Charlemagne?" Desiderata asked, her question hanging in the air. Hildegard could feel her waiting for a response.

"Just do as Ma-Mam asks, Desiderata…if it will keep peace." King Charlemagne sighed audibly, his face a mask of boredom. "I am leaving now. This tumult, this fighting tires me." Hildegard heard his steps move toward the door. She could not believe it. Hilde peeked through the trunks. Charlemagne looked from his mother to his bride, seemingly untouched by feelings for either of them. "Don't be late for the ceremony." His face was a mask. Unbidden, Hildegard thought: I do feel sorry for Desiderata.

"You will see." The Queen Mother made an effort to placate the weeping princess. "Every lady in the court will envy you the dress I offer. It is exquisite, fit for a queen. If you wish to become a queen, my dear," she added, a hint of steel in her commanding voice, "put on this dress."

"I will not—never, never!" Desiderata responded, shaking her head violently. "I will not wear your dress, Queen Bertrada. If you will accept no other gown, go to the priest. Tell him the bride cancels this marriage." She glared into Bertrada's face.

"You will not brow-beat me, neither you nor your son." No one in the room moved. Behind the trunks, Hildegard dropped her face in her hands, willing the argument to end. Desiderata shouted at Queen Bertrada.

"How dare you! Give my dress to me. No one...no one manipulates the Princess of Lombardy. I will not have it! And my father will not countenance it." Hildegard heard feet move across the room; she peeked, again, between the trunks. The Queen Mother held a golden-hued dress out to the Princess. Holding it between two fingers, she acted as if the beautiful cloth had some disease.

"Then, I suppose I will have to accept it. You shame both my son and this court with your deplorable taste." Queen Bertrada answered icily.

"Accept it, you shall." Desiderata's voice was thick with venom. "Beware of flaunting my wishes, Queen Mother. Don't think I accept your direction without question. Understand me." She looked around the room at the countesses, the maids in waiting, even a handful of nuns. "All of you be certain: no one gives me orders—not you Queen Bertrada, not the King, not even the Pope."

"I am surely as strong as you and much younger, Queen M-o-t-h-e-r," she enunciated the word. "Interfere with my wishes, if you dare. Before today's mid-day meal, I shall be the Queen of Frankland. All but the King's soldiers answer to me. Be careful with your commands and directives; I warn you." Two deep lines appeared between Desiderata's eyes; her mouth thinned into a firm ridge. Her cold eyes locked onto Queen Bertrada's face. "You are no longer the only queen of this court." Bertrada nodded curtly, hanging the dress on a peg beside Desiderata. The Princess turned, savoring her triumph—a slight smile on her face, her head high.

"Dress my hair now," the Princess directed one of the maids waiting near-by, "just as we agreed."

Hildegard jumped as Countess Bologna thrust a garment into her hands.

"Put a row of embroidery, vines and flowers, along the hem of this tunic," the Countess whispered. "This must be completed before you go to the ceremony." Hildegard accepted the thread and needle from the countess, sighed, sat back and began to sew.

Looking at the tunic, Hildegard smiled. For most maids, many not accomplished with their needles, this duty would take the rest of the day. But Hilde stitched the same pattern on one of her own tunics and could complete the task quickly. She glanced around the room. There were — fifteen, twenty, maybe more — trunks sitting against the vestry walls, all overflowing with clothing. Interspersed among them were the young women with whom she shared maid-in-waiting duties. Each one was stitching or embroidering some piece of clothing.

"Who do all these garments belong to?" Hildegard asked Marta, the most accomplished seamstress of them all.

"Thank God you were not here for the past two days, Hildegard," Marta answered. "These are the Princess' clothes. Can you imagine? I calculate she does not wear the same tunic more than twice a year." She nodded at the trunks, each filled to the brim. The Countess cleared her throat and gave them both a displeased look. Marta and Hildegard turned their full attention to their sewing and ceased speaking. Hilde sewed steadily, hurrying her stitches but doing the work carefully. Finally, she held the tunic up for the Countess to examine. The Countess checked Hilde's stitches and nodded, pleased.

"Help Marta now, Hildegard. If only we had summoned you the day before yesterday," she added. Marta shot Hildegard an 'I told you' look and smiled.

"You were spared, Hildegard." Marta whispered. "Had I not been in this room, I would never believe the amount of stitching, sewing, and embroidery of the past two days. The noble women, the maids-in-waiting, and Desiderata's entourage of women—all have been busy with wedding-related duties. We sewed, embroidered, redesigned hair arrangements, offered opinions on wedding attire, and admired Desiderata's trousseau. Her jewels, clothing, furniture, tapestries and linens are now re-packed in mammoth trunks, prepared for moving. Unpacking, airing the clothing, putting it away in chests, took an army of maids.

"Hildegard, please look in that gray trunk, the one under the window, and bring me the mauve cloth." Marta directed. Hildegard nodded her assent and, pushing from her seat on the floor, went to the trunk and rummaged around in it. She spotted a piece of mauve linen and pulled at the edge of the cloth. A beautiful, silk scarf emerged from the other clothing. *Oh! It's as soft and slick as it is beautiful!*

"Ahhh..." Hildegard whispered. "This is exquisite, Marta."

"Aye, as is every piece in these trunks. Do you see... the Princess has five trunks—five, Hildegard—of cloth such as this?" She nodded to emphasize her point. "Had she no time to make the cloth into garments before she left home? She must be in some hurry to marry, wouldn't you say?" And Marta grinned good-naturedly.

"It would seem so," Hildegard replied, overwhelmed by the lush color and feel of the scarf. "I must be off, Marta." Hildegard watched for the Countess. "I promised headdresses to one of the young court ladies." Marta nodded, mouthed a 'thank you,' and returned to her embroidery. Hilde slipped from behind the trunks, opened the vestry door and escaped into the corridor.

She hurried to the little staircase and bounded up the stairs. Hildegard quickly evaluated the alcove, verifying no one from below could see into her secret location. She tried to keep her thoughts away from the conflict between Queen Bertrada and Desiderata; but her mind returned to the scene. Her eyes filled with tears as she remembered the dislike of the two women for each other. Considering Charlemagne caught between his mother and Desiderata, Hildegard smiled.

"I wonder how the 'soldier' king will deal with open warfare in his own chambers?" She muttered under her breath. Looking down into the church, she noted the nobles who sat dejectedly; many barely sat upright.

Wine, mead, and ale flowed in the last twenty-four hours, since yesterday at mid-day. Today was a holiday and that, apparently, encouraged everyone to drink. Winter duties and subsequent exercise — mucking stables, riding horses and training dogs, mock fights with sword and dagger, even mending bridles, saddles, and clothing — were all suspended. With much time on their hands and little to do, most of the nobles imbibed early and fell quickly into greedy drinking. The noble ladies, stuffed with tasty, pre-nuptial sweets washed down with potent wine, suffered fates similar to the men, though — mayhap — in less dramatic fashion. Only the bride and her maids, assisted by a handful of noble ladies, remained sober.

The organ music began. Hildegard turned her eyes to the front of the church. The wedding party had gathered there at the door. She heard Charlemagne speak and held her breath to listen.

"It's time to take our positions for the ceremony, Carl," the King said to his brother. "I would not hurry this event; but the time has come. What do I next?" He asked. King Carloman turned to Charlemagne, flashing a smile.

"You're entering the land of adventure, Brother!" Carloman laughed. "None of us realize what we are doing on our wedding day. Believe me, you will not know at the morrow's sunrise either!" All the men in the foyer laughed good-naturedly. They nodded to the King as they reluctantly surrendered their wine cups to the serving maids and turned toward the Church altar.

"Tis not too late, Charlemagne!" Count Janlur laughingly called. "Would you have one of these young men, one unspoken for, take your place this day?" Of a certainty, the count did not want, nor did he expect, a reply. He patted his wife's hand and led her into the nave. Everyone else moved off until only King Charlemagne and King Carloman were left standing together. But Hildegard saw Charlemagne's startled reaction to the count's question. He almost nodded his head affirmatively in reply but caught himself, just in time.

"I wonder; does he not want this marriage?" Hildegard whispered under her breath, looking at Charlemagne anew.

"There you are, Gisela. I began to think I should seek you out." Carl took his sister's hand. They both turned to Charlemagne. "Just say the word, Charley," Carloman whispered to the King. "I'll whisk you away from here, save you from this mistake." Hildegard saw the King's eyes widen; but he nodded negatively. Gisela pressed his hand, seemingly urging Charlemagne to agree. Hildegard frowned, wondering if she heard correctly. She held her breath.

"If I could only make that choice;" Charlemagne responded, looking into their two pairs of eyes, "but I do treasure your concern. It gives me strength." Squeezing Carloman's shoulder and kissing Gisela's cheek, he stepped around them and joined Roland at the center aisle. They walked down the nave toward the chancel together. As Carl and Gisela took a step forward, Carloman crumpled at his sister's feet.

"Carl? Carl? Are you alright?" Gisela bent down quickly, looking into King Carloman's face. "Are you ill, brother? What is it?" She asked, her frantic voice carrying to those near the back of the church. People began turning to identify the problem. Charlemagne turned to come back, but Gisela waved him away.

"I'm fine." King Carloman pushed himself to his feet. "Don't worry," he insisted. "I felt light-headed and, then, found myself on the floor. Nay, nay, please I am recovered. It's merely the excitement of the wedding." He laughed, trying to move people's attention away from his fall. "Come, Gisela, we need to go forward." He placed his sister's hand on his left arm. He bent to whisper in her ear.

"He made his choice, Gisela." Carloman swallowed, forcing down his own regret. "Now he must live a life with that choice. God help him," he murmured.

"We made a valiant effort, Carl, both of us. We offered love, support and understanding—even a way out. It was not enough to move him from his course. For certain, we are blameless in this tragic choice." Hildegard strained to hear Gisela's and Carloman's words. *How I wish I hadn't listened.* She jumped as the huge organ blared forth, alerting all the ceremony had begun. "Tell me if you feel faint." Gisela whispered to Carl. Melodic violins echoed from the walls of the church, marking the triumphant entry of the bride, escorted by her father, the King of Lombardy.

Charlemagne reached the altar. He looked toward the door as Desiderata entered. Hildegard, watching him closely, saw him nod to his Peers and smile slightly to a cluster of countesses. As she watched, she could tell he was unhappy. But he moved, rolled his shoulders, and smiled. Immediately, Hilde-gard noticed the less tense set of his shoulders, his placid stare. He does as he told me. *When unsure of a decision, he deliberately embraces it, closes the choice, and relegates the question to the past.* Tears welled, yet again, in her throat.

Hilde wrenched her eyes from Charlemagne and watched the wedding guests. She forced herself to examine the beauties of the Church. The noble women's silk gowns sparkled in a rainbow of both deep-hued and pastel colors. All of them were equally glowing and beautiful. Their husbands, though elegant in dark tunics and complementary mantles, looked dull by comparison. The men formed a fitting backdrop to the brilliant colors of the ladies' gen-encrusted headdresses and shining belts.

The Peers all smiled, even though Oliver's stance was stilt-ed. Roland was the one to watch; he was the one most privy to the King's thoughts. But Roland frowned. *Who knew what his worried face meant?* Glancing at Roland, the king clasped his shoulder and whispered to him. Immediately, Roland's tense shoulders relaxed; his jaw no longer clenched. The nod of his head to the King was quick and firm. With his eyes on the back of the Church, the King nodded solemnly. There was a quick nod from Desiderius in return. A smile lit the Lombard mon-arch's face as he paused with his daughter, ready to begin the walk down the aisle.

To Hildegard's practiced eye, the countesses' smiles seemed strained. The counts' broad smiles contrasted starkly with those of their wives. Hildegard heard the noble women's com-ments. They did not like this match. They agreed that King Charlemagne went too far afield for a wife. And they were an-gry with themselves. They did not realize Himiltrude was gone permanently when she disappeared. Had they known, they would have championed their own daughters to be the next queen of Frankland.

Of a certainty, they all knew now of Desiderata's temper, as well as her feelings of superiority. Reports of the conflict between her and Bertrada spilled all over the court, from countesses to maids in waiting alike. The noble women were nervous, worried about the peace of their environment. Here in the castle, there were many rooms for escape. This was not so in the tents of their annual circuit.

At that moment, Queen Bertrada peered past Rinaldo who escorted her to the front row pew. "Dear God," Hildegard felt the words escape from her mouth. "She delights in this marriage. Look at her smile! It covers her entire face." Hildegard looked down quickly, ashamed of her judgmental thoughts about the Queen. But the thoughts rose unbidden. She remembered the whispers and endless speculations about the fate of Charlemagne's first wife. "I wonder if Queen Bertrada is responsible for Himiltrude's withdrawal from the court," Hildegard mused.

Entering the altar from behind, a Lombard priest shook the King's hand, smiling at everyone. His dark, purple vestments blended perfectly with the green cedar boughs and red berries around the altar. Just behind the door, Hildegard saw Abbot Fulrad. As she watched, the Abbot attempted to shrug a hand off his shoulder. He seemed agitated. Then, the door behind the altar closed slowly and she lost her view.

At that moment, Desiderata began her long walk down the aisle. The organ music increased in depth and volume. Hilde looked at the bride, watching her closely, trying to find reasons to fault her. But the beauty of the Church, the flickering glow of the candles, the holly and fir branches around the pillars, all seemed to enhance Desiderata's beauty. Brought at great expense, the orange blossoms woven in her hair and their light, heady scent emphasized the perfection of the event.

Surrounded by hundreds of candles, Desiderata seemed bathed in the glow of her pale, blue gown — the color of purity. The wavering flames highlighted the golden embroidery across the bodice, hem, and train of her gown. And gold outlined the turtledoves and quail on her full sleeves. She did well, fighting to wear this gown. Why did Queen Bertrada object to such a gown? Why make such an issue? *Oh, of a certainty, she wants control.* Her hateful words were meant to force Desiderata to do her will.

Desiderata's long, pale, yellow hair curled about her shoulders. The nobles in the Church gazed admiringly at it, wondering if it were as soft as it looked. Because Frankish women covered their hair, the sheer lushness of Desiderata's locks brought admiring glances from everyone, even from her jealous, female acquaintances. Carloman's and Queen Bertrada's gift to the bride — a pair of beautiful, red jasper earrings — dangled from her ears, perfectly matching her opulent necklace and gem-encrusted belt — gifts from the bridegroom. Her hand stroked the necklace, the red jasper brilliant against her white neck and tiny breasts.

The King was elegant in a tunic of dark blue, severe in its narrow cut but startling over his pale blue breeches. His mantle, blue with an emerald green trim, had a collar of snow-white ermine. Hanging around his neck was a pendant of white jasper encircled in silver. The gem symbolized gentleness, Hildegard knew.

Suddenly, Desiderata gave a brilliant smile, her eyes shining. The wedding guests breathed an "ahhh" which echoed throughout the church. She was captivating, a true princess. Hilde moaned softly, wrenching her eyes away from the bride.

As she did, she noticed the brilliance of the other guests.

The Queen Mother, barely glimpsed around Rinaldo's frame, was resplendent in red silk embroidered with silver threads. She looked somewhat like a rather large dragon. Standing next to her mother, Gisela was beautiful in a pale lavender gown. A narrow, purple mantle hung around her shoulders, its side resting inside each of her arms. Her brilliantly-colored mantle had small sapphires sewn along its edge. Mayhap she wore them to highlight her religious vocation. Sapphires are said to mean 'heaven-bound.' They twinkled in the soft light of the candles, suffusing Gisela's face with a mellow glow.

As Hilde gazed down, Gisela looked up, straight into Hildegard's face. She put one hand over her heart and smiled slightly, quickly dropping her eyes once more. Hildegard almost burst into tears.

"To think she feels my pain," she whispered. She felt Gisela's love deep in her soul, renewing her strength. The beautiful silk gowns of the other noble women, their embroidered mantles, their elaborate gem- encrusted headdresses faded from Hilde's eyes. She fumbled in haste for a hand-linen. Gisela's kindness released the tears she suppressed all morning. Hildegard willed herself not to weep. She looked up. The Priest began his homily.

Chapter Eighteen
MARRIED AT LAST

King Charlemagne, flanked by the Lombard priest, Carloman, and Roland -all in tunics and mantles of dove-gray -
looked into the eyes of his people. He appeared to be searching
for someone. His eyes moved all around the church. A final
blast of the organ brought Hildegard's eyes back to the altar.
The priest now turned to give the marriage vows. As Desiderata took her place beside King Charlemagne, the little door behind the nave burst open. Abbot Fulrad hurried to the King.

"Stay! Stay!" He shouted. "The wedding may not go forward; the Pope forbids it." The silence in the Church was total.
No one moved. King Charlemagne stood silent, his eyes boring
into the Abbot. Roland and Oliver looked at each other questioningly. Theo hurried after the Abbot and grabbed him by the
arm.

"What is the meaning of this, Fulrad?" Charlemagne asked
quietly. While everyone's eyes shifted to the Fulrad, Hildegard
caught a glimpse of Theo's face. It was strained and very pale.
He seemed unable to speak.

"I beg you, King Charlemagne." Theo stepped forward. "Do
not chastise the Abbot; he is quite ill." He put his arms around
Abbot Fulrad's shoulders and bent close to his ear. The Abbot
shook his head angrily, doing his best to move away from
Theo. The King looked from one man to the other, paused, and
spoke.

"It's best if you continue, Abbot Fulrad." He suggested very softly. "I'm certain the wedding guests are interested in any message from Pope Stephen." Abbot Fulrad quietened at the King's stare, at his understated words. The Abbot straightened his shoulders and stepped forward.

"Believe me;I am not ill." He glared at Theo and turned back to King Charlemagne. "The Pope does not want you aligned with Lombardy, Sire." He held his hand out in supplication. "He advises you not to move forward with this marriage. The Lombard king is your enemy. You must see what King Desiderius plans...." The Abbot's eyes scanned the church, seemingly aware of his audience for the first time. He lowered his voice. "I warn you, your Majesty; do not defy the Pope's wishes. He is our final authority for God's will." Fulrad raised his hands in supplication to Charlemagne, nodded to the Lombard priest, and, then, seemed to falter. He turned a stricken face to Theo. "Get me out of here."

The King stood where he was until the small door closed quietly behind the two men. Then, he nodded to the congregation and returned to his place in front of the Lombard priest. Looking back, Charlemagne motioned to Desiderata who came to stand beside him once more.

"Begin the ceremony, Father." Charlemagne nodded to the Lombard priest. Just as the King turned his back to the onlookers he caught a quick view of Hildegard. His eyes were soft and kind. She saw him hesitate and, then, look forward to the priest once more. She could feel the embarrassment Fulrad's outburst caused him. His careful words did not erase the bright red color etched on his face. The King nodded at the priest.

The wedding guests shifted where they sat, looked to the neighbor on their right, then to the person on their left. Hilde consciously closed her mouth, her thoughts in a whirl. Her heart fell.

"He will not walk away from this marriage." she muttered. "My hopes are finished."

Hildegard, caught in her own sorrow, did not know — nor would she have cared — how beautiful she looked. But Gisela, seeing her, prayed Hildegard would come to the wedding celebration when the ceremony ended. Hildegard's dark hair shone, picking up slivers of light from the candles. Her figure was enhanced by the low cut of her brilliant brown gown. Sapphires and green jasper decorated her headdress. A string of sapphires hung around her neck, nestled and, then, disappeared between the top mounds of her breasts. Her hair, piled high on her head, escaped her headdress; little tendrils curled around her face. Her mantle, sheer and transparent, had a hem of trailing vines embroidered on it. She looked magnificent! But Hildegard was oblivious to her own looks. She forgot about the Abbot and Theo, about Desiderata and the Queen Mother, as her eyes concentrated on the Lombard priest.

"Do you King Charlemagne of the Franks, Guardian of the Faith, Protector of Widows and Children..." Charlemagne signaled for the priest to dispense with his titles. The priest glanced at Queen Bertrada who glared at him with a frown. But Charlemagne nodded for him to proceed so he began again.

"Charlemagne, King of the Franks, do you vow to honor, to succor and to protect Desiderata, Princess of Lombardy, as your lawfully wedded wife? Do you pledge your troth to live with her in harmony, to forsake all others, and to build together a Christian home? Will you defend her with your strength, protect her with your sword, and cleave only to her as long as you both shall live?"

"...aye, aye and aye!" King Charlemagne responded, winking at Carloman who smiled back. The priest, bowing first to

King Desiderius and to Prince Adelchis, finally turned to Desiderata. Having known her since she was a child, he spoke softly to her, smiling broadly.

"And Desiderata, Princess of Lombardy, respected maid of Pavia, espouser of Christ's teachings, resident ruler of little Pavia castle..." Charlemagne's eyes threatened the priest who quickly cut off his recital of Desiderata's magnificence. "Princess Desiderata, do you freely accept Charlemagne, King of the Franks, as your lawful husband, pledging him your loyalty, your undying support, and your constant concern for his person, as well as for the affairs of his kingdom? Do you promise to honor him, to obey him, and to cleave only to him for as long as you both shall live?"

"Aye, I do." Desiderata answered, a slow smile spreading across her face.

"With the authority of the priesthood and the support of the Holy Father in Rome, I pronounce you man and wife." The priest intoned, speaking slowly, prolonging his final sentence as long as possible. With the priest's last syllable uttered, King Charlemagne turned from the altar, offered his arm to his new wife, and began quickly walking from the Church. Hildegard released her breath. The onlooker's eyes followed the King and his new Queen down the aisle. Hildegard looked down and realized the bride and groom were just below her. She heard Desiderata whisper loudly.

"Charlemagne, please!" Desiderata complained. "We must not run from the Church. Slow down! I fear I will fall on my face!" At her outrage, the King slowed his steps, smiling and thanking the endless line of well-wishers along the aisle. Despite his bride's injunction, the King still left the Church quickly. He hurried his bride to the banquet hall and the celebratory mid-day meal.

As soon as the servants saw the King and Queen step outside the Church, they served the wedding banquet. Hundreds of people milled about, waiting for food and drink, thankful for a happy respite in the midst of the Frankish winter. Children consumed prodigious amounts of fruit tarts, crystallized sugar candy, fried dough sweetened with honey, and honey-crystallized nuts, completely ignoring the food being served.

"Come, come," Roland hurried the celebrants along. "Everyone come to the banquet room! The wedding meal awaits us all." People rushed toward the tables, eager to share in such a sumptuous repast. The wedding banquet consisted of six major courses. First, the servers brought a hearty, meat-based soup which contained carrots, onions, leeks and silvers of mutton and pork, spiced with garlic. Next came the tantalizing aroma of fresh-baked breads: loaves of white and wheat, round loaves of rye, and thick, fruit breads—all offered with a variety of cheeses and preserves: blackberry, red currant, and fig.

Before the guests could identify all the cheeses, much less taste them, the serving maids and squires stumbled to the tables, carrying roast pork, quail steeped in wine, venison, mutton, and roasted peacock. The women were offered quail, turtledove and partridge, allowing for their less hearty appetites. But many of them, having delicately sampled the small birds, called for pork, venison, and mutton as well. All around the hall, trenchers sat, piled high with meat, spiced eggs, and cucumber pickles made crisp in their brine soakings.

As soon as the servers brought the meat, others brought in a smorgasbord of vegetable dishes. Simmered cabbage with celery seeds, carrots drenched in butter, leeks and roasted onions, potatoes garnished with parsley, beets, and parsnips. Various seasonings—ginger, cinnamon, and coriander from Arabia and the Far East—complemented the dishes.

The winter season made fresh fruit impossible, but dried fruits seasoned all manner of tasty sweets: apple bread; custards laced with liquor and dried pears, peaches, and blackberries; crystallized fruits and nuts; fruit tarts; nut-covered slices of dough; pumpkin and squash pies; apple pies and berry cobbler.

With each course, the revelers consumed vast quantities of drink. Italian wines sloshed in the flagons, as did mead, ale, and lager. Cow's and goat's milk, in various fermented forms, found its way to the banquet tables. Finally, nuts: walnuts, pecans, even pistachio nuts - available only to the wealthy -dates, red currents, raisins and mild cheese completed the feast. Hot, mulled wine accompanied this course.

In less than an hour's time, the moans and lethargy of the early, now stuffed, diners surrounded those still eating. The nobles, countesses, and visitors alike made a good accounting of themselves. Even though they drank a great amount of spirits — first one kind, then another — the guests also ate continuously, stuffing their faces with little restraint. And of a certainty, those unfamiliar with the capacities of their own stomachs found themselves retching up all which seemed so delicious a short time before.

The women of the court, the soldiers' wives, visiting noble's wives and daughters, churchwomen who traveled far to witness this grand affair, all ate with abandon. Seldom was so much food available and offered to everyone. Since the meats, pies, and milk custards could not be safely stored, each celebrant consumed as much as he could possibly swallow. The guests literally ate until the food disappeared. Those hearty souls who were not unconscious from all the plenty, those who already rested to renew their appetites, and the few who ate with reason began to enjoy the entertainment which a wedding always provided.

Minstrels, jugglers, and musicians performed as the guests began to eat; but, up to now, they were little noticed. Now, their hunger slaked, individual celebrants laughed and brought others' attention to the entertainers' efforts. The liveliest activity was dancing, always enjoyed by all levels of the population, as it was now by those at the wedding. Musicians hired and recruited from near-by villages moved into the banquet room as squires removed tables and benches. The King's guard removed those already sleeping, and the dancing began.

Feeling he would be well-advised to keep active by dancing off the food in his over-stuffed stomach, Charlemagne asked Desiderata for the first dance and, then, excused himself. From that moment, he danced with women guests but not again with his wife.

"I feel the wine burning off with the speed of my steps," the King laughingly said to Rinaldo who whirled a young woman around. "This excuses one from talking and does make the women happy." Whirling his partner, Rinaldo nodded in appreciation as he stepped energetically alongside the King.

"Aye, Sire, I think this the most pleasant activity of your wedding." Rinaldo said as he turned to the delighted face of his companion. "All the women want to dance." He wished to take the opportunity with as many of them as he could. He admired the King's graceful dancing, especially the ease with which Charlemagne maneuvered one partner to the edge of the dance floor, bowed, and held out his hand to another.

"Strange," Rinaldo commented to his partner as he watched King Charlemagne. "I would wish to dance only with my new wife...if it were my wedding day." His companion nodded and replied.

"My thoughts exactly, Rinaldo. But, of a certainty, kings are

215

not like other men. And King Charlemagne may feel it his duty to assure a good time to everyone." she replied.

"…at his own wedding?" Rinaldo asked, shaking his head in dismay at people's expectations. "I'm thankful I will never be a king, then." Even as the dancing sobered the younger people, Charlemagne saw the older nobles become ever more incapacitated as they continued to drink.

"Of a certainty, they do drink more than they dance." He observed, wondering how many flagons his guests consumed. Momentarily without a partner, the King decided to hunt a vintage Riesling for himself. As he turned toward the wine cellar, he saw Hildegard slip out the hall toward the west wing corridor.

"I've not spoken to her since I delivered the news of my wedding. I am eager to say hello."

"Hilde! Hilde!" Charlemagne called. "Come, I've been waiting to dance with you." He held his hand toward her. Hildegard stopped and looked at him in obvious amazement. Her face, already pale, grew whiter still.

"Surely, you jest." She answered as she fled down the corridor. King Charlemagne, so popular with the ladies, was speechless. His eyes followed her closely until she was out of sight.

Hildegard increased her speed as she entered the corridor. "I did my best to avoid him," she mumbled to herself. In her agitation, she almost stumbled, so completely did the tears cloud her eyes. "I cannot believe him so unfeeling, so unaware." She noticed the library door, stopped suddenly, and went into the chamber. Locking the door, Hildegard sat in front of the low-burning coals of the fire.

"What do I do?" She asked the silence. "I must plan my life, now that my dearest dream is sundered." She dropped her face in her hands, waiting for the tears and loneliness in her heart to subside. I have so few choices, Hildegard thought. *I am caught here until spring when I may return home. I must exhaust myself with difficult, tiring work or I shall go mad from heartbreak!* She stretched her hands out to the fire, realizing they felt as cold as the outside wind. She rose and poured wine from a flagon on the work bench. Sipping the wine slowly, Hildegard sat looking into the newly-roused flames. She startled at a knock on the door.

"...aye?" She answered.

"Hildegard, it's Gisela," came the response. "Let me in." Hildegard unlocked the library door and hugged Gisela as she stepped inside.

"Are you well?" Gisela questioned, a worried smile on her face.

"I am, Gisela." Hildegard replied. "Thanks for your concern. But...why are you here?"

"I saw my stupid brother ask you to dance," Gisela answered, "and knew you were in need of comfort. So, I came." She reached out to hug Hildegard again, kissing her cheek gently. In order not to burst into tears at Gisela's kindness, Hildegard forced calmness on her face.

"I came here to outline my options. Charlemagne forbade my return home." Hildegard said as Gisela shook her head. "And so, I make my plans. I was thinking of you, Gisela, and my other friends here at court: you, Abbot Fulrad, Lord Oliver, Jocelyn, Lord Roland - though I know him less well than the rest. You appear to delight in being around me. You even seek me out, both for my opinions and my company."

"Of a certainty," Gisela confirmed her words. "We all love you, Hilde."

"With such special friends," Hildegard nodded in acceptance of Gisela's affirmation, "I must have some unique gifts or you would not waste your time with me. I even thought of my brother, Geoffrey's, words to me. 'You are intelligent, beautiful, honest, and filled with goodness. How could anyone not like you, not wish to be around you?' She quoted him, smiling as she remembered her brother's intent face.

"I thank God for you and Geoffrey every day, Gisela, especially lately!" She admitted. "You reassure me of my value and of my attractiveness. I need to remember that...just now." Gisela gazed into Hildegard's eyes. She spoke.

"Just because my brother is a fool, Hilde; you must not devalue yourself," Gisela said bluntly. "Men make terrible mistakes, you know."

"Mayhap. I thought I knew one of them well; but, obviously, I did not. Give me advice, Gisela. I beg you. Listen, please, to the choices I have. Do you have time?" She worried. "The wedding celebrations are still going..."

"My greatest pleasure would be to listen to your thoughts, Hilde," Gisela answered. "The games and dances go overlong for my taste." She pulled Hilde on a bench and sat down beside her. "Outline your choices for me."

"I constantly ask myself what I should do," Hildegard admitted. "My life must be constrained from now on....until I can return home to Swabia and to my parents. Let me explain my reasoning." She took a deep breath and squeezed Gisela's hand. "I could still go home. It would be easy to slip away, to claim an illness in my family. But leaving unexpectedly may irritate Queen Bertrada or Charlemagne or both of them." She glanced into Gisela's face and saw only understanding there. "They might punish my parents or react against Geoffrey's rule in Swabia. So, I decided returning home now is not a good idea." Hildegard felt apologetic, talking this way to the King's sister. But she knew Gisela would see her point of view.

"For the same reason, I shall not speak of this to Poppa or to Geoffrey; it would only increase their worries." She shifted on the bench.

"I will continue my activities as before, just with a clearer mind and a less happy heart." She smiled sadly. "I will continue to train the pups, fulfill my duties to Jocelyn, but will reduce my participation in court affairs." Hildegard held her hand up, stopping Gisela's comment. "I don't have the heart to join the social activities, Gisela. My mind turns weak at the thought of interacting with the young noble women and the maids-in-waiting. I need time to heal...away from these shallow people." She dropped her eyes to the floor, afraid she spoke too bluntly of court members.

"I get nothing positive from them, Gisela." Hilde tried to soften her words. "They do so little for others. Their lives are filled with gossip, plans for their own entertainments, criticisms and petty jealousies."

"Why do you think I want to be a nun?" Gisela chortled, laughing deep in her throat. "Aye, court life does seem a deadly existence to me as well." Encouraged by Gisela's comments, Hilde spoke again.

"I would find more useful work, Gisela; but the seneschal and the Queen Mother discourage my interests. We maids may fetch, serve, cower and flatter the nobility; but the Queen Mother wants no true contributions to the life of the court, not from us." She sighed deeply, discouraged at the narrow activities deemed appropriate for her status. Hildegard rose from her chair and walked about the library, pausing at the rolls of parchment along the walls, pulling out one roll and, then, another.

"Why, this is a mess!" She exclaimed to Gisela. "There is no order to these parchments. It's almost impossible to find a particular one. Someone should straighten these out; arrange them in some way." She stopped as her words filled the room. "Oh! I could do that. Here's a task begging to be done…with no one interested in undertaking it." She glanced over at Gisela who was nodding eagerly. "I'll start tomorrow. And, then, I'll identify the parchments devoted to plant lore. I can read them after I've gotten them all arranged. And I will index their location by subject and number, Gisela. Then, anyone interested in a particular one will be able to find it easily." Hildegard smiled slightly, relieved at finding an immediate task, one to fill her mind and help her ignore her heart's pain.

"There's always more to do, Gisela. I'll arrange the library parchments and train the puppies - mayhap some older dogs, too. And I will continue to design and sew clothes for the children of the farm workers. You know about it, don't you?" She asked. At the negative shake of Gisela's head, Hildegard explained.

"It's become my most successful idea," she said. "I noticed the countesses and the young noble women throw away clothing which is perfectly sound. At first, I asked them for the discarded clothing. Sewing in the night, I turned the clothing into garments for the children of the farm workers. They have so little, Gisela." She sighed and continued her explanation.

"The court ladies wish my embroidery on their tunics and gowns, so now we exchange goods—embroidery stitches for castaway clothing." Hildegard's voice strengthened. "The countesses were so positive about my embroidered designs they flooded me with their castoffs. Some of the clothing appeared almost newly made to me, but I used it well. Then, one or two of the countesses came to watch me make over the garments. They wanted to copy my designs in their own handiwork. But I tell you Gisela," here Hildegard tried not to giggle, "many of these women have clumsy fingers." Gisela laughed with delight, having seen her own mother try to embroider and fail miserably. "Because I received so many tunics, breeches, and mantles, I enlisted the aid of some other maids-in-waiting. Now, a bevy of us embroider for the nobility and get discarded clothing in return."

"Hilde, how wonderful this is!" Gisela was impressed. "You must feel very happy, seeing all those children wearing your creations!"

"Aye," Hildegard confirmed. "We all have a very satisfying relationship—clothes shared from one to another." She smiled, gratified Gisela approved of her project.

"I have no worry about you, Hilde." Gisela told her. "You will overcome this unfortunate episode with my brother and move on. You are quite a remarkable young woman, you know." She hugged Hildegard, impressed at her initiative and her enterprising mind.

"My wish is to use my time wisely, Gisela," Hildegard confirmed. "If I stay busy, the days will fly by. Spring will come and I will return home to Swabia. I have learned much here at court and will make a different life for myself there." She looked into Gisela's face. "My love for your brother will fade. With time, life will brighten and, once again, the future will promise much." She nodded solemnly as tears ran down her cheeks. She wiped the tears away, shaking her head.

"The truth is, Gisela," Hildegard continued, "the man I love is gone. Charlemagne is lost. He replicates the old ways, returns to the worst aspects of a traditional ruler: blind obedience to past choices; mindless acceptance of advice from counselors less able or less visionary than himself. He chooses to maintain the court as it has been, rather than how it might be. He forgets or gives up on the new world he envisioned, the world he described to me."

"I pray he finds himself again." Gisela replied, wiping away her own tears at Hilde's characterization of Charlemagne.

"He is not the man I thought, Gisela." Hildegard admitted. "Mayhap, he never was. I didn't see his over-dependency on others' opinions, his fear of challenging tradition, the easy sacrifice of his own decisions to placate another. He is a servant to those he fears to displease!" Hildegard stood up, struggling with her thoughts. "Oh, Gisela, I am well out of his life!" The two young women stared into the flames. Even as the warmth stole over their faces, their legs and feet felt chilled.

"I wonder who Charlemagne really is." Hildegard said, very softly. Gisela's mouth trembled. She would have refuted Hildegard's comments had she not feared, also, for her brother's future.

"He does listen over-much to certain others," she agreed, "and to the wrong others. If he would heed Oliver's words, so much would not be risked. Of all the Peers, Oliver is the least militant, a thinking man. But Charlemagne discounts his opinion for Oliver prefers compromise to battle. We must pray Charlemagne comes to his senses."

"Aye," Hildegard replied, "and soon. But I must strive to think of him no longer, Gisela. He must be in my past. I start a new life. I must move my thoughts away from him...and away from this court."

"I wish you every success, Hilde. Just know I will always be your friend." Gisela reassured her. "I so wished to be your sister, as well." She lifted her eyes to Hilde's. "We shall be sisters, anyway. We don't need my brother for that." Gisela wished Hildegard a good night and left the library. Hilde picked up her headdress and started to follow Gisela out. But, hearing loud talk from the corridor, she quickly closed the library door and stood rooted to the spot. She recognized Charlemagne's voice.

"I would talk with you now," a husky, female voice declared. "You pile mistake upon mistake." The voice- the Queen Mother's voice – reflected impatience, tinged with contempt . "The Abbot escaped from the guard room. Even now, he flees to Rome! He'll criticize you to the Pope, describe your failings in intimate detail; declare you unfit—as a Christian—to rule. What will you say to Pope Stephen? You had best begin planning a response. The Pope may well pay us a visit, journey to this court." Even through the wooden door, Hildegard could feel the glacial thrust of Queen Bertrada's words.

"Be quiet, Ma-Man. I will not hear a single word from you." King Charlemagne declared quietly, ignoring her barbed comments. Hildegard stepped closer to the library door, checking the lock. "It is your insanity which plotted to get the Abbot drunk and detain him. The blame for his leaving rests squarely at your feet. Do not continue with this, Ma-Mam. I will say things you do not like."

"Pshaw!" Queen Bertrada answered. "There is much, indeed, you may say. None of it will amount to a good sentence, Charlemagne. You're unable to make obvious decisions. I must do all I can...in fact, I keep busy trying to repair your mistakes." Her footsteps moved forward another three steps. Hildegard heard the King's steps move backward, away from his mother.

"Why didn't you restrain the Abbot, when he came to you waving the parchment from Pope Stephen? He was livid, demanding we cancel the ceremony. Can you do nothing to silence the foolish man?" She asked intently.

"What would you have me do?" The King asked. "...cut off

his head; imprison him in the castle dungeon?" His voice was subdued. Defeat hovered on the edge of his words. Hilde heard him breathe out slowly. "Come, Ma-Mam, filling him with ale was your doing. You took charge as he left the chancel." Charlemagne ground his boot on the stones.

"You could not wait; let me speak with him! Ohh, Nay! Now, the Queen Mother takes the King's job as well as running everything else!" There was a short silence. "You do stretch my patience."

"I care nothing for how you feel." Queen Bertrada retorted. "I'm protecting the realm; I do what I must."

"You protect nothing, you pompous woman!" Charlemagne raised his voice. "It's your actions which created this situation—your damn betrothal, not mine! Your damn promise—a lie, in fact—swearing I approved this marriage! Ha! You imprison me. You are, of a certainty, a master of deceit." Hildegard heard the grinding of his heel against the floor tiles, once again. "I defy the Pope only because you place me in an impossible situation. For the integrity of my realm, I must honor your word." He thrust his words at her. "My vow would be worth nothing did I refuse this marriage, the vow you so casually make!"

"And you plotted with my most devious enemy to entrap me. Desiderius wants the realm. You give him every opportunity to take it. Take it with the birth of a grandson and with my murder soon after. In your pride, you're a total fool!" Charlemagne stamped his foot and left. Queen Bertrada stood alone. Hildegard held her breath until the Queen's footsteps, too, moved away.

Chapter Nineteen
Mistakes and Regrets

"Congratulations, your Majesty," Count Janlur called as King Charlemagne hurried into the banquet hall. The King pulled his mind from his mother and nodded to the count. "You most assuredly have a beautiful bride. Just raise your hand when you're ready to move to the bridal chamber, Sire," he added. Winking broadly at Charlemagne, he motioned to several men standing nearby. Charlemagne saw Roland, Oliver, and Theo join the group and smiled inwardly.

Carrying the couple to the bridal chamber often gets out of hand, the King thought. He remembered ribald comments, non-stop singing and coarse jokes from years past. *I must hurry it. Desiderata will be offended by the boisterous, bawdry comments and jump to unfortunate assumptions. God! How I wish we could forego this tradition today!*

Hilde's sad face crossed his mind, bringing her pain to him afresh. Bile rose in his throat. May this day end soon, he prayed. Charlemagne beckoned slightly to Oliver who came immediately.

"Sire," Oliver asked, "is there anything we may do for you? Please accept my felicitations at this happy time, your Majesty."

"Thank you, Oliver. Along with those good wishes, I ask a boon of you. Please ensure the path to the bridal chamber is swift. As soon as Desiderata and I cut the cake, in the general confusion, move us down the corridor." Charlemagne held Oliver's eyes. "I shall get her in place for the cake cutting. Don't linger to allow coarse jokes and suggestive leers, if you please." He looked earnestly into Oliver's face, not allowing for any misinterpretation of his words.

"Of a certainty, your Majesty." Oliver answered. "Trust in our speed and skill. Roland and I will do it ourselves. Raise your hand when you're ready, Sire." Best to get it over with, Charlemagne thought.

"Perfect," the King replied; his thoughts grim. *Never did I dread taking a woman to bed.* Shaking his head, he made his way back to Desiderata and whispered in her ear. She nodded agreeably at him, took his hand and moved toward the towering wedding cake.

As they arrived for the wedding, guests from all over the realm took a small, round cake to the cook room. By tradition, the baker arranged the small cakes into one massive tower. Now, standing four feet high and three feet at its base, the 'cake tower' graced the center of the main banquet table. Early this morning, the cook spooned a pale, lemon glaze over the huge cake. The reflected glow of the chamber's candles drew everyone's eyes to the confection.

Seeing Charlemagne and Desiderata approach the table, people gathered around them. To ensure good luck in their marriage, Charlemagne and his bride must kiss each other over the cake without toppling it. Charlemagne took Desiderata's hand.

"Never fear," he reassured her, "I'm a good leaner." He smiled at everyone as he steered his bride to the far side of the cake. Desiderata beamed at her guests. Her face, softened by the candle light, no longer showed its calculating look, its impatient intensity. Truth is; she had what she wanted.

She managed to marry the most powerful man on the continent. She became a queen, an important queen, as soon as the marriage ceremony ended. Now, Desiderata relaxed. Controlling the court and her new husband could begin tomorrow.

Desiderata stepped onto a small trunk which a squire quickly placed beside the banquet table; and, beaming at her groom, the bride leaned over the cake toward the King. From the opposite side, Charlemagne leaned toward her. It was now that his height helped them. He leaned over and stretched his torso over the cake for Desiderata to bestow the expected kiss. She pecked his lips, but then kissed him soundly a second time as the on-lookers roared their approval. Desiderata handed Charlemagne the first slice of cake which he shared with her. As they exchanged bites, serving girls appeared to pass out the delicacy.

"I hope no one breaks his teeth on the nuts inside the cake." Charlemagne whispered to Desiderata. She laughed gaily. She bit one of those nuts herself. She nodded, smiling, as the guests called out their approval of the sweet and their good wishes for her marriage. She turned to one of the serving girls.

"Hasten, do!" She directed. "My ladies sit there, by the fire pit. Take slices to each of them. They are impatient for the confection." A small girl standing at the base of the cake looked at Desiderata in disgust.

"Tell them to get their own cake," she cried. "I've waited sooo long!" Her mother, deep in the crowd, called to her.

"Anja, be quiet! You shall have your cake. Do not speak so to the Queen." Her voice trembled, her fear for her child palpable. Desiderata stared at the small girl and smiled. The smile did not get to her eyes.

"You," she pointed her finger, "shall have no cake this day, not until you learn some manners." All movement, the talking and gentle shoving around the cake, ceased immediately. No one breathed. Everyone stood shocked at Desiderata's words. The silence lengthened.

There was a bustle at the edge of the circle. Lord Oliver excused his way through the crowd, moving toward the small girl. Taking Anja's hand, he picked her up. Holding her in his arms, he spoke to her alone.

"You shall have my cake, little one," he soothed, rubbing her slight shoulder and smiling into her face. "Don't look so worried. Do you like lemon? That's the taste on the outside of the cake. Come, let's you and I get a slice." Oliver smiled at the on-lookers as he made his way to the cake. With his movement, most people around the cake turned and walked away. Many refused the cake offered to them. Desiderata stood beside her wedding cake, isolated as the people around the cake thinned out.

As soon as Desiderata kissed him, King Charlemagne turned to stride about the room, acknowledging the shouted congratulations. He responded enthusiastically, hoping to out-shout some male voices he heard from the edge of the crowd. From the far side of the room, though, like voices broke through the muffled noise of the gathered celebrants.

"Ride her as hard as you like, Sire; you're the master!" A drunk noble roared above the crowd. A young, arrogant voice spoke next.

"As your friends carry her on her back, so should you keep her until the dawn. On the morrow, she will be pliable."

"I do envy you!" Another voice shouted. "That long hair, those slender fingers, what might that body might do as you mount..." The voice faded away.

Ignoring the sexual comments, Charlemagne kept his face immobile, trying to look superior to the blatant words. But their crudeness boiled his blood. Looking back, he saw Desiderata standing alone. King Charlemagne raised his right arm over his head. Immediately, he heard the noise of hurrying feet.

Desiderata looked over her shoulder, trying to identify the sounds. A frown crossed her face; and, then, a short cry of panic burst from her mouth as Roland and Oliver lifted her above their heads. Just beyond, Rinaldo, Adelchis, and Theo lifted Charlemagne. All moved quickly. The lifts were so carefully coordinated and so smoothly executed that most of the merry-makers did not realize when the bridal couple left the banquet room.

"Relax, relax," Oliver whispered as Desiderata began to fight them. "This will be easier if you don't thrash about. This is the bedding, your Majesty. You must get through it; calmly and quietly are best." Desiderata, through her panic, registered Oliver's voice and ceased her struggling.

"What is this 'bedding'?" She asked, gritting her teeth. "...some barbaric custom of this court?" Desiderata vaguely remembered hearing her ladies talk about the bride's journey to the bedchamber. Her breath caught. "If he dares violate me, the Church will geld him," she muttered to herself. The rhythm of the men's feet calmed her; her mind unlocked and took notice of her surroundings. Oliver and Roland held her high, well above the heads of the crowd following them. The corridors appeared to contain more furniture than she remembered. There were benches, flower- bedecked hangings, traveling trunks, leather carrying bags, and shields all along the walls...all the better to slow those in the corridor, Desiderata realized. She relaxed her leg and arm muscles, trusting Oliver and Roland to bear her safely to her bedchamber. But at her door, they kept walking.

"Where do you take me?" She demanded.

"To your bridal chamber, my Queen." Roland replied as they turned the corner and ducked into a room. Desiderata did not struggle; she lay still until Roland and Oliver set her on her feet.

"The King comes momentarily," Oliver announced. "Be ready to lock the door as soon as he stands!" The two men hurried from the room. Desiderata stepped behind the open door, ready to slam it as soon as Charlemagne's carriers delivered him.

At that very moment, Hildegard slowly opened the door of the library. She heard heavy footsteps; many of them hurried down the corridor. "Oh, nay," she exclaimed, as she realized the 'bedding' process was in progress. Trying to keep from gasping, refusing to let her mind think of the bridal chamber, she paused in the open door.

"I will not get caught in this frenzy," she murmured. "I cannot bear it!" She looked around quickly, noting the speed and crush of people moving toward her. She decided to stay in the library until the worse of the activity in the corridor was over. She locked the door and, picking up a sheaf of parchment, sat to read, doing her best to ignore the stampede outside. She heard feet in lock-step pass the library, taking the King to the bridal chamber. Then the corridor erupted; shouts, hoots, and talking increased in volume as people streamed down the corridor - following the King and his bride.

With Charlemagne in the chamber, Desiderata closed the library door quickly. As she did, Roland hung a flower garland on the outside door handle of the bridal chamber.

"No one will dare to enter now." He smiled at Oliver, nodding at the garland, "…as if anyone would have so much courage." The two Peers laughed together, hurrying back to the banquet hall.

"I have no stomach to hear the unsolicited, bawdy advice from this crowd. Shall we try to deflect their enthusiasm?" Roland asked. Oliver nodded in agreement. He turned to face the growing crowd.

"Come, come!" Oliver motioned to the people streaming down the corridor. "Refreshments are waiting in the banquet room!" He whispered to the guards behind him. "Stop them. Don't let all these people into this corridor. Suggest the happy couple took the other hallway. Block this one off." Oliver turned to Roland. "Hurry; move quickly toward the herb garden. Many will follow us because they saw us leave, carrying the princess."

"Aye." Roland agreed. "They've no idea which chamber holds the bride and groom. Here, let's hurry!" He half-ran back to the corner, heading toward the banquet hall and the entrance to the herb garden. Many people, spotting the two men, sped after them. The revelers' enthusiasm cooled rapidly, however, as they hurriedly opened the door and ran into the snow and wind of the herb garden. Lord Roland and Lord Oliver ran toward the far entrance. The crowd surged in that direction.

"The silence in the corridor is even harder to bear than the noise." Hildegard muttered as she heard the crowd turn. But, try as she might, she could not keep her mind on the celebrating crowd. Nay, she imagined King Charlemagne taking Desiderata into his arms. Not knowing the coolness between the two, Hildegard imagined sweet, gentle kisses and paced lovemaking, imagined passion far in excess of its reality. Despite her brave words to Gisela, she loved Charlemagne and lived her own dreams, responding to her yearnings for him, the one she only partially acknowledged before today.

"I can only dream of touching him," she murmured as she thought of his broad shoulders, muscled legs, and massive chest. "Why couldn't I be his bride - I who love him so dearly?" She moaned, unable to think of his body while her heart broke. Tears filled her eyes, ran down her cheeks. She beat her hands against the library table, paced around the chamber, trying to still her despair. But, as quickly as she thought her feelings under control, her eyes would betray her, and tears rained down again.

Through the lonely feelings of abandonment, Hildegard heard other footsteps. They, though, did not know the location of the bridal chamber and loitered along the corridor or rushed quickly away, searching for the procession, she assumed. Hildegard considered drinking the ale sitting on the library's table.

"Mayhap it will lift my spirits," she whispered. "It surely was effective for those inebriated people outside." She stepped away from the door as she heard stumbling steps outside.

"Wait, wait! We're supposed to sing to them!" Three soldiers shouted.

"Open the door!" A drunken reveler cried.

"We have to give Queen Desiderata a Frankish welcome! Come, come!" One matron screeched to those behind her. At her side, young women threw flowers, even though no one saw the bride. "Where is she, where is the Princess - I mean, the Queen!" The effects of the day's drinking, begun soon after the early morning repast, contributed to the general uproar.

"We must take her belt!" One of the tipsy young women called out.

"We have directions and suggestions for their love-making!" The voices calling down the corridor erupted in a frenzy of noise once again.

"Bed her quickly," someone suggested.

"Be gentle, King Charlemagne. That will reap you more than a brutal assault." A quiet, female voice suggested.

"Demand she do her part! Hold her as close as possible!" A voice called out.

"Tear off that fine gown and show her who will rule!" The suggestions hammered Hilde's ears. She folded in upon herself, trying to live through the pain flooding her heart.

Oliver and Roland, in the meantime, circled the castle and came back to the bridal chamber's corridor. They gathered other Peers from the banquet hall and led them down the corridor, hurrying to the corner beside the bridal chamber. Once positioned, Oliver locked his left arm with Roland's right and extended his right arm to Rinaldo. Theo motioned the other Peers and nobles into line and stood in front of them.

"Quiet! Quiet!" Theo shouted. "Everyone move back into the banquet hall. The food and drink are there. The King and his bride deserve a little respect. Come, do as I ask. Move back! Move back!" Theo turned a deaf ear to the cat-calls the drunks directed at him.

"Hell, we just want to have a little fun!"

"You damn Peers…you always ruin the merriment! I have a suggestion for the King. He must spring upon…" The man's voice was lost as someone muffled his words.

"Let me in the room! I'll handle the bride. She'll be begging for the King's touch by the time I finish…" That voice faded away.

Drunken objections and a few curses continued; but the crowd, caught now in the Peers' slow movement down the corridor, turned and moved back to the banquet hall. Oliver breathed a sigh of relief, thankful the Queen heard only a little of these barbarians' comments about the marriage bed.

"Thank God, they do heed Theo," he whispered to Roland. Roland nodded silently, aware of the strained feelings between the two newly-weds and wondering about Desiderata's view of this 'bedding' tradition. "I do not envy the King his duty this day. This uproar cannot have aided any romantic inclinations."

In the library, Hildegard heard the revelers pass by, yet again. But, finally, the corridor was silent. She felt cold all over, cold and exhausted. The feeling was not a chill.

"I will surely freeze to death, so empty is my heart." Hildegard leaned toward the fire, warming her hands. She stood to turn her body back and forth in front of the weak flames. Realizing the coals burned low, she added one, two, three fat logs to the fire; watched the wood smoke, smolder, and then, finally, burst into flames. How long she watched, mesmerized by the burning, she could not guess. She half-lay on the bench, feeling her heart—wounded as it was—continue to beat. She sighed, resigned to the tears coursing, yet again, down her face.

"I will finally," she promised herself, "finish with all these tears. A body can, surely, have only so many of them." This day, steeped in emotion and, for Hildegard, in regret exhausted her. Her bench—cushioned with soft wool and an embroidered cover—was soft; the fire was warm. Hildegard was asleep in moments. When she awoke, it was twilight, though she could hear the still lively music and the continuous clink of dishes. "Can they be eating again?" She raked her hands through her hair and replaced her headdress.

"I can safely return to my chamber now. I'll go through the

garden. It will be cold; but, this way, I'll see no one." Hildegard pulled on her mantle.

King Charlemagne sat on a bench, staring into the fire pit. He heard his bride disrobing behind him, laying her wedding clothes across her trunks. At Desiderata's plea for help, he unlaced the several layers of her clothing and, then, excused himself so she might gather her courage. She admitted her fear to him quite frankly. And he vowed to take care with her, to lead her gently to their marriage bed. But, she seemed to take a lengthy time to disrobe. He looked around at the bedchamber. The nobles ladies spent much time and effort in decorating it. The room was over-warm to him, the fire blazing. On the sleeping bench were the skins of two black bears, glorious in the blackness which picked up the firelight. Dried rose petals, lavender, and honeysuckle blossoms crunched underfoot, a gentle scent wafting from the stones as they walked. Although he did not look in the baskets, he knew there was food from the midday banquet there on the little table. Of a certainty, several flagons of wine sat around the room.

"Would you like wine, Desiderata?" The King asked his bride. "Someone wishes us not to run out of drink! There are six, separate flagons that I can see." He chuckled to himself, waiting for an answer from his new wife. She said not a word. He stooped to take off his foot coverings and began unwinding his leg coverings as well. *I wonder how long it takes for her to remove her clothes. I suspect she's deliberately dawdling.* He opened his mouth and heard her voice.

"Are you coming to bed, husband?" She asked.

Chapter Twenty
BROKEN HOPE

As Hildegard walked quickly and silently toward the herb garden, King Charlemagne stood, pulling his tunic over his head. He could not understand his reluctance, his lack of interest in this new wife. She was comely but, despite this, he had no interest in her. He did not consider her desirable; he did not, even, want to bring her pleasure – much less get pleasure himself. He took off the rest of his clothes and walked over to the sleeping bench. Desiderata's eyes widened as she examined his shoulders and his chest. She looked quickly down his body and, then, swallowed. She moved her eyes quickly to his face.

"You must be cold." She said. "Come here; it will feel warmer between the linens."

"I expect it will." Charlemagne replied, almost laughing aloud. "I will do my best to be gentle, Desiderata." He added. "There will be some pain for you, but I hope there is pleasure as well. Would you like me to rub your shoulders and your back? Often times, touching in that manner helps a woman to relax...and increases her pleasure." Desiderata turned with her back to him. He almost didn't hear her words.

"Just get between the linens. I do not expect pleasure and, of a certainty, no happiness in this...thing...we share." She said. "But it must be done. Undoubtedly, I'll be able to tolerate it; women have for many centuries. I need no reassurance from you, Charlemagne. I will do my duty. And, nay, I do not expect…nor do I want…to enjoy this love-making."

"As you will," Charlemagne answered. He slid on the sleeping bench and gently pulled his new bride into his arms. He slowly traced the line of her neck with his finger. Then, he gently kissed her back from the right shoulder to the left one. Her body jerked and, then, stiffened at his touch. Knowing the first time would, likely, shock her and, perhaps, bring pain, he settled in for lengthy titillation. Always had he brought passion to his love-making: his own, of a certainty, but awakening a woman's passion was an aphrodisiac for him. Because he was unhurried and gentle, women said he had a magic touch, able to increase their passion and make them eager bed partners. He stroked Desiderata's back and, then, gently pulled her shoulder to turn her to face him. But she shrugged off his hand and burrowed into the linens. For the second time, he kissed her back all over; lightly touching her side, moving slowly toward her breast. But she did not respond…just lay there like a piece of wood.

Initially, he felt hopeful, certain his sexual experience could overcome his bride's reluctance. But he quickly learned better. Desiderata had no interest in making love. She was an unwilling bed partner. The King pushed the linens off his body and rolled to the edge of the sleeping bench. He might as well get up.

Understanding his movement, Desiderata turned on her back and reached out to stroke his chest. He groaned and pulled her to him, pressing against her breasts. But, as he slid down and reached to pull her atop him, she withdrew her hand and spoke.

"Your chest is massive, Charlemagne." She whispered. "Being in your arms will always make me feel safe." She snuggled closer, trying to seem eager. Her hand moved up and down his side; but it was a nervous gesture, not meant to be suggestive or stimulating. Charlemagne kissed her earlobes, nuzzled her neck, and pressed his lips against hers. She submitted to the kiss but gave no answering kiss of her own. He tried to decide if he should kiss her again when she sat up, pulled her bed tunic over her head, and slid back under the linens.

All of a sudden, his hands were full of her. Her body, though, still did not respond. It almost seemed she was checking off specific behaviors: gently stroking her bridegroom's chest, giving a compliment, accepting a kiss, removing her sleeping tunic. Charlemagne smiled but kept myself from laughing out loud. What is the point of this? He asked himself. *My little dog, Foxi, gives me more real affection than my new wife.* He wished he had left the sleeping bench at the first thought.

But what if she thinks him incapable of begetting a child? She must know all that entails. After all, the single reason for this marriage is a child: an heir for him, a grandson her father will manipulate, a queenship for her. So, a child it must be. He dared not shirk away from that. If he did not make love with her today, of all days, when would she let him back in her bed? He must do the deed and be finished with it…with this calamity.

Although not done before, Charlemagne steeled himself to get through the love-making. He reached for his wife, a woman for whom he had no feeling. He could say she was beautiful, as did all his Peers; but he was completely untouched by that beauty. And he hesitated and, then, made to leave the sleeping bench again.

Immediately, Desiderata lay across his chest. Her hair draped over his face. He closed his eyes and imagined Hilde was there with him. He wanted Hildegard; she was the one who heated his blood, the woman his heart cried for. He lay still, transported to the orchard where he and Hilde stomped grapes together for making wine. He felt Desiderata shift and, in the next moment, she straddled him. She made abrupt movements with her hips. Her naked flesh against his body, the suggestive thrusts of her hips, her breasts barely touching his chest fed his sexual need. His breathing increased as the new bride sped up her movements. He felt his body's need building. Without thinking, Charlemagne pressed his lips against hers, moving his body below her. In a moment, he recoiled in pain. She bit him!

"No need to draw blood, my dear." He said to her as she stared into his face.

"You know little of kissing. I can attest to that." She caught her breath, apologized and was, of a certainty, embarrassed.

"I'm sorry, Charlemagne. Please, I don't know how that happened." She was horrified at the blood on his mouth. "I didn't mean to..." She buried her face in his chest. As he felt Desiderata's hair tickle his chest, his mind flew back to Hautgard's manor. He could feel Hilde's streaming curls as she rode beside him there. Her bright, laughing face pulsed through his body.

He kissed Desiderata demandingly, all the while thinking of Hildegard. He moved his hands all over Desiderata's body, lightly stroking breasts, thighs, belly - the places that should give her pleasure. But, though she pressed against him and gasped, it was all a sham. She had no true interest in coupling.

Before he thought, Charlemagne entered her and began his rhythmic moving. He wanted to finish, just do his duty and finish. Her eyes flew open as she felt the pain. But she did not cry out nor ask him to stop. She closed her eyes and seemed to leave her body, just gave in until he was done. He did not wish to talk with her or to hold her. He did not whisper sweet words in his bride's ear, nor did he love her again in the night.

Some time later, he stroked her hair, brushed it back from her temples and massaged the back of her neck gently. She was asleep in a few moments. He slipped from the sleeping linens and sat before the dying fire. His despair was complete, even before he pulled on his clothes.

"My body betrays me." Charlemagne mumbled. "I must make some peace with this or my life will be hell from this day forward." He vowed to come to his wife's bed to make a child. It could be a quick deed and, then, he need not 'bother' her again.

"What a hell of a life!" He exclaimed. "I will pray that God, in His wisdom, will make our firstborn a son. Mayhap one more son will be enough. My dream of daughters I must forego." He sighed deeply. "And a true wife I forego as well. There is no wife in this bride, no meeting of life minds, no true care one for the other. God help me!"

The King turned back to his new wife, watched the rise and fall of her breath. He kissed her forehead and left the linens. Sitting before the fire pit, he reviewed his wedding day. Truth be told, he had no joy—only frustration, worry, anger, and regret. But he did try; he did his marital duty. If he were really blessed, Desiderata was with child. If not, he vowed to produce a son.

"I shall feel little for the child's mother. And time will make no difference. I am to be lonely until the day I die." He thought, again, of Hildegard and wiped tears of regret from the corners of his eyes. He looked around for his tunic.

"Hell," he swore quietly. "I might as well dress. Sleep is unlikely to come this night." The King shrugged on his tunic, donned a pair of breeches, and pulled his mantle over his shoulders. He slipped out of the chamber quickly, remembering to leave the flowers hanging on the door. *No one needs to know I've left my bride.* So dejected, he could not even smile at the irony of it all.

"Men would say I married the perfect woman. But despite her beauty, her breeding, her wealth, and her position, she is nothing to me."

Knowing he would find solitude and some measure of peace away from the castle, the King headed for the stables. He cut through the herb garden to shorten his walk and, more importantly, to avoid wedding revelers. No matter what he did, his thoughts returned to Hildegard—the tilt of her head, the way her mouth crinkled when she argued with him, her delighted laugh when he called her on her weakest point. Thinking of her, he smiled, remembering her enthusiasm, the joy she found in little things.

"I must get Hilde out of my mind." Charlemagne admonished himself. "These yearnings must stop. My God! Am I so weak I cannot forget the charms of a young woman I have not even bedded?" He compared his wife and Hildegard. Desiderata came up wanting. It was then he remembered Roland's question those months ago. He wondered at its import.

"What kind of woman would you like, Sire?' Roland had asked.

"One with great passion for living, Roland; one with an enthusiastic spirit." He had answered. "I find the typical woman's conversation boring. I cannot admire any woman whose interests are limited to her beauty, clothing, and entertainments."

"You must look long and hard for an educated woman, Sire,

one with skills you admire." Roland had laughed. 'But, I daresay you will find her.'

"Aye, I found her," the King admitted to himself; "but I let her go." He shook his head in regret and opened the door to the west side of the herb garden. At the icy blast of the wind, he stopped to rethink his route.

As Charlemagne hesitated on the steps into the herb garden, Hildegard hurried down the corridor from the library. Exiting the castle, she took care the door did not squeak as she entered the herb garden from the east. Bending over to balance in the fierce wind, she made her way across the garden, walking toward the west wing. She stopped. There at her feet lay a body, a light scarf spread across its face. *It must have dislodged as he fell.* She noticed the richness of the man's clothing. Hildegard knelt, feeling for the pulse at the man's neck. She pushed the scarf away and gasped.

"King Carloman?" She asked, amazed and frightened to find the Charlemagne's brother unaware, lying on the ground. His pulse was weak but steady. "Dear Father in heaven, don't let him be dying." The King was so gracious to her and spoke so kindly of her parents yesterday night that Hildegard could not bear the thought of his passing. As her cold hands rechecked his pulse, King Carloman's eyes fluttered. Hildegard called his name and shook his shoulder.

"King Carloman? It's Hildegard. Sire. Are you able to stand? I must get help; I cannot lift you alone." Hildegard's heart dropped. *What is he doing, lying here in the snow?* Hildegard shuddered in the cold.

"No need for that, Hildegard," he answered clearly. "Nay, if you will bear my weight, let me lean on you, I can stand. Here, wait a moment." King Carloman sat up, placed his hands to the right of his body and pushed to his knees. "Now, may I have your arm?" She bent down, stretched out her arm, and locked her knees in place as he slowly pulled up. When he was upright, he let go of her arm and sighed.

"You see?" King Carloman said, smiling into her face. "I made it. Now, I will lean on you, just a bit. Please help me walk to my bedchamber."

"Of a certainty, Majesty," Hildegard replied. "But I must fetch a healer. You are ill, Sire. You need someone to ..." Her voice trailed off as Carloman interrupted her.

"Nay, nay, I was lightheaded, only for a moment," he answered. "Believe me, I am capable of walking. I just need a little help." Hildegard extended her arm. He held it and took a small step. Hilde moved her feet to match his tread. But he leaned to one side and would have fallen if she had not grabbed him. As his full weight bore down, though, she could not hold him upright and was forced to ease him slowly to the ground. Hildegard's mantle flapped in the wind as she knelt by the King. At that very moment, she felt uneasy. A figure loomed over them both!

"Please, please, aid me." She said, looking up, trying to identify the large figure bending down toward King Carloman. "King Carloman is very ill! I'm unable to get him into the castle alone," she explained. She knew her words were frantic, but she feared Carloman was dying. "He's so weak."

A large man—all she could tell in the wind and snow—moved to the other side of the King's body, raising him much more easily than Hildegard could do. She looked up to suggest they co-ordinate their efforts and gazed into the eyes of King Charlemagne.

"Thank goodness you're here, Sire!" She almost burst into tears. "Your brother is very ill. I found him lying on the path. He is unable to stand alone and tried to walk. I cannot hold him so eased him to the ground. It's so cold, Sire." Her heart quaked. She was distressed. *Of all the people who might help, it's Charlemagne who appears.* How she hoped not to see him again. To cover her reluctance she began apologizing for her lack of strength. "I did try to hold him, your Majesty, believe me." She assured Charlemagne. "But his weight is more than I can manage." Her voice broke.

"Hildegard?" Charlemagne could scarcely believe it was she. "I was just thinking of you. Thank God you happened into the herb garden. I remember…you have some knowledge of the healing art, do you not?" He was not certain if it were Hilde's presence or the blinding snow; but he blinked rapidly to stop the tears which rose in his eyes. He forced his thoughts back to the garden.

"What are you doing out here? I thought the palace still celebrating…" Damning himself for referring to his marriage, he stopped speaking. Seeing Hildegard's distraught look, he realized Carloman was her only concern.

"Hurry," Charlemagne urged. "Slip your arm around his back; I'll do the same on this side. Together, we can get him into the castle. His bedchamber is but two doors down from this one into the garden." He saw her nod as her arm went around his brother. "One, two, three, lift," the King counted.

Responding to Charlemagne's voice, King Carloman made a huge effort to help them; but he was so weak he could scarcely hold his head upright. King Charlemagne and Hildegard gripped him and walked slowly toward the castle door. Once inside, Charlemagne took all the weight of his brother on himself.

"Hurry, Hilde! Find a healer and bring him to Carl's chamber. I'll get Carl into his room and onto his sleeping bench. Tell the healer that Charlemagne summons him. Hurry; do not linger!" Hildegard nodded and went flying down the corridor. Charlemagne half-carried Carloman to his bed-chamber, surprised to find his brother's family gone. Then, he remembered. Gisela and Queen Gebnega were hosting a party for the visiting children. "That must be where everyone is."

"Carl?" King Charlemagne called his brother's name. "Can you hear me? I'm going to get you into your sleeping linens. Nod if you understand me." But Carloman did not respond. He was unconscious. Charlemagne removed Carl's wet mantle and his foot coverings and got him into dry clothes. The door opened and Hilde rushed in.

"I left word for the healers, Sire. No one is about but the serving boy. Everyone is still celebrating. I told the young lad to send at least two healers as soon as possible." She paused to catch her breath. "We must warm your brother as quickly as we can."

"Aye," Charlemane agreed. "What do you think is the quickest method — lay him down by the fire?"

"Nay, Sire," Hildegard answered immediately. "Nay, someone must... you must get in bed with him. Lie beside him as closely as you can. And take off your mantle, your Majesty." Charlemagne's eyes bulged.

"What did you say?" He asked, staring into Hildegard's face.

"Lie down beside him," Hildegard repeated. Then she looked into the King's face. She laughed. "...body heat, your Majesty. The best warmth for him is body heat and you should have plenty of that." She sobered when she saw Carloman's pale face. "Take off your mantle and those foot coverings; they're wet. Lie on your side beside King Carloman. I'll cover you with linens and wrap some coals for his feet. Please, Sire, do this now." *I wonder why he refuses to take such simple direc-*

tions.

"As you say, Hilde … I shall do whatever you advise." He yanked his mantle off, throwing it beside his brother's. He slipped his right arm under Carloman and pulled his brother close to his body. "Carl isn't conscious, Hilde. I wonder how long he's been lying on the path? How long were you there, helping him?"

"I? …Just as I came into the garden I saw him. I know not how long he was there." Hildegard answered. She walked over to the side table and sniffed a leather tankard. "Ahh, here's some warm tea. Sire, I'll hold it for you to drink. It will maintain your body heat and add to the warming of your body against King Carloman. Here, let me add a bit of honey in it for you." She took the tea to King Charlemagne and held it steady as he took a long drink.

"It is warming." Charlemagne agreed. He moved his head to take another swallow and, finishing it, smiled his thanks at Hildegard. She added more water to the pot and set it just inside the fire pit.

"We'll need more tea...for you and King Carloman," she decided. "Now, let's see if he injured himself in the fall. He has no wound, does he?"

"Nay, no wound. But he arrived here ill, Hilde." Charlemagne replied. "He took ill on his journey to Lombardy. He stayed at the Pavia court for some ten days before coming on to us. When he arrived, he said he was recovered. But he was exhausted and weak, despite his brave words. The last few days he rallied...or so we all thought. "As Charlemagne held his brother up, Hilde examined Carl's chest and his back.

"There are no open wounds on his torso, but his chest is hot to the touch." She explained, frowning. "We must lower this body heat. It is strange; his arms and legs feel cold, but his head and torso are hot." She nodded at Charlemagne. "As you hold him, your body will spread even warmth throughout his. Hold him close a little longer. I will get some snow."

"Snow?" The King asked, "...whatever for?" He looked completely lost. "I don't understand, Hilde. Snow, for what reason?"

"Oh, snow to cool some water..." Hildegard smiled. "We need to wipe his body with cold water. That will reduce the heat of the inner body."

"...truly?" King Charlemagne asked, doubt coloring his voice. "How can a mere wiping do that?"

"Not one wiping, your Majesty," Hildegard explained. "We must cool his body with constant bathing; it does provide some salutary effects."

"I will start the bathing," Charlemagne declared, admiring Hildegard's matter-of-fact description. "This is not a goodly occupation for a maid." Hilde startled, looked quickly into his face.

"You do jest!" She laughed, realizing he did not. "A body is a body, Sire—no more, no less. I do admit our bodies look somewhat different. You are bigger on your bottom, the better to sit long on a horse, mayhap." She grinned at him. "And I am bigger on the top, the part that feeds a babe; but all in all, our bodies are not that different." She chortled at his gaping face. "Cooling the body is the goal. Who provides that cooling is of no consequence." she said calmly. Hildegard spied a bucket on the hearth. She picked it up and nodded encouragement to the King.

"Please hold him close while I'm gone, Sire," she directed. "I shall return immediately." Hildegard went directly to the herb garden and filled the bucket with snow. Rushing back, she met a nun in the corridor.

"Have you experience in nursing the sick, Sister?" She asked.

"Of a certainty, my Lady," the nun, Ruth, replied. "My vocation is healing, especially in the breathing illnesses."

"Then, come with me, please," Hildegard begged. "King Carloman is unconscious in his bedchamber. He seems very ill." She took the nun's arm, pulling her toward Carloman's room.

"I'll be happy to help," Sister Ruth responded, matching Hildegard's pace.

Chapter Twenty-one
LIFE AND DEATH

In the few moments Hildegard was gone, King Charlemagne lived a lifetime of grief. "You and Hilde were in the garden together," he mumbled into his brother's chest. "She has been scarcely seen in the court; but there she is, come to your rescue. You did tell me your marriage is unhappy; but you would not..." His words stopped. His brother did not hear him. "Nay, he would not deny his marriage vows." The King paused as he uttered those words. He, himself, knew feelings for a wife might die, but a child's needs often bound its parents together, even after their feelings for one another changed. He shook his head. *Nay! Nay! Hilde does not flirt with married men nor try to advance their opinion of her. There is nothing between these two.* He sighed, struck by his next thought.

Why do you care? Hildegard is free to follow her inclinations; you killed any chance of retaining her favor. You gave her up. If Charlemagne were not holding his brother, he would have risen from the sleeping bench. But as it was, Carl's weight penned him down. He continued to analyze his sad choices.

"Oh, God," Charlemagne murmured. "I want Hilde's approval. I want...I want...Hildegard's love!" As he admitted this aloud, the door opened quietly and the love he gave up, the one he denied, re-entered the room. Hildegard glanced at Carloman, checking that all was the same. She gasped and held her breath. The King's eyes gazed at her, filled with such longing.

"Hilde?" Charlemagne struggled to call her name. "Hilde? I cannot tell you what I wish…" He allowed his words to trail away. *I must NOT tell her how I feel.* Charlemagne warned himself. *It's too late, too late for us.*

"Your Majesty," she asked carefully, "are you well? Do you feel chilled?" She placed her hand on Charlemagne's forehead, not understanding how he could become ill so quickly. At her touch, he sucked in his breath. Hildegard felt the quick intake and looked into his eyes. Her eyes widened; she shook her head and moved away.

"You frighten me, Sire," she admitted. She nodded toward the nun at the door. "This is Sister Ruth. She's going to help with your brother; she has healing experience." Hildegard added the final sentence, thankful to deflect her thoughts from Charlemagne's yearning look. "You should access King Carloman's health, Sister. He is very weak but I cannot judge the seriousness of his illness." She deferred to the nun. "Mayhap, it's time for me to warm King Carloman." Charlemagne shifted at her words, shaking his head.

"This is a novel method to warm a patient." Sister Ruth smiled. "I applaud you, my Lady. But, for deep heat, we must bathe him. I shall do that." She volunteered. "If you can prepare some coals…" Her voice trailed off as she saw the linens on the hearth, spread out, waiting for the coals to be placed in them.

"Aye, Sister," Charlemagne spoke. "Lady Hildegard told me we needed to wrap coals. I waited for her return to do it. Besides, I've warmed Carl all I can. Will bathing not undo this warming?" Charlemagne extricated himself from the bed linens, stood up, and walked toward the firepit.

"I will warm my body here before the fire," he explained.

"A warm heart I may have; but for now, it needs help." He looked over the nun's head and winked at Hildegard.

"Aye," Sister Ruth answered, "warm yourself. The Lady and I will place coals alongside your brother's body. The coals maintain internal heat as bathing will relieve his skin of its burning," she explained. Hildegard, trying to ignore Charlemagne's wink, placed coals in the linen. The wink confused her. *Winking? He has scarce left his bridal bed; he should not play with me. He does not realize my heart rejoices at his every move.* She looked again at the linen under the coals. *Would a thicker weave be more beneficial in holding the coals?*

"Of a certainty, there must be woolen linens here somewhere," Hildegard commented.

"Aye," King Charlemagne replied. "They are stored in the trunk, there in the corner," he pointed. Hildegard opened the trunk, smiled with delight, and lifted out three additional woolen pieces. Underneath, she found a more closely woven cloth than that of the wool. She held it up to the nun, a questioning look on her face.

"Monks beat the threads." The nun explained. "Then, they cover them with the clear liquid which comes from the joints of butchered animals. That helps the cloth shed water." Hilde looked at Sister Ruth.

"Do you think this cover will retain the heat of the coals?" Hilde asked. "…better than the thin linen, I mean?"

"Aye," the Nun replied, smiling with approval. "Let's try it."

"We'll have the 'coal logs' ready in just a moment." Hildegard remarked, as she poked two coals away from the edge of the linen. Charlemagne watched Hildegard, drinking in her face, her hands, her mussed hair, curling around her shoulders. When the Sister turned to spread the second linen, he dropped his eyes to the floor.

"The coals are scorching this cloth," Hilde said to Sister Ruth. "But the slick linen is not smoking. We must use it." Charlemagne arranged one end of the coal log around Carl's arms and shoulders. Hildegard spread one around and over his chest.

"If you will remove your brother's clothing, Sire," Sister Ruth said, "I will bathe him." Charlemagne nodded. He removed his brother's breeches and, next, the bands around his legs. Hildegard held the sick king's shoulders up as Charlemagne quickly slipped the tunic up to his neck and, then, over his head. Taking a hand-linen from her sleeve, Sister Ruth dropped it into the bucket and squeezed the water from it.

"Hold him, Sire," she suggested. "The cold of this cloth will be a shock to his heated body." At the first cold wipe, Carloman's eyes fluttered; his body jerked, but he did not waken. After a few wipes, he was as still as before, but breathing with greater difficulty.

"Where are the damn healers? Why does it take so much time for them to come?" Turning to Hildegard, Charlemagne asked: "You did tell the fool this was an emergency?"

"Of a certainty, I did, Charlemagne." Hildegard reassured the King, regretting she called him by name. I must be formal with him, she reminded herself, no personal response. "I have some herbs in my bedchamber, Sister. Do you know their uses?" Sister Ruth looked uncomfortable but nodded. "I have studied some with my father's herbalists and recognize the breathing difficulty King Carloman is having." Hildegard continued. "There are other things, though, about his sickness I do not understand."

"Go. Bring the herbs, my Lady," the nun urged. "We must use every bit of knowledge to help him." Hildegard cocked her eyes at Charlemagne, waiting for his permission.

"Hurry back." The King begged, nodding his approval. "I feel insecure here without you." Hildegard sped to her chamber, snatched up her herb apron and rushed back toward her patient. I wonder where everyone is, Hildegard thought to herself. In her walk to the herbalists' chamber and during her return, she met no one. She saw two serving maids returning to the cook room, but not a single noble or visitor. *They are either asleep or drinking still.* Hildegard decided as she slipped back into Carloman's sickroom. She placed her pocketed apron on a side table and unfolded it.

"I need to heat water...to steep the herbs." She explained to Charlemagne and Sister Ruth. Before she extracted the herbs, she pulled the hanging kettle from over the fire, filled two flagons, and added more water. As she dropped pinches of herbs into the flagons, King Charlemagne came to stand beside her. He reached for her hands, but Hildegard shied away. She could not risk her reputation because he needed reassurance!

"Would you mix this potion, Sister?" Hildegard asked the nun as she plucked other herbs from her apron.

"Nay, my knowledge is meager, Lady," Sister Ruth replied. "You have more experience than I...with herbs. You mix, but I will aid you in any other way."

"The herbs will make a tea for King Carloman." Hildegard explained, surprised the Sister demurred. King Charlemagne walked over to the table to examine Hildegard's apron.

"What is this, Hildegard?" He asked, fingering her apron. "Is this your way of carrying the herbs?"

"Aye, my way of transporting herbs from the woods and fields or to take them with me, if someone needs a concoction." She dropped her head, suddenly shy. "The herbalists' roll their herbs in packets. But they are cumbersome. They must recog-

nize the herbs through heavenly influence," she joked, "because all those rolled packets look the same to me!" She opened
one pocket.

"I like storage places," she admitted. "So, I put my herbs in
little pockets which I stitched on this over-tunic. Then, to remind myself, I embroidered the name of each herb on its pocket. It's pretty clear, anyway, because the herbs are arranged by
name. But my apron works for me and allows me to carry
herbs wherever I go. It serves its purpose well."

"You are knowledgeable about herbs, then?" The King
wanted to know.Hildegard's practical approach fascinated him.
"This is clever …to put the name of the herb on its pocket."
When caring for battled-wounded soldiers, he often saw the
herbalists smell their rolls to determine the herbs inside. They
have no organization, he thought.

"You see," the King continued, "your apron is much like
my spice chest. I designed a spice chest for the court's mobile
journeying around the realm. Each small drawer contains
enough spice for the cooks — spices for soups, meats, stews, and
'sweet delights.' It serves until we are back in our winter castle.
Your apron is the same, though on a small — let me say —
medicinal scale." Charlemagne beamed at Hildegard, impressed by the things he learned about her. He smiled, though
his heart squeezed inside his chest. Another skill, she has yet
another skill I never imagined, he thought. He stifled a groan of
despair as he glanced at Sister Ruth.

"You two do, indeed, have like minds," Sister Ruth complimented. Hildegard bobbed a quick 'thank you' and praised
the King's spice chest. She needed to deflect the King's interest
from her. His stares made her uncomfortable.

"You should see the spice chest, Sister Ruth," Hildegard
said. "And we have moveable ones to hold our jewelry." She

looked at Charlemagne eagerly, ignoring the shadow which crossed his face. His present interaction baffled her, so different was he from the man who announced his betrothal to her. *I shall pretend I don't notice.* She promised herself.

"Did you know? Many of your food spices are here in my apron as well, Sire. Herbs are versatile; they can be used to treat illnesses, to enhance the flavor of food, even to calm the spirit. For now, I'm going to rub King Carloman's chest with this oil which contains peppermint. It will help reduce the fullness as he breathes. And I'll ask the cook to add turmeric, ginger, and garlic to his next meal. They will reduce that wooly feeling in his nose."

"We need not worry overmuch about the herbalist, Hildegard," the King observed. As Hilde talked, he became more subdued. His thoughts overwhelmed him. *I cannot bear it! This woman is perfect for me and I gave her up. I have denied my love for her. I have, instead, married a mean-spirited princess who appears to know nothing much about anything.* Charlemagne sighed and attempted to control his voice, despite his despair. "You know as much as they, probably more." He said, beaming his appreciation of her skill and knowledge.

"Oh, thank you, Sire. But I will be more comfortable if the herbalists come quickly. There are many ailments I know little about treating," she explained.

She placed her hand on Carloman's forehead, smiling at his cooler body. "Our hot coals and wipe-downs appear to be working. Would you wipe him down again or should King Charlemagne do it, Sister Ruth?"

Hildegard frowned, suddenly realizing Charlemagne's appreciation of her herbal knowledge. *But, even that would not recommend me to him. He cares nothing for skills and know-how; he married for political gain. But I did not bring an alliance so I could never be his wife. After all, I am not a princess.*

"I'll do it, Sister Ruth. It matters little who does the wiping." The King said. Sister Ruth nodded, handing Charlemagne the bucket containing the snow-cooled water. The King turned to Hildegard. "I wonder, Lady Hildegard, would you grant me a boon?" He saw her hesitate. "It is a small request."

"Of a certainty, I will," Hildegard replied; "you are my King after all. I may not refuse you."

"Not as your King do I ask it," Charlemagne answered, "but as your friend. Would you end this formality in your speech? It makes me uncomfortable and we know each other too well for that." Hildegard shook her head at his words.

"Forgive me, Si…we are acquaintances, rather, I think. But I will endeavor to honor your preferences." Sister Ruth chuckled a little.

"It is often true. None of us has deep knowledge of anyone else," the nun offered. "Seldom do we even know ourselves. Knowing a person often takes a lifetime. Don't you think so, your Majesty?"

"It is true," King Charlemagne agreed. He dipped the hand-linen into the snow bucket and wiped his brother's body. Hilde kept him at arm's length, but he earned that. After he bathed Carl, Hildegard offered him tea, laced with a pinch of lavender and hyssop to ease his spirit and his throat. She saw him swallow repeatedly as he watched his brother's still face.

I can offer him so little comfort, Hilde thought. Although King Carloman's body is cooler, he labors much harder to breathe. *I believe he's failing. I will not lie to Charlemagne, if he asks.* Sister Ruth announced she was going to find the herbalist.

"We, Lady Hildegard, have done all we know to do. The herbalist lingers…to King Carloman's detriment. Where is he? He should have come by now." As the door closed, King Charlemagne and Hildegard moved to the chairs by the fire. They sat side by side.

"The herbalists are most likely drunk," Charlemagne mused, staring into the fire. At Hildegard's gasp of surprise, he nodded quietly. "Truly. Every one, with the exception of you, Carl, and me, has been drinking for hours. I daresay, even Sister Ruth's companions have imbibed deeply since early morning." He grinned at Hildegard and walked over to replace the linen which slipped from Carloman's body. The King returned to the bench in front of the hearth. "I am certain it is the same with the herbalists. After all, anyone who is sick today does not even realize it. Their minds are pickled by strong drink." Charlemagne shook his head. He did not understand the attraction which wine and mead had for the average man. He spoke soberly.

"It would be wise to mistrust any treatment an herbalist might suggest today," he said, "if we value the life of my brother." He settled into his seat. "Rest easy, Hilde. I appreciate your efforts. You did all that you know. I know that." Charlemagne reached over and squeezed her shoulder. Hildegard startled and leaned toward the fire. Seeing her discomfort, he dropped his hand quickly and stared steadily into the flames himself.

"How ill is he, really, Hilde?" The King asked. "It looks very serious to me." Hildegard caught her breath. She dreaded this question, ever since she realized the depth of King Carloman's illness, there on the garden path. *I must speak the truth. He must understand his brother is seriously ill. He may not recover.*

"He's very ill, Sir....Charlemagne. This heat of his body...there is some sickness within. He's fighting; but he's very weak. I do not know if he has strength enough to overcome this. He looked well, some five days ago, when your party went on the hunt," she remembered. "But you said he was ill when he arrived here."

"Aye. The cold and chill of the journey from Lombardy were severe, probably weakening his already over-taxed strength." Charlemagne rubbed his eyes. He stared into Hildegard's eyes, his grief emblazoned on his face. "I pray we do not lose him, Hilde. I need Carl. We've just begun to understand…and to value…each other, after years of avoidance and resentment."

"He's a young man. Pray this weakness is temporary, hope he'll improve steadily over the next few days. He does have a strange rash, though, on his back; and the texture of his hair is odd—a straw-like feel which is not natural." She described additional symptoms which she could not interpret. There was no pattern she could discern. Some symptoms were always evident in specific illnesses but she could not find them here. The King grabbed Hilde's hands, his voice catching as he spoke.

"Hilde! Hilde, what will I do?" Sadness and worry both sat in his eyes. "I need Carl! I cannot rule this realm alone. He is young and makes foolish choices; but we share the realm. It needs us both!" He squeezed her hands so hard Hildegard winced at the pressure. But she did not pull her hands away. "Carl and I together, we don't make one of Poppa. He had such great hopes for us, for what we might create together. He never imagined the loss of either of us, not for many years." The King sighed and covered his face with his hands.

Charlemagne rubbed his temples, his hand shaking ever so slightly. "I've lost Poppa and, now, Fulrad as well. The Abbot fled to Rome, undoubtedly to report to the Pope. I've never seen him as angry as he was at the wedding ceremony." The King gazed out of the window into the darkness.

"You've not lost Abbot Fulrad, Charlemagne. The Abbot

loves you well. He'll say little to the Pope. You cannot seriously distrust him!" Hildegard almost laughed at his foolishness.

"Fulrad will tell the Pope I'm a poor Christian, not fit to rule the realm." Words tumbled from his mouth. "He'll criticize my temper; my decisions; the lack of solemnity in the church; the large number of people lingering, doing nothing in my court. I spoke with him about the need for an heir...one who could command the allegiance of the soldiers. He completely rejected my argument." The King's voice rose. "Fulrad will poison..."

"Nay, he will not!" Hildegard objected, interrupting the King. "He is a priest, your Majesty! He will tell the Pope the truth, as he sees it." The King stared into her face. "Each person has his own version of the truth or, at least, his interpretation of it. Fulrad will report his truth to Pope Stephen. Only if he does not know all of the truth—mayhap your truth, Sire—will he neglect to say it. He'll share everything he knows with Pope Stephen. Is there information you deliberately kept from him...something related to this marriage to the princess?" Hildegard stopped speaking. Charlemagne's face was so hopeful.

"Abbot Fulrad will not betray you, Charlemagne." she reiterated.

"I did fear him false, Hilde." he admitted, her words soothing his troubled mind.

"Has the Abbot ever turned against you? Has he ever taken another's side?" Charlemagne did not answer. "Think of the Abbot's service. Analyze it. You will seldom find him wanting." She finally smiled slightly. "Only if he thinks you commit some grave sin will he judge you." The King nodded his head and, then, bowed it. "Mayhap, you listen overmuch to others who do not support your interests as well as the Abbot?" Charlemagne did not answer; but Hilde felt him turning the question over in his mind. She turned to check on King Carloman.

"Forget these thoughts; use your energy in helping King Carloman recover. He may need to stay here for an extended visit...through the spring perhaps, long enough to rebuild his strength completely. You must stay positive."

Charlemagne raised his eyes to her face. Each moment he saw more and more of Hildegard's value. He stood and walked slowly to the casement overlooking the courtyard. *She is everything I dreamed of. Here is the woman who truly would have shared my life!* He moaned softly. Hearing him, Hildegard thought his pain was worry for his brother. She crossed the room, patted his shoulder, and went to Carloman's bedside.

"Let's change the coals," she told him. "Let's not sacrifice the good we have by chancing a chill."

"Aye," Charlemagne agreed, standing up. "Let me put coals in another set of linens, Hilde. You rest here for a bit." Hildegard nodded, happy to let him retrieve the coals. Crouching by the fire, he picked the coals out, placing them in a deep trencher. "I would share some information with you, Hilde. It might better explain Carl's weakness. But I make this request of you. Tell no one." He waited for her response and hearing none, looked toward her.

"I would not be privy to secrets, please," Hildegard replied, thinking of her attraction to the King. "Secrets are often misconstrued and leave much pain in their wake."

"True," Charlemagne agreed, "but this information is important." He did not wait for her to demur again. "Gisela thinks someone deliberately and slowly poisoned our brother. She speculates the poison weakened his lungs and, thus, he cannot overcome the fullness there." Charlemagne searched Hildegard's face. "With your herbal knowledge, can you evaluate the likelihood of Gisela's suspicions." Hildegard stared into the King's face.

"…poisoned?" She repeated the word. "King Carloman has been poisoned?" Understanding this was Gisela's opinion, Hildegard believed it immediately. Gisela was very circumspect. She would never mouth such a suspicion, even to her brother, if she were not positive of its truth. But there was no way to determine the type of poison and, without that, any effort to counteract the poison might further undermine Carloman's life.

"Could she identify the poison she suspected?" Hildegard questioned.

"Nay. She could not name it; but she believes poison is inside him still. His looks, his inability to walk, his very fragility — those are the things she noted to me. It is only a suspicion." He added. "But I want you to know…in case someone else in the court falls ill."

At that momnt, two herbalists burst into the room. They went directly to King Carloman, felt his brow and listened to his breathing.

"He seems not very ill, Sire," the older herbalist pronounced. "His body is over-warm to the touch, true, but not enough to be concerned. His color seems quite normal." He looked at King Charlemagne, smiling as if the King were a dullard. "I believe you worry unnecessarily." He reached to the table to steady himself.

"Unnecessarily? You drunk fool!" The King shouted. "Get out! Get out, you son of a whoremaster! This lady and I watched for hours, warming and cooling - struggling to keep my brother alive. Where in the hell have you been? We summoned you hours ago, more than once! I should burn you at the stake!" He glared at the herbalist who took one look at the King's face and fled the room, followed rapidly by the other one. The door opened wider. Roland peered in.

"Is anything amiss, Sire?" He asked, nodding to Hildegard.

"...aye! Damn it, aye!" The King answered. "Carloman is very ill, Roland. Come in; come in. I have prevailed upon Hilde's good nature much too long. She did all she knows to do; and the herbalists — so called but as yet unproved — are drunk. I'll not allow them to touch Carl." Hildegard nodded to Roland and went quickly to the King's side. Bending close to Charlemagne's ear, she spoke quietly.

"Sire, sire. You're overwrought. Roland is here to help. Please, calm yourself. There is no need for this shouting. The herbalists are gone." She took his hand. The King dropped his face in his hands and nodded. Roland looked at Charlemagne and, then, looked closely at Hildegard.

"How long have you been here, Hildegard?" He asked her kindly. "You both look exhausted."

"I don't know," Hildegard admitted. "Let me think. Close to sundown, I found King Carloman lying in the herb garden. King Charlemagne and I helped him to this bedchamber and have been tending him. He is very ill, Lord Roland. The herbalists, though called hours ago, just arrived and fled as you came in."

"Hildegard," Roland's face paled. "It's now but three hours before sunrise. You've been tending Carloman throughout the night." He patted Charlemagne's shoulder. "No wonder the King is short-tempered. You both must get some rest. I, myself, will stay with Carloman." He looked at the still-unconscious king. "I daresay I'm a better guardian than the herbalists would be. Is there anything I should do for him?"

"Nay," Hildegard replied. "We just changed the coals...to warm him, Sire," she explained. "And, during the night, his body heat dropped a goodly amount. He seems more peaceful, not struggling as much to breathe as before." She smiled briefly at Roland. "I hope all he needs is rest. I gave him some herbal tea; but he does not need more until mid- morning."

Now hearing Roland mention the long night, Hildegard felt weariness creep into her body. She glanced at Charlemagne; he appeared to be sleeping, sitting up. Roland saw her weariness and her glance at the King.

"Then all is done. Off to your bed linens. Wait, I'll have my squire escort you to your bedchamber. No early rising, sleep as long as you're able." He smiled warmly at Hildegard, imagining the effort she made. "That is an edict from me." He admonished.

"But if King Carloman is..." Hildegard protested.

"If he bears just watching, Hildegard," Roland answered, "I can surely do that. Besides, he may need you again after the sun rises. I beg of you; get some rest. I shall see Charlemagne gets to his chamber as well." He pulled Hildegard to her feet. "Any wedding festivities will have to progress without him this morning, at least." He went to the door and summoned his squire.

"Take Lady Hildegard to her sleeping chamber...in the east wing, is it not, Hildegard?" At her affirmative nod, Roland spread a mantle around her shoulders and led her to the door. He directed his squire. "Tell the young women in her chamber she is exhausted from tending the sick and is to sleep. They are not to question her or try to feed her. Give them this message. Then, return here immediately to help the King." The squire, seeing Hildegard sway with exhaustion, took her arm. King Charlemagne stood, rubbed his eyes, and followed Hildegard and the squire from the chamber. He pulled Hildegard into his arms, gently kissing her cheek.

"For all you've done for Carloman, I thank you." King Charlemagne said. "We are both in your debt."

"Not at all, Sire." Hildegard answered. She was so weary

his kiss barely registered in her mind. If asked, she could not say he kissed her. If he did, he did not act properly. But she didn't know. She'd think about it tomorrow.

"I've done little, your Majesty." Hildegard replied. "I wish no thanks but King Carloman's recovery." Charlemagne nodded to the squire as Hildegard turned toward the east wing.

No one saw Desiderata peep around the corner or watch the blood rush into her face. As Desiderata turned back the way she came, the squire led Hildegard quickly to her bedchamber. At the squire's insistent knock, Maria and Jocelyn stumbled to their door, immediately embarrassed they didn't realize Hildegard was not in her linens. They led her to her sleeping bench, spreading linens over her. As they removed her foot coverings, Hildegard fell asleep.

Chapter Twenty-two

REPERCUSSIONS

Charlemagne walked beside Roland's squire, scarcely aware of his steps. Not until the lad stopped at the bridal chamber did the King realize he was not at his old room. He turned to retrace his steps just as the door banged open. Desiderata stood outlined in the door, her eyes flashing fire, her foot tap, tap, tapping on the stone floor.

"Oh!" She exclaimed. "Sooo! You've decided to return to your wife; have you, husband?" Charlemagne's eyes flew open. He never realized a world of contempt could be packed into one word. But he heard it tonight—in the word 'husband.' He quickly accessed his wife's stance as he motioned the squire away. All his weariness disappeared, replaced by a heightened sense of caution. There was to be hell to pay; he saw that. Charlemagne carefully closed the chamber door and locked it.

"Good morrow to you, Desiderata," he greeted his bride.

"Good morrow! Surely you jest!" She replied. "Good morrow for whom, I would like to know? Where have you been—dear, husband of mine?" Desiderata walked to within an inch of his nose. "Who is the little she-wolf you so sweetly kiss, standing in the corridor of your castle, the very morning after your wedding?" She kicked at him, connecting with his left shin, almost sending him to the floor.

"How dare you? How dare you, when the linens on my sleeping bench are not even cold from your body? How dare you consort with some sniveling serving maid? I'll make you pay, you bastard!" Her fists pressed against her legs. Her face was white but her cheeks were a vivid red. "I will not be humiliated, Charlemagne. I will not be embarrassed by your rutting, your 'man's' needs. I *will* destroy you!" She hissed, her eyes wild with anger, her fists beating around his head. She grabbed his dagger and reached to cut his arm. He turned just in time. Clasping her arm with his right hand, Charlemagne twisted. Desiderata yowled and fell to her knees, screaming her hatred of him.

"Stop. Or I will close your mouth myself, unless you mean to beg on your knees." The King threatened. His voice was cold, his jaw clenched tightly. "Be quiet, Desiderata. I command you."

"You swine! You, you…beast!" Desiderata replied as she tried to stand. Charlemagne turned his hand a quarter-turn, bending her arm at a painful angle. "Ooooo, you're hurting me!" Her desperate cry rang through the chamber, as she clawed at his face with her free hand. He released her and flung her backward. She crumpled to the floor. The King moved behind his wife, lifted her by the arms, and pulled her against his chest. Holding her there, he spoke.

"If you are quite finished," he said softly, "finished with disgusting allegations and maniacal shouts, I will listen to all you have to say." His voice was deadly quiet; his words uttered slowly. "Speak clearly, briefly, and quietly. Raise your voice, even once, and I'll squeeze your neck until you are unable to speak. Do you understand me?" *The last thing I would have is an audience in the corridor. With all the wine which flowed since yesterday, I will be condemned before the telling is finished.*

"Are you going to control your voice?" He asked his bride. She nodded her head. He marched her to the bench in front of the fire pit and dropped his arms. Desiderata backed up three steps, glared at him and took a deep breath.

"Quietly," the King ordered. His wife stepped back again, as if to object to his words, then nodded her head.

"How dare you?" Her face white with anger, she spit the words in his face. "How dare you leave my bridal bed to consort with a maid? I do know the wench's name, not yet. I wonder she would even have a name! Do you think me a fool? I will not be mocked, Charlemagne." She trembled violently. "Go ahead! Flaunt your little whores, you bastard. You'll pay when my father takes your kingdom!" She slowed her breathing and marched half-way around the chamber, struggling to control herself. It was a strong act of will in her fury. Charlemagne stared into her face, holding her attention with his quiet intensity.

"You know nothing." King Charlemagne dismissed her words and her anger. They signified her lack of control. He dismissed the threats. "Your threats are scarcely less debased than your accusations. You continue, moment by moment, to earn my complete disgust." She opened her mouth but Charlemagne held up his finger.

"Not another word." He warned her. "It's my turn to speak, though with truer words than you utter. You are no princess, Desiderata, and of a certainty, not a queen. You may have a king for a father; yet you have not a single royal virtue. Your mouth is even less impressive than your manners." He waved his hand in dismissal. "You accuse with no facts; you scream to no purpose. Are you able to listen? If your pea-sized brain is able to comprehend my words, signal me. Raise your hand, why don't you?"

King Charlemagne sat on the far end of the bench, away from his bride, and waited. She glowered at him, struggled to control her anger, and stamped her feet in staccato against the floor. Charlemagne stared directly into her eyes, showing no emotion. His face, his feelings, his reactions to her were dead.

When Desiderata didn't speak, the King fed two more logs to the fire, removed his leg bands and his over-tunic, and washed his face and hands. Completing his preparations for bed, he turned down the linens and lay on the sleeping bench. *Desiderata and Ma-Mam will kill each other. Neither of them can compromise. There will be constant battle.*

"Explain your behavior," Desiderata demanded, walking to the other side of the sleeping bench. "I will tolerate no lies."

"I tell no lies," Charlemagne replied firmly as he stood. "After this display, appalling in its lack of control, you deserve no explanation. You shout like a fish-monger and undermine your position with every word." He shook his head, deliberately emphasizing his disappointment. "Have you no pride, no ability to speak reasonably?"

"Despite your foolishness, I'll tell you where I've been, what has happened. This is the single explanation you will ever receive from me. Do you understand? Never, never mention this conversation to me again." He turned his back on her and walked to the fire. He faced her once again.

"First, heed my warning. Desiderata. I do not say this lightly. Never again remind me of your words or of your behavior this night. If I hear a syllable of our conversation repeated to anyone, most especially to your father," the King fixed his eyes on her face, "you will never think yourself a queen again." Charlemagne did not blink. "My weariness and grief soften my reaction to you, to this spectacle you create. Otherwise, you would be well on your way back to Lombardy tonight." He raised his right eyebrow as she opened her mouth to speak.

"I do not have to keep you, Desiderata." He showed no

emotion; his very stillness was deadly. Only his mouth moved. "Alliance or not, marriage or not, some things are not worth their pain. You are surely one of them."

"As for my actions tonight, you know nothing of them. Your spies need to improve their information and check its veracity." He did not pause for an answer. "My brother is terribly ill. Carl's most likely dying. He fell in the garden, sometime during the wedding festivities, and might have frozen to death there. A maid-in-waiting, passing on the path, discovered him. I came upon them and, of a certainty, stopped to determine the problem. She and I helped Carl to his bedchamber; she went to summon the healers." His sad visage, worried eyes and gray pallor convinced Desiderata he spoke the truth.

"All in the court are inebriated—celebrating your marriage, my dear. The herbalists are drunk. Even the nuns who know dressing of wounds and the restorative power of teas are useless." He added contemptuously.

"This maid and a passing nun did all they knew for Carl, kept him warm and concocted herbal potions." Charlemagne sighed deeply. It broke his heart to remember Hildegard's concern for his brother, the only sober member in his entire court. He was certain Sister Ruth had a glass or two herself.

"He appears to breathe more easily but their efforts may not save his life. I would give this maid a duchy, if she would accept it. She wants nothing from me. More's the pity, I do assure you. Without her knowledge and care, my brother would be dead already." He gazed steadily into his wife's astonished face.

"Make as much scandal about this as you dare, Desiderata. You will accomplish nothing." His eyes challenged her. "Harangue me; confront her; gossip and spread tales, if you will. Your place by my side is as insecure as your ready mouth." He moved toward the sleeping bench. "Now, I am going to sleep. I am more weary from your tantrums, your ridiculous threats, your malevolent mind, than from worry about Carl." He lay down and pulled the linen over his body. The King smiled to himself as Desiderata left the bedchamber.

"Hah," he whispered, "such a temper." *It may yet be possible to relieve myself of this wife. She'll surely not win Ma-Mam's affection.* He dozed off. Sometime later, he felt Desiderata return to their sleeping linens. Sleep crept up on him. It seemed only a moment later when he felt a hand squeeze his shoulder.

"Sire," Theo whispered. "You must rise. You're needed. Come now." Charlemagne turned on his sleeping bench, noting the light of dawn breaking, just coloring the sky. "I know no other way to tell you. Queen Gebnega asks for last rites for King Carloman." Theo spoke quietly, helping Charlemagne sit upright.

"What? Theo, what did you say?" Charlemagne was totally befuddled. "What are you talking about?"

"Your Majesty, forgive me." Theo's voice was low, filled with sorrow. "King Carloman is dying, Sire. He has little time left."

"Why was I not called?" Charlemagne demanded as he stood. "When I left his chamber, he was improving. There must be some mistake." He grabbed a tunic lying near-by and pulled it over his head. He accepted a pair of breeches from Theo. "Have the healers been summoned?" Charlemagne asked as he pulled on his clothing. "Have you sent for them, for the herbalists?"

"Nay, your Majesty, I have not," Theo replied. "King Carloman is beyond all earthly help, Sire. I'm sorry."

"This has to be a mistake, Theo," Charlemagne answered firmly. "Gebnega surely over-reacts. Come, let's check on

Carl." Desiderata sat up in bed but Charlemagne motioned her not to rise.

"Nay, don't rouse yourself, Desiderata. Wait here for my return." Leaving the room, Charlemagne hurried down the corridor, his heart pumping quickly. As he rounded the corner, he saw Gisela reach for the door of Carl's bedchamber. She looked up, saw him, and ran into his arms. She was already crying.

"How is it possible, Charley, for Carl to be dying?" She asked, her voice thick with tears. "Make haste, let's go in." She pushed out of Charlemagne's arms and, taking his hand, opened the door. They walked hand-in-hand to stand by their brother's sleeping bench. Charlemagne heard Gisela's intake of breath before he looked into his brother's face.

"Merciful Father," he murmured. "What's happened to him?" Carloman's face was whiter than the linen on which he lay. The veins in his neck and along his arms were dark, the blue drawing a startling contrast to the white of his skin. His breathing was labored and wheezing. Every breath he took he earned; his entire body strained to draw air. An herbalist approached King Charlemagne.

"Sire, forgive me. There's nothing we can do," he whispered. "We've tried every herb to relieve the thickness in the lungs. All has been for naught. Though King Carloman appears strained, believe me; he feels no pain. He is beyond pain, your Majesty." King Charlemagne, experienced with battlefield deaths, saw the face of finality resting on his brother.

"Is there nothing to be done?" He beseeched the herbalist. "You tried everything?"

"We have, Sire," was the quiet answer. Hearing the response, Gisela sobbed and lay across Carloman, weeping. She stroked his face and called his name. Gebnega came to her and drew her close, comforting Gisela against her own chest. She mumbled into Gisela's hair and drew her from the sleeping bench. Carloman's sons sat on the other side of a near-by bench, their arms around each other. They looked from their mother, to the herbalists, to King Charlemagne.

Gisela's sobs caught their attention. Together, they stood and went to her, each wrapping a little arm around her waist. She turned to them as Gebnega, also, began weeping. Theo led them to a bench, placed linens around their four shoulders and began talking to them softly. They held hands, silently comforting each other in their shared grief.

Charlemagne knew his brother was no longer aware. Carl's face was taut, his eyes sunk in their sockets. He felt warm to the touch, his skin dry. Charlemagne knelt by the sleeping bench and prayed. He asked God for comfort and for the strength to accept yet another loss.

"Please, Roland, fetch the Queen Mother," he said as Roland came to stand beside him. Roland nodded and left immediately. Charlemagne stood, bent down and hugged Carloman. He whispered to him. "Good journey, Brother. You leave much too soon; but I wish you peace." King Charlemagne stepped back so Queen Gebnega and her sons could say their goodbyes. As he did so, he heard Carloman whisper.

"Take heed, brother, of my words. Do not follow Ma-mam's lead. She will destroy you—if not your rule, your happiness." King Charlemagne turned quickly but Carloman said no more. Hearing Roland's voice, Charlemagne went to the door and took his mother's arm as she stepped inside. He placed his fingers on her lips.

"Ma-Mam," he said, "be brave. Your grandsons need your strength. No cries, no wails—do you hear?"

Queen Bertrada's eyes filled with tears. She clung to Charlemagne's arm and pointed to the sleeping bench. Charlemagne, his arm around her waist, supported her as they moved beside Carloman. The Queen Mother kissed her younger son goodbye and stroked his hair from his forehead. Tears streamed from her eyes.

"My precious son," Queen Bertrada whispered. "Fight this; fight so your people may welcome you home. The whole world will rejoice." She took his hand in hers.

"My fight is over, Ma-Mam," Carl clearly replied. "Consider your own behavior. Leave Charlemagne alone. Let him rule...without your help." His eyes bored into his mother's face and, then, he was still. Charlemagne bent over his brother, his heart jumping with hope. Bertrada gasped, frozen in place. Roland, not hearing Carloman's words, offered the Queen a chair. She sat as Roland nodded at another seat for Charlemagne.

"Nay, Roland," the King whispered. "I will stand, stand in honor of my brother. He has just spoken. I..." Charlemagne stopped talking as Carloman's gasp echoed through the room. Everyone heard him draw his last breath. The silence in the room was total. Queen Gebnega sobbed, stood, and threw her arms around her husband. Her older son pulled her gently away.

"Mother," he whispered. "Poppa's gone. We must not cry." Queen Gebnega stared at her son, nodded, and wiped her eyes.

"Come, my dears," she said to her two boys. "We'll take your Aunt Gisela and your Gran Ma-Mam for tea. We should leave this chamber now, I think." Charlemagne nodded, helped his mother to her feet and walked the grieving family out of the bedchamber. Once in the corridor, Queen Bertrada took Queen Gebnega's arm, a boy on each side of them. Gisela came to Charlemagne, clinging to his arm.

"Oh, Charley," she moaned. "How can this be happening? Carl's gone! How can we bear it?" She dabbed at her eyes, willing the tears to stop.

"I can't believe it, Gisela." Charlemagne answered. "Just last night, he seemed better—weary, over-tired, certainly; but not as ill as this. I will never forgive myself. I didn't understand his pain." He pushed back his tears, regret flooding over him. Gisela tried to comfort him.

"Ohh, God, Gisela! How shall I protect his kingdom? Threats will rise before we get Carl buried. The weasels are here...at our doorstep." Charlemagne squeezed his sister's hand in worry. "I must have time to think!" Seeing Gisela's understanding, King Charlemagne bent to her ear and whispered.

"Can you manage them?" He asked, nodding at Carloman's family and at his mother. "I must have some time alone." He looked into his sister's dear face. "Outside events threaten us, even now. I must plan." At Gisela's nod, he rushed down the corridor, waving Oliver toward his sister.

The King's feet turned toward Hildegard's bedchamber. *I must see her.* He hurried down the corridor, then stopped. *But how do I wake her? All in the chamber will be asleep. Mayhap, I can call quietly to her.* He opened the bedchamber door soundlessly. The fire's logs crackled, burning brightly. In the light he could see Hildegard's sleeping bench was empty. He looked quickly around the room. Jocelyn and Maria were in their alcoves sleeping, but Hildegard was not inside.

The King hastened to the stables, hoping to gather strength and peace among the animals he loved. Opening the stable door, he saw the flicker of a candle. There, sitting among the puppies, was Hildegard. She fed the smallest puppy, trickling milk into its mouth. It wasn't strong enough to fight its litter mates to nurse.

"Hilde, thank God you're here!" The King's voice burst out. "I have need of your calm presence." As he sat, puppies swarmed into his lap, eager to lick his hand and get an ear rub. Charlemagne smiled, comforted by their quick little feet and energy. The sun shined brightly, mocking his sadness.

"They welcome you, Sire. Each one is a miracle." Hildegard observed. "But the small one here is my favorite." Charlemagne scooped up the puppy she identified and stroked its little body.

"They brighten my heart, Hilde," he answered, turning the pup on its back to rub his stomach. "Their hearts are full open to everyone." He stroked first one puppy and, then, another. Hildegard, watching his face, saw the pain in his eyes. The King frowned, a sigh escaping his mouth. *What can be wrong?*

"Are you well, your Majesty?" A shadow settled over Charlemagne's face. As she spoke, Charlemagne dropped his head and pulled Hildegard close to his chest.

"Sire, please," she begged, "unhand me. This is not seemly!" She felt the slow thud of the King's heart. "Let me go, Sire. You are a just-married man." Hildegard pushed against the King's shoulders, wiggling hurriedly away from him. "Please. I must leave the stables!" Hildegard was frantic. Seeing the King at her feet, anyone would jump to unhealthy conclusions. "You will ruin me!"

"Hilde, wait!" Charlemagne spoke softly. "It's Carl, Hilde. My brother's gone. He died." He swallowed quickly, staring into her face. Hildegard could not believe his words. Her mind would not process them.

"Who told you this?" She asked, shaking her head in denial.

"Nay, Sire, he recovers. I asked of him, just as I came to feed this pup..." Her eyes widened, seeing the King's grief. "The guard reported him sleeping soundly." Charlemagne shook his head.

"Nay; it's not true," he answered. "He just died; I myself heard his last breath."

"King Carloman is gone?" Hildegard asked, her voice bewildered.

"Aye," the King confirmed, "... little more than a heartbeat or more ago."

Hildegard saw the truth in the King's eyes and reached for him. He hugged her close as they shared each other's grief — Charlemagne for the brother he had just begun to know, Hildegard for the man she knew so little.

"I share your grief, your majesty." Hildegard said, recovering from the shock of his news. "Please accept my condolences, Sire. I can think of nothing to say." She reached her arms around the King's neck and hugged him tenderly.

"He was a good man, your Majesty... not a soldier, not an enthusiastic hunter, mayhap; but a man who wished to make the right choices. You and he shared a commitment to the Church, to the realm, and to your people. May God comfort you in this great loss." She kissed his cheek gently and pulled away, even though he tried to hold her a little longer.

"I must go, Sire," she whispered, shaking her head. "God forgive me, I didn't do enough! I thought him recovering." She stood, leaning into the King's shoulder.

"Nay, Hilde," King Charlemagne responded. "We could not save him. I suspect God wished him to come home. But us, us HE leaves to grieve for Carl and our loss of him." He reached for Hildegard again, knowing the comfort holding her would bring.

"Is there anything I can do for you, Your Majesty?" Hilde-gard inquired, as she stepped back. "Give me a task. I beg for something to occupy my mind, take it away from this sadness." She took yet another step away from the King's outstretched arms.

"Nay," Charlemagne bowed his head. "Nay, there is noth-ing. I do appreciate your words, Hilde. We did share his nurs-ing and that...that will sustain me." Hildegard nodded, aching to return to his arms but afraid of his response.

"I regret I can do no more." She answered. Charlemagne could see the conflict in her face, the rigid set of her arms along her body.

"Return to your chamber, Hildegard," he advised. "It is enough. I've seen you. It does give me strength." So saying, he squeezed her shoulder, hurriedly patted the sleeping puppies, and walked away.

King Charlemagne, though he bid Hildegard goodbye, lin-gered in the stable, reluctant to return to the cares of the castle, to the decisions he, alone, must make. But, finally, fearing his mother or Desiderata would come searching for him, he stood up to return to the cares of the realm. He found he could not face those grieving faces, not yet. Instead, he went quickly to Samson's stall, saddled him, and whistled for his little dog, Foxi. She bounded ahead of him as they headed across the fields toward the river.

"Please, Sire," the stable boy called, "do not stay away too long. The skies speak of heavy snow before mid-day!" The King looked up, noting the darkening sky, gray and troubled to the west.

"Aye," he called. "I will not linger."

Unknown to the King or to Hildegard, a Lombard squire, filled with wine, slept in the hayloft for his bed. He awoke to the King's voice and watched the scene below.

"Ha," he muttered to himself. "I have news to set the serv-ants' ears on fire…on the morrow." He smiled as he went back to sleep.

Chapter Twenty-three
MORE GRIEVING

Charlemagne cantered Samson along the river's edge, riding out his pain. He felt such regret. He and Carloman misjudged and avoided each other for most of their lives. Now, just as they came together, Carl was gone. In a heartbeat, he was the only male left in his family, the only one to rule the realm. Carloman's sons, though cognizant of their station and their birthright, were small boys, years away from the skills or the knowledge they needed. The petty nobles and powerful counts who scrambled for influence in Carl's realm were, individually and together, limited in ability and foresight. But their limitations would not discourage them from supporting each other, several hoping to take power for themselves. *What shall I do?* Charlemagne stopped beside a sturdy fir to shelter a moment from the wind.

Nearby was an old, gnarled oak, spreading its leafless limbs in a wide arc. *When the spring winds come, they are likely to topple and uproot it. There'll go another old survivor.* Thinking of the probable fate of the tree, Charlemagne imagined his own fate but, more importantly, the fate of his realm. *The old oak, immobile and caught in place, lives its life as it can.* He realized. Bound by location, by rainy or dry conditions, by hot or cold temperatures, by the threat of men's axes, by the peace of nature's cycles, it survives. *But it has no influence over its life.* He stared at the bleak, empty branches of the oak.

"This oak can do nothing to change its life." he mumbled to himself. "But I can...and I must!" He stared off into the forest. "Today, I must plan Carl's funeral. But soon thereafter, I must reclaim my dreams, be true to the vision I shared with Poppa. Otherwise, I am lost—more lost than poor Carl."

King Charlemagne returned to find the court in an uproar. Nobles shouted advice to Queen Bertrada: the best time for the burial ceremony, the need for food preparations; names of men who should carry Carloman's casket, those who should offer remembrances at his funeral.

"Be silent!" King Charlemagne thundered. "What in the hell do you think you're doing? We are in mourning here. Desist! This noise will cease. I'll hear no more. When burial plans are in place, Egginhard will announce them. Until then, go back to your chambers. I want no one in the corridors of the castle." Then, he had a brilliant idea. "So far as we know, Carl may have succumbed from a dread disease." Charlemagne warned. "Stay in your chambers. None of us recognize his illness. But we do know it weakens a body quickly." He would have laughed if the situation itself were not so sorrowful. The nobles and former wedding guests fled like birds, intent in their efforts to distance themselves from each other.

"Fear, worry and uncertainty will keep them all quiet for a bit," Charlemagne said as Gisela mouthed a fervent 'thank you' from across the room.

Charlemagne knew his mother would be of no help in funeral arrangements. He would consult with Gebnega instead. After all, Carloman may have, at some point, spoken of his last wishes with her. *I do doubt it, but courtesy requires me to speak with her.* He went to the new bedchamber given to Gebnega and her sons, away from the room where Carl died.

His sister-in-law and nephews looked up as he knocked and

entered. Although food trenchers stood on the table in front of them, they appeared to eat nothing. The boys just moved the food around on their trenchers. As Charlemagne came toward them, the boys stood, hurrying to him. They gave him long hugs, seeming to relax a little against his body. He spoke gently to them, then sat at the table beside their mother.

"Forgive me, Gebnega," Charlemagne began, "for speaking of this now; but plans must be made. It's not wise to transport Carl's body to Asturia; the journey is too difficult at this time of year." He stopped to swallow. "If you don't object, I shall put him next to Poppa's crypt. They both may derive comfort from the closeness. Do you mind?" Gebnega shook her head.

"Of a certainty, that's fine, Charlemagne." She replied. "We were never certain we would live permanently in Asturia. It was one of the decisions we deferred making...until the spring. So, Carl's resting here — beside your father — is agreeable to me. It is right he lie there." She looked into Charlemagne's grief-stricken face. "He had no preferences for his burial, as far as I know. If the monks could chant, the boys and I would like it. Their voices would comfort us. Carl was a believer, you may be certain." She bowed her head.

"He once told me if he were unmarried, he would enter a monastery. But, not being able to make such a choice, he chose to live surrounded by as much peace and solitude as possible. I often thought him much better suited for a monk's life." She commented. Gebnega fumbled for her hand-linen as the tears slid down her cheeks. "Carl did sometimes rouse my anger," his wife admitted; "but he was a wonderful father and a caring husband."

"He sought the best for us all, Gebnega," King Charlemagne responded, remembering his brother's energetic demands for Charlemagne to make his own life choices.

"Indeed," Gebnega affirmed. "He worked and prayed, hoping for the best for everyone." The King talked quietly to his brother's sons, assuring them of his love and concern for them. He promised to see them later when the family shared the evening meal. He left them to walk to the Church. He had the burial service to plan.

"God, how I wish Fulrad were here to help me," he mumbled. As the King entered the Church, the very church which only yesterday was the scene of so much merriment, the Abbot came from the small chapel where he was praying.

"Fulrad?" Charlemagne asked, unbelieving. "How are you here? I thought you…"

"My son, Oliver sent a messenger to tell me King Carloman's health was failing. I turned back and arrived but moments ago. I join you in this deep sorrow," the Abbot said. He stepped closer to the King. "I must ask you a question, Charlemagne. I know; this is not a good time. But the health of your realm may depend on your answer." He did not take his eyes from the King's face.

"Anything I can answer, Abbot," Charlemagne replied gravely, "I shall." Charlemagne held his breath. *What if he asks about my feelings for Hildegard?* But Abbot Fulrad had something else on his mind.

"Why is Carloman dead?" He asked gently. "This weakness in his lungs…he overcame that, did he not?" Fulrad did not wait for Charlemagne to reply. "The day of the wedding, he appeared to recover his health. He regained so much strength, after he arrived from Lombardy. He laughed without succumbing to a coughing fit."

"I can't explain it, Fulrad." Charlemagne answered. "He weakened rapidly, almost like a star falling."

"It's worrisome," Fulrad commented. "Carloman's death, so

sudden, makes little sense. Is there some evil here, some man's hand in his death?"

"What?" The King asked. "I do not understand your meaning, Abbot."

"The question is: was he poisoned?" The Abbot asked bluntly, looking quietly into Charlemagne's eyes. "Gisela shared her worry with me...about that very possibility...days before the wedding." He saw the King did not give the idea much credence. "She and I talked at length. As she spoke, I realized—even before the wedding—I thought his coloring worrisome. His face was not exactly pale but ill-colored. I believed it came from exhaustion." He watched Charlemagne wrestle with his thoughts. "Can you name the enemy, son? Is there anyone who would go to these lengths?"

Charlemagne held his hand up, delaying any more words from the Abbot. He rubbed his forehead, his eyes closed in thought.

"You know the one I would name, Fulrad," the King responded. "Is the Lombard king capable of it? Aye. Would he do it? Aye, particularly if he were never under suspicion." He looked at the Abbot. "Desiderius of Lombardy would profit most from Carl's death. You and I discussed his ambition before Carl arrived, puzzled he stopped in Lombardy. Remember?"

"Aye," the Abbot acknowledged, "but did he do this; did he poison Carl?"

"I cannot discount it, Fulrad," Charlemagne replied. "But I have no proof."

"The proof may be before us—one of the two Frankish kings is dead, my boy. You are the only one who stands between him and a doubling of his realm. We must protect you, particularly with Desiderius' daughter in your bed. We must ensure your survival." He shook his head in worry.

"But, Fulrad, his daughter is my wife!" Charlemagne blurted out.

"Ambitious men think nothing of such a connection. To Desiderius, it is not even a complication," the Abbot declared. "Let me investigate, if you will. The Church has years of expertise in this sort of thing...and I still must go to Rome." He looked grimly into the King's face. "Have someone taste your food, the little wine you drink as well. Heed me, Charlemagne. Eat nothing from your wife's hand. Do you understand me? ...not a fruit, a nut, especially not a flagon of tea."

Charlemagne turned a shocked face to the Abbot. I don't doubt Desiderata's father may have hastened Carloman's death; but to use his own daughter to....It is unthinkable!

"I cannot fathom it." The Abbot looked at him, a deathly pallor on his face.

"Then, leave the protection to me." He advised. "But don't sleep in the same bedchamber each night. Move about...on a whim if you can pretend well enough to convince others, especially Desiderata. She herself will not bloody her hands. Desiderius' hope is for you to die and for her to live...pregnant, I suspect. He's likely to use a handpicked assassin to kill you. He would be certain of your quick demise."

"Abbot, you do frighten me." Charlemagne admitted.

"I mean to," Fulrad replied. "I try to frighten you, frighten you into taking care and remaining alert. Let Carloman's death be a warning. You are not safe!"

"Should I have Oliver or Janlur investigate....?" Charlemagne began but the Abbot interrupted him.

"Aye, alert the Peers. Put them on watch. But leave the questioning and the information-gathering to me. The Church knows ...poisons. Let me send my spies out, here and to the

Lombard Court. We'll speak again when I have more information." King Charlemagne looked at him questioningly. The Abbot hesitated.

"After Carl's internment, I continue my journey to Rome, Sire. You do understand." The Abbot hurried his words.

"I wish it were not necessary, Abbot," King Charlemagne replied. "But you must do as your conscience dictates. So must we all."

"Aye," Abbot Fulrad replied. "Now, as for the funeral... If Queen Gebnega agrees, I recommend much the same service as we used for your father. Will a like ceremony serve?"

"Aye, Fulrad," the King replied. "It will serve well. I need to think of the burial as little as possible. Though in deep sorrow, I must concentrate on the problems of the realm, the problems Carl's death promises. I'd be grateful for anything you can decide. Gebnega agreed to lay Carl next to Poppa. He had no special wishes." He squeezed the Abbot's arm. "I must think of Frankland. It stands threatened - without, surely; but within as well."

"I'll ask your direction, Sire, only if I have no idea of your or King Carloman's preferences," the Abbot promised. "Thankfully, much of the ceremony is spelled out for us in the liturgy." He patted Charlemagne's shoulder. "All will be well, my son. Don't forget to be cautious, will you?"

"Aye, I shall, Abbot. Thank you," Charlemagne answered, relieved to be spared so many sad decisions.

The morning of the funeral was bright and cold. Charlemagne broke his fast with Gisela and Queen Bertrada, thankful the burying would soon be over. Walking to the chapel, he remembered the happy faces in the Church only two day previous. He thought of the transitory nature of life, of plans changed, of dreams gone. *What is the use of hopes and plans?* As he considered the question, he spied Hildegard coming into the chapel. She was with Jocelyn and Maria.

They entered through the herb garden door and walked quickly to the prayer stools before the chancel. Kneeling with bowed heads, they reminded him of turtle doves — sorrowful and silent, reflecting a peace he could never capture.

"Poor Carl," Charlemagne grieved. "Little did I know our mother foisted so much upon him." He thought again of Carl's marriage, the union which brought him so little joy, of the young age when he became a father. *Ma-mam's manipulation of us only increases. And to what end? Her son is dead; my sister has no trust of her own mother and I question the value of my own decisions. If, at the end of my life, I cannot look back at having fulfilled a single dream of my own, what is the point?*

Charlemagne watched the three young women rise and walk toward the herb garden. He stood also. They saw and recognized him. With no hesitation at all, Hildegard left the other two and turned toward him. She walked the long aisle at a steady pace, never looking to see if her friends followed. Conferring together, Jocelyn and Maria, too, finally turned toward the King.

"King Charlemagne," Hildegard's soft voice soothed his grief. "Let me extend my condolences to you once again. Your brother was a loving, caring man, Sire. I urge you to remember his positive contributions to the realm." She looked into the King's face. "Should you wish to speak of him, I am ever a ready listener," she offered. "Sharing memories does help comfort the heart." She spoke softly, gently squeezing his arm.

"Know I share your sorrow." Hildegard whispered. At that moment, Jocelyn and Maria knelt and curtseyed to the King, each one clasping one of his hands.

"Please accept our condolences, your Majesty," Jocelyn said. "It's difficult to believe King Carloman is gone. Give our love to his wife and children and, of a certainty, to Gisela and Queen Bertrada." The sisters bowed to him and walked quickly away, catching up with Hildegard as she paused at the door of the chapel. Leaving the weeping court workers behind, Charlemagne turned toward Abbot Fulrad's office.

The next days passed in a blur, filled with grieving family, disconsolate friends and the bereaved of the court. At last, the time for interring Carl came. Many of the mourners who celebrated the King's wedding remained for Carl's funeral. As King Charlemagne sat in the nave, Desiderata knocked on the Queen Mother's bedchamber door and slipped inside.

"Good morrow, my dear," Queen Bertrada greeted her quietly. "Thank you for accompanying me to the Church. I feel so weakened by sorrow; your steady arm will serve me well this day."

"I am happy to be of service, Queen Mother," Desiderata replied, "if you will but return the favor." She dropped her eyes to the floor but looked up as Bertrada frowned intently into her face.

"Of a certainty, my dear," Queen Bertrada answered. "You have but to ask. Your wishes are my main concern; you know that." Her smile did not quite hide the calculating look which crossed her features. "Suppose you tell me what you want...before we leave for the service."

"It's a delicate request." Desiderata licked her lips nervously. "I wish to protect Charlemagne from vicious talk, Queen Mother." She explained. "And I, myself, am quite humiliated!"

Her face flushed with anger, though she made an effort to keep her voice subdued.

"Humiliated? What has upset you, Desiderata?" Queen Bertrada asked, focusing her attention on the distraught woman. "What has you so overwrought? Charlemagne is not at his best...who dares to speak against my son?" Seeing Desiderata's eyes flash, her hands ball into fists, Queen Bertrada cautioned: "Calm yourself; do."

"The problem is Charlemagne!" The words jumped from Desiderata's mouth. "He dallied with a maid yesterday night!" The Queen Mother shied, backing up a step. She stared at Desiderata. "I want something done! Banish this harlot from the court! I will not accept such behavior from my husband." She paced around the room, almost marching in her anger. Although buffeted by Desiderata's accusation, the Queen Mother did not accept it.

"I do not believe it. Surely, you jest." She laughed.

"I do not; of a surety, I do not." Desiderata replied coldly, just as Oliver's squire entered the corridor outside. Angry voices halted him, dead-still in front of the Queen Mother's bedchamber. He overheard every word said between the two women.

"I saw them, hugging and kissing each other good night—right there in the corridor! I know what I saw." She hissed, her face red and mottled. "And, there's more. One of my maids swears a squire saw your son hugging a young woman in the stables! Explain that, can you? We've been married no more than two days... What is wrong with him? I dare you to explain!" Queen Bertrada stared into Desiderata's face. She said nothing.

"I want your solemn word, Queen Bertrada. Agree to remove this woman from the court...today. I want your vow."

Desiderata demanded. "An accident which severs her head from her body would not displease me."

"Aye," the Queen replied, "if there is any truth to your accusations, I will remove her immediately. I promise you. But I do not believe your tale. My son is not so foolish as to entertain a maid where anyone can observe him. Were you spying on him, Desiderata?" She asked, holding her hand up to prevent Desiderata's answering.

"Charlemagne would never compromise your good opinion by dallying with a maid, by dallying with anyone. You two have only just married...as you say." The Queen Mother shook her head. "This is quite preposterous. Although men speak of his conquests with envy, he does not flaunt unseemly behavior nor embarrass himself. Nay, you do not have the right of it; I assure you."

"See to her banishment," Desiderata ordered, her face splotched with angry welts. "I want her gone before this day is finished. I know her not but will get her name. And, if you demand proof, she WILL confess." She yanked open the door.

Hearing her steps, Oliver's squire ducked behind the adjacent wall as Desiderata flung wide the door. Luckily for him, she marched off in the direction opposite him. Waiting to be certain the Queen Mother would not enter the hall, the squire turned and ran toward Lord Oliver's room.

"I must tell someone about this," he mumbled to himself. "Of a certainty, Lord Oliver will know what to do."

Chapter Twenty-four

RECOUPING

As Queen Bertrada made her way to the banquet hall for her son's funeral service, Charlemagne arrived from the Church. He nodded to the priest at the side of the coffin. The sight of the coffin disquieted the king, reviving memories of his father's internment.

The officiating priest's amice lay across his head and dropped to his shoulders. The long, white linen alb, the girdle, and the stole of office completed his somber clothing. The maniple band, an embroidered piece of silk with the cross at its bottom, hung from his left arm while the chasuble covered his body. All his clothing was black. The image of a small cross, a reminder of the Christ, shone from the back of the chasuble.

As the bells tolled, the rest of the clergy assembled. The parish priests and Abbot Fulrad's vestments were black as well. One of the priests carried the cross; the other one carried a stoup of holy water. The Abbot looked around the room. Seeing all members of the immediate family, he nodded to the officiating priest.

Charlemagne closed his eyes, vowing not to watch the ceremony. *Mayhap, looking elsewhere will lessen my grief.* He could re-play it all from his father's burial anyway. The sprinkling of holy water, the recitation of Psalm 129, the walk to the Church—all of them King Charlemagne passed, as if in a dream. Even the chanting of the Miserire, as the priests alternated the verses, hummed in the back - not the forefront - of his mind. Being certain Carloman's feet were aligned with the altar, the presiding priest recited the Vespers of the Dead. The Priest's homily broke the King's heart; he struggled not to weep aloud. He saw Gisela breathe deeply, holding desperately to Gebnega who was bent over, sobs wracking her body. Queen Bertrada's eyes, red and swollen, dominated her face. Charlemagne had not seen her dry-eyed since Carl's last breath. Now, she was gulping air, scarcely able to catch her breath. Watching her made the King not sorrowful but furious.

How much pain she caused Carl, Charlemagne thought. *It seems my very weariness has improved my insight. Ironic, isn't it? Now I see the truth, and can do nothing to help my brother.* He stared at the altar, consciously wrenching his thoughts from his mother's failings.

"How much more sadness must we endure?" Gisela asked quietly, looking down at her black clothing. "First, we lost Poppa. Today, we bury my brother. Years ago, sisters before me died, having just been born." She shuddered. "How I wish I were already a nun..." Tears welled, again, in her eyes and slid down her cheeks. Her oldest nephew, Pepin, took her hand. She did not even notice. "Even novitiates take comfort in penances, penances to strengthen their belief. I wonder, will a penance mend a broken heart?" Gebnega gave no answer, just patted her hand.

"Aunt Gisela? Would you like to leave the church?" Young Pepin asked. "I'll come with you."

"Aye, I'd be wise to leave." Gisela replied. Pepin stood immediately, holding his aunt's hand as he led them into the church aisle. Gently, he led her by each pew as the mourners nodded to them.

"The ceremony does go on and on, Pepin, does it not?"

Gisela said to him. "It gives no comfort to either of us... though the candles' light is soothing. That glow is very like your father, Pepin. It is unwavering, stable, and diligent in its duty, just as he was." She turned her eyes back to the priest, hearing him complete the prayers of pardon.

'Enlighten me that I may be enabled to walk

in your holy light all the days of my life. Amen.'

Gisela squeezed her nephew's hand. "I appreciate your strength, Pepin. You and your mother have kept me upright through this difficult time. If not for your mother, I would have collapsed after the Miserere." She gave Pepin a hug. "We must spend more time together," she said to him. "I want to get to know you, know who you really are." She shook her head, watching her tears drop on her black gown. With her hand-linen, she blotted the dark spots there, the spots her tears made as they fell. Gisela and Pepin heard a quiet word behind them. Queen Bertrada motioned to them to wait for her. She put her arm around Gisela's shoulders and leaned down to speak.

"Gisela," Queen Bertrada whispered to her daughter. "Are you ill? Go outside. Wait for me under the oaks next to the church." Pepin nodded, still holding Gisela's hand. "But before you go, I need to ask you something." The Queen Mother lowered her voice even more and whispered.

"Tell me. Do you know who found Carloman lying in the garden? I would thank her for her kindness," she said, tears gathering in her eyes.

"It was Hildegard of Swabia, Ma-Mam," Gisela replied, drawing strength from such a prosaic question. "She prepared a commemorative wreath for Carloman. See? It's there, the one with the fir branch and red berries. Isn't it beautiful?"

"Aye," Bertrada replied. "It is. I must thank her for her efforts."

Finishing the Pater Noster, the Priest walked around the coffin: first he sprinkled it with holy water, then he spread incense. When the Prayer of Absolution began, Rinaldo, Oliver, Roland, and Theo raised the coffin to their shoulders and began its final journey to the crypt. The clergy chanted "In Paradisum."

The priests sang the Canticle Benedictus, asking the Lord for mercy for Carloman's soul.

At the crypt, each of Carl's family threw a handful of dirt over the coffin. Gisela found Charlemagne standing by her side. He squeezed her shoulders and pulled her close. He nodded to her to look forward.

There, Carloman's young squire led his war horse. It was in full combat readiness and looked as regal as any time Carloman rode him. Queen Gebnega and her sons bowed to the priest and presented the horse to him. Later, Charlemagne would pay for the return of the animal and his payment would be given to the poor. Many such gifts, offered in sorrow and thankfulness for the life of the dead king, would ease the lives of the less fortunate.

"I feel as lost and confused as that poor mount looks," King Charlemagne whispered to Gisela as they left the burying ground.

"That is true of us all, brother," Gisela responded. "Look around. People can scarce believe that but four days ago, this court was celebrating a wedding. Now, we attend a funeral. It does tax the mind, Charlemagne. The joy and sadness, the juxtaposition, are difficult to absorb."

"Aye," the King replied. "We must fight, not to go mad. All of us, I daresay, will come to some rude awakenings this day — realizations about life and death, frivolous and serious choices, positive and negative beliefs." Gisela looked at him quickly, noting different emotions racing across his face.

"Think no more about it now," she advised. "Guard your strength for these last moments." The King nodded.

The pallbearers slid King Carloman's coffin into the crypt. Now, the young king rested beside King Pepin, rested there forever. I wonder, King Charlemagne mused, if the departed ever shed tears for us—those of us left in this vale of shadows, those left here without them .The King went to his knees, oblivious to the priests, the organ, his family, the mourners—oblivious to everything but the deadly hopelessness of his heart.

Oliver's squire, Adam, was a mature lad of fourteen. Having served Lord Oliver for two years, he knew well the place of gossip and intrigue among the court's nobles. But the conversation which he overheard between the two queens made him fearful.

"Queen Desiderata's voice was full of hate," he muttered. "Such hate will harm this young woman…whoever she might be. I must find Lord Oliver." He hurried to the castle's crypts. "Thank God!" Adam shouted when he saw Oliver steering the King's sister away from the throng of mourners. "Lord Oliver?" Adam increased his speed. In the mass of people, no one took notice of him. By the time he got to Oliver's side, Roland had Gisela's arm and was walking her back toward the castle.

"Lord Oliver," Adam called again. "I must speak with you, Sir. Directly, if it please you, Sire."Adam was a calm, gentle lad; so when Oliver heard the fear in his voice, he turned immediately.

"Is something amiss, Adam?" He asked, his forehead furrowed at Adam's agitation.

"I fear it may be, Sir; that's the reason I hurried to you," Adam replied. "I must recount something to you...quickly, sir, and privately." Oliver noticed the heightened color in the lad's face, the way he rubbed his hands together behind his back, his rapid breathing.

"Come, then; come with me." Oliver said as he turned toward the apple orchard, the trees now leafless in the bitter cold. "We will walk and talk, son." Oliver gentled his voice. "What is it?"

"Sire, the Queen Mother and Queen Desiderata, they do plot together." Adam forced the words out. "They spoke of banishing a maid-in-waiting....such punishment, for one who has done little harm!" Oliver looked deeply into the boy's eyes. He seems much overwrought. Oliver thought.

"I fear for her," Adam added. "Both the women are very angry. Her life may be forfeit."

"...banishment?" Oliver asked, feeling his heart cramp, "banishment for whom, Adam?" As Adam recounted all he overheard, Oliver's heart plummeted. Oh God, he thought. What is the truth here? Has Charlemagne compromised Hildegard? Oliver shook his head; he did not know what to think. "And you are certain this was the Queen Mother speaking and Queen Desiderata?" He knew the Queen Mother would correct or banish anyone to protect Charlemagne. She'd sent Himlitrude away without a thought. A maid was already lost. Queen Bertrada would consider her nothing.

"Was the name of the maid-in-waiting spoken, Adam?" Oliver asked hurriedly. "It is critical for me to know the identity of the maid!" Adam shook his head and replied.

"The Queen Mother did not ask the name. Queen Desiderata spoke of a kiss between the King and this maid," Adam explained, "a kiss in some corridor. But she did not know the maid's name." He looked worriedly into Oliver's eyes. "Can you guess who she is, Sir Oliver?" His eyes were huge; he swallowed again and again, his heart in his throat. "The new queen said she would get the young maid's name." Then, he remembered Desiderata's words.

"It's likely only one person. The suspicion will fall on the maid who found King Carloman in the garden. She and Charlemagne were caring for him before his untimely death." Oliver made a decision.

"Would you recognize the Lady Hildegard of Swabia, Adam?" He knew Desiderata spoke of Hildegard. "I don't believe Desiderata's accusation; but you are right. Great harm can be done to an innocent person. Will you recognize Lady Hildegard?" Adam nodded, his eyes wide.

"Find her Adam, as quickly as you can." Oliver didn't pause for breath. "She knows all the maids-in-waiting and can identify each one of them for us. If there is any truth to this allegation, Hildegard will know the most likely maid." He hesitated, seeing Adam's uneasiness. "Today, Lady Hildegard wears a dark brown mantle, bordered with small emeralds...pieces of green stone, lad. Her hair is dark and braided under a green mantle with brown embroidery."

"Aye!" Adam laughed with relief. "I saw her this morning, putting flowers near the King's crypt. I will find her and bring her...where? ...to you, Sir?" He asked Oliver. Oliver paused, thinking how he might hide Hildegard from the Queen Mother.

"Nay, take her to the Abbot, Adam," he decided. "Tell him to keep her out of sight for my sake. Now, hurry, lad! There's no time to be lost." Adam ran across the courtyard; Oliver turned back to the castle, frantically searching for the Abbot. Across the yard, Oliver saw King Charlemagne draw Roland aside.

"Send for Ma-Mam," the King said to Roland. "I will meet you in the library." Excusing himself from those offering condolences, he walked quickly to the Aachen library. A few moments later, Roland returned, ushering Queen Bertrada into the room.

"I shall guard the door, Charlemagne," he said as he stepped back out. Charlemagne hugged his mother, giving her an extra squeeze. He imagined she was even wearier than he. These past days, first to celebrate a wedding and, now, to bury Carl demanded much hospitality and reassurances from them both. He, like her, was beginning to look glassy-eyed. But, burial or not, he must plan for the future of the realm.

"Ma-Mam," the King came straight to the point of his summons. "I wish you to escort Queen Gebnega and her sons to Lord Nbolet's manor. Start at tomorrow's sunrise. If we don't move quickly, Desiderius will offer Gebnega his protection. In seeming to be kind and concerned, he will impinge upon my relationship with her and, for certain, with my nephews. He will ingratiate himself to Gebnega, beg her to bring her sons and join him in Lombardy. It's our ill luck that he remained here after the wedding. Had he left that day, his machinations would take a little more time." His mother shook her head, moving to interrupt. The King stared her down.

"Ever does he eye this kingdom, Ma-Mam. He does want it...and Gebnega, like Carl, sets great belief in Desiderius."

Charlemagne did not understand his mother's lack of perception. She failed to understand the most rudimentary ambitions of his father-in-law.

"Gebnega will say Carl wished Desiderius to oversee his lands. Desiderius will happily volunteer to become regent, acting in Carl's stead, securing my nephew's interests. This is the way he will justify it, Ma-Mam." Charlemagne hunched his shoulders, moving them around to release the tension. "Then, there will be war. Desiderius will attempt to wrest the rest of the realm from me."

"There are enough dis-satisfied nobles to lend strength to him and to support his dreams." He looked steadily into his mother's face. "Haven't you seen them...mingling and planning together here? Even before Carl was in his tomb, the vultures circled and plotted." He let his frustration show in his voice. "You must get Gebnega and the boys away from here. Do it quickly." The Queen Mother frowned, planting her feet to argue with the King.

"I warn you," Charlemagne spoke urgently. "Do not delay. Hurry on this journey, do!" He turned toward the door. "Give me leave. I must speak with Fulrad." His mother stopped him with her outstretched hand.

"I must speak with you about another matter," she replied, scarcely seeming to hear his request. The King hesitated and, then, replied.

"So be it, Ma-Mam. I will seek you out after speaking with Fulrad. The transition of the realm must begin immediately. Please, I shall talk to you later." He gave his mother's cheek a peck and left the room, hurrying to Fulrad's office behind the chapel.

"Fulrad," Charlemagne went directly to the point. "I want the kingdom—all of it. Do something to transfer Carl's realm to me. I will be king of all of Frankland. This must be done quickly and peacefully. How long will it take you?" Fulrad's head jerked up from the parchment he was examining.

"I know, I know," the King replied, "this is quite irregular. But it cannot be helped. Everyone expects me to divide Carl's lands between his sons, just as in times past. I cannot do it. The boys are too young; there is no man I trust to appoint regent in their stead. The size of the realm makes stewardship unworkable. The old tradition dies today." He stepped toward the Abbot. "Can you do it, Fulrad?"

"Aye, I can, your Majesty; and I shall." Fulrad answered. "It will be artfully done, I promise." Charlemagne nodded, refusing to show personal satisfaction. With this request, the King knew, Fulrad was even more aware of his ambition ... not necessarily a good thing, but necessary to do what he must.

Fulrad began searching for codices, just as there was a knock on the door. Queen Gebnega stepped inside as the Abbot's squire beckoned to him from the doorway. The Abbot nodded to the Queen, bade Charlemagne goodbye and went out to the boy.

"Forgive me, Charlemagne, for the interruption," Queen Gebnega apologized. "I must speak with you now. I have an issue of pressing concern. It cannot wait."

"Of a certainty, Gebnega," Charlemagne replied. He offered his sister-in-law a seat, looking into her face. "I am glad you've come. I want to offer you all our love and sympathy, Gebnega. With you and your sons, we all mourn Carl's untimely passing. I joyfully offer a home, support and comfort for you and your sons. You are our family; be certain of our concern for you all."

"Thank you, Sire," Gebnega responded. "This is the very subject I have in mind — my boys' futures. They must be named kings of Carloman's realm. I know nothing of rule, Charlemagne, and, of a certainty, have no interest in ruling in my sons' stead. I know some women are comfortable, even eager, to assume such responsibility. I am unable." She paused, speaking more forcefully.

"Desiderius of Lombardy has generously offered me his service in ruling Carl's lands." She smiled. "You will advise and guard my sons' interest, of a certainty. I appreciate that. But," she paused, thinking deeply. "The realm needs daily oversight and you are far away."

Gebnega knew the realm was in danger, certainly from without. With Carl not even buried, she already received two cloaked, marriage proposals and was almost frantic at the implications of that for her sons' futures. "I know it impossible for you to spend a lengthy time in our realm, Sire."

"I believe Carloman's soldiers would give their allegiance to his old friend, Desiderius. As you know, he spent many days with us in our realm, as we have done in Lombardy. Our nobles joke, declaring we share everything with the Lombards — food, sons and daughters, good times, illnesses, common enemies. Desiderius offers me protection and help with the realm as adviser to my boys. I ask you to name Desiderius regent." She paused and looked at Charlemagne.

"What say you to this idea, your Majesty?" This, the longest speech the King ever heard Gebnega make, gave him a moment to compose himself, to avoid an abrupt disavowal of her proposal.

"Desiderus remembers precedent, Gebnega." Charlemagne replied. "In the past, the mayors of the castle always divided the realm among sons...or grandsons." He nodded slowly. "Even though we must not allow the realm to be considered unprotected, the sorrow of these recent days must lessen before we can speak about this question." The King dropped his eyes to the floor. "I beg you...may I summon Desiderius to meet with us some days hence? At this moment, my heart is too heavy to think upon it." Charlemagne sat down abruptly, so quickly Queen Gebnega thought him either ill or overcome with grief.

"Do not, I beg you!" She exclaimed. "Do not think me insensitive! Carloman's brief illness was virulent in its effects. I watched him struggle at the Lombard court and, then, during his journey here. I was, mayhap, less shocked than you at his untimely death." Gebnega was overcome; tears seeped from her eyes. "Let us speak tomorrow." She fled the room. Charlemagne congratulated himself on not giving his sister-in-law a clear response.

"How bold Desiderius becomes. Not two days after Carl's death, he offers his service to Carl's widow! He lost no time." His face grew red; his jaws clenched. "I will not name Desiderius regent; I cannot allow it." Charlemagne stood quickly. "I must hurry Fulrad along." King Charlemagne thought to seek advice from his mother; but he caught himself and, instead, called to his guard.

"Aye, Sire?" The guard said.

"Please, Hans, bring food from the cook room, roast and bread. My stomach protests."

"Aye, Sire," Hans replied compassionately. "Sadness doesn't support much of an appetite, I know. I'll return directly, Sire."

"I don't need the Queen Mother," King Charlemagne assured himself. "She failed me again...not getting Gebnega away from here."

The guard returned with a wooden trencher filled with stew; heavy, brown bread; softly cooked apples; and a thick slice of roast. Charlemagne placed the roast on the bread and began to eat. As he ate, he outlined his options. After several moments of thought, he smiled. *If I move quickly, take the realm, and Fulrad supports it, most people will applaud my daring and confidence.* He pushed his food aside and walked to the door.

"Hans, summon Lord Oliver," he directed. In a few moments, Hans returned with Oliver who hurried inside.

"You sent for me, your Majesty?" Oliver asked.

"Aye," Charlemagne replied, motioning Oliver to sit. "I want your honest evaluation of my next course of action, Oliver. The realm is at risk. Already, Desiderius works to control Carl's lands." He shrugged. "Queen Gebnega requests that I name Desiderius regent for her sons. If I make such a decision, many of the nobility will defect and support Desiderius, hoping to gain more concessions from service to him than to me. In no time, he will murder me and become king of Frankland. I believe he will not wait for Desiderata to give me a child. After all, the child could be a girl."

"I have no choice; I must absorb Carl's lands into my own. Carl's soldiers, being Frankish, will see this as a natural transition and will rejoice at their place in my army. It is the single way I can protect the entire realm."

"Interesting you ask me, Sire," Oliver answered. "Our views on protocol do vary widely. But, in this instance, I agree with your assessment completely. This is the only solution." He smiled into the King's widening eyes.

"...new realms, Sire, new visions. They do require different ways of thinking, of acting. Aye, your Majesty, you must rejoin the two parts of your father's kingdom. It is the only logical choice. Had you grown nephews, the choice would be different. May I ask the Queen Mother's opinion, Sire? What did she recommend?"

"I have not asked her opinion. Quickly, Oliver," Charlemagne continued, "this must be done quickly. If you will…" They both turned at a knock on the door.

"It's your mother, Charlemagne." Queen Bertrada called. "I must see you before I retire." Charlemagne nodded to Oliver to wait in the small alcove of the library. As Oliver quietly entered the little chamber, the King opened the door to his mother.*What can she want now?* His mother swept into the chamber.

"Might we postpone this until the morrow, Ma-Mam? We both had a long, exhausting day."

"Nay," his mother replied. "Bad currents follow each other. Let's dispose of this tonight so the morrow may be fresh and new."

"…bad currents?" The King asked, offering a seat. "I have no strength to deal with 'bad currents,' whatever they may be." His mother's face was red, her brows drawn angrily together. *What have I done this time?* He waited, refusing to guess at her concern.

"What do you know of Hildegard of Swabia?" Queen Bertrada asked. Charlemagne was so shocked by the question he answered immediately. His lack of hesitation convinced Queen Bertrada her son had no interest in the young woman, if he even knew her.

"She is the young woman who joined the court with Count Hautgard's daughters, Ma-Mam. She is the maid who found Carl in the garden. Her herbal knowledge did extend his life…though not long enough." He added.

"I am weary," Queen Bertrada admitted, "so I will get to the heart of this. Your bride believes that you have…ahh… you were familiar… you…" Her voice trailed off. She was suddenly wary of discussing sexual allegations with her son.

"Familiar with?" Charlemagne stood with his mouth open. "What are you suggesting?" He asked, his eyes glaring into his mother's face. "My wife? Do you speak for Desiderata... or of your own suspicions, Ma-Mam?"

"Desiderata demands this young woman be ... Hildegard, is it? She requires I banish Hildegard from court. Your wife says you had...improper contact with her." Queen Bertrada replied, somewhat uncomfortably. "She claims she saw you hug and kiss the girl. She called it 'whoring around,' as I remember – some words of that caliber." She looked into her son's face, surprised at the anger and, then, the horror blazing there.

"I'm usually tolerant of male behavior, but I must say, this is unexpected. You've been married only a few days, son." She glanced at the King. "And, in any case, anything which distresses your wife must be rectified as quickly as possible. I shall banish this Hildegard tomorrow."

Charlemagne's eyes never left his mother's face. He was livid and frightened - his mother and his wife in collusion? Dear God; here was a serious threat! His brother's admonitions ran through Charlemagne's mind. He masked his face, showing absolutely no emotion to his mother.

"I resent such insinuations, such words from my new wife, Ma-Mam," Charlemagne replied coldly, putting as much contempt in his voice as he could. "You surely do not believe such dribble. Do you think me insane...to marry a woman and be unfaithful to her on the very night of our wedding? This is ludicrous, though Desiderata must think little of her own charms. You are both sick." He marched to the door, opened it, and nodded for his mother to leave.

"Never mention this incident to me again." He warned. "Continue with this, repeat this to anyone and I shall ruin Desiderata. I promise you." King Charlemagne slowly flexed his balled fist. "I shall tell every man in court she was not a virgin on our wedding night."

"The truth is she is much too accomplished in bed to be an innocent princess; her sexual needs are perverted." He saw his mother recoil, unable to believe his words. "I will, also, offer proof of your unfaithfulness to Poppa." Queen Bertrada held her hands up, as if to ward off his words.

"You wouldn't dare." She spit out.

"Spin filth about others, including your own son, and it will come back to stick on you." Charlemagne predicted. "Don't take the chance, Ma-Mam." He almost growled as he pushed her from the room and locked the door behind her. The King turned quickly as Oliver re-entered the room.

Chapter Twenty-five
RIGHTING LIVES

"What can we do to protect Hilde?" King Charlemagne demanded of Oliver.

"Get her away from here, now." Oliver replied as he crossed the chamber. "I shall see it done." The King squeezed Oliver's shoulder and, then, left for the stables, bedding down in the straw of Samson's stall. He couldn't bear to re-enter the muck of the castle's walls. And he could not bear to imagine Hildegard's confused and frightened face as Oliver described her danger.

As Queen Bertrada entered the chamber, Abbot Fulrad saw Adam approaching him. The lad was almost running down the corridor. The Abbot stepped into a small alcove and beckoned to him. Adam whispered quickly to the Abbot, telling him the same story he recounted to Lord Oliver.

"Queen Bertrada agreed to banish this young woman?" The Abbot asked. "You are certain, Adam?"

"Aye, Abbot Fulrad; she agreed, though she did not seem to believe Queen Desiderata's story. Lord Oliver sent me to find you. He asks you to take the maid from the castle. With your leave, I am to fetch her and bring her to you, according to Lord Oliver's directions, Sir." Adam answered. "But where am I to bring her? ...not to the chapel, surely?" His brow creased with worry.

"Aye," the Abbot concurred. "We must remove her quickly,

get her away from court." He turned to the young squire. "Do you know Lady Hildegard, Adam; would you recognize her?" At Adam's nod, Fulrad urged the lad to hurry. "Do not linger; find her quickly. Take my horse; ride double with the young woman. Go to the small manor house at the crook of the river. Do you know the one, son?" Adam nodded again.

"Leave her there and return my horse to the King's stables. I want no one to know the horse moved." As he talked he wrote his name on a small piece of parchment.

"Give this parchment to Lady Hildegard. Say this signature guarantees I sent you. Tell her, as gently as you can, lad, that her life is in danger. She will, I pray, do as you ask. Tell her I will speak with her later tonight. Don't forget to tell her this. Now, hurry, my boy," the Abbot urged. "Hurry and find her!"

Adam tucked the parchment in his neck bag and ran directly toward the stables. He saddled the Abbot's horse, rode to the rose garden and tethered him near the east wing of the castle. He went in search of Hildegard, the woman in the brown mantle. Luck was with him. As he entered the garden, he saw the lady leave the castle, turning toward the west wing.

"Forgive me, Lady," Adam apologized as he hurried forward toward her. "I have a message for you. It's urgent. You are Lady Hildegard, are you not?" Hildegard stopped, surprised at his appearance. Looking at him, she recognized Oliver's squire and smiled.

"Aye, I am. Are you sure your message is for me? I don't often get summoned by squires." She cocked her head at Adam, looking serious.

"You are the one I seek." Adam confirmed. "The message is for you, for certain. The Abbot directed me to find you. You are to come with me." Adam hurried on. "He feels you are in danger." He looked at the ground, then back into Hildegard's eyes.

"I can say no more than this. But as you trust Abbot Fulrad, please come with me." He pointed at the signature as he handed Hildegard the parchment signed in the Abbot's own hand.

"Aye, I do trust him." Hildegard confirmed. "I know his hand. Where do we go?" She asked Adam, not even flinching at his words.

"To his manor, Lady," Adam replied, taking her hand. "We must hurry." He led Hildegard to the Abbot's horse, mounted and pulled her up behind him. Quickly, he cantered toward the river beyond the fields.

The Abbot returned to his office beside the chapel and prepared the documents needed to transfer Carloman's land to Charlemagne's realm. He delivered the documents to the scriptorium to obtain additional copies. Giving instructions for the dispersal of the documents throughout the realm, the Abbot gathered his traveling bag and stuffed it with all manner of parchments. He turned to his squire.

"I leave for Rome on the morrow. Summon Lord Oliver for me and, then, return to my manor. Tell Gerta I will be home before sundown." Deciding to confide in Oliver, the Abbot made his plans. A few minutes later, Oliver hurried into the chapel. The Abbot assured Oliver Hildegard was safe and described his upcoming journey. He asked Oliver to be certain the courier carrying the land transfer documents got on his way the following morning.

"I am concocting a destination for Hildegard, Oliver. Don't be surprised by anything you hear about the court. Likely, none of it is true." Oliver nodded and bade him 'Godspeed.' The Abbot excused himself, mounted his horse, and rode directly to his manor. He found Hildegard in his courtyard calmly drinking tea, waiting for his arrival.

"My dear Hildegard," the Abbot greeted her. "Please forgive our stealth in spiriting you away. Have my people made you comfortable?" This was the Abbot's personal manor. It ran like a well-manned catapult. The manor was a gift from King Pepin and served as the Abbot's retreat. He maintained a small, loyal staff to farm the acreage, care for the animals and oversee his home. They were never surprised or inconvenienced by his occasional visits and were totally devoted to his well-being.

"This is a lovely home, Abbot," Hildegard complimented him. "If I were you, I'd move my office here and go to the court only when necessary." She laughed at her boldness and smiled at the Abbot.

"...exactly my thoughts, Hildegard, exactly. But, as you imagine, my 'necessary' is quite different from the king's. Unfortunately, he requires me to stay at court. It is a great sacrifice, I admit to you." He smiled at Hildegard, noting the weary lines around her eyes, the slight trembling about her mouth.

"But not to keep you in suspense, my dear, let me explain the reason for your visit here." He paused, searching for words which would alert her to danger but not frighten her overmuch. "Oliver and I thought it best to remove you from court. We would not see you browbeaten, embarrassed or harmed."

"Abbot," Hildegard replied, a frown between her eyes, "what have I done...to earn such danger?" Her eyes were wide with confusion and fear. "Please, tell me; tell me all of it. I can think of nothing untoward in my behavior or in my speech."

"Nay, my dear, I did not say you earned any of these reactions, merely that you may suffer. I know not how to soften it, Hildegard. You have somehow earned the wrath of the two queens." The Abbot looked uncomfortable.

"But I did nothing! I have not even spoken to the new queen. And the Queen Mother? I doubt she even knows my name!" Hildegard protested.

"No one judged you poorly to me, Hildegard," the Abbot assured her. "I have heard only this: Desiderata is jealous of you." Hildegard's hand went to her mouth, her eyes widened.

"Jealous? Jealous of what? Abbot, there is no reason. I've done nothing. How does she even know who I am?" Hildegard's eyes darkened with fear.

"Aye, I daresay you did nothing—nothing to stir up feelings of jealousy or anything else." The Abbot responded. "But it seems Desiderata saw the King hug you and kiss your forehead. She drew her own conclusions." Hildegard's face was blank. She did not remember such affection from the King. Ever since he told her of his betrothal, she kept as much distance between them as she could.

"I do not recall a kiss, Abbot," she admitted.

"I think Desiderata did not create the tale, entirely," Abbot Fulrad replied. "Did he hug you when you left King Carloman's chamber—you to go to your bed and he to the bridal chamber? Such is the affection mentioned." He watched Hildegard closely, already knowing she was blameless. When Desiderata arrived at court, he noticed her selfish, demanding personality and had no doubt she would create offense in order to punish some perceived slight.

"Did he kiss me, Abbot?" Hildegard shook her head, not remembering. "I was weary beyond description—after the long night caring for King Carloman. The King did put his arm around my shoulders," she remembered, "but a kiss? I don't know. And if he did, it was meaningless, Abbot Fulrad."

"Well, Queen Desiderata embellished his thanks to you to the Queen Mother and demands your banishment from court." At his words, Hildegard's face crumpled, looking even more frightened. "Nay, nay," the Abbot cried. "I will not let it happen, my dear. We must counteract this allegation, here and now; or Desiderata's claims will ruin your reputation. Don't look so frightened. I have a plan." He turned to a serving wench who entered the room.

"Marta, please bring a late meal. Neither I nor the lady here ate at mid-day. Include a light ale, if you please."

"I can never thank you enough for this, Abbot," Hildegard answered, her eyes filling up. "You have no reason to be concerned and no responsibility to..." She sat quickly, afraid her legs would buckle. Abbot Fulrad hurried to calm her, bolstering her confidence and verifying he believed her words.

"Aye, but I do, my dear," the Abbot reassured her. "Any untruth said against an innocent person, any miscarriage of truth in the hands of a tyrant or, even, of a mere liar...it becomes my job." Marta returned to the room with a tray filled with food. The Abbot bustled about, offering Hildegard venison and boiled potatoes.

"Eat, eat. I'll explain my plan. Let me know if you think the court ladies will believe it." Hildegard—comforted by the Abbot's reassurance, warmed by the fire and beginning a hot meal—relaxed and smiled.

"Luckily," he reminded her, "I have a journey to Rome to complete. I will be leaving after mid-day on the morrow. It will not seem unusual if you accompany me. Among my acquaintances in Rome is an older noble who has a marriageable son. The duke is forever begging me to find a wife for the young man. Amado is shy and gentle, not easily able to attract female interest. This is my plan. I will announce you are traveling with me to Rome to meet your future husband." Hildegard's eyes popped open in shock, then disbelief.

"But, Abbot, I do not know this man. I have no interest in...."

"Of a certainty you don't, Hildegard!" Abbot Fulrad

laughed with delight. "I didn't say you would be his bride. We will say you will travel with me to Rome. This is a ruse, my dear, to get you away. It is an offer I can announce — with you blushing prettily beside me, I hope — to the entire court." He smiled at her open mouth. At her stricken look, the Abbot laughed even harder.

"Hildegard!" He cried. "Use your imagination. Know this journey will protect you and your reputation. After all, this could be true — if you were interested, I mean." He nodded as the light of understanding dawned on Hildegard's face. "I will add your gentle care of King Carloman convinced me of your wifely abilities." The Abbot stopped teasing Hilde and sobered. "I do think this is rather clever, my girl, from an old, straight-as-an-arrow, provincial priest, don't you?" His eyes twinkled; his mouth turned up happily. The Abbot beamed at her.

"I do appreciate your efforts," Hildegard hurried to assure him, "but I don't want you lying to get me out of this predicament."

"Lying, my dear?" The Abbot rolled his eyes. "What a harsh word! Nay, I do not lie. The truth is…this young man would beg you to be his wife. You are perfect for him." The Abbot took Hildegard's hands in his.

"I will not allow either of these selfish queens to ruin your life, my dear, neither Bertrada or Desiderata. It will not happen," he assured her. "But you have not heard the best part of my scheme….ummm…my plan." At Hildegard's wary face, he chortled, even louder than before.

"You will not actually come with me to Rome," he announced. "I shall leave you here to enjoy my manor. My people will keep your presence a secret, warn you if anyone approaches, and hide you — if it should be necessary. Nay, you will stay here and brighten the lives of those who serve this house." He

stopped speaking, giving Hildegard time to consider his proposal and to react to it. Placing their trenchers to the side, he
offered her dried apple slices, cheese and raisins and waited for
her answer.

"Will you play this little game with me, my dear?" He
asked, seeing her worried frown. "Oh, I do neglect an important point. Of a certainty, as soon as spring weather allows
you to travel, I will send you home to your father's house. If
anyone asks about the proposed marriage, I will say the young
man was not accomplished enough for the Lady Hildegard and
you returned home after our journey." Abbot Fulrad was very
pleased with himself. Seldom did he get the opportunity to do
good and have fun in the process.

"Aye, Abbot," Hildegard answered, smiling. "I wholeheart-
edly endorse your plan and will give it my best performance."
Then she looked at him seriously. "I do thank you for helping
me, Sire. My life is worth little...even now, as we speak." At
the thought, she dropped her head, doing her best not to weep.

"Your life *is* significant, Hildegard," the Abbot softly scold-
ed her, "else why would I fight to protect it? You are precious
to God, to me, and to many others. You must believe me, my
girl." He held out his hand to help her rise. "Now, go to your
bedchamber and sleep. We travel to the court first thing on the
morrow to announce your engagement. Shortly after, we set
out for Rome."

At court the following morning, the Abbot announced
Charlemagne's appropriation of his brother's lands and conferred with Oliver. A courier to the Pope began his journey

while other messengers were sent throughout both realms. Sometime in the early afternoon, Gebnega and her sons slipped away. They fled to Lombardy with Desiderius.

"Why didn't you act as I asked you, Ma-Mam? I begged you to remove Gebnega and the boys from the court." King Charlemagne vented his frustration on his mother. "Now, all three of them are lost to us. And you have given Desiderius time and opportunity to turn the nobility against me. How could you have lingered, Ma-Mam?" Charlemagne paced the library, slapping his thigh repeatedly.

"Don't you see the threat Desiderius poses? How many times must I warn you?" He scowled into his mother's face. "You do glory in defying me."

The Queen Mother could only hang her head. Finally giving due attention to Charlemagne's words, she remembered Desiderius' long-standing hunger to rule the kingdom, even before King Pepin became mayor of the palace. Even though Pepin received the hereditary post from his father, Desideridus attempted to get the mayoral post for himself, doing his best to undermine Pepin.

"Gebnega is attempting to assure her sons' futures," Queen Bertrada muttered to cover her tardy understanding. "I could never fault her for that."

"Aye, I am certain you cannot." King Charlemagne retorted. "You never find fault with your own behavior. Think on this reality. Were Desiderius to defeat me in battle, he will not treat you with courtesy or respect." The King took her face in his large hands, holding it immobile.

"You are not the ruler of this realm...or of Carl's lands, for that matter.You rule nothing. Do you understand me? I will tolerate your meddling no longer." Queen Bertrada wrenched her face from his hand.

"How dare you question me! You have no right. I do as I know best. You must follow my lead." She glowered at him, her face flushed, her eyes bulging. Charlemagne almost laughed. She looked exactly like an old bull dog. But he did not mention the comparison, though he was sorely tempted.

"I have a surprise for you, Ma-Mam." King Charlemagne replied, shrugging, though his voice was deadly quiet. "You are not the king; you will never be the king. You may be the Queen Mother but you have no power. Even your position is now insecure." The more his mother ignored him, the less patience he had. Her mindless tenacity to her own goals interfered with his ability to plan. Charlemagne paced the room.

"I will not continue to suffer from your decisions. You want what you want, and you will use anyone to get it." Queen Bertrada stepped back and looked at her son in horror.

"How can you say such things?" She screeched. "Everything I do is for you! You are inexperienced; you have no knowledge of court protocol…"

"…inexperienced, am I?" King Charlemagne exploded. "Tell me. Who spent his life training me on the practice field? Who discussed strategies and battle plans with me? Who described the strengths and weaknesses of our military commanders so I understood their abilities and temperaments? Who drilled me on troop deployments, on the planting schedule for spring crops, on the personality of an effective guard dog, on land yields needed to pass the winter?" His mother did not reply.

"Who described the thoughts of an Arab sheik, the land dreams of a second son, the family expectations of a count's daughter? You have been my teacher, my spiritual guide, my friend, have you? Nay, Ma-Mam, you have undermined me, belittled my own interests, scoffed at my ideas. I will hear nothing more from you. Do nothing, nothing to help me from this day forth. Do you understand?" Ignoring Charlemagne's anger and hurt, the Queen Mother attempted to set things right.

"We must negotiate with Desiderius and Gebnega," she replied. "In fact, if we can separate Desiderius' ambition from Gebnega's claim — promise him more than she can offer — it would add immeasurably to our relations with him." She did not look at the King. "I'll approach him. My failing encouraged this unholy alliance; I must…"

"You will do no such thing." Charlemagne objected. "Nay, I forbid you to contact Desiderius. Be silent. Say nothing to anyone about the future of this kingdom." He left the room, his mother staring after him. *I must ask Fulrad to send a spy to watch her. Her previous freedom can continue no longer.* Hurrying from the chamber, he dismissed his mother from his mind.

Charlemagne told Janlur to double the guards on his wife and his mother. He pressed Roland to deploy a defensive, secret guard about the castle. He asked Rinaldo to spearhead a foray among the courts' nobles to identify plots and whispers against his interests. Only then did the King feel it safe to return to the banquet hall for the evening meal. As Charlemagne walked toward the raised table, he saw Abbot Fulrad stand and tap the table to get everyone's attention. Fulrad tapped until the hall quieted. Every face turned toward him.

"I wish to make two announcements." Fulrad looked over the chamber. "The first is this: I begin my journey to Rome tomorrow at first light. I began this same journey some three days ago; but, hearing of King Carloman's illness, I returned to court. The Pope still awaits my presence. All of you, try to behave yourselves while I'm gone." He smiled as the diners laughed their appreciation.

"The second announcement is much more exciting," he continued. "I am escorting Lady Hildegard of Swabia to her new husband in Rome. She wishes to take leave of all her friends tonight. Our journey begins early on the morrow. Do rejoice with her." The Abbot turned to beam at Hildegard. "She is to wed Duke Franco, the sole heir to the duchy of Tuscany. He awaits her with much anticipation. Please, wish us both God speed." Fulrad sat down as applause filled the chamber. The ladies of the court immediately jumped up, flocking to exclaim over Hildegard and ask questions about her bridegroom. King Charlemagne stood rooted to the floor.

Hilde? Hilde is to marry? The words rolled around and around in his head. *But what shall I do? I cannot live without her.* His eyes closed at the thought, closed out her happy face, glimpsed through the bevy of women around her. The King looked toward his wife and his mother. They sat on either side of his chair, staring at each other in shock. Queen Bertrada shook her head back and forth, denying vehemently she had any knowledge of the betrothal. Desiderata's face darkened with anger. The King walked straight toward Hildegard, pushed his way through the well-wishers, and took her hand.

"My best, most heart-felt good wishes to you, Lady Hildegard," he said. "Your betrothed cannot know the treasure he is getting; God speed, my dear." And he backed away.

"Thank you, your Majesty," Hildegard replied, confused by the tightening of the King's jaw and the blank look in his eyes.

Chapter Twenty-six
CHANGES ONCE AGAIN

After breaking her fast the next morning, Hildegard readied luggage in her bedchamber for the announced journey with the Abbot. A knock sounded on the door as Roland stuck his head inside.

"The King wishes to bid you adieu, my Lady." Roland explained, handing her the King's summons.

"But I told the King farewell yesterday night," Hildegard objected. "I have only a few minutes, Roland." Hildegard tried to wiggle out of meeting the King again. "Abbot Fulrad wishes to leave quickly for Rome."

"King Charlemagne knows, my Lady. He insists you come to the library. I am to escort you there." Hildegard nodded slowly but sent a message to the Abbot. She penned she would join him at the stables as soon as she spoke with the King. She followed Roland to the library. He knocked on the door.

"Come; enter." Charlemagne called. Roland nodded her inside. Hearing light steps, the King turned to see Hildegard enter the library. Catching himself before saying 'my dear,' he welcomed her neutrally.

"Hildegard," the King said, "thank you for coming."

"You gave me no choice, your Majesty," she responded. "A command is a command, Sire. Lord Roland was clear. I must obey your summons, he said, though I do not wish to delay the Abbot's journey."

Hildegard looked into the King's face. She startled and frowned, then stepped back. His regard for her shone in his face. His eyes were tender, his face flushed. His hands were clasped together—as if to keep from reaching for her. Hildegard ignored his behavior, reminding herself he did not return her love. He married another. She waited for him to speak.

"Aye," King Charlemagne replied. "I treasure your appearance and appreciate your promptness. I know you are ever punctual." Hildegard stared at the King. *Am I here for useless conversation?* She smiled slightly, admitting he always kept her guessing.

"That smile," the King pointed out, "what does it mean?"

"Only this, Sire. I cannot fathom the reason for your asking me here." Hildegard responded. "We said our goodbyes yesterday night."

"Ah, well...I wished to say 'goodbye' again." Charlemagne declared with no apology. He gazed at her longingly; but, steeling himself against her more clearly realized charms, he raised his hand, as if in surrender, and spoke again.

"First, I want you to know I have rethought my vision for the realm. As a result, my behavior will change." He smiled at her wistfully.

"Majesty," Hildegard answered, "I did not question your behavior. I merely..." His voice overrode hers.

"Aye, Hilde," the King replied, "you did, in truth, question my behavior. You declared I was not the man you knew. The statement is a fault-finding assertion, I assure you." He smiled briefly and, then, looked into her face. "I thank you for it. I did, for a time, lose my way." Hildegard nodded and sat on a nearby bench. She was reluctant to look up, knowing the king would see relief in her eyes.

"You insisted the realm falters. I evaluated your statement

and discovered its truth. In fact, the only aspect of my kingdom which appears to be sound is my military. But even that one encouraging thought does not tell the whole story. As soldiers, my men fight well, recover, and fight again. They, also, nurse their wounded comrades back to health. But when they leave soldiering, they return to wives and children who are hungry almost all of the year, to women who die by their thirtieth birthdays, to children so stunted in growth they succumb to any passing illness, and to huts which protect them from neither the elements nor the outlaws of Frankland." The King shook his head, saddened by the want among his people.

"This is not success, Hildegard, as you clearly pointed out. I will not bore you with details. I'm changed. I re-discovered the man you used to know, the soldier-king driven by dreams of change and improvement for his people." Hildegard stirred and, then, looked with bright, excited eyes into the King's face. Charlemagne almost cried out, seeing the relief and hope reflected there.

"I tell you this before anyone else," he declared, "except for Fulrad who helped me take an important step. I am, as of today, the only ruler of the Frankish realm. I took Carl's lands for my own, integrated them into my kingdom. I shall govern them myself. My Peers will aid me, I trust; and I am certain Pope Stephen will wish to offer me his counsel." He smiled slightly.

"I have found my way again, little bird." The King's mouth caressed her nick-name. "I wanted you to know...from my own lips." Hildegard stared at Charlemagne, the tears forming in her eyes. She made a mighty effort, so mighty only a small tear escaped. As it wound down her face, she smiled tremulously at Charlemagne and quietly spoke.

"I prayed for this, Sire," she assured him. "You have the

strength and the skills to save the realm. Temporarily, you lost your vision." She paused. "God must have wakened you and infused you with purpose to create the new world you've dreamed of." The King shook his head slowly, gratified her faith in him could was so resilient.

"I know one thing, Hilde. You support my vision. And, for now, that is enough." He saw her mouth tremble, her hands clasp each other; her will prevent her from taking a step toward him. "Thank you for your words. You, alone in the kingdom, made me stop — stop to consider the choices I made. You made me remember Roland's advice...much like yours." He approached her slowly, softly touched her arm.

"I owe you my life, Hilde, and the hope of a better life for the entire realm." King Charlemagne stopped speaking. He stood, loving Hildegard with all his heart, though he knew he may never call her his own.

"You owe me nothing, Sire," Hildegard answered. "I only identified the man I feared lost. Your return..." Her voice trailed away. Smiling shyly, she continued. "Your return gives me new hope for tomorrow."

"Ahh," the King replied. "Tomorrow is the only hope I have — for you, for me, for the Frankish people. I wish much happiness for you, much happiness." With those words, the King knelt to her, kissed her hand, and left the library.

Hildegard looked at her hand. She could feel the outline of the King's lips against it. Tears filled her eyes as she gazed out of the window, struggling not to weep. *It matters not. It matters not. He is newly-married, not free to care about you now.* She learned against the window, her eyes turned toward the horizon.

"Create new dreams for yourself." She whispered. "You must!" Hildegard sat to compose herself, finally realizing this chapter of her life was over. A new door must open. "And I will begin at the Abbot's manor," she promised as she left the castle for the stable where Abbot Fulrad's escort loaded her luggage.

Hildegard almost wished she were going with the Abbot to Rome. *What an adventure that would be!* Spring was finally inching its way over winter. The long-frozen streams and ponds had a lattice-work of ice across their surfaces. Stretching fingers of slow-moving water showed between the broken edges of ice. Icicles no longer hung, frozen in place, from the stable's roof. They melted to nothing two days ago, disappearing in the warming sun. Dirty, gray heaps of snow dissolved into large puddles which wet everyone's foot coverings and breeches, so deep was it in the low spots. The cows and brood mares gazed longingly at small, green shoots in the fields, even as their bellies, swollen with babies yet to be born, slowed their steps. Swallows and wrens hurried from their hiding places under the buildings' eaves, wheeling and soaring about the treetops.

"Take good care, Hildegard." The Abbot whispered to her, as his squire helped her mount her horse. " 'Tis not likely you'll see anyone from court. But stay close to my manor. The King is leaving for the spring assembly next week and, as usual, the army marches with him. I heard Oliver and Roland speaking of invaders. Seems every tribe on the continent has visions of taking Frankish lands from us. Be cautious as you move about." He smiled and patted her shoulder.

"We cannot seem to be parting, so wave happily to anyone you see watching." Hildegard complied, smiling broadly at the maids-in-waiting and an occasional countess gathered outside the stable. At the Abbot's slight nod, she rode her horse over beside him. He spoke quietly, for her ears alone.

"If you have any questions, need anything while I am away,

ask my manor man, Gregg. Although he refuses the title of 'seneschal,' he is one in everything but name." The Abbot laughed, as if sharing jokes with Hildegard. "This is a pleasant time to spend in my manor. Relax, eat, sleep. The gifts and promise of spring will restore your spirits and your hope. The countesses will not call for you here. Just draw no attention to yourself and stay away from the castle!" He checked the bag he hung around his pommel. "I hope to return within two fortnights, my dear. But the journey to Rome is long. Let us hope the roads are clear and passable." He shook his head as the deep mud sucked at his horse's hoofs. "If we have much of this," he pointed to the mud, "I won't see Rome before Eastertide."

The small party rode away, the Aachen castle receding behind them. At the second crook in the road, the Abbot motioned Hildegard to his right. She and Gerta, the house maid who was to accompany Hildegard on her journey back to the Abbot's manor, turned aside.

"Safe journey, Abbot. Godspeed." Hildegard wished him as the Abbot waved his farewell. She watched the little group until they were only dots in the distance. Then, Hildegard turned to Gerta and spoke.

"Tell me, Gerta." They turned toward the Abbot's manor. "Is there anyone, do you think, among the children, who would like to learn sums? Can you tell me?" Gerta shifted in her saddle, her mouth dropping open in amazement at Hildegard's question.

"...truly, Lady?" she asked. At Hildegard's serious nod, words burst from Gerta's mouth. "...why, everyone! We all do, adults and children, wish to learn sums. Can you teach us Lady? Are you able to do that...to see three chickens in a pen, two ducks on the pond, and one bird on high...and tell the whole number of them?"

"Aye," Hildegard answered simply. "And I am going to teach you, all of you who want to learn. We begin tomorrow. If there'll be several students, we'll meet in the stable after the mid-day meal. There is less happening then in the manor; so more will be free of duties at that time." She looked into Gerta's hopeful face. "Please spread the invitation around. Everyone who wants to learn to sum should come. The Abbot asked me to teach some of the lads. I would as lief teach all of you as three or four boys."

"Aye, Lady Hildegard," Gerta replied. "I will let everyone know."

The excitement of the day and the sadness of the Abbot's departure added to Hildegard's weariness. She asked the cook for a fruit tart before she retired to her bedchamber, early though it was. Changing into her sleeping tunic, Hildegard planned her mathematics lesson for the following afternoon. As she snuffed out her candle, the chamber maid responsible for linens knocked on the door. Timidly, Jenna put her head inside as Hildegard answered her quiet knock.

"My Lady," Jenna said. "I have coals for your feet."

"Wonderful!" Hildegard exclaimed. "Though the air is warmer, my toes are cold. Goodness, you have even better comforts here than I saw at court. It was not often I got coals for my feet there. It was late in the night, after all the countesses and their daughters were warm and dreaming, when coals were offered...if they were offered at all."

"Aye, my lady," Jenna replied. "I do have them for you now." She hurried to Hildegard's sleeping bench and thrust a wrapped bundle at her feet. Hildegard felt the warm glow of the coals through the linens.

"Thank you," she said as she looked at the young maid.

"The warmth will guarantee my sleep." Jenna smiled at her, waiting for any other requests Hildegard might make. It was then Hildegard noticed how tightly the young woman's tunic pulled across her chest.

"Is your tunic comfortable?" Hildegard asked before she thought.

"Aye," the girl answered. "It's good, Lady. It does not fit me as well as it did my sister, though." Jenna laughed. "I'm more...well, lady...more bosomy than Adrienne." She smiled shyly and looked away.

"Mayhap, we can make it a little bigger," Hildegard offered. The maid's eyes widened. Her lips turned up in a delighted smile.

"If so, I'll breathe easier." She moved closer. Hildegard reached out and flipped the bottom of the tunic up, examining the side seam."

"Aye, it can be done," she confirmed, looking into Jenna's face. "The seams have plenty of room; it will take only a few moments. Come tomorrow morning to wake me," she directed. "We'll fix it then."

"I will, my Lady, I will." The girl agreed. "I'll be happy to learn such a thing." But Hildegard did not hear, she was snuggling into her linens, already half-asleep.

She awakened as the sun streamed into her window and the bedchamber door opened, squeaking in protest. Hildegard raised her head as the young maid from last night brought herbal tea to her bedside.

"It's a lovely morning, my Lady," Jenna commented. "Though the wind is cold, the sun does give hope to every living thing!" She smiled broadly at Hildegard, holding out the tea. Hildegard took a sip from the leather cup, tasting the honey and rolling the tea around her tongue.

"Hummm," she sighed. "What delicious tea. It wakens me with such sweetness."

"Aye, the honey from this manor is famous here-abouts. We even sell it to the nobles' manors." Jenna announced with pride.

"I understand the reason. It tastes of apple blossoms and pears." Seeing Jenna waiting, Hildegard remembered her promise of the night before.

"Here," Hildegard said, as she hopped out of bed, "let me wash the sleep from my eyes and we'll work on your tunic." The young maid's face beamed as she pulled her tunic over her head and handed the garment to Hildegard. "If you'll bring me cheese and bread to break my fast, I'll dress and be ready to sew when you return. "Put on this tunic of mine to go to the cook room."

"…oh, nay; I couldn't!" The young woman protested. "It wouldn't be proper."

"Nonsense," Hildegard replied. "You need to cover your-self. Put it on and hurry back with my bread and cheese." The young woman slipped the tunic on, grinned widely and hurried from the chamber. Hildegard smiled.

"Mayhap I can teach these young maids some methods for altering clothes. They would get better usage from the garments they have." She sat down to think as she put on her foot coverings. "I provided extra clothes for the stable hands' children at court; but, now, I understand the servant girls need help as well." She grimaced, realizing anew the want through-out the realm.

"Where might I get extra garments?" She brushed and braided her hair and was ready when Jenna returned with her food. As Hildegard ate, she asked Jenna to remove the seams under the arms of the tunic. Although Jenna assured Hildegard she could sew, she knew only the rudiments of stitching. Hildegard showed her how to remove the seams' threads gently and set her to work.

"I did sew a little in my father's house," Jenna confided. "But we had no new linen. We patched and repaired our tunics over and over. Here, the Abbot brings us linen; but I do not know how to cut it." She dropped her eyes, her face reddening. "I can't patch my tunics again; the cloth is too weak. And my May Day tunic from last year will soon be too small," she admitted. Hildegard nodded in understanding.

"Oh, dear," Hildegard whispered.

"What's wrong?" Jenna asked, her voice worried.

"There's not as much room in these seams as I hoped. Let me think a minute." She told the maid, to keep her from talking. "Aye, I know what to do." From her traveling pack, she pulled out a piece of linen which she used to tuck around her legs in Charlemagne's banquet hall — to cut the wind blowing from the cold corridor into the chamber.

"I have it, Jenna! We'll sew an extra strip of cloth to the side of each seam and, then, sew the seams back together. That should give you more room on each side."

"I brought a knife, if you need one, Lady Hildegard," Jenna said. "But take care. It's very sharp."

Hildegard took the knife, laid the shawl on the floor stones and pulled a log on top. She cut along the edge of the log twice. Those two strips she matched with the tunic seams. She sewed one seam; Jenna sewed the second one. As Jenna sewed, Hildegard stood and spread the linens on her sleeping bench. Jenna bounced to her feet.

"Nay, nay, my lady," she protested. "This is my work...to cover the sleeping bench. Forgive me. I was so hopeful about the sewing..." Jenna began to explain.

"Never mind, Jenna. Spreading the linens is no work. Nay, it is better for you to do the stitching. Then, you'll know what to do if I am not around. Go, sew. Together, we shall get the work done." Hildegard reassured the girl. Jenna nodded thankfully and returned to her sewing, a satisfied smile on her intent face. Soon, she handed the tunic to Hildegard, a question in her eyes.

"Good. You sew very fine stitches, Jenna," Hilde complimented her. "Now, watch me fold over these ends; and we'll have this done." She took the needle from Jenna and finished the seam. She handed the tunic to the maid and watched as she slid it over her head. The tunic now hung over the girl's body, smooth and even, not pulling across her breasts as before.

"Thank you! Thank you, my Lady!" She exclaimed to Hildegard. "I can breathe deeply again!" Jenna laughed in delight.

"Good," Hildegard answered. "You'll be more comfortable now as you work. Can you show the other women how to do this?"

"Aye, if you listen as I tell them. I'd rest easier if you're there," she replied.

"I will be," Hildegard agreed. "Now, let's check to see if the cook needs any help. If not, I shall embroider cushion coverings for the benches in the Abbot's entryway. The ones there are much too plain for that lovely room!" They both startled as a dull noise came through the window.

"What is it?" Hildegard asked, her eyes wide as she turned to Jenna.

"It's the army, my lady. The men march to the annual meeting."

"I never noticed the sound before," Hildegard explained, "mayhap, because I was behind the army, marching with them. I never knew how loud it was! No wonder all soldiers worry about stealth!"

"Every year the Abbot leaves us," Jenna explained, "so we know the meaning of that sound. They march north, a little northeast." At Hilde's surprise expression, Jenna smiled. "We tell from the sound of the march. Each direction sounds a little different." They both moved to look out of the window. Of a certainty, the army headed northeast.

The days flew by, each one warmer and more beautiful than the one before. Hildegard, Jenna, and Gerta often sewed or embroidered in the garden to enjoy the sunshine and warm breezes as they worked.

Chapter Twenty-seven
REWARDS OF USEFUL WORK

"Would you like to help me teach the younger boys their numbers, Hardy?" Hildegard asked one of the stable lads some ten days later. He learned his numbers, both to recognize the written number and the meaning of it, long before her other students. Hardy stared into her face, completely shocked by her question.

"Teach them, my Lady? Me?" He asked, dumfounded. "I don't know about teaching. I only know a little myself." He dropped his head, looking at Hilde from almost closed lids. "Don't tease me, my Lady. Please." Color rushed to Hildegard's face. *Oh, nay! I didn't mean to embarrass the lad.* She looked at him again and saw the fear in his eyes, in his body's stiff posture.

"I don't tease." Hildegard hurried to respond. "You know enough to teach, Hardy. I've no doubt. And, it is said no one ever truly knows a thing until he can teach it to another." She smiled at him and squeezed his shoulder. "Come with me. I'll prove it to you."

Hardy straightened his back, shrugged, and followed Hildegard to the end of the garden where three young boys, five and six years old, were playing chase.

"Boys, boys!" Hildegard called to them. "Come here, please. You've run enough for today. Sit here and let Hardy help you learn to count." The boys' eyes widened as they ran to Hildegard, each one sitting as close to her as he could get. Their attention never wavered, their eyes alive with curiosity and excitement.

"Now, Hardy, show your students the difference between three stones and four stones." Hardy looked into Hildegard's face. She could see the panicked expression in his eyes. "How can you show them what 'three' is?" Hardy expelled a huge sigh and began gathering stones. He piled the stones in front of the boys.

"Here," he said to them, "how many stones do I have in my pile?" He looked from one face to another. "Let's see if you can count them. He took two stones from the pile and pointed to them. "Is this one stone?"

"Nay," one of the boys quietly said. "We have one stone and one stone again."

"Aye," Hardly smiled. "So, how many stones do we have?" The boys just looked at him. "If you count one but there is another stone, what is the next counting word?" Hardy asked.

"One, then two..." the oldest boy replied. He looked intently at the stones Hardy was touching. "We have two stones."

"Aye, good!" Hardy answered. "You are correct. We have one stone, and, then, another stone...which means we have two stones in this small pile." He looked at Hildegard who nodded. Hardy made another pile and turned to the boys. Hildegard watched Hardy teach, gratified as his confidence grew, inspired by the boys' eagerness to learn. Noting their enthusiasm, Hildegard's thoughts turned to the Abbot's trip.

If only I were eager for the marriage possibility the Abbot mentioned, she thought, I could start a new life. *I cannot dream of Charlemagne indefinitely. Nothing will change his marital situation. I must start a life of my own.* Her thoughts were interrupted by a shout from the youngest boy, Larkt. Hildegard raised her eyes to look at the three boys.

Larkt was full of excitement. He waved his hands, begging Hardy for a chance to answer a question. Hardy nodded at the boy.

"Count them aloud for us." Hardy suggested.

"There's one stone; here's another, and the last stone makes three!" Larkt shouted as he understood. He held his breath, looking from Hardy to Hildegard.

"Very good; that's right." Hardy answered. "Aye, we have three stones here; this is the number '3'." He drew the number on the ground. "Now, each of you go and fine me three objects. Bring them here. Get three of the same thing: twigs, bits of wood, blades of grass. Don't pick the little buds, though." He waved his hand for the boys to begin. Hardy looked at Hildegard, his face worried.

"Am I doing right?" he asked her. "I know nothing about teaching."

"You're doing fine, Hardy," Hildegard reassured him. "Give it a little time. The boys' enthusiasm to learn will help you teach them." The boys returned, each one smiling. They walked carefully, balancing objects in their hats. Hardy examined the contents of the hats carefully, praising the boys as he counted out their objects.

"You've done well," Hardy told them. "Meet me here tomorrow after the mid-day meal. We'll talk about 'four' then." He promised as he turned away.

"Nay, nay!" The boys chimed in together.

"Nay," Carl shouted. "We want to talk about four, five, and six today!"

"Aye!" Han said. "Today, we want to learn more!"

Hildegard took five pieces of baked sweet dough and five pieces of crystallized candy from her basket.

"Teach your students as much as they can learn, Hardy," she told him. "And reward them each with a piece of candy and a dough strip, only one piece of each." She handed the 'delights' to Hardy. "The rest are for their teacher." Hardy's eyes widened as he nodded happily at Hildegard.

"Aye," he agreed, "thank you."

Hardy proved to be the most able of Hildegard's students. As the days slipped by, Hardy taught one group of children while Hildegard taught the others. Even the baker came to learn to sum, swearing that summing was sure to improve his breads and cakes. Hildegard discovered Hardy had a talent for math; he grasped the principles of subtraction as quickly as those for sums. With his help, their students acquired a good understanding of basic math.

Hildegard surprised her students with picnics beside the river, horse rides as rewards for mathematical competitions, and baked tarts and puddings for their hard work. Some of the children's parents even joined the classes, slipping in and out as they completed their daily duties. Hildegard quickly became known as 'The Teacher,' her words quoted several times a day.

Hardy, much aware of his status, nevertheless was ever humble, asking Hildegard for direction and evaluation.

By early April of that year, Hildegard's students were quite adept at simple math. She knew planting season would interrupt and postpone their studies; but, already, many of the children were coming for lessons on Sunday afternoons.

There was one fearful time for Hildegard during those work-filled but pleasant days. Before anyone could shout a warning, a messenger from Aachen castle cantered down the road to the Abbot's manor. Hildegard was in the barn, showing two squires how to handle twelve new puppies. Hearing the horses' hooves, one of the lads peeked out of the hay loft above the stable.

"Rider!" He shouted. "...a rider from the King!" The mounted soldier carried a small banner and sat his horse with pride. The lad, Josh, who happened to peer out and see the King's colors, beckoned to Hildegard and hurried her up the ladder to the hay loft.

"Hasten, speed up," he directed. "I'll cover you with hay. 'Tis not likely a soldier will climb those steps to investigate up here." Even though Fulrad's captain of the guards hailed the soldier from the courtyard, the soldier turned his horse and rode directly to the stable door. Hildegard, scrambling up the steps two at a time, dived into the remnants of last year's hay. Josh handed her a reed and, making a breathing motion with it, forked straw over her. At that moment, they heard a man's voice at the bottom of the stairs.

"Lad? You in the hay loft." the soldier called, "Come where I can see you." Hildegard's rescuer hurried to the top of the stairs.

"A good...a good morrow to you, Sire," Josh spoke as he looked down into the soldier's eyes. The man nodded, his eyes darting all around the stable.

"My bridle is fraying," the soldier said. "May I borrow a bridle for my ride back to Aachen? I'll return it to you long before the Abbot returns from Rome."

"Aye, Sir, aye," Josh answered, starting to descend the ladder. "The Abbot would not want you to ride with a frayed bridle. I'll get you one this very moment!" Eyeing the hay stack, he backed down the stairs. Josh knew if he talked to the man, it would prevent his lingering too long at the manor.

"Sire, have you any word of the Abbot's homeward journey? We wish to prepare a welcome-home feast for him," he explained.

"Aye," the soldier answered. "The King expects him by the end of this week or early next week, mayhap one or two days before Sunday. But we hear the roads are barely passable out of Italy—much flooding, the scouts say. So he may be delayed. Don't make bread for the welcome party yet, lad." He added as Josh handed him a bridle.

"That hay up there in the loft," the soldier inclined his head. "Was it harvested from the same field as this one here, this stack in the corner?"

"Aye, Sir, the north field—as the Abbot calls it. That's the field above the river, Sire." He added by way of explaining the field's location.

"I want a bundle of that...for my rabbit hutch," the soldier said.

"If the morrow is not too late, I'll bring it on the cart to you after mid-day, Sir. The stable-master is going to Aachen to deliver eggs and cheese. Will that suit?" Josh asked. "Anything to keep him out of that hay loft," he mumbled to himself.

"Perfect," the soldier grinned. "Your offer will save me from having to bear scratches from carrying this hay. Good. Find me on the morrow, at the horse line, boy." He left the stable and mounted his horse.

"...on the morrow, then!" Josh called, sitting down to rest his quivering knees. Under her hay cover, Hildegard breathed through the reed. Finally, in the distance, she heard the sound of the horse's hooves. She crawled from under the hay as Josh leaned to pull hay from around her.

"Thank you, Josh," Hildegard said to him. "You may have saved me from much embarrassment...and from the King's anger. Thank you for your quick thinking!"

"You are much welcome, my Lady," Josh grinned. "It's my duty to keep my teacher safe...especially one as pretty as you."

He dropped his eyes to the floor. Hildegard startled, then smiled.

"What a wonderful compliment." She changed the subject. "Did I hear correctly? The Abbot is on his way home?" Her eyes widened as she felt her heart jump. *I should prepare for my journey home.* Hilde was, all at once, conscious of the passage of time. "I will alert the manor." She ran from the stable, though her stride slowed. *I wish to return home, but I consider this dear place my home, too. The Abbot served me well, giving me the privilege of living at his manor.*

Living away from all she knew, Hildegard wondered – despite her best intentions –about the new queen. How did Desiderata fare: in a new home, in a different court, away from her family and friends? Rumors bubbled, even here in the Abbot's manor. Some said the new queen was pleased with her marriage; others objected saying Desiderata and Charlemagne were almost strangers. Hildegard didn't know what to believe so she thought of them as little as possible. Charlemagne, she continued to yearn for but it was pleasant to be away from the court and the demands of the noble women.

She prayed every day, before the mid-day meal, for the soldiers' safety, naming the King, Roland, Oliver and Rinaldo. Her only regret was that, if any were hurt, she would be weeks in hearing the news. She did not consider the danger of a mortal wound for any one of them. It was inconceivable.

Weeks later reports of the battles would make their way back to Aachen and, from there, to the Abbot's manor. Those left behind could do nothing for the court or the soldiers now…just plant, gather, and harvest foods for the winter.

Preparations for the Abbot's return filled the minds of everyone at his manor. They swept, cleaned, dusted, arranged spring blossoms everywhere and, then, cleaned again. Hildegard unpacked her trunk and re-evaluated her clothing. Since I'm going home, she thought, I'll give some of my older clothes to the young women here. The serving girls' tunics and aprons were worn and most knew only the rudiments of sewing. Hildegard knew much of the clothing, even the sleeping linens, would find its way to the women's families. They took little for themselves, saying their younger brothers and sisters needed new clothing more than they.

"I can get more clothing from the Countesses." Hildegard muttered. "I'll send it here to Jenna. She well knows how to re-design and cut the garments and, with a little more practice, will be skilled enough to sew a finished garment."

A mere three days later, the Abbot's return was announced by a single 'Haloo in the manor' wafting through the summer air. The Abbot waved wildly, even though everyone easily spotted three of the Pope's guards, their red mantles blazing in the morning sun. The guards smiled as the manor's residents rushed to the courtyard. The cooks and serving girls, Gerta and Josh, Jenna and Todd were spell-bound by the entourage.

"Close your mouths, my children," Abbot Fulrad laughed. "I return with a guard from Pope Hadrian. Only the tapestries in the holy church match their magnificence. Come, come," he beckoned. "We must catch up on each other's news. Is everyone here well?"

The people of his manor rushed to help the Abbot from his mount, to take his mantle, to bring him refreshments. He was gentle and kind to them, ever eager to share in their joys and their pain. Despite the length of his journey, the Abbot was in good spirits, eager to receive updates on all manor activities. Hildegard welcomed the Abbot, then stood beside him as everyone reported his own news.

In an impromptu moment, Hardy's three students who were now quite proficient in math—as long as no one questioned them about numbers more than twenty—displayed their skills to the Abbot. He did not spare his delight in their accomplishment and praised them again and again. Finally, he looked around the room at the people who loved him best and spoke.

"My beloved friends, my family," the Abbot began, "words are not enough to express my gratitude for my good fortune...for my home and for those who dwell with me. It's wonderful to be among you again! I spent several reassuring days with Pope Hadrian. But, even seeing him, does not match my delight in returning to you. I know, once again; you are dearer to me than anything else. I know, also, each of you developed new, important skills while I traveled. To celebrate our good fortune with each other, there are surprise gifts for everyone." The children of the manor cheered with good spirits, pushing each other aside to get closer to the Abbot's chair.

"I have nothing here at the table," he assured them. "The surprises are on the pack horses in the stable. Josh, take the little ones with you to the stable. Unpack the horses. Every gift has a name on it. When the children have their gifts, bring the ones left for the 'big' people here to the manor!" Josh nodded, pleased to have this honor. He took the hands of two of the smallest children and, like the pied-piper, marched to the stables with his followers. Hildegard laughed and squeezed the Abbot's arm.

"Abbot," she said, "it's wonderful to have you back. As fine as is your manor, it's only half a home without you in it." She smiled and kissed his cheek.

"My dear," the Abbot beamed at her, "from all I hear, including praises sung about 'our Lady,' I know you've transformed my manor." He frowned. "I remember your warning about learning being dangerous, Hildegard," he said. "But it brings so much pleasure to my people that I cannot fear it. Thank you for all your efforts here."

"Oh, Abbot, thank you for the privilege of becoming a member of your family. Each is wonderful, every one!" She exclaimed, her eyes sparkling, her face a big smile. The Abbot nodded, rose to kiss her cheek, and spoke.

"On the morrow, I shall report to King Charlemagne, Hildegard." He told her. "Suffice it to say this: my trip to Rome was partially successful. The King has much to make up to his Holiness. The newly selected Pope, Hadrian, like his predecessor — Stephen — is angry about Charlemagne's hasty marriage."

"I don't understand." Hildegard replied. "What's the reason? Did he have someone in mind for the king to marry? Does he dislike Desiderata herself and, if so, why? She brings an alliance which should decrease fighting. I think saving lives should be most positive to the Holy Father." She remembered Fulrad's stricken words at Charlemagne's wedding — 'The Pope is against this marriage.'

"Desiderata's father wants to control the Roman Church, Hildegard," the Abbot responded. "Unlike King Pepin or Charlemagne, Desiderius actively plans to take power from the Pope and transfer it to himself. The Pope fears him…with good reason, I think. He knows Desiderius hopes to undermine the Church, to weaken it. Pope Stephen forbade Charlemagne's alliance with the Lombard king. Such a partnership makes him sleepless at night." The Abbot rubbed his forehead.

"Governing and religion," he continued, "they make court

intrigue seem like child's play."

"Tis sad, Abbot, for the Pope to worry about such temporal things. He would, I know, prefer to be about God's work." Abbot Fulrad nodded at Hildegard's words but said nothing. If religious men would think of God, Hildegard, he thought, the Church would be a much more effective instrument for HIS will.

"I suppose the Pope does the best he can, Hildegard, much like the rest of us." Putting this topic aside, Fulrad motioned Hildegard inside where they sat down companionably together.

"I, reluctantly, remember my promise to you — to send you home," Fulrad said. "I will honor that, despite many misgivings." At Hildegard's frown, the Abbot laughed. "Everyone in this household whispers, begs me to keep you here, my dear!" He admitted. "But I don't forget the threat to you at court. I believe it no longer an issue, forgotten. We will make it so by removing you from them. So, let's talk about the future. When I return to court tomorrow, will you come with me to gather the rest of your things from Aachen? I know you left a trunk with Gisela. I'm determined to send you homeward with no delay, hoping you'll return to us soon."

"Thank you, Abbot," Hildegard replied. "Aye, I should like to return to the court; but, mainly, to bid my friends goodbye. My family is eager for my return so I would leave quickly." She stopped the Abbot as he turned to leave.

"You know the army marched." At his surprised look, she added. "Aye, they left Aachen a few days after you began your trip to Rome. We heard there was a Saxon uprising, but know nothing for certain." The Abbot nodded.

"Tomorrow, at the castle, I've no doubt we'll hear the details." He said. "This disturbs me. The Saxons are always rebelling. So, Charlemagne marched early, then, well before the battle season usually begins." He shook his head. "The summer promises to be long, my dear." He left to consult with his seneschal, to walk about his manor, and to be updated on all events since he left.

That evening Hildegard slept little, nervous about being in the same house as Queen Desiderata and the Queen Mother on the morrow.

"But I shall not stay there long." She promised herself. "I will avoid all of them, the court entirely. I want only to bid Gisela, Oliver, and Roland a personal farewell. All else was done...weeks ago."

When Hildegard and Abbot Fulrad awoke the next morning, they discovered King Charlemagne was in the castle. He preceded the army, arriving home near to midnight. He sent a missive seeking their presence on the morrow, emphasizing he anxiously anticipated talking to Abbot Fulrad.

After arriving at the court, Hildegard shared tea and tarts with Gisela. She and Hildegard relaxed together, sharing memories and strengthening their friendship before Hildegard continued her journey homeward. The Abbot planned to send her on her way today after the mid-day meal. As they laughed and talked together, there was a knock on the door. A guard handed Gisela a folded parchment with Hilde's name of it and hurried away. Gisela brought the note to Hildegard.

"It must be from Charlemagne or the Abbot," she said, knowing the King and Fulrad closeted themselves together as soon as the Abbot arrived. Hildegard unfolded the parchment and scanned it rapidly. She released her breath in relief.

"He says," she reported as she looked over at Gisela, "he and the Abbot have much work yet and asks me to remain at the castle tonight. Abbot Fulrad will summon me when he is ready to return to his manor in the morning." Hildegard frowned. She hoped the Abbot brought Charlemagne a positive message form Pope Hadrian but, mayhap, such was not the case. I'm caught here this night, she thought. But she smiled and asked Gisela.

"Will you aid a poor, Swabian lass, Gisela, and give me a bed for the night?" Hildegard asked.

"I would give you my own bed," Gisela responded, "if it would wipe the worried look off your face!" She laughed at Hildegard's surprised reaction. "You seem aloof and unaffect-ed to others, Hilde," she teased; "but I can read your face, and you are troubled. What is it?" Hildegard smiled at Gisela. Alt-hough she knew Charlemagne confided in his sister, Hildegard did not want to worry her unnecessarily, so she answered eva-sively.

"I hoped Abbot Fulrad would be reporting only pleasant greetings from the Pope," she answered. "Your brother needs all the friends he can attract."

"Aye," Gisela agreed. "If only I could do something to de-fuse the Pope's temper. He expects much from this court; he always has." Hildegard listened to Gisela's words with half an ear. What would please the Holy Father, she wondered. *What was of equal import as the King's recent marriage?* Hildegard started to stand, then sat back down quickly. That's it, she real-ized, her mind jumping. *Gisela's broken engagement would be im-portant to Pope Hadrian! And it would put the King in a good light.*

"Gisela," Hildegard began, "did you inform Pope Hadrian your betrothal to Adelchis is finished?" Gisela looked up sharp-ly, searching Hildegard's face.

"Nay, I did not," she replied. "Should I?" She saw Hilde-gard's fingers tapping on the writing bench. Why would the Pope care about that? Gisela asked herself. Her mouth dropped open. "Why, if that marriage happened, I'd be marrying into the Lombard kingdom, too." She said. "...the *very* thing the Abbot said the Pope hated!" She glanced at Hildegard. Watching Gisela's face, Hildegard nodded, seeing Gisela understood the political implications of the broken betrothal, just as she did the marriage of her brother.

"I believe the Pope would be very pleased to hear about your broken betrothal, Gisela." Hildegard pointed out. "And he would be even more reassured were you to tell him Charlemagne and Carloman both objected to the betrothal, that they rejected your mother's wishes and condemned her meddling."

"Aye," Gisela nodded thoughtfully. "Should I have the Abbot deliver the message, Hildegard?" She asked. Hildegard was silent, thinking.

"Nay," she answered. "You write the Pope a missive yourself. Tell him you wanted him to know. Tell him you're officially a novice and you long to be an abbess." Gisela whooped with disbelief at Hilde's words.

"An abbess! Oh, nay, Hildegard!" She responded. "I just want to be a nun. I have no such ambitions."

"Why not, Gisela?" Hildegard asked. "You will be a wonderful nun, all the more reason to become an abbess, a model for all those young women!" Gisela shook her head meekly but put pen to paper to write to Pope Hadrian. Hildegard helped her phrase her message. When the letter was complete, Hildegard rose, beckoning to Gisela.

"Come with me," she invited. "I will show you the tunics and breeches I'm leaving behind, the ones I want you to send to the Abbot's manor. His maid there, Jenna, is already planning the clothes she will redesign and sew for her sisters and nieces."

"How I wish I had such a wholesome occupation!" Gisela

moaned as she and Hildegard left her bedchamber. "Such a responsibility would be sweet, indeed."

Gisela accompanied Hildegard as she bid Oliver and Roland adieu. Next, Hildegard stopped by her old bedchamber to say her goodbyes to Jocelyn and Maria; but neither was there. Hildegard wrote them a farewell note, propping it on Jocelyn's sleeping bench. She wished Maria special happiness, for Gisela told her Maria accepted a marriage proposal from a noble's second son. Time flew by and it was time for the evening meal. The two young women skipped the court meal at day's end, eating companionably in Gisela's bedchamber.

Chapter Twenty-eight
SURPRISES, INDEED

Back in the banquet hall, King Charlemagne looked around. *Where the hell is Hildegard?* He asked himself. He so looked forward to seeing her at the evening meal. Now, he realized his sister was not in the room either. *Ahhh, they're together, probably in Gisela's chamber.* He frowned, happening to glance at his wife. She stared over the heads of the diners, pre-occupied as always. Desiderata felt the King look at her and turned to face him.

"I would speak with you, Charlemagne." Desiderata said to her husband. Sitting beside her at the great table in the hall. Startled, Charlemagne looked at her; his face puzzled. She spoke to him so rarely he was momentarily speechless.

"At your pleasure, my lady," he replied. "In a few moments, one of the younger poets is reading. After that, we'll have a stroll in the gardens. Would this please you?"

"Aye; thank you, Charlemagne. A walk in the garden pleases me very much." She accepted a piece of roast he offered her. Desiderata ate with better appetite this night. After her decision to speak with the King, she found life looked much more hopeful, more hopeful now than since her father told her of the betrothal. She glanced at the King again. He never changed. Even now, when she asked to speak to him, he seemed to care little. Of a certainty, though, little changed in his life after the wedding, despite the massive changes in hers. He was in his own court, among his own people – hero to them all.

As usual, Charlemagne ate with gusto, beckoning to the serving maid for another piece of his favorite meat, grilled roast. His huge frame allowed him to carry more weight than the average man; and he was so active, soldiering almost three days out of four, he was always hungry. Yet, he listened eagerly as one of the young poets read both his own work and a piece of a Roman master. Charlemagne often wrote his own laws, even penning religious essays. But he swore he could never be a poet.

"Bravo! Bravo!" He shouted as the young poet finished his reading.

"If I could only speak that way, what a king I would be!" He said to the beaming man. "Thank you; you have added sweetness to this meal, much more so than the honey." The fledging poet blushed with pleasure.

"Would you grace Count Hautgard's court with your poetry?" The King asked the young man. Hearing an affirmative reply, he summoned the Abbot to write to Hautgard forthwith to offer the young poet's services. The Abbot rose to speak with the young poet whose face beamed with pride and excitement.

Because Desiderata was eager to talk to her husband, the poetry readings seemed slow to her. But, eventually, the King rose, beamed at everyone in the hall, and announced he and his lady-wife were going for a walk in the rose garden. Desiderata left the hall on his arm and gathered her courage.

How to go about this delicate task? They talked in desultory fashion about his day-long ride, her growing interest in fruit trees, the time of the next spring assembly, and other neutral subjects. Just as she felt the King ready himself to ask why she requested a talk, Desiderata plunged into her decision about her future.

"Charlemagne," she began, "I'm going home; I'm returning to my father's house."

"For certain," Charlemagne replied. "I'll go with you. It's time for me to visit the villages in the direction of Lombardy. The people are always happier and easier to control if I appear before them. It's been almost a year since I moved through that part of the realm, just before we were married, in fact. Aye, this is an ideal time for such a journey. Do you mind moving at a slow pace? I'll need...we'll need to stop and pass our nights with nobles along the way. Such visits build loyalty."

"Nay, I don't object to such a trip," Desiderata answered. "But you misunderstand. I'm going home for good. I can think of no reason to continue this charade of a marriage. We remain strangers, you and I, and are not likely to become friends...or lovers." She lowered her eyes as the heat of her embarrassment crept up her neck.

"I must accept some responsibility for that," she admitted.

"I know so little about men. And I realize you find me odd. I surely do not like this so-called 'woman's duty;' but loving is not our only difficulty." She held her breath and continued. "You can, of a certainty, forbid my return to my father. But, before you do, please, think of our last weeks together; tell me we should stay wed. Is there any defense for it?" Charlemagne sat down abruptly on a garden bench and stared at her face.

"Forgive me, Desiderata," he muttered. "You have me at a disadvantage. I didn't realize your unhappiness was this deep. Do I greatly wrong you, so much you wish to leave the marriage? It's true; I'm often absent. My duties to the realm are many. Mock maneuvers, military planning, sword-play take much of my time. But battles must be fought; lands must be held. Friendships and alliances must be cultivated each and every day." He stared at her.

"How can you so calmly say: 'I am returning to my father's house?" Desiderta stared into his face. She could see Charlemagne was dumfounded. He did not understand her!

"I say this based on our relationship." Desiderate tried again. "The truth is we have no marriage, Sir! We smile remotely at one another and play a game of caring. But we bring each other no pleasure, no pride, no warmth. I have no idea who you are, and you make no effort to know or to understand me; you seldom speak. What do you imagine…that I wish to live a stranger to my own husband, never to share a common thought with you? There will be no heir for we take no delight in each other – not in bed, not in talk, not in affairs of the court. Queen Bertrada makes every decision. She will never willingly surrender duties to me. I am nothing here, nothing to you, to the members of your court, or even to myself."

"You loved before with another wife. How, then, can you want such a union as we have? I know little of men but there must be…contact…to make a child. Without that, I count for nothing. Why this pretense, this shell of a life we pass together? Nay, Nay, Nay! I want to lose myself in living. Here, I wait and wait for life to begin!" She paused to control her emotions. "Do, please, consider all I say and let us talk again in another day or two." Charlemagne nodded mutely; Desiderata pressed his hand and left.

"Oh, my!" She thought. "I didn't anticipate this shock, this inability to believe my words. I thought he might get angry; he does that so easily. But does he expect less than I? Or is it pride?" Desiderata's worries followed each other quickly through her mind, one by one. Her face paled; tears sprang to her eyes.

"What mistake did I make? I was not subtle. I didn't speak about his disappointments." she moaned. "Ohh, Father, help me! He will refuse to release me!" Her eyes bulged with fear as her quiet wail quivered in the air. "Mayhap, he'll not consent to an annulment. I must have one, I must! Otherwise, I have no future...no future at all."

Charlemagne could not process Desiderata's words. Going home? Leaving me? Ending the marriage? He was speechless. Of all the things he expected of this marriage, Desiderata's rejection of him was surely not one of them.

"What is she saying?" Charlemagne muttered to himself. "She wants to leave, to end the marriage? Why?" King Charlemagne tried to be hurt by Desiderata's threat. But, truth be told, he wasn't even angry. This is a rejection, he told himself. *Why do I feel so little? I don't care. But how will I explain her departure? I wonder what people in the realm will say; what will the nobles say?*

"Ha!" The King laughed. "My wife and I foisted a joke on the entire realm. We have no marriage, almost no relationship at all! I have no regret; I actually have little concern." He stilled, considering his thoughts. "She's leaving me and I don't care!" When that realization came, Charlemagne's mouth dropped open; he stood immobile.

"How could such a thing happen? Marriages are supposed to be built on mutual respect, shared goals, and, eventually, on loving commitment. But not one of those attributes described his current union. *Why not divorce?* There is no union to save, and despite his need for an heir, there is no child."

"This is a reasonable decision, the very course to take!" The King muttered to himself. "I'll suggest Desiderata leave quickly. And for a couple of days, I'll spend my nights in the soldiers' tents and be scarce in the day. The court can believe she and I journey to the Lombard court together. Such a tale will tame speculation for a time. Time will pass and cover any lingering questions."

"I vow," Charlemagne promised himself. "My next wife will come to me willingly, by God. She will want me. I'll have no more of this ice in a woman's veins and no bitter words!" The King smiled to himself, already developing an explanation for his court.

"I don't need to deal with the court whispers," he promised himself. "I'll say Desiderata began her journey home without me. In a few more days, the truth will come out; but she will be gone by then." King Charlemagne smiled to himself, hurrying toward his soldiers' tents, anxious to lose himself in their midst.

By this time, Gisela and Hildegard were long in their sleeping linens. Hildegard wished to be fresh on the morrow to begin her homeward journey. But, despite the tension and sadness of her leave-taking, she couldn't sleep. The air felt overcast, almost brooding, as if something were yet to come. Hildegard, gazing out of her window, saw the doors of the courtyard swing open. What is going on? She asked herself. People seldom left the court this deep in the night. She hoped there was not bad news, another rebellion or rapid marauders. Her mouth dropped open as she saw soldiers bend down to tie cloths to their horses' feet.

"Who leaves with such stealth?" Hildegard whispered. "And why? I never heard of any such secrecy in this court!" Her breath caught as she saw Queen Desiderata mount her horse. Hildegard stood spell-bound by the window, looking out long after the Queen and her escort departed. Now, as the sun's rays lightened the east, the mystery of the Queen's leave-taking remained.

Hildegard paced the floor, feeling her heart beat, surprising her with hope. She swallowed convulsively as she told herself not to resurrect her dreams of the King. A knock on the door announced Count Hautgard's daughters. Early to break their fast, they heard two countesses remark that Desiderata was not in her bedchamber. People scarcely ate; rumors began. A maid reported to Countess Marsono that the Queen's clothing and personal furniture were nowhere to be found. Her Lombard ladies could not be located, and her heavy traveling trunk was missing.

Neither Jocelyn nor Maria brought reports from anyone who knew of the Queen's whereabouts. And there were as many speculations as there were noble women. Still, Hildegard knew one fact: Desiderata and her large escort left the court furtively, deep in the night. But she said nothing. Jocelyn and Maria hurried away in an attempt to learn more. *Where is Charlemagne? Does he know his wife slipped away from the court?* The questions haunted Hildegard.

"He must know; how can she leave without him?" The lack of answers crowded together in her mind. "I know Desiderata left," Hildegard murmured; "but I didn't see the King with her."

At the mid-day meal, Egginhard announced the court's departure date for journeying to the spring assembly. He did not mention the queen nor the mobile court's expected route. He also cancelled a long-planned trip to Strassburg at summer's end. Widespread disappointment greeted the announcement; court ladies and courtiers so looked forward to the destination that they began their preparations months ago.

Hildegard, confused and groggy from falling asleep on a chair, heard a knock on the door.

"Come." Hildegard called. She looked up expectantly and, just as quickly, was downcast again. Gisela stood in the doorway.

"Were you expecting someone, Hilde? I can return later."

Gisela offered. "I sent my letter to the Pope with the King's messenger. But on my return, that nervous Lady Barsonne stopped me. The court is atwitter over Desiderata's disappearance."

"Did you learn anything?" Hildegard asked. "Forgive me, Gisela. I hoped to hear from Charlemagne and, mayhap, news of Queen Desiderata—from him, I mean." She amended. "Where can he be, Gisela? Desiderata left the court in the night. I saw her escort gather. Soldiers muffled their horses' hooves! What happened? Do you know anything about it?" Hildegard's eyes dropped at her question, trying to conceal her intensity from Gisela. She was unsure how much Gisela guessed about her current feelings for Charlemagne. Gisela hurried from the door to give Hildegard a squeeze.

"Nay, I cannot find him. No one has seen him." She reported. I know Hilde adores my brother, Gisela thought. But if he knows of Desiderata's departure, I'm not certain. She frowned. *He **must** know. Desiderata would never dare incite his anger by just disappearing from the court, would she?*

"I can't think she would leave without his knowledge." Gisela said as she heard the intake of Hildegard's breath and turned to her. "Speculation is rampant but even the King's retainers know nothing. No one can explain Desiderata's sudden departure. Everyone denies any knowledge of it. Someone even voiced the thought she might be pregnant and, therefore, anxious to return to her father's house. But this makes no sense; we would all know such important news." Gisela repeated the rumor, knowing it would give Hildegard scant comfort. She was as confused as Hildegard was troubled.

"Why doesn't Charlemagne come, let us know what happened?" Hildegard muttered. He should explain this himself, she thought. "If Desiderata began a journey, any journey, surely she must tell her husband. Gisela, I just don't understand the secrecy! It appears the Queen is fleeing, running away from something! Of course, the court doesn't know she left in the dead of night." She stopped speaking, suddenly realizing she speculated to Charlemagne's sister. "I shouldn't make guesses, I know." Hildegard admitted. "The King will announce his news in his own good time." She saw Gisela shake her head, her eyes downcast, and realized the King's sister knew her feelings. Hilde ran into Gisela's arms.

"Gisela, Gisela! I love him. I've tried my best to put him out of my heart; but I've failed." Hildegard sighed. "Now, just for a moment, I did hope he realized this marriage was a mistake. But...it's a false hope, I know." She sat slowly on a bench. "Wouldn't he tell you of a change in his marriage, an unexpected journey, a change in Desiderata's schedule?" Gisela nodded her head.

"I like to think so." She confirmed to Hildegard. "But does he know Desiderata left the court? I can't answer the question. I'm as confused as you, Hilde."

"This change in plans may mean nothing. Mayhap, Desiderata is off to plan some Easter surprise for the King. And there may be the hope of an heir; you can never be sure." Voicing her biggest fear, Hildegard collapsed on the floor, stricken at the thought of a child.

"If there's a pregnancy, I have no hope. A child will cement this loveless marriage." Her heart contracted. *I will not become a mistress to the King. I will not.* She vowed to herself. *He severed his life from mine; I have to accept that. If he has feelings for me, surely he would come to say so.* Unable to control herself, Hildegard burst into tears, hanging onto Gisela as though she were drowning.

Oblivious to the court's uproar and to Hildegard's distress,

King Charlemagne strode around his soldiers' eastern camp. He shared venison roast at three campfires and enjoyed two servings of blackberry cobbler, made with dried berries.

"Sire? Your Majesty?" A voice called as Charlemagne walked to the fourth campfire. "Sire, might I speak with you? I entreat you." The voice continued a little more loudly. The King stopped, turned, and recognized Adelchis, Desiderius' son and heir, and Desiderata's brother. He smiled; Adelchis hurried toward him.

"Good day to you, Adelchis. Come; join me at Grant's camp.We're to have venison and eggs to break our fast. He promised turkey, also; but, knowing his eye with a bow, I think not." The King laughed aloud.

"Thank you, Sire," Adelchis answered. "Would that I could join you; but I come to bid you farewell. My days here at your court and your table are finished." Adelchis scuffed the earth with his foot covering, looking distinctly uncomfortable at the King's invitation.

"Oh, come," Charlemagne insisted. "Whatever your journey, you will travel better on a full belly. You're taking your leave?" Charlemagne faltered as understanding came. "Oh, hell, of a certainty, you would be leaving! Forgive me." the King continued. "My mind is cloudy." He smiled slowly but asked again.

"Must you leave, Adelchis? Is there no possibility you could direct your allegiance to my court?" The King growled, caught between regret and reality.

"Oh that I could, Sire! But I am my father's chattel. Be certain. His constant threat is banishment. In some ways, I would welcome it. But the Lombards are my people, your Majesty. I must go home. Desiderata spoke of her journey to me, Sire," he clarified. He looked around and added softly. "My mother will be distraught and embarrassed by this failed marriage, as you can imagine, and will need my presence." He shook his head slowly. "I regret leaving your court, Sire."

"You shall always be my sovereign, if not my daily commander. I must ride; I can speak no more!" Adelchis bowed to the King; stopped a moment to say a word to Oliver, hugged him, and ran for his horse.

Adelchis' departure sent a cold chill through the court. Everyone liked him, much more than they did his sister, Desiderata. His leaving pressed Queen Bertrada to announce Desiderata was on a journey home. She missed her family. The Queen's words, her obvious regret at her daughter-in-law's leaving, puzzled the court. No one dreamed the Queen Mother saw herself in Desiderata and wished, even more, for the new queen to succeed. The Queen knew, of a certainty, Desiderata would not return. Bertrada's machinations, her defiance of her son's wishes, her meddling earned her nothing in the end.

Court members, secretly relieved at Desiderata's absence, shrugged their shoulders at the news, and turned to speculate on the King's next choice of bride. All knew the pressure Queen Bertrada exerted on him, ever demanding an heir. Of a certainty, no one knew Charlemagne spoke with Abbot Fulrad before he, too, disappeared.

"Use any excuse, Fulrad, to keep Hildegard here. I do not ask your counsel or your opinion. You will only quote Church doctrine to me and it is of little use. I, myself, will send an escort with Lady Hildegard when she returns to her father's house. A few more days can be of little moment."

Despite his better judgment, the Abbot postponed Hilde's journey. Later in the day, he discovered the roads toward Swabia were treacherous, many impassable from the spring downpours. At the least, his decision seemed right, even were it not honest.

"We must delay your departure, Hildegard," the Abbot said to her. "I do not regret delaying this journey, my dear. You've become a daughter to me and my manor. We all are loathe to see you leave." Hildegard dropped her head; she was eager to see her home again.

"As you say, Sir." She replied.

King Charlemagne, removed from court talk and speculation, spent the next two days among his soldiers, hearing of their exploits against the Saxons and comforting the wounded. On the third day, Charlemagne bathed in the freezing river, carefully dressed, and went in search of Hildegard. I close my mind to Desiderata, the King told himself. *She is in my past.*

"I shall think only of Hilde from this day forth," he vowed, "even until the end of my days." He rode quickly toward the Abbot's manor, knowing the Abbot kept her yet there.

With no word from the Abbot when she might journey home, Hildegard thought of unpacking her travel bags. But her heart was not in it. Not wanting to worry and pine in the manor, she joined the workers in pulling weeds from the crops. She worked for three hours but began to feel faint. Since her return from the court, she was never hungry and ate little. Now, as she pulled and chopped in the field, weakness came upon her. I need to eat, she thought to herself.

"Truth be told," Hildegard muttered, "Charlemagne truly cares little for me. Otherwise, he would come; he would tell me of Desiderata's leaving and of his plans." She left the field and walked back to the manor, entering the now-deserted cook room from the garden door. No one was about. She found a rye loaf, cheese and some very young onions. She carried them to the herb garden.

King Charlemagne, riding toward the Abbot's manor, memorized his words to Hildegard. *I don't have my speech perfect*, he admitted to himself, *but Hildegard will hear my sincerity. She cannot deny the love she will hear in my voice.* At the front of the manor, the King understood no one was about. As he turned back toward Aachen, he heard a slight sound, seemingly a door closing. He listened intently and surmised someone was on the far side of the house.

"Mayhap, a maid came from the cook room into Fulrad's herb garden," he mumbled. "She will know which field the Abbot weeds today. This person can tell me where to find Hildegard." He mumbled as he turned Samson's head. He hurried to the back of Fulrad's manor and opened the gate to the herb garden.

Hildegard was there, sitting under a maple tree, eating bread and cheese. The King took a deep breath and, smiling, went into the garden. She will finally be my wife, as soon as the annulment is granted, he thought joyously.

The garden gate creaked; Hildegard looked up. In a moment she was on her feet, dropping the King a curtsy.

"Your Majesty," she choked. "Good morrow, Sire."

"Good morrow to you, my love." Charlemagne replied as tenderly as he was able.

"What do you here, sitting in the garden alone?"

"Just breaking my fast, late though it is," Hildegard replied, ignoring his endearment. "The entire household is in the lower field chopping weeds, Sire. Lucky for us, the rain holds off."

"Aye," the King replied. "Spring was doubly welcome this year, after such a harsh winter and the heart-breaking trials all of us endured. This one is a season of hope, like no other. And, now, early summer bathes us in its heat."

Hildegard wondered at Charlemagne's gentle smile toward her. He seemed almost a young boy. But, then, she guessed the warmer weather, as he suggested, brought out the hope and child in everyone.

"I did not think to see you again, your Majesty," Hildegard observed, "before I set out for home. This visit is a surprise." She paused as the King's face changed, his smile replaced by a displeased frown. Ought I not speak of leaving, Hildegard wondered.

"You do know the Abbot is at court?" She asked, thinking to deflect the King's thoughts.

"Fulrad?" Charlemagne replied. "Aye, I talked to him yesterday night. He said he would return here by mid-day." The King answered, though it was clear his mind was not on the Abbot. He looked into Hilde's eyes and spoke.

"Going home? You still mean to return to your father's house?"

"Of a certainty, Sire; you must remember." Hildegard bristled. She did not believe he teased her this way, playing as if she did not yearn for home. He was the very one who kept her here, refusing his permission for her journey! "You promised I might return to my father's house in the spring. Spring is past. Summer comes. Abbot Fulrad arranged my journey."

"I can't let you go." Charlemagne King answered. His face reddened, a vein throbbed at his temple. "Nay, I forbid it. You cannot leave. I do not wish it!" He exclaimed. Hildegard stared at him in shock. Then, she recovered herself and stood. She took three steps toward him and stopped, her jaw thrust forward.

"Ha!" Hildegard laughed bitterly. "I no longer care for your wishes, Sire! I do return home…as soon as the Abbot gives me leave. His men, my friends, are escorting me home." She paused to control her reaction. Then, she continued more calmly. "Although I'm sad to leave the Abbot and this wonderful manor, I'm eager to return to my family. My time in your court has been difficult, Sire, difficult and demanding. You cannot imagine." She watched the King's face.

"We shall talk after the mid-day meal, the King stated. "I don't wish you to return to Swabia. Not now. Humor me; I am your King."

"Nay, Sire." Hildegard answered firmly. "You promised I could return home in the spring. Preparations are made. And I am going, your Majesty. As for our talking, we must speak now, this moment. The manor's folk are working in the south field. A picnic is scheduled for the mid-day meal. Even the cooks are helping in the fields, breaking the soil, removing weeds. I must return there; they wait for me." She paused for this information to be absorbed.

"Do you wish to speak? Then, you must speak now. Know, though, there is nothing you can say to keep me here or in your court. I am going home." The king said nothing.

"You can have no objection to my journey. I did as you commanded." Hildegard repeated. "The roads are clear; the weather is amenable. I ask you for nothing. I merely wish to return to my home." She had a new thought. "My parents feel my obligations to your court are fulfilled. At the least, my family values me."

"I regret the weeks and months I spent here. I was but a servant to your nobility. Though I am well-educated and proficient in many things, no one values my skills, my abilities," Hildegard was not sure the King was listening, so unaware did he seem. She ceased speaking and waited. As she paused,

Charlemagne begged.

"Hilde, please!" He cried. "You wound me, break my heart! I adore you; I know you care for me!" His eyes were wide and pleading. "What you choose…it makes no sense." Hildegard shuddered, shook her head, and looked at the ground.

"Why say this to me? Why now? I accept you do not care for me." She shook her head.

"Please, I beg you, my love." Charlemagne found his voice again. "Give this up. We will marry. I give you my solemn promise." His face turned whiter still as Hilde turned an angry face to him.

"Marry! Marry?" She spat the word. "When shall we marry…after you bed all the princesses on the continent, when another two or three young women refuse your offer?" She shook her head. "I did have feelings for you before you married Desiderata. Did that predispose you to me then…when you were able to wed again? Nay, you passed me by, Charlemagne. My feelings were of no consequence." She stared into his eyes. "I loved you and lost you. You can't think my heart can be enticed yet again. I doubt your words, your sincerity. You speak but there is no feeling behind your words." She moved to leave the garden. "You ask too much. Leave me, please." He came toward her, his hands outstretched.

"You play with me. Get out!" The King wilted, turned toward the manor, and, then, stopped.

"Nay, damn it! I will not leave." His words spilled out. "I refuse to leave…not until you explain this change of heart. It's impossible to love as we did and, then, declare the love gone. I cannot accept you no longer love me, Hilde; I will not!" He stated, holding his anger inside. Hildegard said nothing. "Give me the reasons for your rejection of me. Explain the change in your affections!" Hildegard tried to walk pass him. He blocked her way.

"Explain myself?" Hildegard laughed bitterly. "Nay, Sire. Explain yourself!" She paused, looking weary. "But, mayhap not. Your 'mouthings' serve no purpose. In fact, explanations will earn you nothing." She looked into the King's face, her eyes blazing with anger. "If you are truly this unable to understand, God must bless you with an especially intelligent wife, less your children be idiots." Charlemagne winced at the venom in her voice but remained solidly where he stood. Hildegard shrugged. "You love me, you say. Then, share my pain. Mayhap I can make you see my wounds, my hurt."

"Was the entire court to be told of your next choice for wife before you informed me, Charlemagne?" She asked softly. Her shoulders slumped; her voice cracked. "I saw Desiderata leave the court in the early hours of the morning. Three days ago, was it not?" She waited for him to speak. "You stand here and say you love me. Yet, you did not come to me when your wife departed. Nor did you come in these last three days - despite all the mystery and speculation around her leave-taking." Hildegard walked back toward the garden bench, the better to stand away from the King.

"We who love you best, Gisela and I, received no word from you. Now, you come; you stand here and say you love me. Come, come Sire! You must believe me a fool!" King Charlemagne stared into Hildegard's face. He saw the effort Hildegard commanded to hold her body still and upright. His own stance visibly shrank as he realized the depth of her pain, the degree of his betrayal. He stepped toward her, wanting to hold her, to soothe those wounds. She held out her arms, warning him to come no closer.

"A man who loved me," Hildegard continued, "would rush to me, hurry to bring tidings of the change in his circumstance—less the worst be imagined." Hilde pulled her shawl around her shoulders and moved toward the garden gate again.

"Hilde." Charlemagne called her name. "She followed my injunctions, was so careful not to compromise my name, and loved me with no promise of a future. How could I not tell her of the failure of my marriage?" He could not believe his stupidity.

"Forgive me, little bird; forgive me! I didn't come to you because I had to be certain Desiderata left. If she guessed I loved another, she would be here yet...just to spite me. Nay, she would stay to haunt my entire, miserable life! In my love for you, my wish to protect you, I feared she would harm you, that she and my mother would spirit you to some far distant place." He bowed his head in shame.

"Don't you know?" He asked. "My mother banished my first wife from the court, ordered her taken away, both Himiltrude and my little son! I knew nothing of her plans, not did I know their destination! The two Frankish queens—Desiderata and my mother—you cannot know. They are capable of great harm. I had to remove myself from the court, act ignorant of Desiderata's leave-taking, to protect you, to encourage her to leave, to keep my feelings for you a secret!" He grabbed Hilde's hands.

"Don't you understand, Hilde? I'm finally free! I can love anyone I wish." He caressed her cheek. "I love only you. The marriage to Desiderata was a huge mistake. Please, please, my love, believe me," the King begged. "Forgive me: forgive my stupidity, dear one. I beg you." Tears splashed from Hildegard's eyes; her shoulders shook as she moved directly in front of him.

"We all bear the consequences of our actions, Charlemagne," she whispered sadly. "I have nothing but your words. You speak carelessly and late, very late. Your lips mouth words of love; your behavior shows just the opposite. I no long believe your words, Sire, not anymore." She turned back to the King as she reached the garden gate.

"Who are you really, Charlemagne?" Hildegard's voice was formal once more. "You spend your time and your energy bowing to the demands of others—those who advance their own interests. But in doing so, you lose yourself. You talked to me of finding yourself again; but I see no evidence of that. You do as you wish in choosing a bride but it is *Abbot Fulrad* who labors to put things right with Pope Hadrian. Your *Peers* plan a joust for your soldiers but it is your *new wife* who makes the list of guests. This wife leaves the court in secret and you hide among your soldiers. Three days later, *your mother* announces your wife's visit to her father's house. My God, are you the ruler of this realm?"

Hildegard wrapped her shawl more tightly around her shoulders. Even here in the sun, she felt cold. She raised her eyes back to King Charlemagne's face.

"I have no idea who you are, what you value, the kind of realm you wish to build." She paused to wipe the tears from her cheeks. "But I know I will not be a part of it. I do not want your love, not anymore." Hildegard ran from the garden. Her voice drifted back to the King.

"The shame is not in making mistakes," she called softly. "The shame is in doing nothing." Charlemagne saw Hildegard stop suddenly. She turned toward him and added. "You turned your back on my love. You gave me no reason to think you ever loved me. I cannot trust your words. You do not live them." She ran out of sight.

The King felt for a bench, sitting in shock. He never imagined Hildegard's love for him would die, that he would drive her from him. And her disappointment, it was more than he could bear! Hildegard's words played and replayed in his ears. How could he convince her he had found his way, that he loved her more dearly than life, that he wanted only her as his wife—forever? Hearing voices, the King hurried out of the garden to his horse.

He unhitched Samson and rode quickly out of the courtyard toward the river. Riding Samson along the river, back toward the Aachen castle, he knew his court prepared to march. Battle season was upon them. Seeing a large party coming from the castle, he veered away from the river into the shelter of the lush, green, oak and birch leaves, their brilliant hues sparkling in the mid-day sun.

Charlemagne sat under the trees, willing the tears not to form in his eyes. But his will lost. His eyes filled until the leaves, even the river, were a blur. Weeping quietly to himself, the King got up to hobble Samson. He didn't hear a horse approaching, but he did hear someone call his name. He looked up into the eyes of his sister. The King opened his arms; she hurried to him, hugging him strongly.

"I was riding with the group that passed," she said, "and seeing you could tell I should stop. What is it, Charley? You look so sad, so full of despair."

"I told Hildegard of my love for her, of my regret of the last few months." He hung his head. "She rejected me, saying my words are worth nothing to her." He wiped his eyes. "And well she should," he admitted. "I treated her in such an odious manner—misleading and hurting her, belittling her feelings, acting the king, denying my love and my need for her. What can I do, Gisela? She won't listen, will not believe anything I say."

Chapter Twenty-nine
NEEDS OF THE PEOPLE

"You wound her, also, if you don't appreciate her efforts for our people." Gisela told him. "Do you know of those?" She asked her brother, her grieving eyes boring into his face.

"Aye," Charlemagne answered. "I know she gathers little-used clothing for the manor's children. I know she and the Abbess in Rouen work for the poor. I know..."

"You know nothing, Charley." Gisela interrupted him, shaking her head. "Let me tell you the efforts Hildegard made after joining the court, not to mention the teaching she did at Abbot Fulrad's manor." His sister motioned for him to sit on a near-by stump. "Let me describe her activities to you. Remember now, these are in addition to her duties as a maid-in-waiting. Think of that," she urged the King.

"As you say, she helps the manor's children. But listen the methods she used to do that. Not a fortnight after arrival at the court, she worked to provide extra food and clothing for the widows and children in Aachen. She collected clothing which the court's ladies discarded, redesigned it and sewed it into garments suitable for children. She did the sewing herself, Brother." Gisela emphasized. "Knowing many garments are thrown away, she enlisted the aid of the Abbess in Rouen. The two of them encouraged Lady Hautgard, Lord Janlur's wife, and several countesses here to replicate their efforts."

"In her spare time, she trained the squires to conduct obedience exercises for all the puppies under one year old in your stables. Lord Roland asked her to come to Brittainy to pass this knowledge on to his family there.

"In an inspired decision, I think," Gisela continued, "she obtained seeds and planting instructions from the Aachen monks to encourage the children of Fulrad's manor to plant small gardens of their own. She, in addition, instructed those children in hoeing, planting, and watering herbs and vegetables. The gardens will have 'little farmers' when she leaves."

"She enlisted the Abbot's help in her efforts to grow additional food. She copies, in her own hand, directions for rotating crops—wheat, potatoes, turnips—so that each monk in the monasteries will know of the technique. The Abbot urges the bishops to implement this cultivating technique." Gisela paused, waiting for her brother to absorb the information. He stared to speak.

"There's more." Gisela said primly. "In Abbot Fulrad's manor, she used her own skills to teach his house maid, Jenna, to redesign and sew used clothing into new clothes for the farmer's children...and for her own brothers and sisters. Hilde donated her own clothes for this project." The King stirred but Gisela shook her head negatively. "And," she continued, smiling broadly, "Hildegard risked the Abbot's wrath by planning and implementing instruction in math for the children of his manor. Some adults attend her classes as well."

"Hildegard, Jocelyn, and I applied pressure on the noble women of your court, urging them to enlist their own children in planting gardens. If the noble children plant gardens and give them to local children as the court makes its annual circuit, good feelings will arise among the young people of your realm. Isn't that brilliant?" Gisela asked, her eyes laughing with delight.

"I cannot believe it, Gisela," Charlemagne acknowledged, "all this activity right under my nose." His face changed suddenly. "And I made no effort to discover this. I didn't open my mind to new possibilities...or new methods or even think someone else would have useful ideas." He sighed deeply. "Such energy and enthusiasm, Gisela - all for the sake of the people." Gisela remained silent as she saw Charlemagne thinking. His eyes were moist with admiration.

"While I and the men of the court frolick at Ma-Mam's hunting parties, while the countesses gossip and play their games, while the nobles drink and complain, Hildegard worked, worked herself— think of all that stitching— and created work for others! She got the fortunate to help those less so!"

"It's impossible for me to love her more, Gisela," he admitted quietly, "even with these good, positive deeds. I must find a way to prove my love and my renewed dedication to her."

Gisela nodded, determined she would not suggest anything to her brother. He must find his own way back into Hildegard's heart...if such were possible. Gisela jumped as a horn blast split the air. Charlemagne stood immediately, turning in the direction of the sound. He saw Roland riding toward him at break-neck speed.

"Sire?" Roland called. "A missive has come from Pope Hadrian. Abbot Fulrad summons you immediately." Riding up to the King, Roland continued. "Forgive me for interrupting your conversation, Sire. But the Abbot is upset."

"Don't apologize, Roland. I linger too long from the challenges of the realm." Charlemagne answered. He and Roland bade Gisela farewell and galloped toward the castle. Gisela rode hard to catch up to the group she left. Abbot Fulrad met them as they cantered up.

"It's Desiderius again, Sire. At the same time he undermines you," he reported, "he challenges the authority of the Pope. He hopes to weaken him and, eventually, control the Roman Church." The Abbot handed parchments to the King. "I have missives from Soisson and Rome. The Lombard king already besieges Papal territory, spreads fear and havoc. His army murders, sets fires, and plunders. He occupies both Blera and Otricoli and ventures almost into Rome itself. He most certainly wants Ravenna." Fulrad relayed the gist of the messages. Charlemagne frowned, his face tightening, as he read them.

"I marvel Pope Hadrian did not call you for help right away." Fulrad continued. "Mayhap, he understands you are caught in battles with the Saxons. They take all our resources, I know. They are the kings of rebellion." Charlemagne nodded at Fulrad's insight. "And, the holy Father appreciates your efforts to introduce Christianity to the heathen. Might it be he thinks that effort worth the immediate, but not the permanent, sacrifice of the Papal lands?"

"I feel certain Hadrian would not go that far, Fulrad!" The King laughed. "But he does favor us…by leaving us alone!" He grimaced and turned to Roland.

"Roland, go to the soldiers' tents, go among as many of the captains as you can. Determine if anyone is privy to Desiderius' plans. Bring me reports of any nobles who support him, openly or not." He held up his hand in caution. "Work in stealth. Be creative; don't ask direct questions. I must know Desiderius' strength, that hidden among my supposedly 'loyal' nobility." The King glanced at the Abbot.

"I know the Lombard king continues to placate Gebnega, to poison her sons' minds against me, and to urge nobles as far south as Provence and as far north as Asutrasia to break their oaths of allegiance to me."

"I can't think they'd drop their allegiance to you, Sire." Rinaldo objected as he rode up. "They have nothing to gain."

"Oh, but they hope for more lands, more wealth, Rinaldo! Desiderius guarantees them positions when he rules the Frankish empire...or so he says!" King Charlemagne smiled at the Peers who responded to the Abbot's summons. "Ever do these nobles hope for unlimited choices. They believe the Lombard army can support and protect them all, that they will have less to do. What foolishness," he concluded. Charlemagne turned, again, to Roland.

"Roland, be certain of the traitors in our court. I want no man accused unjustly."

Before King Charlemagne had time to consider any decisions about the evil machinations of the Lombard king, there was another warning about the Saxons. Some two weeks ago at the spring assembly, nobles and spies alike reported movement in the Saxon tribes. Small and large Saxon bands already gathered. Surreptitiously listening to Saxon conversations, Roland's spies verified the Saxons met to plan rebellion against the King. In fact, their most-loved activity was submitting to Charlemagne's rule and, then, rebelling – just as they did with his father, King Pepin. All at the assembly encouraged – some demanded – Charlemagne march immediately. Charlemagne summoned Count Janlur.

"Move the army out, Janlur. The Saxons call once again. We march toward Cologne and, from there, into Saxon territory. Confer with the commanders; we'll meet after the evening repast. When you finish, send Oliver and Theo to me." Roland, conferring with Bernard, hurried to the King.

"Sire, what are you orders?" Already dressed for battle, he held the Frankish banner on his pommel. Charlemagne smiled.

"We employ the pincer movement, Roland. As before, bring

your troops from the south as Oliver marches from the west. I and my soldiers join you from the east. No one, yet, seems to anticipate our 'pincer,' do they? Or, mayhap, they have no action to counteract it." The King laughed. "So much the better for us, we will win this battle." He nudged his horse, delighting in the strength of Samson's leap. The horse was ever eager for military action.

King Charlemagne marched his troops hard; they marched after dark and began again before dawn. Scouts ranged ahead of the army, ever alert for enemy soldiers. But they saw no one. For every day they marched, they felt more emboldened. Did the enemy do no forward scouting? The King wanted to come upon the enemy as quickly, as unexpectedly, as possible. Often the court and the army did not unpack, just cooked over ground pits and slept rolled in their linens.

Charlemagne's troops, buttressed by a core of professional soldiers, marched steadily day after day. Under the cover of darkness, soldiers practiced their maneuvers, always moving with stealth. After weary days, over rough terrain, the Frankish army was within a half-league of the Saxon enemy. Charlemagne summoned his commanders.

"We rest until the hour before dusk." He told them. "Then, we march rapidly toward the Saxon camp. Our scouts report no practice sessions and little discipline in the camp. As the sun begins to set, shining in their eyes, we attack."

"Do you not worry about the difficulty of seeing, seeing to fight effectively, I mean?" Bernard questioned.

"I think it won't be an issue. The Saxons first camped in this place almost two weeks ago. Our spies report no battle preparations, no mock battle, nothing to hone their skills. Confident they must be... to maintain their skills so poorly. I think this will hardly be a battle, Bernard. Pray it is so." The King replied.

Unbelievable as it was, Charlemagne's army attacked before the Saxons knew they were in the area. With neither the numbers, the training, nor, the organization of Charlemagne's army, the Saxons fell to defeat and surrendered.

King Charlemagne led Ganelon and his archers into the Saxon's religious sanctuary, conscious of having protection at his back. In the middle of the sanctuary, stood a pillar of stones - the 'Irminsul, sacred to the Germanic Saxons. He left the archers, always under Ganelon's command, to confront the Saxon leaders.

Customarily in the first battle of the season, King Charlemagne allowed the soldiers to keep whatever booty they could carry. On Ganelon's command, the archers and, then, other Frankish soldiers spread throughout the main plaza. They crushed sacred artifacts and idols, overturning them and bashing them with their axes. The soldiers roamed freely over both the sacred sanctuary and the enemy camp, hoping to enrich themselves with booty. As the looting ended and the men prepared to withdraw, Ganelon pointed to the giant pillar, the symbol of the Saxon's world view.

"Destroy it!" He called. Ganelon himself flung his ax against the stone pillar. Men grabbed limbs from beside a cooking pit and threw them at the pillar's base. Other Frankish soldiers came forward to help in the destruction of the symbol. Saxon soldiers, seeing the flames, fell to their knees, keening in sorrow. Although apparently made of stone, the pillar smoked and cracked, raining stones around its foundation. As stones dislodged and moved, the pillar shuddered, leaned, and eventually fell.

"...Nayyyyy! Ohhhhh, nay!" Saxon voices soared in sorrow and protest. "Ahh, the sacred pillar! We are destroyed! He burns the sacred pillar! Naaaay! Naaaay!"

"We are doomed!" They cried. Saxon soldiers writhed on the ground, tears streaming down their faces. Their combined prayers, uttered reverently—though in great despair—rose to the heavens.

"Irminsul, Irminsul! You burn!"

The Frankish soldiers watched their enemies in astonishment, unable to understand this love for a pillar! Eventually, the pillar was no more; stones, large and small, littered the ground.

The Saxon soldiers, their faces glassy with grief, stumbled after their captors, shaking their heads and moaning. Charlemagne, some distance away, began the ceremony of oath-taking. He was oblivious to the burning.

"Oliver," King Charlemagne called to his Peer after the last Saxon leader gave his oath. "We must establish a garrison here at Eresburg. It's the perfect location for a northern, Frankish outpost - the Diemel River below, the Eder River beyond. A garrison built between the two rivers will afford us protection from all sides." Oliver nodded, seeing the defensive benefit.

"Come; summon Ganelon; he will be in charge of constructing the fort."

"Aye, Sire." Oliver replied. "Mayhap a permanent garrison here will discourage the Saxon tribes' efforts to merge their fighting men. I'll seek Ganelon now and send him to you." Within minutes, Oliver returned with Ganelon riding beside him.

"Ganelon," King Charlemagne nodded to Roland's stepfather. "Your job now is to construct a fort—build it and man it. We'll establish a garrison here. It should be located equal distance between the rivers. Choose your soldiers. I shall send stonemasons and wood workers from Aachen and Tours as well. As soon as the army marches, begin your work. The rest of us must journey toward Rome, I'm afraid. The Pope needs our strength."

"Aye, Sire," Ganelon answered, thankful his fighting was over for the season. "We begin work on the morrow."

Before marching to Rome, the king urged his army to rest, to heal their wounded and to recoup their strength. Sitting atop Samson's back, King Charlemagne looked over the trampled battlefield. Despite the churned earth, he saw bloody, red patches - some large puddles, some only flecks against the dark soil. *Can there be another way to deal with an enemy? Oliver is correct; this is not God's will – this killing. But how do I restrain men's love of power? How do I defend those under my protection without the sword, the dagger, the love of the fight?* He rubbed Samson's neck, infusing new energy into his exhausted horse. But no matter how hard he searched, how much thought he gave to it, he could find no alternative to battle.

Later that same night, Charlemagne and Abbot Fulrad sat by the camp fire, there near the river. Behind them, Frankish commanders shouted orders as they bedded down Saxon prisoners.

"Look at them, Fulrad. These Saxons, they are decimated by our forces. But this surrender will not last." Charlemagne predicted. "Why do they resist so much? As the year turns, they fight us and lose—year after year— just as they fought Poppa. This Saxon spirit, where does it come from? These wars are nothing but sacrifices of their men."

"They wish to live free, Sire." Fulrad replied, admiring such tenacity."They want to worship their own gods, follow their own customs, to be in charge of their own lives."

"Free they may be, free in the Christian realm of Frankland." King Charlemagne responded. "This is their only choice." Hearing hoof beats, the two men turned.

"King Charlemagne!" Roland called to the king as he crested the hill. "Sire, there's a Saxon commander who would speak with you. He is gravely wounded or I wouldn't ask you. He begs to see the King. I don't believe he will last through the speaking. He bleeds profusely."

"Aye," Charlemagne responded, "I'll speak with him. What Christian would refuse a dying man's last request?" Fulrad settled by the fire as the King left.

"He has no weapons, your Majesty. We made certain of that." Oliver said as the King rode up. Charlemagne followed Oliver to a nearby gulley where a wounded Saxon lay on the ground. Roland tried to give the soldier a drink; but the water spilled all over his chest.

"He cannot swallow," Oliver noted as Charlemagne dismounted. His eyes were sorrowful as he shook his head slightly at the King.

"Well met, brave soldier," Charlemagne greeted him. "I'm King of the Franks. Speak as you will." He moved closer to the man and squatted down so the dying soldier could look into his face.

"I would say much but have not time. I'm dying. You cannot kill me twice, so I say this to you. You think by destroying the Irminsul, you destroy the Saxons' will. But this be not so! The great pillar was our talisman, our hope—the very soul of Saxony. By your act, your lack of reverence, you have condemned us to fight forever. You thought to destroy a symbol; but you unleashed a dragon." The soldier's voice faded. He pushed up on his arm, looking into the King's face.

"May your God protect you," he said. "May my god spite..." Blood bubbled from the soldier's mouth. He was forever silent. As the soldier spoke, Charlemagne paled visibly. But, as in times past with non-Christian warriors, his anger surged.

"All he says is blasphemy! I conquer all lands to bring them to the only GOD and to his son, the Christ! Your curse or your blessing means nothing to me. I do what I must." The King left, cursing the soldier and all his comrades.

Later, spreading his linens beside the fire, Charlemagne summoned Oliver.

"What is this Irminsul, Oliver?" He asked. "I saw no 'pillar' on the Saxon's sacred hill."

"It is, it was the symbol of Saxony, your Majesty—a much beloved pillar. In some way, the Saxons feel it holds their spirit. Each tribe carries a small pillar, often carved from wood, to represent the Irminsul. This pillar is sacred to them."

"They feel this, the people's spirit, in a pillar?" Charlemagne questioned. "That soldier...he accused us of destroying it. What did the Saxon soldier mean?"

"As Ganelon's soldiers searched for booty, Sire, they pulled the pillar to the ground...there in the sacred space."

"What was the point?" Charlemagne asked. "I don't understand. How did this come about?" The King asked. "The pillar did no harm, surely..."

"Our soldiers overran the Saxon camp, Sire, and the scared area. They came upon the pillar. Our soldiers tore it down as they looted the Saxon courtyard for booty, just over there." Oliver looked quickly toward the dark fields. Watching him, Charlemagne saw there was more to the tale than Oliver said.

"And who led the burning?" He caught Oliver's eyes with his own, demanding the truth.

"Ganelon struck the first blow, Charlemagne, with the massive ax he carries. His men followed him. The pillar crumbled from those blows and the heat of fire at its base." Oliver explained. Charlemagne shifted his head to hear Oliver's words, so quietly did he speak.

"Was the destruction of this pillar needed?"

"Nay, not in any manner I can see." Oliver answered, his face pale, his jaw clenched. "Ganelon seldom considers 'need,' Sire. You know how quickly his violence flares." The King nodded and walked back to his horse, his head bowed in thought.

Near to the 'witching' hour of the night, King Charlemagne left his linens to find Roland. He awakened him gently.

"Do you know when Hildegard planned to leave the Abbot's manor for Swabia?" King Charlemagne asked. Roland, still weary from the battle, grimaced.

"I am neither a messenger nor a guard, Sire. The Lady Hildegard did not confide her travel plans to me." He replied.

"Nay, I daresay she did not," the King answered testily. "Do you know if she left Fulrad's manor before we marched."

"She was to leave the manor the day after we rode to join the army, some four days after you arrived back in Aachen. Someone said the Abbot worried about flooding." Roland answered. "I know not if she left for Swabia, however." Charlemagne nodded.

"But where else would she go?" He asked.

"I repeat the little I know, Sire. Rinaldo said she was no longer at the Abbot's manor. Jocelyn and Maria wished her to visit them at the court, but she declined, gave some excuse." At Charlemagne's surprised expression, Roland explained. "Rinaldo and Maria were 'friends,' Sire. Their interest was not consistent and neither was the time they spent together."

"Ahhh…" Charlemagne understood. "It's likely Hilde is not too far along the road then." He whispered into Roland's ear. "I go to find her, Roland." At Roland's shocked stare, the King confided. "She is the woman I love; the only one I love. I must convince her of my sincerity, of the love I have for her." He paused. "I travel alone. Rest easy; I will return by tomorrow's daybreak. Send no one to seek me. Do you understand?"

"Sire," Roland spoke. "This is foolish. Anyone, seeing you alone on the road, may attack. I cannot allow you to take such a chance — not with Saxons and Lombards both after your head!"

"Send no one, Roland. I will travel in stealth and be circumspect. I cannot afford to die just yet!" Charlemagne laughed. "I'm leaving now; see you after tomorrow's evening meal. Don't worry. I will be safe." He touched his forehead, mounted Samson and was quickly lost in the night's deepening darkness. Roland climbed the highest hill and watched the King ride out of sight.

Chapter Thirty

CONFESSION, AT LAST

There was only one main road which Hildegard's escort could travel. The King was certain he would not miss them along the way. He vowed to be careful, not to startle her or, God forbid, alert her escort to his presence. She must not call for help or alert her guards. They would, without a doubt, detain him or embarrass her, thinking of Queen Desiderata. He wanted to see her alone, to declare his love for her. No one else could know he was anywhere around.

Charlemagne rode easily. He was intent on his course. Only an act of God would prevent his carrying it out. He pressed Samson as hard as he dared. Finally, after many leagues, he spied a cold campfire at the bottom of a small hillock. The number of tents and the horses' shadows matched the Abbot's likely escort, but Charlemagne must make certain. He tied Samson to a sheltered oak and darted between trees until he came close to the campsite. There, hanging on one tent along with the banner of the Governor of Swabia, was a small copy of his own banner.

"Ahhh, it is she." Charlemagne whispered to himself as his heart thudded. "Now, I sneak into her tent." He dropped to his knees and began crawling toward a group of bushes. Just as he got on his knees to crawl from the shelter of the low-lying bushes, two guards came around the back of the tent.

"Why are we patrolling behind the tent?" One of the guards

complained. "We are safe here; everyone says so."

"We are safe because we are careful," was the reply. The older guard looked around slowly, double checking the stakes which held the tent to the ground. "All seems to be in order." He nodded as he moved toward the campfire.

Not waiting a minute, the King crawled quickly to the back of the tent, slit a wide hole above the ground and wiggled inside. Once there, he turned, pushed his mantle against the hole and pressed a small trunk against the mantle. *That will, I hope, cover my entrance.* Looking toward the light, he gasped.

Hildegard sat on her sleeping bench, trying to straighten the covers around her legs. King Charlemagne watched, transfixed, as her ebony hair fell in gentle waves, almost to her waist. He could almost feel its silkiness against his face. *She has never looked more beautiful.* He drank in her lovely face, her white neck, her gently protruding breasts. He waited until Hildegard rose, fearing if he startled her from behind, she would raise an alarm. She went to tie the flaps of her tent closed. Charlemagne stood and stepped to the center of the tent.

"Hilde?" He saw her flinch, and spoke rapidly. "It's Charlemagne, little bird. Please, I've come to talk with you one last time. Please, don't be afraid." He whispered. Hildegard turned quickly, her face worried, her arms tense at her sides.

"What do you here?" She asked in a neutral voice. "This is dangerous, sneaking around in the dark."

"Nay, not nearly as dangerous as losing the woman I love." King Charlemagne replied. "I've come to convince you of my love for you, Hilde." He found he never wanted to stop talking to her. Talking to her was the most important thing in his life. "I must have your love; I must. Life is meaningless without you, fearing you may not still care for me. What must I do to prove my devotion, Hilde?" His question was almost a prayer.

"There is nothing to be done." Hildegard answered, her eyes dropping to the ground. "Your words are easily spoken but you…" Charlemagne moved quickly to gather her into his arms. He gently touched the back of her head and aligned her mouth with his. And, then, looking deeply into the eyes he loved so much, he kissed her. He felt her body quiver and, soon, she was kissing him back. Anything else, he forgot.

Charlemagne pulled Hildegard closer and closer to his chest. He felt he would explode with longing; but he could not bear the idea of pulling away from those lips. She shifted in his arms, moving her mouth from his. Almost immediately, her mouth found his again. And, then, he thought no more.

He gave himself up to the feelings: his body's growing warmth; the happiness he felt, holding her in his arms; the passion building as their lips devoured each other; the sweet sound of her moans as her hands caressed his chest.

"I love you, my precious girl," the King whispered. "Life is nothing for me, if you are not by my side. I want to hide in your hair, lose myself in the curve of your neck, drown in your kisses, burn at the fire which your touch begins. Please, please, my love, tell me I have not lost you." He talked and kissed and caressed. Through it all, he waited. It did seem a long wait. But, finally, Hildegard spoke the words he so longed to hear.

"Aye, God help me, I do love you." she whispered. "I have loved you forever, my dear. I did despair you would ever come to your senses."

"I did despair myself." Charlemagne felt Hildegard shake with merriment. "But, no more…!" He whispered vehemently into her neck. "No more; I have found you! My life will never be the same again…thank God."

"I distrust your words, my love," Hildegard admitted. "You must prove you love me and you must do it now." Her tone brooked no dissent.

"I am your obedient servant." Charlemagne returned her banter. "Of all the tasks you ever set me to do, this is the easiest and the sweetest one I will have." He cuddled her in his arms. "And how do I prove my love?" He asked.

"Love me." Hildegard replied simply, turning her lips to his.

He kissed the palms of her hands, the tips of her ears, the sweet dip below her neck with as much tenderness as he could summon. He lightly caressed her back, brushed a hand over her breasts, and, then, slipped both hands beneath her sleeping tunic. As his hands touched her naked flesh, Hildegard pushed closer against him, pressing her breasts against him, moaning ever so slightly, her mouth teasing his neck. He put his arms around her waist, picked her up, and carried her to the sleeping linens. As he lay down, she raised her arms and slipped her tunic over her head. Charlemagne stopped in mid-motion.

"Dear Father," he exclaimed. "You're so beautiful!" He moved his hands all over her, trying to memorize such loveliness. Her breasts seemed to reach out to him, begging to be touched. Her mouth tightened on his as her tongue licked his lips. The King thrust his tongue into her mouth and heard a quick gasp before she smothered his tongue with her own. Their limbs wound around each other, trying desperately to merge. The King's passion built and built, enhanced by Hildegard's body, warming every part of him she touched. He heard her little pants, her effort to breathe, and felt crazed. Their bodies, yearning for each other, could no longer be denied. They curled and twined their bodies together. Hilde matched the King's passion with an equal one of her own.

Every shift in his body, every touch he made, every sigh, she returned to him. She long imagined his body under her fingers, her breasts against his chest, her legs wrapped around his waist. As the King worshipped her body, his heart sang. As she nestled in his arms, his mouth could not stop caressing her name. As her fingers teased and stroked, as her lips kissed his nipples, his ears, his thighs, he could not think. Charlemagne gave himself totally to her loving and matched her step for step. *If she wishes me to feel this, she must wish it for herself.* They loved once, in a great hurry. And, then, they loved again in slow, almost stately procession.

The months of denial and need culminated in one, long sharing as they reached a pinnacle together. They clung to each other, their bodies trembling at the intensity of their joining. Many moments later, Charlemagne spoke.

"I am at peace, my love. I love you with no limits. And I dedicate myself to making you happy." Hildegard smiled sadly at him, shaking her head slightly. "I do not know how it will be done," he admitted, "but I will find a way. I cannot live without you."

"And I will no longer live without you," Hildegard warned him. "Leave now, if any of this is a game, Charlemagne. If you stay but two moments beyond this time, you are mine forever, forever. I will no longer sit and wait for you to come to me. I will demand your presence and expect you to love me unceasingly."

"I can think of nothing more desirable," Charlemagne murmured in her ear. "I will love you forever...and even beyond." They lay together in peace, the peace which only comes after weeks of denial, hopelessness, and fear. They talked; they kissed; they hugged each other joyously.

"I love you, Hilde," King Charlemagne whispered again, "more than you can ever comprehend. My little bird, it is the gift of my life, to have you in my arms this very moment!"

"But why have you come? Why now?" She smiled, unsure how the King could respond to her questions. His lips were too busy on her forehead, on her cheeks, now in the crease of her neck. "Ohhh, my love." She murmured as he squeezed her to him. She shifted ever so slightly as the King sat up on the sleeping linens. Hilde leaned her head on his shoulder, content in knowing this was where she truly belonged. "Why have you come here?" She repeated.

"I come to take you home," Charlemagne answered. "I come to beg you to be my wife. I come to lay my heart, unworthy as it may be, at your feet. I come for you, Hilde—for you, little bird!" The King's smile warmed the room; his happiness covered them; his love for Hilde transfused her heart.

"My love," Hildegard whispered, "I have missed you so!" His lips met hers again. It was then, in that magical place, that she knew the long months of waiting were over. Charlemagne came for her; she was home.

"I don't know what to say. My heart overflows with love for you: for your laugh, for your quick smile, for your questing mind. I have had no life since you left the court," he admitted. "Not that I blame you, Hilde, I was abominable. I am overwhelmed with shame when I remember how badly I treated you, how much I didn't understand. Nay, I did not think and, as a result, kept hurting you. Please, forgive me, Hilde. Please. I do vow to spend the rest of my days in bondage for your forgiveness." Hildegard laughed.

"Of a certainty, you shall not," she assured him. "You may feel a slave to me, but it cannot last. We have a new kingdom to build together, Sire. Neither of us is capable of realizing our dreams alone, so we must help one another." She looked longingly into his eyes. "But I must go home. My parents have waited these many months for my return. You cannot deny them my visit." Charlemagne nodded in understanding and drew her back into his arms. They loved each other once more. All too soon, the deep dark of the night was gone.

"Hilde, as soon as I can come, I will journey to your father's house," Charlemagne announced, slipping from the linens. "Be certain of my arrival." He dropped his tunic over his head. "I will see you very soon, my love." He slipped out of the back of the tent and returned to his army.

The large size of Charlemagne's soldiers required a slow journey, but one which moved steadily. They must keep moving. There was not food enough in one place to sustain them. Although the soldiers had to circle deep puddles of water from over-flowing rivers, the heavily-laden wheat and oats, and the nubs of blackberries on the sides of the road promised a bountiful harvest. The air was hot. Birds became couples again, their babies now grown and away from the nest. Leaves, still holding their green, nevertheless, promised days of riotous color.

The army marched, passing the days with tales, ballads, and stories of mythic heroes; with deep, warm reminiscences of the past; with large bonfires and early encampments at the end of the day. Their large force made slow but steady progress. During the second week of their march, Charlemagne's court finally caught up with them. Receiving word of the Saxons defeat, Egginhard moved the court expeditiously toward the army. Great was the rejoicing in the court when they joined up again.

Even though Charlemagne and Pope Hadrian exchanged many missives, the King did not often visit Rome. It was too far to the south for his liking and he disliked the long days with little activity. Now, though, still mellow from his night with Hildegard, Charlemagne looked forward to greeting Pope Hadrian in person. It was to be a long march; but one he dare not postpone. Already, his promise to the Pope to come to Rome was two years old.

Still thinking of Desiderius' threat and, then, of Gebnega and his nephews, the King spoke to Oliver about the boys and the Lombard king's growing influence over them.

"It's the loss of the boys which grieves me," he worried to Oliver, surreptitiously wiping moisture from his eyes. "They would learn more and know their family better, if they were with us." Oliver saw Charlemagne's genuine regret over the loss of his nephews and wondered again at the gentle side of this strong, vengeful warrior. The King's concern for Carl's two sons was a direct reflection of his concern for all the children of his kingdom.

As if hearing Oliver's thoughts, Charlemagne began describing his views for a palace school, one to serve as a model for schools throughout the realm.

"This will not be a school just for the nobility's sons in my court, Oliver," he said. "It will be a school for all the children. Instruction will include the soldiery arts, of a certainty; but we'll also teach reading and writing, the ability to debate, a love of literature, as well as mathematical skills. Our students will learn to appreciate poetry, folklore and music. Then, when we reward these same students with stewardship or duchies, with organizational duties, they needn't feel unworthy or uncomfortable at court." He smiled, thinking of the learning and skills the school would teach.

"The knowledge I received from the monks in my youth encourages wide interests — my love of words, for example. And I'm certain this makes me a better king." Charlemagne explained. "If everyone in the kingdom has the opportunity to learn, the realm will be blessed. The daily lives of our people cannot help but improve. I will find the best teachers on the continent and bring them to our academy." Even though well-educated himself, Oliver never understood the power of words until he watched Charlemagne at work.

"Aye." Fulrad later replied to Oliver's admiration of the King's goals. "King Charlemagne uses language well. He speaks with authority to the Pope and clergy, influencing them with his words alone. I think education for girls is useless," the Abbot admitted. "But the King is adamant, as I'm sure you've noticed."

"He is," Oliver agreed. "You need only watch Gisela to understand. She is a fireball, dedicated to speaking her mind and obtaining just what she sets out to do." Oliver believed the King's ideas far-reaching. Charlemagne's ideas will become far more important than his many conquests, he thought. Already Charlemagne was a credit to King Pepin. Many of these dreams for the Frankish people arose first in his father's fertile mind. "I know Charlemagne is delighted with Gisela. He takes her thoughts, as well as those of Hildegard, very seriously. Those two are a pair; they would help all the people of Frankland, native and conquered alike."

"That's true," the Abbot concurred. "But neither the King's wish to educate his people or his hope for his nephews will deflect the coming confrontation - the war with Desiderius of Lombardy. It cannot be avoided, Oliver. God grant it is not upon us too soon."

Now ten days into their march, Charlemagne blearily opened his eyes to a new day. Birds singing to the sun, horses' neighing for their riders, snakes and rodents hunting morning breakfasts all around, urged him to rise from his linens; but he felt sluggish and very weary. Pushing with his arms, he watched his vision tilt, first one way and, then, the other. With a sigh, he laid his head back. Moments later, lifting his head again, the King experienced the same giddiness.

"Am I wounded?" He wondered and, then, remembered the same feeling from years ago. When struck by an arrow of unknown origin, he suffered from this same, disoriented feeling. *But I had a raging fever then and a terrible headache.* Raising his hand to his forehead, Charlemagne drew a sharp breath. His brow was alive with heat! Just then, Roland stuck his head in the tent door.

"Sire, are you ready to break your fast?" He inquired cheerily. Getting no reply, he entered the tent, intending to wake the King. The King's feeble wave drew Roland to him quickly.

"I seem to be ill, Roland," the King admitted. "My head is turning; my eyes will not focus. Please call one of the healers and the Abbot, if you will." He turned his head away from the light of the tent door and moaned.

"Right away, Sire!" Roland almost saluted with his words. "I'll be back immediately. Don't try to stand!" A slight smile touched Charlemagne's lips as he heard Roland's admonition.

"If I could stand, Roland, I would," he mumbled before he lost consciousness. Some moments later, Abbot Fulrad hurried in and began wiping the King's forehead, wondering aloud at the sudden onset of this illness.

"How can he be so ill so quickly?" But he said no more. Any time he saw such a high fever, he thought immediately of Carloman. Carl's deterioration was rapid after the onset of a particularly hot, body temperature. The Abbot wiped the King's body down again, sending his squire scurrying for fresh, cold, river water.

By mid-day, the king was no better. He came in and out of

consciousness but, clearly, did not know where he was. Fulrad summoned a healer and a herbalist. The healer, Hadrod by name, listened attentively to all the potions his colleague previously gave the King. He nodded at the Abbot and spoke.

"Herbalist Braun has done all I know to do, Sir. Time will give us an outcome." His face furrowed in thought.

"In this case, I fear time will do harm." Roland responded as he walked up beside the Abbot. "Without a change, Charlemagne is going to die. You know nothing else to try?" He asked in a quiet voice. Both men shook their heads sorrowfully. Roland felt Charlemagne's forehead. It was burning with fever, even hotter than in the morning , if that were possible. Roland tried to rouse the King.

"…Sire? Charlemagne? Please answer me." He shook the King gently by his shoulders. But the King's head only lolled about. He was incapable of speaking, even if he heard Roland's voice. "We must do something!" Roland said to Rinaldo and the Abbot. "The Swabian governor rules the realm some leagues distant. I'll ride there and seek help. I don't know the land here about, but, no matter. I must go." He mounted his horse and, waving goodbye, raced off. Rinaldo hurried after Roland, leading an extra mount.

"Roland, Roland, wait!" Rinaldo called. At his call, Roland reined his horse and turned, riding back.

"Here, take this mount. Ride one and spare one." Rinaldo suggested. "Ride as long as your strength holds. Want me to come with you?"

"Nay, Rinaldo. Stay with the King," Roland replied. "Guard him well and keep giving him water. Force him to drink, if you must, and wipe his body down. I will return as speedily as I can." He turned, his image soon lost in the distance. Rinaldo settled down for a long wait, wiping the King's sweating forehead, changing the linens on which he lay, and praying for improvement.

Oliver and Abbot Fulrad appeared after breaking their fast. They immediately called the other Peers together to develop a plan. Rinaldo told them Roland rode toward Swabia to seek help. They nodded grimly.

"Mayhap I should ride in a different direction," Oliver suggested a few moments later. "I may find a knowledgeable healer before Roland. We cannot depend on just one of us looking." He did not wait for anyone's response. He left the King's tent, mounted his horse and rode north.

Well after mid-day, Roland spotted signs of a fire. He slowed his horse and walked toward the gray haze in the sky. He dismounted, hobbled his horse near some grass alongside a stream, and began a careful, stealthy climb up a nearby hill. Peeping over the hill, Roland spotted two men and a woman, he thought. One of the three appeared busomy and had a head covering, but wore men's clothing; so he couldn't be sure. Suddenly, this person raised an arm and pulled the head covering off. Roland caught his breath.

"Why, it's Hildegard!" He cried in surprise. Remembering Hildegard's care of King Carloman, Roland forgot any possibility of danger and began running down the hill.

"Hilde! Hildegard!" He called, waving frantically at the three people. The younger man drew his sword and looked in surprise at the woman who began running toward Roland. Roland covered the distance quickly and shouted, again, before he reached her.

"The King, the King, Hildegard! He's very ill. The herbalists know nothing else to do. Please, please, come." Hildegard put her hands out to steady herself, just as Roland caught her arm. Together, they slowed each other's frantic pace. "God has answered my prayers." Roland whispered. "Come, Hilde. Come with me." He and Hildegard turned back toward her father and brother. Her father nodded at Roland, looking from him to Hildegard in perplexity.

"Is there some emergency, daughter?" He asked.

"Aye, Father, the King is ill." Hildegard spoke quickly. "His army is marching to Rome. Roland says he is felled by some sickness. Oh! Father, this is Roland of Brittainy. Roland, my Father and my brother, Gerold."

"Please excuse my haste, Duke Baden," Roland apologized to Hildegard's father. "I'm begging your daughter for help." His pale countenance, his constantly moving eyes, relayed his distress. "I have an extra horse, Sire, if you would allow Hildegard to accompany me." Roland continued, holding his breath. Duke Baden's eyes questioned his daughter.

"Do you wish to go, my dear?" At Hildegard's nod, he frowned. "Of a certainty, then, if that is your choice." The Duke replied. "Gerold and I will follow at a slower pace. Or, mayhap, I should return to our manor and bring something from there?" He asked.

"Nay, Sire, thank you," Roland replied. "I am ever in your debt. We house the King in a cave, about five leagues, down near the curve of the river. He was struck ill in the night. I pray on my return, he improves." He turned to Hildegard who seemed ready to bolt. "We must hurry, Hildegard. The King was, of a certainty, failing when I rode out." He took Hildegard's hand and ran back toward the hill. Recklessly, they ran up and down the other side where they mounted the two horses and rode off.

Roland set a steady pace, not wanting to tire Hildegard or to push the horses beyond their strength. By mid-afternoon, the two of them reached Charlemagne's tent and rushed inside.

Hildegard's breath caught in her throat. She knew at once; the King was gravely ill. She rushed to his side and fell on his chest. Then, she realized all eyes were upon her: Roland, Abbot Fulrad and Theo were in the tent. Hildegard moved her ear close to the King's chest and closed her eyes, trying to convince the on-lookers she listened to the King's heartbeat. She sighed audibly and stood. His heart beat fast but steadily.

"There are too many people in this tent," she declared. "The King must have air stirring, all the better to cool his body. Please, all of you but Roland vacate the tent. If you would help, each of you, bring a bucket of water. Leave it outside under the trees, if you will." Roland nodded and ushered each man out, urging them to lift the sides of the tent near the ground to allow more air to enter. He turned back to the tent and spoke to Hildegard.

"What would you have me do?" Although exhausted, Roland wanted to aid her.

"Get some food from the cook. Bring spirits; wine is best. Then, sit down right here and eat." She smiled at him. "You're exhausted and, I think, hungry. Please, Roland, eat. I may need your strength later." Roland nodded and left the tent. After he left, Hildegard examined Charlemagne's body, frightened by the heat radiating from the King. She did not spare a minute to gaze at him, no matter how much she wished to take him into her arms. *I must heal him. Loving will come later.*

Returning with trenchers of food, Roland pushed open the tent flap, setting food on the table, as well as three bottles of wine.

"Please, Roland, help me turn the King over." Hildegard said. "I need to examine his body for a wound. There must be something; his body is afire." Roland hurried to the King and pushed the sleeping linens aside. He wiggled his arms under the King's back and pushed slowly. King Charlemagne's body inched over. Hildegard held the King's head as Roland turned him onto his stomach. She began examining him from the back, starting with his feet.

"Here it is." She pointed to the King's ankle. Roland peered at the King's right foot and saw a small puncture wound, just below the ankle. "Do you see the red markings below the wound?" Hildegard asked. "And see the puffiness all about the ankle?" Roland nodded wordlessly. "That's the source of his problem. Don't give up hope, Roland. We'll save him yet. This is a wound which we can treat."

So saying, she took a pot from over the fire pit and poured hot water from it into a smaller vessel into which she dropped a white powder. This, she mixed together; and, soaking a hand-linen, she washed the King's right foot. She, then, washed the other foot, making sure there was no wound there as well.

"I must make a poultice, Roland. Is there salt?" Roland nodded and handed her a wrapped bundle from the table. "Here are parsley and comfrey," she said as she took herbs from her apron. "Mix them together with hot water for me. Add the salt and make a paste. I want to encourage the wound to drain." Roland was intent, mixing the herbs and the water with care.

"That's good," Hildegard told him. "Let's slather this over the puncture wound. Give me the paste." She spread the paste over and around the wound under the King's ankle. Then, she soaked pieces of linen in hot water and gently put them over the ankle, pressing the linen against the skin. King Charlemagne moaned and tried to move his leg. Hildegard rubbed his back slowly, grimacing at the pain his deep frown suggested.

"We'll change this poultice every hour or so. I'm hoping the paste will draw the corruption out."

"Is there anything else we can do, Hildegard?" Roland asked. "I would make him more comfortable."

"Aye, as we change the poultice, we will pour this wine over the wound. That should help clean it. Get some of this wine down the King's throat, as well," she suggested. "It may not help the swelling; but he will feel less pain." She smiled a little at Roland at Roland's worried face.

"I think I need a little myself," Roland admitted.

"That's the reason I asked you to bring more than one flagon," Hildegard replied somberly.

She checked on him repeatedly during the afternoon but could see no change in his condition. Her heart skipped a beat. Be patient, she advised herself. *He's very ill; it will take time for the poultice to work, if it can help him.* Near to dusk, Hildegard approached Charlemagne's sleeping bench yet again. She looked closely at him. His breathing seemed less labored and his face was less pale, at least so it seemed to her eyes.

"His forehead is definitely cooler." Roland said as he placed his hand on the King. "And the linen over the poultice is stained yellow by the draining." He shook his head. "At least, the swelling lessens, Hildegard. Look." He pointed. It was true; the area below the King's ankle was no longer tight and firm; the air seemed to have escaped from his skin.

At just that moment, Oliver burst into the tent. He looked from Roland to Hildegard. Seeing her, his mouth fell open; Hildegard saw the tears spring to his eyes.

"Hildegard?" Oliver mouthed. "Is it really you?" He asked as he found his voice. He saw the linens on the King's foot, noticed the King's face was no longer pasty white. "You've saved his life." He dropped to his knees and took her hands in his.

"Nay, Oliver, it's too soon to say. Let's hope the progress of the illness is interrupted." She gazed at Charlemagne, her heart in her eyes. "I do think his color is better, don't you, Roland?" Despite her effort to keep her voice positive, she heard it tremble.

"Aye," Roland agreed. "He seems considerably better. But, let's be cautious. We must expect little until multiple applications of your herbs and this wine have time to work, Hildegard."

"I'll sit with him," Hildegard said. "You two get some sleep. He'll need watching by each of us tomorrow." She saw Roland hesitate. "It's best if I take this watch, Roland. I know other herbs to use is he grows hot again or gets restless." She smiled at both men. "Go; get some sleep while you can. He will need you later."

Because the night was mild, Roland and Oliver brought their linens to sleep outside the King's tent should Hildegard need anything of them. They insisted she eat and promised her rest as quickly as they could sleep a bit themselves.

Chapter Thirty-one

HER FATHER'S WARNING

At any other stop in an army's journey, men felt relief, jubilant not to have to engage the enemy. A stop meant another day of marching and that signaled another day of peace. On the road to Rome, all were weary from the Saxon battle, the tension of the march and the fear which comes to even the most battle-hearty. But over their relief at the limited fighting hung their anxiety about Charlemagne. Little, squabbling fights - ridiculous reactions to negligible, often unfairly perceived, slights - took on huge proportions as the men waited for word of his health. Seeking activities for the soldiers, the Peers organized competitions. The rewards were participation in an autumn hunt.

"We must resume our march." Theodoric said to Oliver and Roland the morning following Hilde's arrival. "We require more foodstuffs than the region can supply. The berries, the squirrels and rabbits are too great a temptation for the men to pass up." He looked around, heartened by the understanding on the Peers' faces. "The local people will starve this winter if we do not move the army forward."

"I agree. Two or three of us can stay with the King until he recovers; we'll leave an escort, of a certainty. But who dares predict our reception in Rome? We know Desiderius is likely marching there before us. Let's proceed, albeit slowly." Oliver suggested. The men nodded their approval.

"Who will stay?" Oliver asked. Roland and Rinaldo volunteered to stay with Charlemagne, supported by a small contingent of men and horses. Oliver was to lead the army forward and respond to any altercations which might arise along the way. All the Peers trusted his slow, sensible judgment. Rinaldo promised to send a messenger every day to report on the King's condition.

Oliver ordered the soldiers to pack their tents and gear. The great army marched after the mid-day meal. King Charlemagne frowned and stirred on his linens as the sounds of the moving army carried into his tent. But he did not awaken. The Abbot agreed to move with the army after Hildegard assured him the army needed his presence.

Hildegard, Rinaldo, and Roland took turns in the night, wiping down the King's body with wet, cool linens. Near to sunrise on the third day after Hildegard's arrival, Charlemagne opened his eyes and gazed into Rinaldo's concerned face.

"Sire, how are you?" Rinaldo whispered, worried the King did not understand his words but afraid to confirm it. Seeing Charlemagne understood his words, he asked again: "How do you feel?"

"Not as hot as before. I am hungry, very hungry, Rinaldo." The King answered, a wisp of a smile around his mouth. He noticed a movement beside him and, then, believed himself dead and in heaven. "Hilde?" He asked, his heartbeat rising with every breath. "Hilde? Is it really your or is my fever causing me to imagine you?"

"Aye," Rinaldo grinned. "It **is** Lady Hildegard, Sire. She saved your life. I'm telling you; you have no idea all the effort she..." Hildegard smiled and put her hand on Rinaldo's arm.

"Rinaldo, tell the King all you want later. Now, though, he's hungry. If you would go to the cook tent...?"

"Aye, of a certainty! What would you..." He stopped speaking and smiled. "I will bring a little of everything, Sire. Don't fall back to sleep before I return." He cautioned joyously as he left the tent.

"My dear Hilde." Charlemagne murmured her name. "Rinaldo has no idea how you saved me, does he, my little bird?" He smiled at her and looked around. "How are you here? In fact, where are we? I slept for a long time..." He moved and winced as his leg pained him. "Tell me what happened." He laid his head back on the linens.

"I will tell you all, Charlemagne." Hilde promised. "But you must lie quietly. Conserve the little strength you have. Be still and rest." Hildegard sat beside the King, alternately kissing his hand and wiping his forehead. It was enough to look into his eyes, to see his love there, and to hold his hand. Soon, Rinaldo returned with trenchers laden with food. He set them eagerly on the table.

"Do not give him overmuch, Rinaldo," Hildegard cautioned as Rinaldo brought a trencher to the King. "Nay." Hildegard held up her hand and shook her head. "He may have one-third of your serving of roast, much less cheese, and only one hunk of bread. Add more sour plums and those dried persimmons for him."

"But Lady Hildegard!" Rinaldo's concern registered on his face and in his voice. "That's not enough food for the King. He must regain his strength. You feed him like a bird!"

"Aye," Hildegard responded. "He must regain his strength with lighter foods, not those which lie in his stomach, those which feel heavy. Give him dried fruit, a very little cheese." She smiled to reassure Rinaldo. "He will not be so hungry as you imagine or as he thinks, I daresay." She laughed at the King's look. "Trust me." Rinaldo nodded and, reluctantly, sat the half-filled trencher beside the King.

"Forgive me, Sire. I must put the food into your mouth; don't bite my hand!" He joked. "You should not sit up, not yet." Charlemagne nodded and obediently opened his mouth as Rinaldo described the food he was putting in. The King smacked nosily at each bite.

The following day Charlemagne asked Roland to move him beside the river. The Peers rigged a taut piece of linen between two horses and transported the King who was still too shaky to stand. They lay him under a towering oak tree about fifty feet from the river's edge. At mid-day, Hildegard came with soup thickened with squirrel and barley.

"I return to my father's house today, Charlemagne." He tried to rise but was yet too weak.

"So soon, Hilde? I hoped you would accompany me back to court," he answered.

"Nay, I cannot," she replied. "I came to help you in your sickness and you now recover. I will return to my home." The King, then, noticed the weariness in her face, her slow movements; and his heart fell.

"Are you well, Hilde?" He asked with great concern. "Mayhap, you should rest a few days before making the journey back."

"Nay, not a few days," Hildegard replied. "I will rest best in my own linens, dear one. Poppa and Gerold waited, at my request, for your recovery. We will return home together. I know my mother worries about us." She looked quickly around them. Seeing no one, she kissed the King gently on the cheek.

"Worry for nothing and mend quickly. I will stay for another day or two to be certain you continue to mend."

The King lay under the huge limbs of the oak for the duration of the day, snoozing and resting as the soft breezes ruffled his hair. Rarely, he would call for Roland or Rinaldo; but, mostly, he wished to be alone to think. He thought mostly about Hildegard. *If she is beside me, I am equal to any challenge.* As his body healed, his spirit calmed. I *must recover Hildegard's respect.*

"That's my first concern." He spoke aloud, so intent was he on his thoughts. "She must see I am a man of change, a man who does — not one who just speaks pretty words. My behavior must show a sure commitment, a dedication to my own ideals." He smiled, remembering her sweet kisses, the love in her eyes, the gentle caresses on his back.

"I can imagine no life without her. Hell! I want no life without her; all would be meaningless." Then, he reviewed the three years since his father's death.

"I've talked and dreamed but done little to improve life in the Frankish realm." Startled by his thoughts; Charlemagne sat bolt upright. "That's it! I must implement my dreams. I can prove my dedication to Hilde and my commitment to my people by initiating changes in governance throughout the Frankish realm. I must undertake an overhaul of the church - its organization is suitable for governing but its corruption undermines its effectiveness. Now's the time to tend the dreams Hilde and I share." King Charlemagne pulled his legs up, rolled onto his knees, pressed down and pushed himself up. He stood and walked, one small step after another.

The nest day, the King could sit his horse. He was weak but wanted to ride with Hilde before she left for home. They rode slowly beside the river, enjoying the hope which the late spring season brings to every living being. Birds sang of sun-filled days to come; baby rabbits darted back and forth around the horses' feet; squirrels chattered nosily at each other, promising all kinds of dire revenge. Hildegard preferred to ride in her 'man's clothing,' breeches and a tunic almost to her feet.

Dismounting to allow the horses to graze, Charlemagne gasped. Hilde looked over at him, following the focus of his gaze. He stared, mesmerized, it appeared, by her stomach. She looked down and smiled. As she prepared to dismount, her tunic pulled tightly across her little mound of a belly. Before she could move, Charlemagne reached up and lifted her from the saddle onto the ground.

"I carry your child, Sire." She told him.

Charlemagne was beside himself with happiness. He kissed Hildegard; he spun her around the meadow; he grinned and hugged her repeatedly.

"...a child, Hilde, a child!" He shouted. At her slow, delighted smile, he walked hurriedly around the meadow, just like a little boy working off his intense excitement. At her injunction not to run, the King laughed.

"I can scarcely contain myself." he admitted. "If I weren't so weak, I'd dash, dash all around this meadow!" He hurried back to Hildegard's side, his smile running from ear to ear. "We must go to your parents, Hilde. Although I did not follow the courting ritual in quite the correct order, I must declare my love of you and ask for your hand."

Hildegard felt the tears gather in her eyes. She did not expect such a gesture. The past few weeks were agonizing. She didn't know, couldn't decide, if the King would be pleased by her pregnancy or not. She knew he loved her. But he loved her before...and chose another for his bride.

Charlemagne could not hug Hildegard enough. Excitement, remorse, awareness of his narrow thinking threatened to overwhelm him. *I must learn from her—both how to love well and, then, how to see the needs of others. She has a natural ability, some God-given talent, for helping and encouraging people.* The King said none of this. There was so much to say words completely escaped him.

"Charley," Hildegard said, her heart in her throat, "you are pleased?" His answer would seal her life. If he rejected her and the child, what alternative did she have? He may ask her to become his mistress, not mention a word of marriage. What would she do? In the past few weeks, she lived a thousand deaths. She had no way to foresee the King's reaction. She, of a certainty, did not even know if he would keep his vow, if he would come back for her.

Hildegard recalled her mother's constantly strained face, her father's barely controlled anger, her brother's concern for her future. She would not repeat the question; she would be strong. If he did not answer her, if he *were* displeased, what then? Hildegard pressed her lips together.

"Pleased, my precious Hilde?" The King finally found his voice. Sensing all the questions and worry in her inquiry, he fought to find the most reassuring, most joyous words he could. "My love," the King exclaimed, "I am the happiest man on this earth...mayhap, the happiest of all time! To have won the most beautiful, the most loving, the most insightful woman on the continent and to hear she is carrying my child! Ohhh, Hilde! I am overwhelmed with happiness. I must thank God for this greatest of gifts." Thinking again of the surprise of this announcement, he sought to determine her feelings.

"Why didn't you write me? Why keep this a secret? You must know I adore you, want only to spend my life with you. You can never, never doubt my devotion again. Agreed?" He asked as he spun her around. He stopped short.

"Oh! Hilde! That whirling...it did not sicken you, did it?" He carefully sat her on a nearby tree stump. "Tell me I did not hurt you or the child." The King begged, his eyes bulging in his now pale face. "I wished only to show you my delight. Do you feel sick in your belly?" He placed his huge hand on her stomach, gazing into Hildegard's face, looking for any hint of concern or pain. Hildegard laughed and wrapped her arms around his waist.

"Nay! Nay, my darling! I'm fine! The sickness of the morning...? Aye, I did have it. But it is long gone. I feel good, truly. I did not write because you were on the battlefield. And this news...a woman likes to give face-to-face." She laughed with relief, then grabbed his face and kissed him warmly, all the doubt of the past weeks leaking from her overwhelmed heart.

"I will never have a happier day than this one." She whispered into his neck.

"I shall ride to your home with you. I would speak with Duke Baden and his Duchess. Mayhap, I'll ask them, and Gerold as well, for your hand?" He suggested, smiling.

"Aye," Hildegard agreed. "Words from you would comfort them, Charlemagne. They worry much about my state of mind and, obviously, about my future."

Roland and Rinaldo escorted the King and Hildegard to her home. As the small group spied her father's manor in the distance, Roland spoke.

"Please give my regards to your family, Hildegard, and our thanks," Roland requested. "Rinaldo and I will see you in a couple of days and renew our acquaintance with your family. By allowing you to accompany me, they helped save Charlemagne's life." Hildegard nodded, giving Roland and Rinaldo quick pecks on their cheeks and bidding them goodbye. The two Peers returned to the small, 'sick' camp, to pack it up.

Charlemagne and Hilde turned toward her father's manor.

"Welcome, King Charlemagne," a voice boomed out. "We are honored by your visit to our duchy." Charlemagne froze in place. He gazed into the faces of Hildegard's father and brother. In addition to feeling apologetic, he was distinctly embarrassed. Not until this very moment did he give any thought to their reception of him, their evaluation of his behavior with their daughter and sister.

"Rise, please rise," the King urged them. "This is not necessary. I'm delighted to see you. I thank you deeply for your solicitude in my recent illness and, most especially, for your unselfishness in sharing Hildegard with me. She did save my life. Make no mistake. And I am grateful, grateful to you all."

"Allow us to welcome you, King Charlemagne." Duke Baden and his son said in unison. "It is an honor to have you visit our manor, even if it is to return our daughter, Sire. Please dismount; come in and refresh yourselves. I pray you will spend some time with us." Hildegard's father came to her, gave her a kiss, and stood with his arm around her shoulder. Gerold smiled and kissed Hildegard's cheek, bowing to Charlemagne.

"If you would, Gerold," Charlemagne bowed, "I would speak with your father for just a few minutes. Hildegard wishes to see her mother. We two shall join you in a short while." Gerold nodded, took his sister's arm and asked her to describe the herbs she used during her care of the King. The two walked toward the manor. Charlemagne turned to the Duke. He found himself almost tongue-tied at the awkward position in which he found himself.

"I would speak with you about Hildegard, Sir," he managed to say. The Duke nodded, staring into the King's eyes. He neither smiled nor encouraged the King to continue. He hadn't a hint of friendliness or deference in his face.

"Might we move inside toward a fire, Sire?" The Duke inquired. "I find myself more than a little chilled...all of a sudden." The King nodded in agreement, fearing the Duke's reaction to his coming words.

"Only the fact you are my sovereign prevents me from taking your life." The Duke said softly to the King. Charlemagne looked quickly into the Duke's face and saw the firm resolve in his eyes. "My dearest wish is for your death."

"Sire!" Charlemagne's voice caught, even as he understood Duke Baden's anger. "I can't blame you. But, please, try to forgive me. I have come here specifically to convince you of my love for Hildegard and to beg your pardon. I do beg your forgiveness, Sir. I wronged your daughter and your house. Although I did earn your hatred, I assure you, my actions were not deliberately evil." Charlemagne would attack, if he did not kill, any other man who said such words to him. But before Hildegard's father, he had no defense.

"You broke my daughter's heart," the Duke replied. "Your presence in her life, in her heart, turned my happy, bright, energetic child into a young woman who could only gaze into the distance, who longed for you with no hope for her future. Some days, she is totally unengaged with her life. I cannot deem her unhappy," the Duke saw the King's troubled look; "but she, gradually, day by day does lose her spirit."

"Forgive me, Sir," Charlemagne begged. "I spoke with Hildegard about my intentions before this opportunity brought me here. I do vow to you. I love your daughter with all my heart and wish to spend my life proving that dedication." The King's own words astounded him. Never had he so completely let his guard down...and to the father of the woman he loved!

I'm losing my faculties. Charlemagne thought to himself. I must seem a lovesick moose—my head hanging down, my eyes glazed, my speech tortured. He laughed aloud.

"Forgive my unorthodox conduct, Sir," he continued. "I regret not coming to my senses long before this; but it was not to be. Happily, I now know the path I must follow. And the journey demands Hildegard be my wife. I cannot live without her, Sire. I cannot. I love her dearly, Duke Baden. I assure you. Please overlook my foolish behavior and forgive my failures. They both come from my own lack of knowledge about myself. I'm a fool, if not worse. With God's help, I rediscovered my own best instincts and reclaimed your daughter's love—a gift I will spend the rest of my life praising." The Duke nodded his head, although King Charlemagne saw his doubt, his hesitation.

"She says her heart belongs to you, Sire," the Duke admitted. "I would never choose this for her, but I'm doubly relieved you return her affection. Not to be a typical father, your Majesty; but I must hear your intentions. You may love, Hildegard. That is not for me to dispute. However, you do have an unacceptable way of showing your love." His troubled face showed his concern.

"I will not have her cry herself to sleep over you, nor wait for something impossible. She deserves better, as I am sure you must realize." The Duke spoke deliberately and firmly. "Hilde tells me you labor to better the kingdom. She, too, would improve the lot of every living thing: children, dogs, bees, everything! I, often, do not understand her intensity, her impatience—though I do admire her persistence." Duke Baden shook his head slowly. "Why must she struggle so steadfastly?"

"Because she loves deeply, Sir," Charlemagne replied, "because she strives each day to help others, to reflect your faith in her selflessness." The Duke gazed into the King's face; then he smiled.

"I believe she did truly win your heart, son," he answered, smiling himself. "All of us here know her worth. I'm relieved to see you do as well...finally." He paused. "I have no reason to be pleased with your treatment of her... before this day."

"Aye, I acknowledge my shortcomings, as dire as they are," the King replied, dropping his head. "I asked Hildegard to be my wife and, late it is true, I seek your permission, yours and her mother's." He spoke quickly. "I know my request is late, Sir. I do beg forgiveness. I bring Hildegard to you today only to take her back to court. As soon as possible, we shall be married." He stopped speaking to look into the Duke's face.

"You know the sorry tales of my marital exploits, I do fear," he added. "Suffice it to say it brings me no pleasure to speak of them to you. All of it is painful. But, I lay my heart bare to you. And now, may I meet your Duchess?" Hildegard's father nodded and walked King Charlemagne to his wife's day chamber. They spoke pleasantly along the way; Charlemagne asked if any puppies from the spring litters were ready for training. As they came to the Duchess' door, the Duke withdrew his sword and handed its handle to the King.

"Should you hurt Hildegard again, my liege; distress her in any way, her brother and I shall earn our deaths, but not before we have brought about your own." The Duke bowed once and knocked on the door of his wife's chamber. At her response, he motioned Charlemagne in. "I shall expect you in the entrance hall for refreshments when you are finished here."

Chapter Thirty-two
CRISIS IN ROME

As her father closed the door, Hildegard came and took the King's hand. She placed his hand in her mother's as the Duchess curtseyed to the King and bid him welcome.

"I am honored to meet you, Duchess," Charlemagne responded as he kissed her hand. "I wish to apologize to you in person, apologize for the worry my behavior has given you and for the unfairness in my courtship of your daughter. It's true I did not value her nearly as I should." The Duchess nodded gravely, assessing the King as he spoke. "My only excuse is I needed to grow my strength. Your daughter has assisted me in this. And, though I did treat her much less well than she deserves, I do vow she shall never doubt my affection again, nor weep from any mistreatment from my hand." Duchess Baden inclined her head slightly.

"I appreciate your words, Sire." the Duchess said, looking directly into his face. "I do hope your love and care can erase Hildegard's sleepless, worried nights. She suffered much, Sire, in her love for you."

"I know." Charlemagne acknowledged. "And I am thankful her love for me still burns steadily. I did sorely test it, I acknowledge my stupidity." He beamed at Hildegard. "She will never regret her love for me, Duchess, from this moment forward. I do promise you." The Duchess curtseyed to the King and, then, gently kissed his cheek.

"Hildegard is a very special person, Sire," she said. "Please care for her well and cherish her good nature."

"You have my word for all time." Charlemagne declared. He returned the Duchess' kiss and left her chamber.

Late that afternoon, King Charlemagne, Roland, and Rinaldo camped near-by, giving Hildegard one last night with her family. The following morning preparations for Hildegard's return to court got underway early. Greeting the Duke, King Charlemagne asked to see his hunting dogs. As Roland and the Duke discussed training methods, the King walked quickly to the stables, searching for the most recent litter of pups. Following in Charlemagne's wake, Roland assured Hildegard's father of Charlemagne's long-standing, if undeclared, love for Hildegard.

As Roland and the Duke came into the stable which housed the dogs, they found Charlemagne evaluating the puppies. He chose one for his bride, a sweet-tempered female full of energy and high spirits. It was a happy three-some which, a few minutes later, joined the Duchess and Hildegard to break their morning fast.

The pressing nature of Desiderius' threats to Charlemagne, however, foreshadowed a confrontation and hurried the packing of Hildegard's treasures: a writing desk she received for her tenth name day; a trunk of beautifully embroidered silk gowns; a spice cabinet which contained her store of medicinal herbs; another trunk of tunics and embroidered linens; and a small collection of parchment, writing tools, and jewelry. The Duke and Duchess reluctantly bade Hilde 'goodbye,' buoyed by the joy and delight on their daughter's face.

Just as the group was ready to begin their journey, hoof beats sounded down the road. Around the bend came a rider, almost reckless in his speed.

"Why, that's Oliver!" Roland cried as he kneed his mount forward. He and Oliver met several hundred meters from Lord Bader's manor. They all saw Roland shake his head. He and Oliver rode toward those waiting.

"Good morrow to you all," Oliver greeted them, dismounting and bowing before Lord Bader and his lady. "Forgive my haste. But I have an urgent message for the King." He turned to King Charlemagne, nodding at Rinaldo.

"Good morrow, Sire, or – mayhap - it is not. I regret to bring bad news but our spies confirm Desiderius prepares a march on Rome. Our core army camps at Milan; but we need to extend a call for the rest. The Lombard army's preparations began two days ago, so he won't march immediately. Word is he awaits a contingent from Venice."

"He marches for Rome already?" Charlemagne asked, frowning. "We must hurry." He turned to Hildegard.

"My love, I beg your forgiveness again. I must go to Pavia, stop King Desiderius. Will you stay here with your family and wait for me to return? I cannot think of your riding with us. The journey is too far. It will debilitate you. Oh, Hilde, I do so hate to leave you!"

"Aye, I will wait for you here, Charley. My family will worry unnecessarily if I make such a journey. Please keep safe." She turned to Oliver, Rinaldo, and Roland.

"All of you take good care. And spare Charlemagne as much as you can. He still recovers."

Charlemagne took Hildegard into his arms and held her. He appeared more heartbroken than she at the separation. But he knew she was better off in her own home than on a hurried march and, then, possibly adjacent to a battle.

"As soon as possible, I'll return for you." He promised.

"Roland, you and Rinaldo go to the west; Oliver and I go

south. Let our dukes and counts know the army marches soon. We need any soldiers they can spare. I know, I know! This is the wrong time of the year to march. But we cannot wait for the spring battles. Gather as many soldiers as you can. Alert our soldiers in Geneva to ready for a march; we'll meet them there. Send a message to Theo in Milan. Tell him we march toward Italy as soon as we can." Charlemagne paused. "Wait a bit, though. We need to hear Oliver's news of the realm." He turned to Oliver, a questioning look on his face.

"Queen Bertrada declares she and the mobile court will join our army. She, somehow, senses you are ill, though no messenger went to her. I made certain of it, Sire." Charlemagne nodded. Trust Ma-mam to sense something, he thought.

"When I get an idea of Desiderius' intentions, we'll send for the court. I know all therein feel insecure away from us."

"I promised never to speak the Princess' name again in your hearing, Sire; but you asked for news. Bernard returned from a journey to Bavaria some five days ago. He reports your most recent wife, Desiderata, is betrothed to a very wealthy merchant in Ravenna. It's said the marriage will take place next year in the late summer."

"Optimistic, isn't she?" Charlemagne answered. "Desiderius must be certain the Pope will annul our marriage. Oh, I wish he would hurry! When did we ask his help...some six months ago?"

"It is only when we are anxious that things appear to take much time." Oliver offered.

"Ha!" Charlemagne laughed. "You are the master of understatement, Oliver.

But six months, a half-year seems sufficient time to me."

"In a missive separate from the one from the Queen Mother, Egginhard reports the court well provisioned for the spring battle season. And wants to know the effect the Saxon battle had on summer plans." Oliver looked seriously at the King. "Rome is a long journey; the troops we bring from Geneva will need rest. This marching back and fro; it does exhaust us all."

"I agree." Charlemagne replied. "But I do not choose these battles, Oliver. We respond to the threats. Thank God, only the Saxons called us forth. As you know, Pope Hadrian's missives find me anywhere. He is frightened of Desiderius and, this time, I think him correct. We've no choice about the Lombards. Mayhap, we can defeat them for good and all this time. Here, take a look at Hadrian's latest missive." He placed the parchment in Oliver's hands.

My dear brother, King Charlemagne:
Defender of the Faith
Servant of the Holy Church
Ruler of the mighty Frankish Realm
Esteemed Father of the Realm
Lord Commander of God's Soldiers

Your sister-in-law, Queen Gebnega, has asked that I name her oldest son ruler of King Carloman's lands. She fails to realize the papacy has never supported the ambitions of a Lombard ruler, certainly not one cloaked in a widow's request. Several counts in the Lombard court assure me that Desiderius is the mind behind Gebnega's plea.

Please, Charlemagne; come to Rome. Defend your Church. Help me, my son, help me. I fear Desiderius prepares to invade the Holy City. You must find a way to control Desiderius. It is impossible for the Church to do its work with his constant effort to control us, to wrest power from the papacy. I will delay my answer to Gebnega as long as possi-

411

ble; but I fear Desiderius will attack and overwhelm us. I beg
you, Charlemagne. Come; save us!

Yours in the faith,
Pope Hadrian

"We will finally fight Desiderius; it's inevitable." Charlemagne acknowledged. "But, let's first respond to Hadrian's call, ignore Desiderius, and evaluate the result. Mayhap, our Army's strength will deter him, make it possible for us to be magnanimous in our judgments and, possibly, to defeat Desiderius' ambitions in the process."

"Aye," Roland agreed. "We must march, so let's be off. Mayhap we can go and return before the snows get too deep."

"I pray our presence in Rome will be all that's necessary," King Charlemagne said. "If we fight, I'm afraid the battle will have little heart in it. This battle year stretches interminably. But if we must fight, let us begin." The Peers deployed messengers far and wide, searching for soldiers.

Once Charlemagne and his Peers reached Geneva, the army came together quickly. Many temporary soldiers, called to bolster the army's numbers,responded to the king's plea, convinced that booty from Rome was more desirable than wages from planting or harvesting. Charlemagne told them frankly; his hope was to avert battle. But, no one was able to predict exactly what would happen once they reached the Holy City. They marched hard, even into the dark of summer nights.

Camped some five leagues from Rome, King Desiderius planned to march on Rome on the morrow. As he met with his commanders, two scouts raced to him with news. The Frankish army marched - not only marched, it was near Rome! The Lombard king thought Charlemagne in Frankish lands, resting his army after the Saxon war. Desiderius ordered his army to strike camp and sent scouts north of Rome. They returned earlier than expected with reports of Charlemagne's great army not even a half-day away.

Desiderius, shocked and embarrassed at his own miscalculations, labored to evaluate his now-reduced possibilities. He never believed the Pope intended to summon Charlemagne or, indeed, that the Frankish King would respond. How was it possible for him to arrive in Rome so quickly?

"Damn him to hell and back!" Desiderius swore. "My spies assured me the Frankish army toyed with the Saxons. They predicted massive bloodshed and many days of fighting. The campaign there cannot be finished. I wonder...? Is it my ill luck? Can Charlemagne be coming for a visit, just to see the pope? They appear to support each other at every turn." He paused, thinking.

"Mayhap, this is coincidence—his appearing as I prepare to attack. I must speak with Hadrian; determine if he knows Charlemagne is within a day's march of Rome."

He hurried into the Holy City, sending commanders ahead to announce his arrival to the pope. Arriving at the basilica, he beckoned to three of those commanders to accompany him. Desiderius dismounted and handed his reins to a papal initiate. His commanders followed his lead.

"Welcome to Rome and to my city." Pope Hadrian said, his voice very quiet. "Come, let us talk." Hadrian ushered Desiderius into a rich chamber, ornately decorated with gold embroidered tapestries and marble benches.

"State your business here, King Desiderius." Pope Hadrian

wasted no time on niceties. His own scouts, returning to Rome ahead of the Lombard King, informed him of the location of the Lombard army and of Desiderius' hectic sprint to the city. This morning they, also, confirmed the front section of the Frankish army was within sight.

The Pope knew Desiderius' ambition. He cared nothing for the fate of soldiers! Aye, Lombard soldiers could fight, die, and march home. But, after the battle, Frankish soldiers — only following orders like all the rest — must march weeks to get home, transporting wounded men whose moans and cries he could imagine even now. Hadrian was angry; the anger changed to disgust. Blaspheming the Holy City with blood and conquest was bad enough. But worse was Desiderius' lack of respect for the coming Yuletide, for the hope which the season brought its believers - the hope of love and peace. *Even Desiderius, fool that he is, should know better.* Hadrian shook his head, imagining the huge death toll likely to result from a pitched battle.

"If only the Church could protect itself," Hadrian mumbled. And, suddenly, he smiled. Desiderius, seeing the smile, made a mistake. He believed the Pope attempted to be friendly and agreeable. He decided to play the conqueror, before anything else disrupted his plans.

"You have one choice, Hadrian. Surrender the city to me." Desiderius demanded. "I give you my solemn oath: surrender and no one will be hurt. Be responsible; honor your vows. Choose the way of peace. After all, it will soon be the season of peace." He smiled, his eyes radiating contempt.

"Responsible? Aye! I labor to be responsible, King Desiderius." The Pope replied. "It's the very reason I will never surrender my city to you. You are a war-monger and worse. You are a heathen, marching on the Holy City, bringing death and destruction. Your ambition strips the populace of hope, of any belief that war - that most evil of man's actions—will ever end."

"Attack Rome, if you will. I will not name King Carloman's son to rule a kingdom, just as I will never surrender Rome to a man like you. I advise you to turn your army around and go home." Desiderius laughed loudly, pretending great amusement at the Pope's words.

"I will have Carloman's lands." Desiderius declared. "If he died as he ought, expired at my court last year, all this would be unnecessary."

"Men do not often die on another's timetable, unless evil is afoot. God determines a man's birth and his death. Who are you to decide when another must die? Aye, who gave you the right to pit these men against me, against the Holy Church?" Hadrian asked.

"You are lost, Pope Hadrian lost! Mayhap, you are destined for hell." Desiderius threatened. The Pope caught his breath, then shook his head slowly. His eyes were mournful, his lips turned down at the corners.

"I **will** be King of this world!" Desiderius exclaimed. "My effort to take the crown from Carloman failed. He refused to name me joint ruler. He didn't even succumb to my poisons until he journeyed back to his beloved Aachen! Nay! I will not be deterred again. Rome is mine. Charlemagne's realm is next. It shall all be mine."

"Take one aggressive step against the Church or, indeed, against Rome herself, I dare you. I shall excommunicate you and every one of your soldiers, from your commanders to your squires." The Pope threatened. He stepped directly in front of Desiderius, staring into his eyes.

"Order your soldiers back. I do not countenance your wish for war, for destruction. I have a great army at my back, as you undoubtedly know. Desist, Desiderius! Withdraw your army now, before the Franks bathe you in your own blood." Pope Hadrian folded his arms and waited, secure in his most recent reports of Charlemagne's presence. He knew the King rode well ahead of his army; he would be here within moments. Unknown to them both, Charlemagne entered the outskirts of Rome.

Desiderius heard his squire's feet slap the marble floor. Without his leave, the squire fled the room, taking the excommunication threat to the Lombard commanders. In a moment, Desiderius heard the shuffling of his soldiers' feet, the scratch of swords being unsheathed, the staccato beat of hundreds of horses' hooves as the infantry waited for orders. He felt his commanders walking among the troops, trying to reassure them. Two of the three commanders with him began climbing the steps to the portico.

"Excommunicated? ...such an empty threat, Hadrian! A Pope would never excommunicate the men of an entire realm. You try to dupe me." Desiderius smiled, hoping to deflect his commanders' worry, trying to outmaneuver the Pope.

"Do you test me, Desiderius?" Pope Hadrian asked quietly. "Will you risk God's eternal disapproval of you and of the Lombard men who follow you?"

"I *will* destroy you, Hadrian." Desiderius threatened. "If not today, in the future; no mere priest should have the power you possess...be it from God or from men's connivance. I promise you; I will destroy you and your church." So saying, he turned, ran from the chamber, and ordered his army from Rome.

Chapter Thirty-three
RESOLUTION AND LOSS

Charlemagne's great army marched toward the city. The soldiers steeled themselves for horrendous fighting and massive loss of life. Charlemagne, well ahead of his army, scanned Roman streets for Rinaldo and Oliver. Yesterday night the two peers left him under the cover of darkness to gauge Desiderius' strength and to monitor his soldiers' movements. The King, seeing Rinaldo riding toward him, held up his hand.

"Sire! Sire! Desiderius marches with Rome at his back. The front contingent of Lombard troops, even now, passes through the Roman gate. They move slowly but are headed north." Rinaldo grinned with relief, mopping his forehead with a scarf. Oliver rode up a few minutes later and confirmed the report.

"The Lombard army retreats, Sire." He re-iterated. "They withdraw!" The three men grinned at each other, each relieved the expected confrontation wasn't going to materialize, at least, not immediately. War was averted...for today.

Charlemagne sent Rinaldo to the Frankish troops, bidding them to make camp. Oliver said he would walk the streets, verifying that all Lombard troops had, indeed, left. The King nodded and rode to the basilica. Pope Hadrian met him on the steps; they both rejoiced at Desiderius' hasty departure.

The two men, the soldier and the priest, spent two days closeted away, discussing the future of Charlemagne's realm and the needs of the Church. Late in the second day, King

Charlemagne took his leave of the Pope. He wished to delay his homeward march not a minute longer.

"We must march, Pope Hadrian. Although the sun shines here, winter moves toward the northern climes. The ice and snow come, along with chilling winds and biting cold. Both delay our speed and sap our strength. I bid you a plentiful harvest and a joyous Yuletide. We, you and I, have much to thank God for this season." He stepped from the portico but turned back.

"So, Desiderius killed Carloman, did he?" Charlemagne asked. Pope Hadrian nodded, his eyes moist, deep regret on his face.

"My son, I'm sorry. He told me himself. I did not get the chance, even, to mention Carl. I'd like to doubt Desiderius; but, in this, I fear he boasts. And in the boasting is the truth. He poisoned Carl, little by little. But, undoubtedly, the poison acted more slowly than Desiderius expected. Carl didn't die in Pavia; he journeyed to your realm. If Carl died there in Desiderius' city, Desiderius thought taking Frankland would be easy, a move Queen Gebnega could be persuaded to support. But it was not to be. Carloman, bless him, must have fought the poison with all his being! Who knows how long Desiderius gave it to him? They spent days together, did they not, hunting and 'strengthening' their alliance?"

"Aye, they visited each other, time and again. I warned Carl to beware of him; but he refused to take me seriously. Carl did fight, Father. He fought for his life, though I think he never suspected the betrayal. Thank God, he wasn't conscious of it." Charlemagne hung his head then looked into Pope Hadrian's eyes.

"He was too good a man for this world, Father. I discovered that truth late, but I am positive of it. Mayhap, that's the reason

God took him home."

The army did not break stride as it marched. Although Lyon, their destination, was a considerable distance, everyone moved with a lighter heart. No one wished harm to the Holy City and all knew the destruction war brought to populated places. Although summer still reined in Italy, cold, drenching rains dogged the troops. And as they wound north, colder air pricked at their faces, promising even more chilling downpours and hazardous travel ahead. Finally, after several days march, they camped to dry their clothes, to eat a hot meal, and to rest.

Having more time to think, King Charlemagne again considered the Lombard threat. The pope's parting words echoed in his mind. 'You must stop Desiderius now. Otherwise, he will be a constant sword in your side.' Charlemagne shook his head. How he longed to go home! He knew his soldiers were weary, little enriched with booty from this campaign. They yearned for home and rest as much as did he. It was with a heavy heart he re-examined the strength of the Lombard army and the single-minded aim of its king.

Not an hour before the mid-day meal, he heard someone approaching, shouting with great enthusiasm. Charlemagne ducked his head and left his battle tent. Abbot Fulrad cantered some quarter mile away.

"It has come!" The Abbot called as he rode toward Charlemagne. He pulled his band cincture off and waved it, seeking the King's attention. "Sire! Sire, word has come!" In a few moments, he abruptly pulled his mount up beside the King.

"It?" Charlemagne asked, smiling at the Abbot's enthusiasm. "Is there good news, Fulrad? What has happened to so enthuse you?"

"Sire, the messenger followed in our wake." Fulrad paused to catch his breath. "The annulment, it's granted! Here, see this missive from the pope!" He dangled a piece of parchment in front of the King's face. "The dispensation is right here, signed in the Pope's own hand, effective some four days previous, your Majesty." He beamed at the King, all too aware of the child Hildegard carried. His anger at that news, he admitted, was ferocious. But how could he bewail a child's birth? He could not sustain his anger. Here was another new, unblemished soul for the Church. He would be the child's spiritual father.

"It has come." He repeated. Slowly, Charlemagne took the parchment from the Abbot's hand. He unrolled it gingerly, afraid to believe he was free of the Lombard princess at last.

"Aye, Fulrad, aye!" he exclaimed. "God be praised. It does annul the marriage, this very parchment. Thank God! Let us pray, Fulrad. I must thank the Lord for this great blessing." With those words the King fell to his knees as Fulrad knelt beside him. The Peers and their squires hurriedly did likewise. When everyone knelt, Fulrad intoned a heartfelt prayer to the heavenly Father.

"For your goodness and mercy, Father, we do thank Thee.
"For this special blessing you give King Charlemagne,
"For your love of the Frankish people,
"For your forgiveness and great mercy, we do exalt Thee!
"We are blessed with your all-encompassing comfort and support,
"For your care of each of us. Amen"

Every soldier within hearing echoed the Abbot's fervent

'Amen.' King Charlemagne stood quickly, tapping the parchment against his palm. That very night, Charlemagne sent Roland with an escort to bring Hildegard to Lyon.

"The distance is vast, Roland, more demanding than a march. But I can't wait to see her! Don't head for home, though, until you get a message from me. It's best if you wait for two messages."

"Sire, I don't understand. Don't we march to Lyon?" Roland asked.

"I'm not certain. Today's threat from Desiderius is not all we'll hear from him. As one day follows another, his ambition will rise again. I distrust him. His sights still rest on Rome. Rome or Frankland, Frankland or Rome, he will have one or the other. And, then, he'll try for both. I must consider his next move." He spread his hands in perplexity. "But I'll send a courier to you as soon as I know our next destination."

"I pray we're together before the next year, Charlemagne. This trip for Hildegard cannot be made in a few days - no matter how fleet are our horses."

"Nay, it cannot." The King agreed. "As always, I am in your debt...in this life and the next. Wouldn't you say?"

"I never disagree with my king." Roland replied slowly, a small smile hovering over his lips.

"Of a certainty, you don't." The King answered and, then, laughed mightily. King Charlemagne declared a few more days rest as he thought about Desiderius. Pavia, the Lombard king's stronghold, was before them. This was the time to consider an offensive attack against Desiderius; the Frankish army was almost at his doorstep. It was true: Desiderius' confrontation with Pope Hadrian ended this battle but it did not end Desiderius' long-term dream.

Roland and his escort, the same men who always traveled with him on errands for the king, rode hard. They stopped only to hunt, to eat, and to sleep. The days grew colder but rabbit, squirrel, and an occasional deer were plentiful. Blackberries still clung to dried stalks and wild parsnips, though stringy and chewy, added to their meals. They even spied bobcats slinking along the edges of ravines, hunting cover. But they didn't stop to hunt large animals for fur or for meat. They had no way to cure the pelts or to preserve large haunches.

If not for their errand, to return with Lady Hildegard, the men might have slowed their pace and reveled in their relative freedom. But, time was of the essence as heavy snow clouds in the distance warned them. Many days later, they rode down a small hill, the southern entrance to Lord Baden's manor.

Jordy, who had the best eyes in the group, scouted ahead of them. He rode back to report seeing no horses, livestock, or people in the distance. Of a certainty, it was cold; people were inside. But Roland wondered at the lack of activity around the prosperous manor house.

As they drew nearer, all of them felt disquieted. The silence and stillness were eerie. In the distance, they picked out the fence around the stable, the pig sty, and the coops for the chickens. Nothing moved. Roland felt fear replace his previous disquiet. It rose in the back of his throat.

"What do you make of this?" He asked his companions. "There seems no need to approach cautiously. There's no one about. Can you explain it? At the least, we should see sheep, pigs, and fowl."

"The manor is, of a certainty, deserted, Sir," Jordy confirmed, "no workers, no animals. Even the duck pond is empty." At Jordy's declaration, the men rode in tandem to the manor. They checked the barn - nothing. Even the barn cats were gone.

"What do we do?" Marcel asked, voicing everyone's silent question.

"I don't know." Roland replied. "Neither the King or I expected this. Someone or something frightened Lord Baden and the people of this manor. Nothing seems out of place so we must assume they did not leave in a hurry. But, then, we don't know how long ago they left. Let me think." The men dismounted, took hay from the barn for their horses, and built a fire. They sat in the meager light of the afternoon sunshine speculating about the Baden's whereabouts.

"Let's make our beds in the hay loft tonight. It'll be far warmer inside than rolled in blankets, even in a lean-to." Roland suggested. "By the morn, I'll decide what to do."

His companions spread their linens in the hayloft. They were well content. The sweet smell of the hay; its clean warmth; the relative safety off the ground with a view of the road; the mist hanging over the barn but not settling in their linens - all promised a good night's rest. Johann assured Roland none of them objected to several days spent here.

"Unless we determine where Lord Baden and his family are, we have no reason to linger." Roland told them. "I, for one, am ready for a winter respite. Let's hope the mobile court settles in Lyon. Mayhap, we can unpack for a month or more." Bright and early the next morning, the men were ready to depart.

"We turn back toward the army." Roland told them. "Along the way, we'll ask about Lord Baden and his family. Mayhap, someone will have information about their travel or will know their destination." Even though the manors around Baden's home were far apart, the neighboring families were at home. None of them had any knowledge about Hildegard's family. The far-flung neighbors agreed that the family often attended a wedding or a burial and, in such a case, were absent for several days. But no one informed them of such a trip this time.

"We've talked to everyone we can find. Further roaming is unlikely to yield us more information." Roland said to his companions. "I can tell you, though; this is very troubling. Basically, we have no information. I can see nothing else to do. We'll move slowly south until we get a missive from the king. Let's pray he sends his destination to us soon. Then, we turn in that direction." Sure enough, on their second day southward, a messenger hailed them from a half-league away. It was Gareth, one of the latest squires to become a Peer.

"Well met, Gareth." Roland greeted him. "How are things with you and with King Charlemagne?"

"The King and I are well, Sir Roland. But I come to let you know; your destination is Geneva again. King Charlemagne distrusts Desiderius and plans to lay siege to his city, Pavia. It will, he says, likely be an extended endeavor; the city appears well-provisioned for the winter." The men looked at each other, clearly surprised.

"So, we're to cross the Alps in ice and snow, huh?" Marcel answered.

"It seems likely." Gareth replied, his voice low.

"Do we march through the Susa Valley?" Johann asked another question. "I thought the fortifications there forbidding to outsiders. The Lombards man them at all times, do they not?"

"I have no knowledge of the King's battle strategy or of his route, Johann." Gareth replied. "I am delivering the King's message. That is all." Roland moved to de-accelerate the conversation.

"You are just in time, Gareth. We were ready to turn toward Pavia, having found no one at the Baden manor."

"No one? How strange. King Charlemagne will be vastly disappointed."

"Aye, my thoughts exactly." Roland caught the eyes of his men. "Let's be on our way then. We've a long journey, regardless."

On hearing a small band approach from the north, King Charlemagne mounted Samson and rode rapidly toward Roland and his men. Hailing them from a quarter of a league away, Charlemagne scanned the group anxiously. Roland returned so quickly he knew Hildegard must be with them. But he could make out no extra riders, no traveling cart, and no hurry in their measured pace.

"Well met, friends!" He shouted. "Where is my bride-to-be?" He called, grinning as he covered the space left between them. Roland caught his breath, wondering how to tell the king.

"She is not with us, Sire." He called, shaking his head. King Charlemagne almost stood in his stirrups. He reined Samson in and looked all around the escort.

"How dare you return without her, Roland! Explain this." The muscles in his jaw clenched. Roland saw him slowly relax his fists. Charlemagne rode up beside him.

"We did not find her, Charlemagne. There was not a living soul at Lord Baden's manor; it was deserted."

"Deserted? How can that be?" Charlemagne asked, his face

paling.

"No one was there, Charlemagne - no people, no animals, no activity of any kind."

"But, Roland! This makes no sense! Hildegard, her parents, her brother – they all knew I planned to return for her. I gave them my oath! We planned our reunion!" Roland took the King's arm and walked him toward the river.

"No one was there, Sire; no one at all." Roland answered.

About The Author

Acacia Oak, a dedicated researcher and academic, has dreamed of fictionalizing Charlemagne's story since she taught 'History of the Book' in 1969. In a world which cries for heroes, Charlemagne's vision for his people claims our attention. He redefined our concept of king, a leader who seeks to improve his country and the welfare of its citizens. His vision of a progressive, humane nation which educates its children — boys and girls alike; which values the differences of its neighbors; which anchors its society around the tenets of brotherhood are ideals we need for our own century. How amazing they are reflected in the world view of an eighth-century barbarian king!

"We all need heroes," she says, "even with their ever-present feet of clay."

Acacia Oak is a southerner by birth, a world citizen by outlook, and a hopeful writer by inclination. She lives near Seattle with her family and their three 'girls,' rescue dogs who keep life mellow as well as interesting.

For the continuing story of Charlemagne's banished first wife, read *The Banished Medieval Queen* by Acacia Oak.